About the Author

S. E. Ney was a teacher for
for a lot longer (since she w...
fascinated with the concept of time travel after watching
the 1960 film of The Time Machine when she was
somewhere between knee high to a grasshopper and shin
high to a small rodent. As a result, after completing her BA
in Philosophy at the University of Durham, she stayed on
and did her PhD on *The Logical Possibility of Time Travel*. Her
conclusion (that time travel within one possible world was
logically impossible) put her off time travel in film and
television for ten years.

She has since recovered.

In her spare time she has been a hospital radio show
host, ghost writer, barmaid, magazine editor, secretary and
trainer.

Read more at https://oslacs-odyssey.co.uk/

Also by the Author

NOVELS

The Anquerian Alternative

Ystrian Dreams

The Dragons of Mithgryr

Entrapment In Oestragar

Book I of Oslac's Odyssey

S. E. Ney

∞0-0 Publishing∞

This is a work of fiction. Names, characters, places, and incidents either are the product of the author's imagination or are used fictitiously, and any resemblance to any persons, living or dead, business establishments, events, or locales is entirely coincidental.

First published in Great Britain by
0-0 Publishing
Copyright © 2018 S. E. Ney
All rights reserved

This paperback edition 2021
3

ISBN-9781085829151

The moral right of S. E. Ney to be identified as the author of this work has been asserted by her in accordance with the Copyright, Designs and Patents Act, 1988.

No part of this publication may be reproduced, stored in a retrieval system, or transmitted in any form or by any means, electronic, mechanical, photo copying, recording or otherwise without the prior written permission of the publishers.

This book may not be lent, hired out, resold or otherwise disposed of by any way of trade in any form of binding or cover other than that in which it is published, without the prior consent of the publishers.

Cover design by T-Jay

This book is dedicated to Matt, Lucy, T-Jay, Gayle and Elise without whose help, support and keen eyes I would have floundered. Any errors remaining are entirely my fault.

Introductory note

While several chapters in this book are set during actual historical events, the characters are either products of the author's imagination or fictionalised versions of real people.

Chapter 1

Dr Alex Oslac nodded as the woman on the other side of the desk repeated her litany of grievances.

"I do understand, Mrs Garrison, but Thomas has been told repeatedly that his timetable has changed. The updated version is on the system and I, personally, gave him a corrected copy. He has no excuse for failing to attend his Monday morning class."

Alex glanced at the clock on the wall. Surrounded by posters, graphics and other 'learning aids' appropriate to history, the red second hand diligently swept around the white face, dragging the black minute hand into place as it passed the 12. 8.55 pm. Trust one of the difficult ones to turn up right near the end of the parents' evening and then drag out a twenty-minute meeting to an hour. The rain had finally let up and now only drops slid down the windows, collecting their allies to gather speed before slipping out of sight. Wishing she could do the same, Alex returned her focus to Mrs Garrison and pasted a concerned smile on her face.

Frankly, the class ran a lot more smoothly without Thomas's constant interruptions, so his absence had been a welcome respite. Alex desperately wanted to tell this woman her son's behaviour was so far outside academic focus as to be laughable. He had zero self-discipline, he was constantly checking his mobile phone, he made comments aloud that had nothing whatsoever to do with history and he was a distraction to all the other students. Unfortunately, funding problems being as they were, the college would do everything shy of kicking him out. It was quite apparent Mrs Garrison had not taught her son the basics of courtesy and consideration, and listening to her now Alex fully understood why her son was such a pain in the backside. Like his mother, Thomas expected everyone else to work around him rather than the usual give and take of civilised society. The fact his mother seemed to think he could do no wrong added to the problem. Thomas had clearly never been forced to consider others or question his right to special treatment.

"Thomas tells me he never received a corrected timetable, and I cannot accept he would wilfully miss a class. Be assured, Miss Oslac, I will be taking this up with the Principal. We'll see what he has to say about this!" With a huff, the lady rose from her seat and headed for the classroom door.

Alex shook her head, rubbing her temples where a headache was building fast. She knew full well the Principal would back her – given that she was not the only member of staff who was complaining about Thomas's poor attendance (amongst other things), and there were thorough records of every meeting, including the one in which she had handed over the timetable – but having to play nice with a woman who was utterly convinced her son was a budding Nobel prize-winner was wearing. The fact Mrs Garrison had declined to use Alex's proper title said much about the parent's opinion of her as a teacher.

"Hey, Alex!" She looked up to see Phil, one of her colleagues, grinning at her from the doorway. "Wanna hear something amazing?"

"Sure, I could use it right now. What?"

He walked in and leaned down conspiratorially. "Apparently, once upon a time, parents believed teaching staff knew what they were talking about and listened to them!"

"No!" Alex gasped, feigning surprise. "Next thing, you'll be telling me the Easter Bunny is real!"

He pulled back in shock. "You mean he isn't?"

"She. Didn't you get the memo?" She grinned at the by-play. Phil always had a way of cheering her up.

"Probably," he replied, pulling up a chair and settling into it, "but between updates, alerts, delayed essays, reminders, newsletters, the canteen menu and the other detritus in my inbox, I could easily have missed it." He took in Alex's expression. "You're not worried about Mrs Garrison, are you?"

With a sigh Alex rested her elbows on the desk and rubbed the back of her neck. "No, I just wish there was some way to get her son engaged. He's telling one story to her, a different one to us, and he's laughing all the way to wherever it is he goes with his mates. The fact he's playing us off against each other is proof he's not an idiot, I just wish I could find some way to redirect that intelligence into something useful – like his classwork!"

"There speaks a young teacher. Only one as yet unbowed by years of disappointments could still believe there's hope for lads like Thomas. Trust me, he's a lost cause."

"I've been teaching for over twenty years," she reminded him, "and I refuse to believe any student is a lost cause unless they decide to be. Probably not even then." She glanced up to see Phil cocking one eyebrow at her. "But I will admit in his case I am near the end of my rope."

"You've given him every chance. What more is there? Apart from corporal punishment which, sadly, is no longer an option. Mind you," he added thoughtfully, leaning back in his chair and stuffing his hands in his trouser pockets, "in his case there could be an argument for something rather more permanent. The other day one of my ethics students told me she thought capital punishment was a bit extreme for failure to submit an essay."

Alex chuckled. "Did you explain the mistake?"

He shrugged. "Nah, I just asked her, if we were to use it, which version of capital punishment she thought might be appropriate: the gas chamber, needle or firing squad." He laughed.

"Reminds me of that essay you handed around a few years back where the student referred to the 'phallicy of Freudian thinking'." She turned to her laptop to make some notes on the meeting with Thomas's mother while it was still fresh in her mind.

"Now that was a classic! I even asked him after class to spell fallacy and he still got it wrong. Problem is," he said, leaning forward once more, "these days the buggers don't read. Actually, that's not quite true, they read a lot provided it's on Twitter or Facebook or some other damned thing on those mobile phones of theirs. Now in my day..."

She paused in her typing and looked at him with a grin. "Back in nineteen hundred and frozen to death?"

"Precisely. I look good in furs." He tugged the lapels of his jacket. Alex shook her head and returned to her note-taking. "Anyway, we didn't have computers or mobile phones or more than 3 channels on the television. We went out, we climbed trees, read books..."

"Got bored..." she added, reading through what she had written.

"Exactly. Perfect practice for real life. Kids nowadays don't have the opportunity to get bored. The second there's the slightest chance of it they move on to something else. No incentive to stick with anything. It's all about arriving and who cares how you get there? All of which can make struggling through qualifications that require years of work a bit... passé?" He looked at his watch. "Speaking of... I believe our shift is over, unless you're planning on staying here all night in case Jonas's parents show up?"

She shook her head, shutting down her computer. "Nope. I don't give up on the kids; parents are a different matter altogether. I've been here since 7 o'clock this morning and fourteen hours for a shift is quite long enough, thank you. I'm outta here!"

"Amen!"

Together they shut down the classroom, making sure doors and windows were locked and the lights off, then headed out, smiling to the security guard who was waiting to lock up after them. The cool evening was a shock after the overheated classroom, but Alex found it a welcome relief. She took some deep breaths of the clean night air, the smell tinted with the fresh scent of pine from the trees that lined the road to the staff car-park and the loam-rich smell of wet earth.

Phil strolled alongside and kicked a stone off the road. "I gather you're going along on the trip this summer?" he commented, looking to fill the silence.

"Um hmm. Long time since I could afford a holiday, and since Pat dropped out they need another 'responsible adult' along for the ride. Not sure how I qualify, but..." They shared a look.

"Dr Oslac!"

Alex closed her eyes, counted to five and then turned to the Vice-Principal who had hailed her from the door of his office that opened onto the road. The glow of his computer screen reflected on the windows indicated he was still working. "Bernard, what can I do for you?"

"I know you want to get home, so I won't keep you long. I just wondered if you could pop into my office tomorrow, say around 2? I've got a project I want to get started and I think you'd be perfect for the job."

"Oh?"

"Only if you want to, of course."

Alex sighed. That meant there was absolutely no danger of any financial remuneration and the job was probably massive. She opened the back door of her small and somewhat aged car and dumped her laptop bag on the seat.

"I'll come 'round, but I make no promises. I'm drowning in marking already."

"That's all I ask. Have a safe journey home, the pair of you. Thanks for tonight."

Alex waved as Bernard disappeared back into his office. Phil stuffed his hands back in his pockets and shook his head.

"For all he knows, we could have been formulating a coup all evening. He never leaves that office of his unless it's to grab something from the cafeteria or use the facilities." He pulled out his car keys. "See you tomorrow?"

"Uh huh, 'though at this hour it hardly seems worth the drive home! See you."

***

At 2 pm the following day, Alex knocked on the Vice-Principal's door, the muffled 'come in' assuring her she hadn't wasted the trip.

"Ah, Alex. Sit down." She did so and Bernard warmed quickly to his task. "As you know, Herabridge College will be celebrating its five hundredth anniversary next year. Quite an achievement. We're all rather proud of it, and we want to do something special."

Alex nodded but kept her mouth shut. She wasn't about to volunteer for anything until she knew what was involved. Bernard paused and then, off her polite smile, continued.

"So, we had a meeting and decided a website dedicated to the history of the college, highlighting a few of our more illustrious alumni, might be a good start. We'll print stuff out to put up around the halls as well, of course, but the website could be linked to our main one and give potential students a chance to see our strong academic tradition."

She nodded. The fact they were due an Ofsted inspection within the next year or so was almost certainly a contributory factor.

"Sounds like a good idea," she offered, warily.

"Exactly, and given you're our lead historian and have a good grasp of IT..."

'Uh oh, here it comes,' Alex thought, bracing herself.

"...it was thought you might be the best person to do it."

There was a pause as Alex contemplated the meteor that had just landed in front of her.

"Me?! I told you last night I'm drowning. My classes are too full, I'm trying to prep stuff for the summer trip as well, you gave me two tutorial groups... where on earth am I going to find time to research the college history?!" *'even if I wanted to'* she added, mentally.

"Oh, you won't have to research it," he assured her, pointing to a large cabinet. "All the records are kept in here."

He got up, walked around his desk and withdrew a rather old key from his waistcoat pocket, which he used to open the massive oak cabinet. Immediately the lock was released, the door creaked open and a large pile of aged papers tied with ribbon dropped out to land with a thud on the floor. This was followed by a raft of yellowed sheets that fell like rain on top of it, the avalanche stalling as a second diverse collection jammed on the other door. Squatting to pick them up, Alex stared at the piles of paperwork stacked on every shelf while Bernard carefully nudged the papers back into place so he could fully open the cabinet. On the one hand, this was a disorganised nightmare. On the other, her historian's mind was eagerly cataloguing the original manuscripts she would have the opportunity to look at. Some still had large seals attached.

"You keep such valuable documents in an old cabinet in a room without any climate control?" she squawked, incredulous. That the seals hadn't melted into a puddle of wax was a minor miracle given the sweltering summer they'd had.

"Not ideal, I admit, but that's one of the reasons we want to put as much of it as we can online. That way, if anything happens to them we won't lose them altogether."

Alex rolled her eyes. That Bernard thought a scan was almost as good as the original was a sad comment on the Vice-Principal.

"Am I moving offices? Because I can't keep coming in here every time I need to grab a new document."

"Ahh, no. But we thought maybe if you took a box at a time?"

"Is there a catalogue, so we can keep a record of what's in and what's out?"

"Um, not really. That was something else we thought you might help with. Just a quick note for each one."

"You have GOT to be kidding me! There must be hundreds in there!"

"Probably," he replied, utterly sanguine, but then he would be: he wasn't being tasked with archiving K2. "That's why we wanted to get this started now. You have a whole year to get it done."

"With all due respect, Bernard, if you think I'm going to be doing this over the summer vacation for free, you've got another think coming."

"Obviously not. You'll be abroad for two weeks." He gave her a grin which faded as she eyed him, her expression implacable. "Look, do what you can in term time. I'll have a talk with the governors and see if we can find a way of funding this."

Still staring at the mountain, she considered his suggestion.

"I'll take a look and see if I can construct some sort of narrative. I make no promises," she added quickly, when his eyes lit up with what were undoubtedly images of a fully archived and recorded history appearing online in the next month, "and some of these documents look like they'll take some time to read."

She tilted her head, trying to make out the handwriting on one of the sheets, the seal hanging precariously over the edge of the shelf. With care, she supported the heavy seal, lifted the documents above it and then realised she needed a third hand.

"Hold these a moment, would you?" Bernard promptly took over supporting the upper layers. "Put them on the table... carefully! If I don't get this one out it'll tear."

He did as requested, eager to encourage her. The Board of Governors had already investigated the costs of hiring a professional archivist and the amount had been eye-watering. That was when he'd suggested Alex. With funds as tight as they were, he doubted they'd be able to offer much, but in the name of such a deserving cause he felt sure he could persuade the college it was a worthwhile investment.

Alex eased the ancient document out of the cupboard, supporting the seal, and then looked for somewhere she could put it down. Bernard quickly cleared away his keyboard and notes and she laid it on his desk. With a practised eye she scanned the document. After a while she drew a breath, shaking her head.

"This is in pretty poor shape, but as far as I can tell this is the original charter. Have you any idea how much this is worth?! It needs to go to a professional conservationist. There's some mildew that should be treated before the entire thing is destroyed, and they could mount it so it could be on show. At the very least it needs to be kept flat."

"Hang on," he replied, and stepped outside.

Alex sat down at his desk, peering at the elaborate penmanship. As with most documents this age it wasn't easy to read, and the fact there were tears and cracks in the vellum certainly didn't help. Bernard returned with a couple of large boxes.

"Reprographics just had a delivery and I seized these before they went to recycling. Big enough?"

They were. Alex really would have preferred some acid free paper to place around the charter, but this was better than nothing. Wary of adding the oils from her hands to the problems it already had given its significance, she used Bernard's (thankfully clean) desk blotter to lift it and place it in the box.

"Seriously, this has to be taken to a professional as fast as possible."

"Can we scan it, first?"

She blinked. He really was clueless.

"The light from a scanner would do even more damage. Talk to the local museum. They may have the equipment to deal with this." With a last, wistful look, she placed the lid on the box, then turned back to the cabinet. "I'll grab some of the more recent documents and when I get a break I'll start going through the rest to see if there's anything else that needs conservation." With a sigh she started lifting papers and sorting them. What had she got herself into?

***

A few weeks later she was willing to admit that while the job was huge, it was interesting. She had even managed to incorporate using some of the records in her history class. As they were looking at the First World War she had selected all she could find from 1900 to 1920 and brought them into one of her extra classes for the more gifted students. All of them appreciated the value of what they had and were treating the documents with considerably more care than the college had.

"Dr Oslac. Look what I've found!" cried Lindsey, waving her white-gloved hand.

Alex had gone to the chemists and bought boxes of cotton gloves for the class – a lesson in the correct way to treat valuable original records that the students appreciated. Bernard had questioned her when she submitted the receipt, but she pointed out the job would be done quicker with help from her students and this way the college could boast about their help later, including displays for open days. Mollified he had submitted the receipt for her remuneration.

She walked to the desk to see Lindsey and some of her fellow students looking at a photograph.

"Well, who have we here?" She turned the photograph over and noted someone had made black ink notes on the back of it. Squinting at the cursive script she read aloud. "'Captain Daniel Lancaster MC. Killed 12th October, 1917'. Now why is he here, do you think?"

"I know!" yelled Gregory, who had a newspaper sheet on his desk.

As one, the students and Alex, who still held the photograph, walked to his desk as Gregory began to read.

"'The Herabridge Herald is saddened to have to report that Captain Daniel Gordon Lancaster (39), former history teacher at Herabridge Grammar School, was killed in action on the 12th October. Captain Lancaster, a well-respected member of our community, recently won the MC for his heroic actions at Ypres. His wife, Elizabeth, née Williams (28) died in childbirth on the 25th of September. The Herald offers its condolences to his family and friends for their great loss.'"

"Oh, that's really sad," Lindsey commented. "I wonder if he knew his wife had died?"

"Well, if he didn't know before he was killed, he found out soon after," Dermot said, and was rewarded with glares from several of the students.

Alex refrained from comment. Whether or not there was an afterlife was not part of her purview – she'd leave that to Sarah Bourne, who taught Religious Studies – history, on the other hand...

"All right, October 12th, 1917. Which battle was that?"

Harriet, who had shown a remarkable enthusiasm for their present study, shot her hand up.

"Passchendaele."

"Well done! The First Battle, to be specific. Now we know someone who was there, why don't we take a look at what happened?" She glanced at her watch. "Whoops. Amazing how time flies when you're having fun. We'd best put this lot away."

A chorus of 'Awws!' greeted her comment and she smiled. It was always nice to teach students who wanted to be there.

"You can do some research between now and our next class and it'll give me time to copy some of this stuff. Greg, leave that newspaper out for me. The rest of you, see if there's anything else we've got on Captain Lancaster so I can put together a fact sheet."

The students did as requested and soon Alex had a second newspaper sheet (reporting the MC) and a few other records that showed the Captain had been hired by the school in 1908 and had apparently made quite an impression.

"Gloves!" she yelled as the students started to head to their next lesson.

A few at the door paused and quickly pulled off their gloves and dropped them in the box Alex provided before leaving.

Alone in her classroom, she looked at the picture of Captain Lancaster.

"You're a handsome one, aren't you?" she muttered, taking in the man's features.

A moustached officer looked back over her left shoulder. High cheekbones, hooded but kind eyes, a narrow, straight nose, strong jaw, and laughter lines at the corner of his eyes to offset the frown line between them made her think this man was probably firm but fair with a good sense of humour. She found his college record and discovered he had got a first in history at university. A letter from a parent thanking the school for the support he gave a student after an unexpected bereavement gave Alex pause. Men of Captain Lancaster's time weren't well known for their care of children, and teachers were more likely to think along the lines of 'spare the rod and spoil the child', yet he seemed to have gone out of his way to support and protect the boy, apparently tracking him down when he ran off in the middle of the night and taking the time to listen as the boy sobbed out his loss.

"I bet you were a good officer," Alex mused aloud.

"Who was?"

She looked up to see Phil standing in the doorway. He grinned and sauntered in, looking over her shoulder to examine the photograph and articles on her desk.

"Captain Lancaster. He was a history teacher here at the school, joined up and was killed in 1917. Even won the MC."

Phil raised his eyebrows. "Military Cross, eh? Impressive. I wonder what he did?"

"Not a clue, but as he's one of the school's alumni, I'll be checking the records to find out." She patted her laptop. "Shouldn't be hard to do a search. Thank God for the internet!"

"I prefer to thank Sir Tim, but whatever. How's it going?"

She sighed. "There's a lot to get through, but between you, me and the gatepost," she lowered her voice, "I'm actually enjoying myself." She raised a warning finger. "Don't tell Bernard!"

"As if. I came to ask you, did Dermot give you his cheque for the trip?"

Alex closed her eyes. "Damn! I forgot to ask him. We got straight into this stuff and it went clean out of my head."

"No worries. I've got him last period. Oh, and Jenny asked me to remind you we have a faculty meeting tomorrow night. She knows you tend to miss those invites in your inbox."

"Oh joy, oh rapture," she replied, the sarcasm dripping from her lips.

Phil merely grunted his agreement. "What have you got now?"

"For a miracle, nothing. The class I was due to have are all on a field trip to the Houses of Parliament, so I get to go home early for a change."

"You didn't have to provide a back-up 'mature adult'?"

She grinned. "Nah. Knowing I was doing this I was let off this year. Not that I'm complaining. Our MP could bore for Britain and he always gives the same spiel when we do the tour. I think I could recite it word for word by now."

He waved at the papers strewn across her desk. "Leaving this stuff here or taking it home?"

"Home. I need to scan some of this into the computer to make a handout for the kids and for the college. You know what the copiers are like when you ask them to scan. I'll get a better one if I use my printer at home. There's nothing here old enough to be damaged by the experience," she added, remembering her complaint to Bernard when this whole thing started.

"Let me help you," he said, grabbing the box from the floor and placing it on the desk.

"Thanks."

Together they collected the paperwork, Alex putting the articles and paperwork on Captain Lancaster on the top so she could find it quickly when she got home. While she carried her laptop, Phil carried the box and together they made their way to the car-park. Once the box was stowed on the floor in the back and her laptop on the seat, she turned to her companion. "Thanks, Phil. See you tomorrow?"

"Unless I win the lottery. In that case, you won't see me for dust."

"Helps if you buy a ticket."

He grunted. "Listen, Alex... I, um. Well, do you want to go out for a coffee or something?"

"Now? I thought you had a class?"

"No, I mean, after class, or on Saturday, or whenever."

She looked at him, curiously. "Are you asking me out on a date?"

"No! I mean yes... I... Look, it's just coffee. Get to know each other a bit better outside in the real world? My treat."

She considered him for a moment, then grinned. "OK. You're on. Just for coffee, mind you. And we'll go Dutch."

"If you insist. Don't say I didn't offer."

"Your chivalry is noted. Let me know when."

"How about tomorrow, before the meeting? We've both got a free period."

She considered his suggestion. She had intended to use the time to get some marking done, but that was before she knew they had a faculty meeting. Without it she could have got stuck in and carried on for a couple of hours before leaving for home. Now she would barely have got started before she'd have to pack up and attend the meeting.

"Good idea," she smiled.

***

When she got home, she looped the laptop bag's strap over her shoulder and then hefted the box. Walking to the block of flats' front entrance, she balanced the box on her raised knee while she fumbled for her door key. Kitty, a neighbour from downstairs, suddenly opened it for her.

"Oh, thanks Kitty! How are you?"

"Fine, for the moment. Simon brought home a lovely present from school... Chickenpox! I hope you've already had it."

"Yep. How about you?"

"Yes, thank god! Mind, they say you can still get shingles so be warned." She stepped aside to let Alex in. "I'm just going to get some calamine lotion from the chemists. Need anything while I'm in town?"

"No, I'm fine. Is someone watching Simon to make sure he doesn't scratch his skin off?"

"He's sitting in a bath filled with the last of the calamine. He'll be fine for twenty minutes and it should calm the itching."

"I can keep an ear out if you want me to," Alex offered, shifting the box to a more comfortable position.

"No, he'll be OK, but thanks for the offer. You guys up at the grammar school better brace yourselves if this is going around. Won't take long to move."

With a wave Kitty headed out of the door, pulling it closed behind her.

"I'll warn them. Thanks," Alex got out before the door clicked shut.

She did the same balancing act at her door, cursing when her laptop bag swung forward, nearly knocking the box to the floor. Finally she walked into her flat, doing a little jiggle to reseat the laptop bag temporarily while placing the box on the coffee table in her lounge. Pulling off the laptop strap she gratefully dumped it on the settee and went to the kitchen to make herself a mug of tea. With her mug in her hand, she walked to her lounge (which doubled as her office) and sat at her desk.

Her room was quite large, for a flat, and one of the reasons she leapt at the rental when it presented itself. Her TV was gathering dust as she typically used her computer for that purpose, and it sat to the right of her desk, standing on top of a rack with a DVD and Blu-ray player beneath it. Bookcases overflowed with everything from academic textbooks to novels and humour. Even more resided in boxes in the spare room. Somehow, she had never found the time to completely unpack, but she had what she needed and the rest could wait. A few carefully chosen pictures decorated the walls. Her desk was large but the space limited by the detritus spread across it. A phone, some papers she was marking, speakers, a metal cabinet of drawers (which was an effort to introduce order that never quite worked), a spindle of blank CDs that might as well be trashed given the modern predilection for using memory sticks, a collection of said memory sticks – most full or close to it – a notepad and a carved wooden box full of pens, many of which needed new ink but, once again, she had never got around to buying any and couldn't bring herself to throw out the pens, many of which were quite old. An LED desk lamp for when she was marking sat atop the cabinet. With so much now done on-line, she didn't need that as much as she used to, but it remained there just in case.

Taking a gulp of her tea, she settled it on a coaster and then quickly went through her private email, trashing nearly half of the messages. She replied to a few, checked the news to see if anything had happened since that morning, did a quick perusal of her favourite sites and then sat back, gazing at her wallpaper – a misty sunset through the trees on an autumn day.

Something had been niggling at her since her gifted and talented class and she couldn't put her finger on it. Finishing her tea, she went to the box and took out the items at the top, including the photograph of Captain Lancaster, deciding to scan that first. In moments she had her printer on, the photograph on the plate and the software on-screen. She decided on a high resolution to capture all the details that might not be as easy to see otherwise and clicked OK.

Once the picture had been scanned, she opened some photo-manipulation software and dragged it in, staring at the image presented to her. What was it about this man that seemed so familiar? She racked her brain. A parent? Someone she'd seen at the movies? He was certainly handsome enough for the latter. Staring at the black and white to sepia photograph she found herself drawn to his eyes and a part of her knew them. For a moment the picture transformed to colour before her. His reddish-brown hair, khaki uniform and deep, penetrating blue gaze that seemed to look through her were all there. She blinked and the illusion was gone. Shaking her head, she glanced at her watch. It was getting late. If she wanted to get the newspapers and other relevant materials scanned ready for the class and grab something to eat, she'd have to stop day-dreaming and start focussing.

A few hours later she had everything scanned and collated for her students. Another glance at her watch and she realised a proper meal was no longer viable, so she selected a microwave-friendly option from the freezer. Settling down with it in front of her computer she continued to read the articles her students had found.

Captain Lancaster had achieved a first at Oxford, so what was he doing in this backwater? He had been appointed by the then Headmaster, a Mr Pitlock, to take charge of the boys' military training. Not unusual in a school such as this, especially before it went mixed, but from the records he was not the first choice, nor did he seem overeager, turning the post down initially and only taking over when the master tasked with it proved hopeless. Several of the boys had signed up when war began, and she gazed sadly at the list of names: young men who never returned. That seemed to have been the driving force behind Lancaster's decision to leave his pregnant wife and join up. Identified as officer material, he left officer training as a Second Lieutenant, rising to full Lieutenant within months of arriving in France. Once assigned to the front she found he'd got a Mention in Dispatches for rescuing a soldier caught on the wire. His promotion to Captain came shortly thereafter. His MC was the result of action on the Menin Road, where he had led an attack on a fiercely defended enemy trench and taken out a machine gun position apparently single-handedly after most of his men were gunned down. Alex had the feeling that horror at what had happened to his men combined with white-hot fury had driven him to put an end to the slaughter at the risk of his own life. What had happened at Passchendaele was not recorded, but given what she knew of the battle she could guess. The fact the news of his wife and child's deaths probably arrived shortly before he went over the top would have undoubtedly impaired his focus, but in that battle, focused or not, your chances of survival were slim.

Rifling through the pages she'd scanned, she found some of his student records. He seemed to take an interest not just in their academic ability, but their well-being. Again, not unknown but certainly not common for the time period. She returned, once more, to the photograph.

"Why do I think I know you?" she mused aloud. Checking the computer clock, she realised she needed to go to bed. With a final look she turned off the screen and headed to the bathroom, still lost in thought.

***

As Alex brushed her teeth she continued to mull over the Captain's familiarity. Spitting out the spent toothpaste she stood up and found the Captain looking at her from the mirror. Alex stilled her urge to turn around. There was no way he was there – the room was too small for him to fit in the space between her and the shower without her feeling him – and too many late-night horror films told her if she looked he'd vanish, so instead she focused on the reflection.

As she'd suspected, his eyes were a piercing blue – astonishingly so. His hair, now visible instead of hidden under an officer's cap, was chestnut, the red tinges highlighted in the bathroom light.

"OK, I know you're not really there, so how come I can see you?" she mused aloud.

The image remained impassive. She reached behind her, still staring at the mirror, and felt nothing.

"If I turn around I know you'll vanish, so I'm not going to. I am, however, going to bed, because if I'm seeing someone who's been dead for a century, I'm way over-tired."

Giving the image a determined last glare she headed for the door and then paused and turned around. Sure enough, the bathroom was empty. She returned to the mirror and found it reflected only herself.

"Way, way over-tired," she muttered and made her way to bed.

***

After a rather noisy day, coffee before the meeting was a quiet affair. While the lively banter of the students had distracted Alex for most of the day (amazing how a bit of wind could make them so much more rambunctious), in the relative peace of the coffee shop her thoughts were once again distracted by the image of Captain Lancaster. In fact, it wasn't until Phil called her on it she realised what she was doing.

"Earth to Alex? Are you in there?"

"Hmm?" She redirected her gaze and then looked chagrined. "Sorry, Phil. Had a bit of an odd day."

"The joys of being a teacher when they've got the wind up them. Be nice if we older folks got the same burst of energy on days like this." He chuckled. "Then again, the thought of the Principal prancing around the playground and challenging his staff to conkers doesn't appeal much." He laughed softly at the image, then paused and gazed at Alex who was once again distracted. "OK, that's not the only thing that's bothering you. Come on, out with it. What's happened?"

She took a deep breath. "Thanks, but I already think I'm nuts. I don't need someone else confirming it."

"Nah, you're just going sane in an insane world. We all go through that. C'mon, spill. I promise not to fetch the jacket with the optional long sleeves."

She paused, eyeing him to see if he meant it. When he gave her an encouraging nod she dove in.

"I saw Captain Lancaster last night in my mirror."

"This is the guy who's been dead for over a hundred years?"

"Yep. Told you I was going nuts."

"Probably just because he was on your mind, and you did find that photograph."

She nodded. This was a reasonable deduction except...

"Yes, but the reflection was in full colour, minus his cap. I know for a fact I've not seen him like that, but I knew that was what he looked like."

"Can't say I believe in ghosts, but there's probably a scientific explanation, or maybe a psychological one."

"For a philosophy teacher, you missed your calling. You should have done physics or something."

"Hey, philosophy isn't a wishy-washy subject. We've had two thousand years to refine our methodology. We're rooted in solid logic. Logic dictates people who've been dead a hundred years do not suddenly appear in mirrors, ergo, there has to be a scientific explanation: you were over-tired; you've got a very lively imagination... or you're nuts." He grinned and she returned it. "I take it he wasn't actually behind you?"

She shook her head. "I reached behind to check. Empty space."

"You had time to do that? I think I'd've run screaming from the house."

"You'd think so, but somehow... I dunno. I didn't feel threatened or afraid. Just sad. Ever since I saw that photograph I could swear blind I know the man, or knew him. I've been racking my brain trying to figure out where I might have seen him before and..." she raised her hands in frustration, "zip city."

"I guess I should be grateful he's shuffled off this mortal coil... or am I competing with a ghost?"

She snorted. "Hardly. Besides, this is 'just coffee', remember?"

He reached out for her hand that was resting on the table.

"Yes, but I'd happily consider a re-evaluation."

She looked down at their joined hands and then up at his face.

"Phil. I do appreciate the compliment, but I'm not sure I'm up for anything more than friendship right now."

He pulled away and shrugged.

"Can't blame a bloke for trying."

He considered the frown on her face, knowing she was once again lost in her musings.

"Here's an idea – and given you're the IT whizz I'm surprised you haven't thought of it – put the photograph into the search engine and see what it finds."

She blinked and stared at him.

"Brilliant! Why on earth didn't I think of that?"

She grabbed her coffee, fully intending to down it and start on the search immediately.

"After the meeting? We've got fifteen more minutes of freedom before we have to deal with an hour and a half of boredom."

She looked at her watch.

"Bugger. Still, if we go back a wee bit early I could get the search going before the meeting starts." She turned pleading eyes on him.

"Me and my big mouth! Come on, then. There'll be no intelligent conversation until you do it."

They downed their coffees and headed back to the school. In Alex's room she pulled out a memory stick on which she'd put all the data on Captain Lancaster, resized the image and then dropped it into the search engine. It chugged away for a while and then a bunch of images appeared. Both Alex and Phil stared.

"Apparently, your Captain has a very popular appearance."

She nodded. "For rather a long time. Look at this! Paintings, sculpture..."

Phil was staring at a painting that showed a young couple from the sixteen hundreds.

"Alex... that's you!"

He pointed and Alex clicked on the image.

"What the...?"

She stared. Sure enough, a man looking a lot like Captain Lancaster was standing formally with a woman who looked a lot like Alex, albeit with longer hair and a dress Alex wouldn't have been seen dead in.

"Okay," Phil drawled, expanding the vowels of the word to breaking point. "I'm now officially freaked out. Who is it?"

She squinted at the caption, the words small on her college laptop.

"'Unknown couple, circa 1643'," she read. "Well that's a fat lot of use. Doesn't even say where the picture is."

"The joys of the internet." He looked at his watch. "We'd better shift. Save the page and you can investigate when we're done."

She saved the page, then unplugged her laptop from the mains and tucked it under her arm.

"I can investigate while we're in there."

"Tut, tut! Hardly appropriate behaviour!" he mocked.

"No, but a darn sight more interesting than this meeting."

"No argument there."

***

The meeting was focused almost entirely on how the college was marketing itself, its financial status, yet another warning that Ofsted was due and the importance of keeping paperwork up to date, and some new forms that had to be filled in for marking purposes. A mass groan filled the air at that one.

"Why?" asked Ellie, head of languages. "We already mark their work in compliance to half a dozen edicts. If we fill in a form we're just repeating what's already on the essay."

"The point of this one," the Senior Tutor, Scott Hamilton, replied, "is so you can highlight whether they're hitting the exam specifications. As you can see," he pointed to the PowerPoint slide that showed the form, "you can grade them anywhere from unsatisfactory to excellent on each of the key exam markers."

"I already do that!" Sean Peters from the English department pointed out.

"Yes, *you* do, Sean, but this is to make sure everyone's doing it."

"Just to clarify," Phil interjected, "is this on top of the marking we do on their work, or instead of it?"

"This is instead of it," Scott smiled, but was surprised when all he got was a series of moans. "It should reduce your workload!" he pointed out.

"And doesn't help the students at all!" Sean cried. "How are they supposed to relate that to their homework if there's nothing written on the homework to highlight where the problems are?"

"There's space to put comments," Scott defended. At the chatter and groans he raised his voice. "And at the end there's a place where you can summarise. You return the work with this on the top, then the student has a space to put a comment on your marking."

"But that leaves the same problem," Sean insisted. "If I tell them on there they're unsatisfactory on A02 I have to show them WHERE in the essay they missed it, AND what sort of things they could put there to meet that need, so I'm still making comments on the essay as well as filling that out at the end." He raised his hands in defeat. "It's bloody madness!"

Phil shook his head as if trying to clear something. "Let me get this straight. We comment on their work, then they comment on our comment on their work? Do we then have to comment on their comment on our comment, or is there an end to this lunacy?"

"Only if their comment needs a reply," came the glib response.

"And where in my timetable am I supposed to find the extra time to double up on every essay?" Sean moaned.

Alex zoned out. They could keep this up for ages and the result would be the same: they'd be filling in that paperwork on top of everything else. The results of her search were proving much more interesting. Not only was Captain Lancaster, in many forms, to be found across the internet, but so was she, and often in his company. She'd even found a Roman house painting that showed them. She was contemplating this new revelation when Phil nudged her.

"Scott wants you to tell people what you're up to with the records," he whispered.

She looked up to see Scott looking at her and she coughed, embarrassed at her faux pas.

"Sorry, got a bit lost in my research," she explained.

"Wonderful that you're so engaged. Would you like to take over?" He pointed to his laptop.

Pulling out her memory stick she walked to the front and popped it in.

"I won't take up much of your time. I'm sure all of us would like to go home. I know I would!"

Her comment was greeted with chuckles and nods.

She outlined what she had found so far and gave a brief mention of the charter and Captain Lancaster, showing images of the former (courtesy of the local museum, who'd been delighted to oblige provided they could keep a copy) and the sample poster she'd done for the Captain that was going to be put up somewhere in the school.

"There's a lot to get through, and for the time being I've been concentrating on those things that can be used in my history class – sorry about that, but it was too good an opportunity to pass up. If anyone suddenly finds themselves suffering from some bizarre need to do more work, I could certainly use the help, but otherwise posters will appear bit by bit as I uncover more material. I'm sure the college understands my actual classes have to come first." She eyed Scott who nodded. "Then that's it. Thanks." She turned to Scott. "Next time, a little warning would be good?" she whispered.

"I sent you an email," he defended in an equally low tone.

"When?"

"An hour ago."

"Perhaps a little **more** warning, then?"

"You did splendidly. Thank you!"

With a grunt she returned to her seat. Scott went on to health and safety issues and any other business during which Alex remembered to warn them of the chickenpox outbreak at the local comprehensive. A groan greeted her comment.

"Here we go again," Ellie muttered.

As an older member of staff, she'd experienced such outbreaks before and knew how it could devastate a classroom.

"I'll get a letter sent out to parents to warn them," Scott said, nodding to Jenny, the secretary, who was minuting the meeting. She quickly made a note. "Keep an eye open and you'd best prepare work that can be done at home for those who succumb. We'll just have to pray the worst of it hits after the exams."

With that the meeting was closed. Suzie, who was in the art department, leaned over to look at the image of Captain Lancaster now up on Alex's screen.

"He's a handsome feller, isn't he?" she observed.

"Hmm," Alex agreed. "Not sure how much history I would have learned with him teaching it. Might have found myself a bit distracted."

"Or you'd have got A's across the board," she winked. "Is there any chance the original plans for the school are in amongst the records?"

"Quite possibly, but I've not found them yet."

"I vaguely recall there was a landscaped garden at the back of the main building at one time. I'd be interested to see what it looked like. I'll come over and give you a hand to track it down."

Warning bells rang in Alex's head. If every member of staff dove in just to find something they were interested in, the records would be in an even bigger mess than they were already and archiving them was hard enough as it was. She honestly hadn't thought anyone would volunteer, but if they had it was supposed to be for the whole job, not merely the bits they were interested in.

"Tell you what. I'll keep an eye open and if I find it I'll give you a shout, then you can make it a special project for your class. We can scan it in to keep it safe, then all your students can have a copy to work on."

The thought of some student spilling paint over it by accident didn't bear consideration.

"Great idea! Thanks!"

As Suzie walked away, Phil leaned over.

"That was a close call," he muttered, watching as Suzie banged into an end table. The teacher's clumsiness was legendary. "Have you seen her art room? A direct hit by nuclear missile would count as gentrification."

Alex nodded.

"My thoughts exactly."

"If you want some real help, for all of it, I don't mind. Apart from anything else, I'm curious to find out if we have any more characters who've cornered the history market."

Alex brought up the Roman painting and Phil shook his head.

"I'm trying to come up with a scientific explanation, and I'm afraid none is forthcoming. Are you a time traveller on the side? If you are, when were you planning on sharing with the rest of us?"

"I wish! Imagine if you could step out of time, do your marking, then return it the same day even though you've taken a few holidays in between."

"And you'd explain the suddenly grey hair how, exactly?"

"Oh, I wasn't planning on ageing. I said outside of time, remember?"

"Time must pass for you in order for you to do the marking and take the holidays, ergo, you will age. Sorry. Logic strikes again."

"Spoilsport!"

"Besides, if you had all the time in the world you probably wouldn't get any of it done. There's something to be said for deadlines: they give us a reason to get on with things. You know what they say: if you want something done, ask a busy man."

"That's true," she agreed, "but sometimes it would be nice to be slightly less busy?"

***

The rest of the term was the usual mix of teaching and prep, marking, reports, extra revision classes, exam practice and first-year classes while the second years had study break and exams. The dreaded chickenpox outbreak was largely avoided thanks to the warning going out to parents, with second years too busy revising to go out where the germs might be lurking. First-year classes did have a few gaps, but not as many as feared. However, on the day of the flight there was one casualty, much to Phil's amusement.

"You remember how we struggled to get the money out of Dermot?" he said, reading the text on his mobile phone.

"Uh huh," Alex replied as they queued up to check in their baggage.

He pointed to the text.

"Looks like he may have had a premonition. Guess who's down with chickenpox?"

"Typical. Of all the kids it could have been. At least the bulk are here."

They were nearing the front of the queue and Phil, who had done the trip many times before, pulled out the collected tickets and passports to hand over while Alex watched the students to make sure they behaved themselves. Luckily, as several were second years celebrating the end of their time at the college and using the trip to prepare for their university studies, they knew better than to risk everything by misbehaving at this late stage, and they were determined to keep the first years in line lest one wrong move put the whole lot in jeopardy.

Without being asked the second years had spread themselves around, watching the first years and delivering words of wisdom and warning should any step out of line. Alex frowned at one who delivered a clip round the back of the head to one noisy first year. The second year, David, shrugged and pointed to the miscreant with a 'what can you do with them?' look on his face. Alex was inclined to agree but shook her head and mouthed 'talk!' to him. He nodded and focused on his charge. No way was young Stephen going to err on David's watch.

Once they were in the departure lounge, with reminders to the students that unless they were over eighteen they weren't to even consider grabbing duty free alcohol, and that any gifts were better bought on the other side where they'd be cheaper still, Alex, Phil and a couple of other staff headed for a coffee shop while the students found their own ways of passing the time until the flight.

Sitting around, chatting and joking now the pressures of the summer term were finally over, the teaching staff were feeling the holiday had already begun.

"Here ya go, Alex," Phil said as he placed a latte and a plate of cakes and assorted treats on the table.

"Pushing the boat out a bit, aren't you?" she replied, gratefully accepting the coffee and taking a quick gulp.

"My payback for that coffee where we went Dutch."

"That feels like a lifetime ago."

She bit into an almond croissant, the sugar dusting spilling on her clothes. Quickly, she wiped her hands and then swept the mess from her top. When she looked up Phil laughed and pointed to the end of her nose, which was now white. Going cross-eyed she saw the source of his mirth and wiped it off.

"Only problem with those, but they certainly taste good."

"A little sweet for me, but help yourself." He took a swig from his coffee, then eyed her. "Any more weird dreams?" Alex suddenly found the table-top fascinating. "That means yes. Let's hear it, I could use some entertainment for the journey."

"Probably better if I save this one for after we get there," she replied, taking another bite out of the croissant, although suddenly it wasn't so tasty.

"Aw, come on. So far I've learned about domestic life in Ancient Rome, the glories of the French Revolution..." he paused as Alex shuddered. That one had featured Madame la Guillotine and Alex had experienced the device up close and personal, "OK, so maybe that one we could have lived without. Then there was frontier life in the old West and a nurse's station in World War 1. I may not be able to explain it, but your nightlife is certainly fascinating."

Ever since her first sight of Captain Lancaster, Alex had been experiencing rather vivid dreams. While initially reluctant to share, when she investigated and found they were historically accurate she'd felt the need to talk to someone who was at least aware there was something odd going on. Unable to explain them she'd made a point of recording them as soon as she awakened, but last night's was not one she cared to share as it seemed more premonition than history. Images of snow, flashes of light, and sensations of plummeting downwards had dominated. She shook her head.

"Definitely not. Besides, it wasn't that clear, just scary as hell. I'll pass, thanks."

"Did you look up that medieval couple you said you were going to investigate?"

"Um hmm. Took me a while to go through the records."

"And?"

"Same as all the others. They existed. I don't remember reading about them when I was at university," she shrugged, "but I guess I must have."

"I thought denial was a river in Egypt? Come on, Alex! Even I have to admit the evidence is stacking up here."

"For reincarnation? Give me a break!"

"What else is there?"

"A well-read historian with an overactive imagination who's spent a term working her way through documents covering most of the periods she's dreamt about."

It was the only explanation she could come up with that made sense, and she was sticking to it no matter what.

Phil refused to be deterred.

"That doesn't explain those times you found pictures that clearly show you and that Captain Lancaster, or whatever his name is."

"Nature reuses patterns. There's a limit to how many variations on a theme are possible given the demands of a human face. There are bound to be repeats. Now we can digitise images we can find them, but that just goes to show people don't change."

He shook his head.

"Alex, I tried my own image and I used the staff mugshots from the college website to try those. Yours is the only one that yields that plethora of results and nearly every time you're with a man, it's him."

"Not me, just someone who looks like me. Are you jealous?" she offered, refusing to concede his point. That way lay madness.

"Hardly. If I saw him walking around here I might be." He looked up to scan the departure lounge just in case. Satisfied, he continued. "But since he isn't, I think my options are still open. Besides, I'm gentleman enough to believe it's up to you."

She gave a small bow.

"Thank you for that, at least." She stirred her latte and then licked the long spoon. "Phil, I'm not stupid. I get there's a problem, but I can't see a simple explanation or a way to investigate the more convoluted ones. If it is reincarnation – and I'm not admitting it is," she added quickly when he looked about to crow his victory, "then fine, but I have no means of proving it. It's not like I can go back in time to talk to them and find out if they sound like me. Even if they did, I run into people every day who think things similar to me. That doesn't make them me. It's weird, yes. If it's true, then apparently I've been around the block a few times. Whoop-de-do. I don't remember any of them; I've gained no benefit and I can't explain how I did it. I'm still the same old Alex Oslac I've always been. Nothing special."

He reached out and covered her hand.

"I happen to think you're very special, and not just because of this."

She looked up and smiled, then, glancing over his shoulder, quietly pulled her hand away. Harriet, together with her best friend Ellie, were walking over.

"Dr Oslac, they're calling our flight," Harriet supplied.

"Huh. I didn't hear that call," Phil commented, downing the last of his coffee. "D'you think I have time to pop to the loo?"

"I'll save you a place," Alex smiled, gathering her stuff together.

She noted Ellie nudging Harriet as the two exchanged looks and rolled her eyes. They hadn't escaped observation, which meant the next two weeks were going to be filled with prying questions and having to be on their best behaviour to ensure they didn't get any comeback from irate parents. She'd have to have a quiet word with Phil once they got to their seats.

"Help yourselves," she added when she saw Harriet eyeing the plate Phil had provided. "No reason to let them go to waste."

The girls quickly dove in as Alex made her way to the gate.

***

Unfortunately, or perhaps fortunately depending on your point of view, Alex and Phil were not seated together, so the conversation would have to wait. The rather large gentleman she was sat next to quickly settled down to reading a book, allowing Alex to focus on her inner thoughts.

She totally agreed with Phil, there was something very odd here but, as she had told him, she had absolutely no explanation. She had no memory of past lives outside of her dreams – which were hazy by the mornings. She'd taken to keeping her phone's voice record app ready so she could verbally recall any relevant information when she woke up, and the detail she did remember in those first few minutes was startling when listened to later. As well as events, she did her best to include sounds, smells and other sensory experiences. Since some of those that included Captain Lancaster were not for general consumption, she'd taken to moving the recordings from her phone and archiving them under a password. When she got back from the vacation she'd take a little time transcribing them, but for now she found her memory more than up to the task. She closed her eyes, remembering one particularly vivid and somewhat X-rated encounter and a smile touched her lips. That was immediately stalled when she heard giggling. She opened her eyes to see Ellie quickly turning back to whisper to Harriet.

"Oh boy," she whispered. Louder she said, "Ellie, is there something you'd like to share?"

"No, Doctor Oslac," Ellie replied, her voice laced with giggles.

"I'm sure if you asked they'd move you and Mr Peters closer together," Harriet offered, trying for innocent and failing miserably.

"And why would that be beneficial? I can keep a much better eye on you two from back here. Are you strapped in?"

"Yes, Doctor Oslac."

Alex glanced to her side and noticed her large neighbour was eyeing her curiously.

Forestalling what she was sure was coming she said, "Since we're not in school, you can call me Alex. You'll have to check with the other staff if they're happy to be called by their first names during this trip and *only* during this trip, understood?"

"Fine by me!" Phil called, turning to grin at the students. "I'm here to enjoy myself just as much as the rest of you."

Alex closed her eyes, wincing at his word choice, her fear reinforced when she heard Ellie mutter, "I bet you are." Thankfully, at that moment the aircraft started to trundle down towards the runway and the cabin crew began their safety briefing, which forestalled further comment. Since many of the students hadn't flown before they paid attention – something Alex had no doubt would not happen in the future: one safety briefing was much the same as another. She took quick note of the exits, checked her carry-on was safely stowed and then settled back. She had a feeling this was going to be a long flight.

***

"I'm just saying we need to play it a bit cool," Alex muttered to Phil as they stood, ostensibly with her waiting for the toilet and him asking the stewardess for some tea. "The last thing we need is Ellie's parents accusing us of unprofessional behaviour. You know what she's like!"

"Why is it always the mothers?" Phil lamented. "And what's unprofessional about standing around talking?"

"Nothing, but Harriet and Ellie saw you take my hand earlier. They're already gossiping fit to bust."

"Let 'em gossip. It's not like they don't get up to much worse, and in full sight of the rest of us. I saw Harriet with Bobby Simpson in the corridor only last week trying to remove each other's tonsils with their tongues."

"I know, but teachers are supposed to be like Caesar's wife: above suspicion. We're more celibate than the Vatican, remember?"

The toilet door opened and the occupant made his way to back to his seat.

"Let's just keep anything that can be labelled even remotely personal to after they've gone to bed."

Reluctantly, Phil nodded and accepted his tea from the stewardess. As he made his way back to his seat, Harry Thompsett gave him a smile.

"Decided not to join the mile-high club, eh sir?"

Phil frowned, put his tea down on his tray and then returned to Harry.

"Mr Thompsett, I find that remark in extremely bad taste. Dr Oslac and I are colleagues and friends, which may come as a surprise to you but it happens. It is actually possible for two people to talk to each other without feeling the need to leap into bed or whatever sordid shenanigans your teenage mind can conjure."

"Aww, come on, sir! We saw..."

At that moment the plane shuddered violently. The seatbelt sign came on and stewards and stewardesses quickly went down the gangways, clearing any cups and saucers, including Phil's refreshed one.

"Sir?" Harry said, a hint of nerves in his voice.

"Just a bit of turbulence. Buckle up. These things happen over mountain ranges."

As calmly as he could Phil returned to his seat, exhaling a sigh of relief when he saw Alex return to the cabin and quickly strap herself in. That wasn't turbulence. He'd felt turbulence on flights before and what had just happened was considerably rougher.

Alex tightened her seatbelt and glanced out of the window. Below them she could see the Alps and images from her dream suddenly flooded her mind. Feeling sick she gripped the armrests. Of all the dreams she'd had of late, that was the one she absolutely did not want to come true.

A voice came over the speakers.

"This is your captain speaking. Ladies and gentlemen, nothing to worry about. We've hit some very rough turbulence. We're not sure how long this is going to last, so for the time being and for your safety we ask everyone to take their seats. Cabin crew, please take your positions. Senior cabin crew to the flight deck. We'll keep you updated."

Phil frowned. Senior cabin crew would normally remain in the main cabin in rough weather. Something wasn't adding up. He turned in his seat and saw Alex looking pale as though she was about to be sick. He called out.

"Hey, Alex? You OK there?"

She shook her head, her eyes squeezed shut.

"Hey, it's just a bit of rough air. We'll be fine."

But Alex was stiff as a board and her lips kept shaping the same word over and over.

"No! No! No!"

The plane shook violently and then dropped. Some of the passengers screamed, everyone now aware this was rather more serious than poor flight conditions. A loud bang was heard and one of the children cried out.

"The engine's on fire!"

Now the screaming was coming from all directions. Phil raised his voice to be heard.

"Students. Calm down! An aircraft can still fly with two engines gone, so we'll be fine."

The plane dropped again and now even Phil could see the black smoke billowing past the portholes on the left side of the aircraft. A few seconds later the masks dropped from the ceiling.

Alex opened her eyes, gritting her teeth. She knew what was going to happen next. She'd seen it. The only thing to do now was to make sure everyone stayed as calm as possible.

"Students! You saw the safety drill. Put the masks over your face and breathe normally."

The voice of the head stewardess came over the speakers.

"Ladies and gentlemen, please assume crash positions."

Alex turned to the man in the seat next to her. He was wide-eyed, shaking and sweat was beading on his forehead. He was clearly terrified. She placed a calming hand on his wrist.

"It'll be OK," she assured him, putting every ounce of conviction she could find into her voice.

He nodded and faked a smile, but he was obviously unconvinced. They both bowed their heads and braced themselves.

Another loud bang and the aircraft started to plummet. Alex could feel the bile rising in her throat and she fought it down. The noise of screaming engines and passengers was deafening. As they were thrown around Alex whispered a prayer. Not that she believed, but right now it seemed the only thing she could do.

"I don't care what happens to me, but let all the kids be OK. Please!"

The noise, the rush, the panic all built to a horrifying crescendo and then there was blackness.

***

Alex found herself in snow. She blinked up at the almost cloudless sky for a moment, picked herself up and was astonished to realise she felt fine. Surveying the scene, she could see bits of the aircraft strewn around her, the bulk of it having ploughed into a snowbank. The port wing, the engines of which had caused the disaster, was now torn off and lay separate from the rest of the aircraft. Blackened and mangled from the events, the fire was at least out, so there was no fear of any further danger from that quarter. Alex made her way to the open rear of the aircraft where the tail had sheared off, but the plane had ploughed into the snow at an angle and it was too high for her to climb inside. Moving forward, she found a door and opened it. Most of the passengers were still in their seats, and the sounds of groans and crying indicated they were still very much alive. Climbing up the inclined gangway she made her way to Phil. He was sporting a nasty cut on his forehead, but he was breathing.

"Phil? Phil, come on! The kids need us."

She felt down his back to make sure there was nothing broken, then eased his head back and pushed back an eyelid. There was some pupil dilation but it wasn't blown completely, indicating concussion but nothing too serious.

"Phil, we need to check on the students."

With a groan he raised a hand to his forehead, blinking to focus his eyes.

"Alex? You OK? You look kinda weird."

"That'll be the concussion. You'll be fine. We need to make sure the kids stay in the cabin until the rescue services get to us. It's too cold outside for them."

"Where are we?" he murmured, wiping a trickle of blood as it dripped from his eyebrow.

He looked at his hand and then reached into a pocket and pulled out a clean handkerchief, pressing it to the wound.

"We've landed in a gorge in the mountains. I was thrown clear when the rear of the aircraft sheared off."

He looked up as sharply as his injury would allow, but still he winced.

"Blimey, are you OK?"

"Feel fine. Come on, let's see how the students are doing."

Between them they worked their way through the cabin, checking on the students. For a miracle, everyone was uninjured, albeit shaken and very frightened. Gazing at the back of the aircraft Alex realised there were probably some students out in the snow. Leaving Phil and the other teachers to calm those inside the fuselage she went back outside and made her way over to the tail.

A few pairs of seats were dotted in the snow and she went to the nearest. Harriet and Ellie were shivering in their seat but they were alive. Alex helped them out of their seat belts and led them to the door, ushering them inside. Once she had handed them over to Phil she went back out to see if she could find any more. A few trips and all the students were accounted for. She breathed a sigh of relief. How the entire group had survived the crash was beyond her, but she was grateful and raised her eyes to the sky.

"If you are up there, thank you," she muttered.

Lowering her eyes once more she spotted another pair of seats she'd missed before. The snow had piled up behind them, obscuring them from view. She realised the one person she hadn't seen was the man who had been sitting next to her, so she guessed that had to be their seat. She made her way over to it, mentally rehearsing what she was going to do if the large gentleman was unconscious. There was no way she could lift him back to the fuselage on her own. Although... she paused and realised that she'd not struggled at all with any of the passengers she'd rescued. Even the larger ones were feather-light.

"Hmph! That's weird. Must be the adrenaline rush."

She rounded the snowbank and figuratively froze. She wouldn't have to worry about shifting him back to the aircraft. It was clear he hadn't made it. What had her heart in her mouth, however, wasn't the sight of his dead body so much as the sight of her own.

"What the...?"

She looked down at herself and then back at her remains or, more accurately, the remains of her remains, mangled in its seat.

"But I'm alive! I've been helping people! How can I be there?!"

She gripped her own arm and to her it felt solid. She reached out to the arm of her body still strapped in the seat, but snatched her hand back before touching it. There were limits and she'd just reached hers.

She looked back at the aircraft and only now noticed there were no footprints. She'd criss-crossed the snow over and over collecting passengers, supporting them back to the safety of the cabin and checking the wreckage, but the snow was pristine. She looked down and saw she was above the snow rather than in it. She held her hands out in front of her. They looked solid enough but when she dropped to her knees to plunge them into the drift they passed through it without making a hole. Pulling them back she noticed they were sparkling slightly. Phil's words echoed in her head. *"Alex? You OK? You look kinda weird."*

"Oh my God, I'm a ghost!"

Her rational mind kicked in. How was she here? If she wasn't solid, how was it she didn't simply fall through to the centre of the earth and out again, or float into space? Could she fly? Move things at a distance? Change her clothes? A bizarre mish-mash of thoughts and ideas sailed through her head in a kaleidoscope that made her dizzy. She looked back at the aircraft – or what was left of it. Knowing what she knew now, she couldn't return. How would she explain what had happened? It would terrify some of the students while the more outlandish would probably want her to perform tricks! What was she to do? She couldn't stay out here in the snow indefinitely, she could start walking but to where? Surely there was some provision for when people died? The earth couldn't simply be filled with spirits wandering about, confused and lost. If that was the case, where was her seat companion? He should be in spirit form beside her, or at least nearby, but there was no sign of him.

She looked back at the bodies. It really wasn't pretty. Apparently this one seat had taken the brunt of the damage while the rest had survived intact. A miracle of some sort, and if the choice was between her or the children, she was happy with the outcome, especially as she seemed to have survived anyway, albeit in a different form. The fact was the one thing the other passengers didn't need was to stumble upon this gruesome sight, especially the students. Frowning, she stepped closer and then raised her hands, willing the snow to cover the seats. She figured it was worth a shot. Amazed, she watched as the snow did as ordered, and before long her body's last resting place and that of her companion had been hidden from sight. Perhaps she'd hang around until the emergency services arrived, then uncover it once the bulk of the aircraft's passengers had been taken to safety. While she didn't care too much about her own remains, and she had no living relatives to worry about, her companion probably had loved ones who would like to know what had happened to him and be allowed to lay him to rest.

As she was contemplating this she felt a tug. It was as though someone had reached through her outer skin and was now dragging her physically from the inside. It wasn't painful, but it was a strange sensation, particularly as there seemed no direction in the space around her to which she was being pulled. It was more she was being yanked out of space and time altogether. She took a last look at the aircraft.

"Take care, Phil," she whispered. "You're a good man."

It was a pathetic farewell, but she couldn't think what else to say. She liked him, yes, but not as much as he liked her. She consoled herself with the thought he'd find someone else and be much happier than he ever could have been had she lived. Another thought barged in and demanded attention. Maybe now she'd finally get to meet Captain Lancaster and find out what the hell was going on.

Chapter 2

The voice was gentle but firm, urging her from the depths and demanding her attention.

"There you go. Give it a moment and you'll be fine. That was a bit of a rough one at the end. Do you want erasure?"

Alex shook her head slowly. She felt so heavy she was convinced she would be crushed by her own mass. Even her eyelids weighed an impossible amount and she couldn't open them. None of this made sense. Wait! What did he say? Erasure? Surely within moments of becoming a ghost she wasn't going to be exorcised like some evil wraith? Well, evil several megaton something or other.

"What?"

She struggled to get up, but in addition to having no control over her body, someone was holding her down.

"Hold on there," the gentle voice continued, "You of all people should know not to go running about just after a training session."

"Running? Training session? What on earth...?"

She stilled as memories flooded back into her mind and suddenly she knew where she was. Instantly she relaxed and smiled. The weight vanished and all was well.

"I'm fine, Almega, thank you."

"And so it returns."

She could feel her companion pull back and there was a hint of humour in his voice.

"You're sure you don't want erasure?"

"When have I ever?"

She sat up and opened her eyes to see an apparently old man smiling down at her.

"Why do you insist on that look? I'm at least as old as you are and I don't take that option."

Almega shrugged. "I'm supposed to be looking after you all. A little maturity adds gravitas, don't you think?"

He drew himself up, trying to look a little pompous, but he couldn't maintain it and quickly gave up.

She chuckled.

"Like any of us need it. You remind me of Phil... or Phil reminds me of you?"

"He was a program. The sources have to come from somewhere."

She nodded to herself.

"Ahh, that's why I didn't fully connect."

"You always could tell the difference, even when you shouldn't be able to. Why is that, do you suppose?"

She swung her legs off the couch and sat up.

"No idea."

She looked down at her clothing, which was a hangover from her previous training session, and shook her head.

"Nope. Don't like this anymore. Alex was kinda fun."

She morphed her Edwardian clothes into something more in keeping with her previous avatar – practical and comfortable, not too stylish and not too laid back.

"Hmm, not sure Daniel will approve," her companion commented, looking her up and down.

She chuckled, shaking her head.

"Is he still sticking with that avatar?"

"Moved away from the rest of us, refuses to talk to anyone, refuses erasure. He's still mad at the system and at all of us – me in particular."

"You didn't force him to take that training."

"But I initiate, and I am there when you return, ergo, I'm the focus of his ire."

"I was hoping my being away might have brought him to his senses." Off Almega's frown she added, "or at least given him the chance to cool off a bit. We exchanged some rather harsh words before I left." This time a raised eyebrow was all the incentive provided for elucidation. "Well, harsh by our standards. I suggested he join me, he turned me down flat and said some other things. I wasn't in the mood to argue with him, so I walked out. He's not settled down at all?"

"After last time?" Almega shook his head. "No." He stood up. "No," he sighed, "I'm afraid Eridar is lost in a hell of his own making."

Alex considered her own moniker.

"Funny how I managed to keep my own name this time."

"Oslac is hardly a common one, I agree, but there it is."

"I think Alex suits me better, though."

She stood up, stretched and spun in place.

"What do you think? Back to Oslac or keep Alex?"

Almega shrugged.

"Up to you, as always."

"And Eridar? Do you think he will accept the new me? If I ask very nicely, of course."

"I'm afraid he's not accepting anyone, and he certainly won't accept you if you call him Eridar. But if anyone can get through to him, it'll be you. You two always have been close. Closer than is usual for us."

He gave her a look that she waved away and followed her with his eyes as she wandered the room, reacquainting herself with her stuff – souvenirs of past training sessions.

The room was airy and comfortable without being overcrowded. Images of her last residence flooded her mind and she compared the two. In comparison, this place looked austere. The couch to rest on while in training, of course, two comfortable chairs – one of which presently held Almega – and art work from various time periods including some rarities that would be lost within the program but that she had preserved for her own enjoyment. In front of her was a table with many tiers that held a mish-mash of objects. There was a space for one from her most recent session and she regarded it blankly.

"Nothing for a memento?"

"About the only thing I was constantly working on was my computer, and that's as associated with misery as with pleasure. Some of my students were a delight. Others... not so much, and right now I don't want an image of one of them staring at me all day. I'll think about it."

"And was teaching all you thought it would be?"

She cast her mind back. "Some of it. At the start when the focus was on enthusing and encouraging, yes. By the end it was all about getting them bits of paper, even if they didn't know anything, and filling out forms. I'm just grateful we don't have paperwork here."

Almega raised an eyebrow and she grinned.

"Well, none I have to deal with, and you do a wonderful job."

He sketched a slight bow of thanks.

"Anyone else out of training at the moment?"

"Only you and Eridar... sorry, Daniel. He refuses to go back in and he seems content with his books and studies."

"I suppose I should visit him. Let him know I've returned."

"I'd put up a shield. He's taken to throwing things at guests."

She rolled her eyes.

"Thanks for the warning."

***

"Go away!"

"Eri... Daniel? It's Oslac."

The door to the re-creation Edwardian home was flung open.

"What part of go away don't you understand? Did they not speak a recognisable language on your last training session?" He glared daggers at her. "I can give it to you in thousands of other languages or just send a bolt of lightning at your fleeing back if you prefer."

"Almega warned me, so that won't work. Please, Daniel? I encountered you in my last session."

He walked away but left the door open and Alex took that as tacit invitation to join him.

"Impossible. I've been here the whole time."

"Your previous self. The one you seem to be preserving."

She indicated his handsome form and their early twentieth century surroundings.

"I must admit, even though it's old fashioned, it does suit you. The beard is new, though."

He self-consciously stroked the short, well-kept beard that adorned his face.

"My choice, now I can," he replied, his tone defensive. "An officer in the army isn't allowed a beard on active duty. That's only allowed in the navy."

She followed him to the main room where he had clearly been working.

"Within the program..."

"That program was a thousand times more real than anything here!" he roared, flinging the papers from his desk.

Alex looked around. His room was full of books. A grandfather clock in the corner ticked loudly, even though there was no real time to record. A black and white photograph of a woman adorned one alcove and Alex guessed that was his avatar's wife, Elizabeth. A petite woman, even through the formalness of the photograph Alex could see she had kind eyes. The mess on the floor indicated his desk had been groaning under a weight of books and papers. What he was working on was unclear, but that he had been doing so diligently was obvious. A fountain pen was leaking ink onto the rug that adorned the centre of the wooden floor and, with a flick of her hand, she returned the strewn conglomeration to their original positions, obliterating the ink stain. With a thought she put the pen in its holder, just in case it leaked onto his work.

"Don't do that," he muttered, staring out of the diamond-leaded windows onto the garden that surrounded the house.

"Hardly an effort."

"Which is why I don't want you to do that."

He marched to the table and swept the stuff back onto the floor, 'though this time avoiding the pen.

"I'll pick it up myself, by hand, when I'm good and ready."

"But why?" she asked reasonably.

"Because I wish it! Do I need any other explanation?!" he replied, his voice barely shy of a snarl.

Seeing her approach wasn't working but determined they should sort out their differences, she walked calmly to an armchair and sat down.

"Almega is worried about you. Frankly, so am I."

"Tell that janitor to mind his own business! I'm perfectly happy, thank you."

She raised her eyebrows.

"Tell that to your face. You don't look happy. Or sound it. All this could be behind you if only you'd take erasure."

He spun on his heel. "No!"

"All right," she replied gently, raising her hands to ward off his fury, "then explain to me the benefit of keeping those horrors in your head. Truly, I want to understand. I was a teacher at the same school you attended in my last session and I read what happened to you. No one should have to exist with those images."

"The place is still standing, then?" When she refused to allow him to distract her, he sighed, "Because otherwise there's no point to anything."

He paced the room and then, finding he was stepping on his papers, bent to retrieve them, stacking them bit by bit on his desk and then sorting them so those he'd been working on were at the top. Alex remained silent, recognising he needed this moment. When he eventually settled into the Victorian-style leather and oak desk chair he was using he remained there, staring at the floor for so long that Alex began to wonder if he was reliving his experience again. Finally, he turned the chair, its castors protesting the movement, until he was facing her.

"Why do we go into the training sessions?" he asked.

"To experience something different. To pass eternity. To learn..."

"Precisely," he interrupted, seizing on her words. "To learn. And what chance have we of learning anything if we erase all the negatives?"

"We can learn a lot from positives."

He inclined his head. "I agree, but not alone. The negatives allow us to appreciate the positives. I know you won't have erased anything from your last session. In fact, you never do."

"No."

"And was it all positive?"

"Mostly. I could have done without the plane crash at the end."

"So why don't you take erasure?"

She sighed and leaned back. The chair was comfortable, if a little noisy. She glanced at him and he waved his hand. The leather instantly quieted.

"Thank you. And in answer to your question, I guess because I'm like you. I want to experience all of it, the good and the bad, but I haven't had as bad a time of it as you. If I'd experienced Passchendaele, I think I'd seriously consider erasure."

He pointed an accusing finger at her.

"*Consider*. I note you didn't say you'd do it."

"Depends on what happened. From what I can tell, you got the worst version."

"Paxto was there as one of my men, did you know that?"

"Paxto? He's never mentioned it."

"He took erasure. He doesn't remember the details of how he met his end, but I do. He asked me, knowing I was there, to tell him after he had removed the memory. So I did."

"Rather mitigates the point of erasure."

"You'd think so, wouldn't you? I told him, he shrugged, nodded, said thanks and that was that. Without the emotion, without the smells and the feelings that go with the memory, you might as well be reading a history book. Not to mention as immortals the notion of death doesn't hold the same fear for us as it does for mortals."

"There is that," she agreed. "It's as well they don't know mortality for them means an end to everything. And what about you? You never did say exactly what happened. I only got the basic headline 'killed in action'. I take it you got the news about your wife and child before the attack?"

He glanced over at the photograph, confirming her earlier suspicion.

"Two days before. If I'd been a private they probably would have kept it until afterwards, but officers were supposed to be able to handle such things. I was given the option for compassionate leave, but I turned it down. I couldn't leave my men. Looking back, they may have done better without me. Paxto in particular."

"I wasn't there, but I was a history teacher in my last training. Surviving that battle was a matter of luck, not skill," she replied, trying to reassure him.

"You too, huh? Strange we both did the same job at the same school at different times."

She remained impassive, gesturing for him to continue his narrative. After a pause he acquiesced.

"I saw the flash before it focused on us. I knew there was a machine gun there. I didn't react fast enough."

"And if that one hadn't got you, another one would have. It was a slaughterhouse," she replied, matter-of-factly.

"Some made it."

"Probably thanks to your sacrifice, and probably not for long. You know the scenario as well as I do. Better, I suspect."

She indicated the books on his shelves, some of which, she'd noticed, were replica histories of World War 1.

"You know what really stuck in my craw?" When she shook her head, he continued. "My wife was a program. She wasn't real, so I let an avatar get his guts blown into the mud for nothing."

"And Paxto is fine, so no harm done. He doesn't even remember it."

He stared at her incredulously.

"No harm? I lay there, unable to move with a bullet in my spine and watched a man trying to put his own muddied entrails back into his stomach, all the while crying for his mother. I saw another staggering around with half his face blown off. In the end I drowned because I couldn't lift myself out of the mud. How is that no harm?"

"Because you're here and they were programs!"

"The private crying for his mother was Paxto."

"All right, but he's fine because he took erasure, and I don't blame him. You may be an Eternal, but you're suffering from what, in that program, they would later call post-traumatic stress disorder. Do you think, if they had the option to erase a specific traumatizing memory, they wouldn't leap at it with both hands?"

"And it's because we're Eternals we shouldn't do that! Don't you see?"

He stood up and resumed his pacing, his movement becoming increasingly agitated.

"Nothing here is real. Not the house, not the garden, not the books, nothing. It's all recreated. If it wasn't for the programs we'd do nothing all day. Without an end date on our existence, we waste our time. Remembering that life, no matter how unreal it was, is what's kept me working and focused. Everything here is optional. Do you know, Gracti has never, ever taken a training with any pain or suffering whatsoever? She picks an easy one every single time."

"And she's an air-head. So?"

"So, don't you think there are benefits to being mortal?"

"And we're not, thus we have the programs to give us that experience. We get a life full of purpose and meaning so long as it lasts, then we get to try a different one."

"All unreal. How is that any different to any of this?"

Daniel waved his arm and the house and all its contents vanished, leaving them standing in a blank space.

"You, me and the other Eternals; we're the only things that are real," he continued. "Even our appearances are merely for convenience."

His shape dissolved until a floating ball of light hovered in front of her. Hands on hips she cocked her head at him, then morphed herself into her true form.

"And the illusion of talking in any given language, a fantasy when we could just as easily communicate directly." His words were instantly in her mind, transferred by thought alone. "We, like this, are the only things that are real in the entire universe."

"And Omskep," she replied, referring to the system that gave them their mortal experiences.

"And there's another curiosity. I don't remember building that thing. Do you?"

"No. Maybe one of the others."

"No. I asked all of them while you were off on your latest training session. Not one remembers creating it, not even Almega."

"Maybe one of them is a very convincing liar."

In her mind she could see him looking at her like she'd dribbled on her shirt and she sent back a shrug. Lying was impossible given their state and methods of communication.

"All right, maybe whichever one created it had the knowledge erased so they could enjoy it as much as the rest of us."

"And none of us noticed that one moment it wasn't there and the next it was?"

"OK, so all of us had our memories erased so we could all enjoy it. One of us built it, all of us built it... What difference does it make? We all use it. It gives us a way to experience lives that matter while we're in them..."

"And then we erase anything we don't like. That's my point. We don't learn from it if we don't remember it, and I mean all of it."

"Eridar..."

A blaze of white-hot fury burned through her and she offered the mental equivalent of raising her hands to placate him.

"Daniel," she corrected, "I get it. It's why I don't erase things. It gives us something to think about, to talk about – albeit only with you given the others don't understand why we keep the negatives – but ultimately, it's a way of passing eternity. We're here and there's nothing we can do about it."

"Have you ever tried?" he asked.

With a thought the house was restored as was his body, and he sat down heavily in the desk chair. Alex matched him, resuming her own seat.

"No. Not seriously, anyway. The usual playing around to see what would happen. Are you saying you did?"

He gave a grunt and leaned back.

"After you went into your last session, I took myself off, away from everyone. I tried quite literally everything I could think of to end my existence. Obviously, nothing worked."

"Did you think it would? As you just demonstrated, nothing here is real except us, so nothing you could use has the reality to kill us."

"I even went so far as getting some help."

"From whom?" she replied, shocked any of the Eternals would indulge him.

"It doesn't matter," he dismissed, staring at the carpet under his feet. "It still didn't work."

"You mean they were willing to test it?! I can't even see Fortan doing that, and he can't stand you!"

"It wasn't Fortan. The one who helped didn't really understand I was serious. They thought it was a game."

"Then it was Hentric. He's the only one who'd indulge you if he thought it was a game."

He bowed, acknowledging her perspicacity, then turned his attention back to the photograph of his human wife.

"She wasn't real, but I find I miss her."

Alex leaned forward, her voice gentle. "She was real, inside the program. If it couldn't convince us while we're engaged there'd be no point in it."

He stood up and fetched the photograph from the wall.

"She died in childbirth. I checked. It was a son and he was a program too."

"If you hadn't been away, would they have survived?"

He put the photograph carefully on his desk.

"You know Omskep doesn't give us what-ifs. The paths are set."

"Maybe not," she replied thoughtfully. When he cocked his head curiously she expanded on her comment. "I had an odd one at the end of my latest. For a while there, I was a ghost in the machine."

He frowned. "I know occasionally we get ghost effects from old programs that haven't been properly filed. Never heard of one of us managing it. What was it like?"

"Bizarre. I didn't even realise I was a ghost until I found the body I'd used."

She shuddered. That was an image that would stay with her for a while.

"I didn't know what was going on, of course. I mean, I realised I was a ghost, but I didn't know I was an avatar. I was just wondering what I was supposed to do next when

I was yanked out, but for a little while I was... in between? I could help people, rescue the kids I was with, but I left no mark. I can only assume I was carrying everyone, otherwise there'd have been footprints across the snow, if only from them. Looking at my own body – and it was as horrible as the images you describe on the front..."

He winced in sympathy and she smiled. Only Eridar (she slapped herself. Daniel! She had to keep reminding herself or he'd get upset again) would appreciate the feeling. If she'd told this to one of the others they'd have simply accepted it as a fact and moved on.

"Thanks. That was the most surreal experience I've ever had as an avatar. Still, I suppose I should be grateful for the error. Without it I wouldn't have been able to rescue the kids."

He raised an eyebrow.

"Your own?"

"No," she chuckled. "It was a school trip. I remember praying they'd survive, and they all did. Well, unless exposure gets them before the emergency services arrive, but I haven't checked that. Not sure I want to know." She leaned forward. "Do you think my prayer affected the program?"

"Unlikely. As I said, the path is set."

"Explains the dream I had the night before." When he raised a curious eyebrow, she elaborated. "I had a premonition about the flight. There's another odd thing. I was dreaming about my past training sessions inside the program."

"Never heard of that before. Did you get all of them?"

"Only the ones before the time I was in. At least, those are the only ones I remember. Can you imagine how I would have reacted as a mortal to visions of the far future?" She laughed. "Phil thought I was nuts anyway."

"Phil?"

"One of the other teachers. Fancied me." She winked. His growl made her smile. "That's more like it. Don't worry. He wasn't you so it didn't go anywhere."

"I should think not."

"Hey! You fell in love with Elizabeth."

"Beth, and that's different," he replied, turning his gaze once more to the photograph.

"How is it different?" she gasped, astonished he could dismiss the similarity so easily.

He turned back to her. "I don't know whether I'm with an avatar or a program and I've never remembered anything outside a program while I'm in it. You always know which is which. I've never seen you strike up anything but friendship with a program character. Besides, you weren't around." His gaze returned to the photograph.

"As a matter of fact, I was." When he looked up sharply she added, "I was at a nursing station in France. I did try to tell you before we went in, but you were having one of your tantrums and wouldn't listen."

He sat up straighter.

"I do not have tantrums. You make me sound like a child!"

"A foul mood, then, and you can't say you don't have those. You've been in one ever since you returned from your last training session, and there's no use pretending you haven't. Almega filled me in before I came."

"That trench rat should mind his own business!"

She rolled her eyes at his language. "Are you going to stick with this alter-ego for the rest of eternity?"

"Are you going to stick with yours... Alex?"

He waved to indicate her present attire. While he was in a three-piece tweed suit, as appropriate for a teacher in the early twentieth century of the program, her trousers and untucked open-necked shirt with flat shoes was far more in keeping with the time-period of her last training session.

She gave him a sheepish smile. One of the disadvantages of communicating directly was that nothing could be held back if another Eternal wanted to know. In those moments while they were in their true form, she had learned what she wanted to know about his present state and he'd learned whatever he wanted from her last training session. It was why they observed the more solid state most of the time. It was a barrier that propriety demanded be recognised. If you wanted to dig you had to ask. So far as Oslac was aware, only she and Eridar regularly transformed to share their experiences without censure or restriction of any kind. It was why they were so close.

"Nice to know you still care," she smiled.

"Of course."

"Almega doesn't approve, you know."

"Almega..."

"Should mind his own business, I know. All right, I'm happy to know Daniel if you're happy with Alex."

"Not sure I should approve. A rather manly name, isn't it?"

"Our perceived gender isn't any more real than this house, as you well know," she admonished.

"Hmm. D'you remember that time we swapped just to see what it would be like while we were together?"

She laughed and he joined in.

"The look on your face when I proposed!"

"I would have done it first if it wasn't socially unacceptable in that time-period!" he insisted.

"You know the others tried it after we set the trend?"

"I bet Gracti didn't!" he laughed.

"No. She's the one hold-out. She likes to be waited on hand and foot."

"Knew there was a reason I couldn't stand her." He stood up. "I find I have developed a taste for afternoon tea. Care to join me?"

"Instant, or are you going the long way 'round?"

He looked at her from under lowered eyebrows.

"Now what is the point of instant when it's the process that's part of the pleasure?"

She chuckled, shaking her head. "Of course. Do you mind if I create some cake to go with? I gave a load of them to my students in the departure lounge before my ill-fated flight. I find I'd like to enjoy them now... the company is better."

"Well I can't cook, so unless you're planning on moving in, that would probably be for the best. Besides, I think the tea will have gone cold if we do it the traditional way."

He offered his hand and she accepted, rising from her seat.

"And you can tell me all that's been going on with you lately," he said.

"You already know, just as I know what you've been going through."

"I didn't dig that deep. Spoils the fun." He led her to the kitchen. "There's a lot to be said for taking the long way 'round."

***

While they chatted over tea and cakes, catching up as old friends are wont to do, Almega was waiting for Fortan to exit from his latest training session. Not one of his favourite characters, Fortan was a stubborn, opinionated, arrogant Eternal who expected others to respect his experience and strength of character, with a temper that could intimidate nearly all when challenged. Almega knew Oslac and Eridar (*Alex and Daniel* he reminded himself. He'd need to remember that, even though of all the Eternals they'd be the most forgiving of his error) struggled to tolerate Fortan. Alex could talk to him, at least, though it was with forced civility. Daniel would leave the minute Fortan hove into view, regardless of what he was doing at the time. Daniel was curiosity, change and (mostly) positive passions; always delighted to have his beliefs challenged. He felt things deeply, even if he kept those feelings under tight wraps with all but, Almega suspected, Alex. Fortan was stolid, abhorred change in any form, thought curiosity a feature unworthy of Eternals, expressed himself without censure and considered Daniel to be flippant. In sum, he was negative energy incarnate. He'd been delighted when Daniel had excused himself from the Eternals' company, saying it was about time he realised his 'puerile ways' (as Fortan had termed them) were inappropriate for beings such as themselves.

Still, Almega's self-imposed duty (he assumed it was self-imposed as there were no higher authorities to order any of them around) was to be there when the training sessions ended to ensure the Eternal would realise who and what they were before they started flinging thunderbolts or otherwise disrupting the relative peace of Oestragar. Not that they could harm anyone or anything beyond simple and instant repair, but previous bad re-integrations had upset the status quo, and Almega was keen to avoid that if at all possible, especially with Fortan's surly temper.

He looked around Fortan's home base, which was lacking in any character or even creature comforts. Almega had been forced to summon a chair for himself and would have to dismiss it before Fortan became fully conscious or endure another tirade about unnecessary luxuries. For a while, Fortan had insisted on lying on the floor, until a particularly bad re-integration had led to him smashing his head repeatedly on the hard surface. Now he had a bare bones couch, which was as much as he was prepared to concede. For a while he'd also tried maintaining his energy state in defiance of usual custom, but repeated admonishments from the others when he inadvertently gathered their thoughts and then acted on them had forced him to abandon that approach as well. Fortan considered himself a purist and everyone else beneath contempt for ignoring their true nature. When he entered the program, he typically chose positions of some power and relished regaling his peers with tales of his natural command in a crisis. The fact he was merely conforming to the program and could do nothing else seemed to completely escape him, and Almega feared he was in for another lengthy description of whatever he'd been doing, and how wonderful he was at doing it.

Waiting in the empty room time could have dragged, but Almega was fully aware that strictly speaking there was no time to drag, and he had waited until the last possible instant before arriving at Fortan's accommodations. Still, there did seem to be a rather lengthy pause. He mentally tapped into Omskep to see how much longer he had to wait in case, by some improbable miscalculation, he'd chosen a pause rather than an ending. What he saw caused him to suspend his musings and frown, digging further.

"But that's impossible!" he muttered, looking at Fortan who remained silent and unresponsive.

In a moment he had dematerialised from Fortan's side and re-materialised inside the domed, crystalline form that was Omskep. Flashes of light blinked in and out of existence around him, images and sounds and other sensations were realised and then ceased as the various Eternal's experiences ran in parallel. Instantly he identified Fortan's present session. Being the character he was, Fortan had insisted on one-upping Daniel, deciding if 'that sorry excuse for an Eternal' could handle the First World War trenches, Fortan could handle the horrors of a later war that included acid attacks and multiple virus bombings, telling Almega before he began that he intended to keep the memories no matter what, just to prove it was possible to experience nightmares with no after-effects. Proof, in his opinion, that he was a better Eternal than Daniel would ever be.

Almega brought Fortan's session to the fore so he could see what was happening. Not that he couldn't directly interface with Omskep at any time and in any location, but seeing it in situ 'felt right'. He shook his head.

He was sounding more like Alex and Daniel. Given their respective characters were fixed in this timeless realm called Oestragar, except for changes brought about while they were within the training sessions (and Almega hadn't entered a session simply because there was always another Eternal in one and he wanted to be there for them), that was odd in itself. He shrugged. That was a concern that could be explored at a later time. Right now, he wanted to confirm whether there was something going wrong with Omskep, not himself.

Flicking with increasing rapidity through the program he was soon a blur of activity, watching a section, backtracking, moving forward, racing ahead and investigating every facet until finally all he could do was shake his head in bewilderment.

"But that's not how it's supposed to play out!" he cried, staring at the images. "That's not the program!"

Going from his solid form to his natural state, Almega quickly explored all the programs that were running. As it happened, all the other Eternals had chosen training sessions that occurred after Fortan's time within the program, and what he witnessed left him stunned. The ones closest to Fortan's session were starting to change, the ones later were still following their prescribed patterns, but the alterations were creeping up on them. Turning back to Fortan's program, he centred his attention on fixing the error. Not that he was in a hurry to talk to Fortan, but the Eternal would be even more difficult if his issues weren't dealt with first. Almega focused his power, intent on rewriting the code to put the program back on the right course. Not only did the program resist his efforts – something that should have been as impossible as it going wrong in the first place – it entered a loop. No matter what he did, he couldn't prevent the repetition. Pulling back he resumed his material state, staring at Omskep.

"I need help," he muttered at last, and vanished.

He reappeared outside Daniel's re-creation house and tugged on the brass door pull, hearing the bell jangling inside.

***

"You expecting visitors?" Alex asked, taking another sip of her tea.

"Hardly. I've done my best to terrify everyone into staying away. Besides, there's only you and Almega not presently in a session, so far as I know."

"Then it must be Almega. I'll let him in."

She waved her hand and a few seconds later Almega entered, looking decidedly upset. Given his calm and placid manner, Alex instantly became concerned. She put her mug down and rose to greet him. Daniel, though not as good as Alex at picking up emotions unless in his natural form, could also see there was a problem.

"Almega?" he asked calmly. "What has you over here in such a state?"

"It's Omskep. As impossible as this sounds, it's developed a programming error."

Alex frowned.

"That **is** impossible," she agreed. "Something that runs flawlessly for eternity can't develop an error. You must be misreading it."

She focused on Omskep, trying to see the problem for herself. Almega paced the room.

"It's Fortan's session that alerted me. It changed, so I went in to fix it, and now it's stuck in a loop."

"Oh, of course it had to be him," Daniel growled.

"What do you mean it changed?" Alex asked, giving Daniel a quelling look that he shrugged off. "They can't change. At least one of us has been to nearly every point in the time line and has memories to match. If the program changes, the events we experienced didn't happen, and that's illogical. It has to stay the same for us to have the memories we have."

There were advantages and disadvantages to residing outside space and linear time, but this was the first time a major disadvantage had appeared in the entirety of Alex's existence. The program didn't run like the ones she'd grown accustomed to in her previous session. It Was, Is and Will Be. A FACT with every capital landing with a thud that echoed through eternity. The entirety of the program existed as a whole, and you picked your moment to enter it, moving along its timeline from outside. There were no re-runs or repeats. The program happened once. Given both she and Daniel had been to the end of the universe (just to see it happen), that meant everything leading up to that moment was already fixed. Self-determination and freedom were illusions generated by ignorance of the future once you were inside the program.

"I know that," Almega replied, his frustration lacing his tone, causing Alex and Daniel to exchange looks, "but I tell you it rewrote itself."

Alex sat back, staring at what she could see in her mind's eye.

"He's right. And it's not just Fortan's section. The whole lot has changed after that."

"What?!" Daniel switched his attention to Omskep and saw the same thing.

"You know," Alex said turning to Almega, "I think this was going wrong during my last trip. I was telling Daniel that I had dreams about my other sessions, I dreamt about the plane crash that killed me, I saw both Daniel and myself in our other incarnations inside the program, and to top it off I stayed in there as a ghost and helped people even though my mortal body was no longer living. I talked to the programs in that state. That's never happened to me before."

The look on Almega's face made something crawl up Alex's back.

"How many of the children aboard that aircraft died in the crash?" he asked carefully.

"None of them. When I left they were all alive."

Almega pulled up that section of the program, confirming her claim.

"And yet, I know that eight of them should have died."

Alex frowned.

"You must be mistaken."

He levelled her with a look.

"Have you ever known me to be mistaken about such a thing?"

She had to concede his point.

"I always check the ending so I can be ready. Eight of those school children should have been killed on impact or died from hypothermia."

"Well, I helped them back into the fuselage once I was a ghost, so I'm afraid at least part of that was down to me, but in my defence, I didn't know who I really was."

"Doesn't matter. You shouldn't have been able to do it at all."

Daniel released a sigh and rose from his seat.

"As much as the thought of trapping that miserable sniper Fortan in the machine indefinitely has its appeal, we'd better figure out a way to get him out of there. He'll be insufferable, I've no doubt, and find a way to blame me for his misfortune, but the longer we leave him in there, the worse he'll be."

As one they dematerialised, re-materialising inside Omskep as pure energy – the better to interface with the system. After reconnoitring the system as a whole, they concentrated on Fortan's program as that one was stuck in a loop and seemed most likely to generate a devastating cascade error, making the situation even worse for the Eternals occupying later time periods. Again, the system itself seemed to be fighting them – something all three were quick to pick up on. Deciding to attack several different sections simultaneously in an effort to thwart whatever malevolence was fighting them, they succeeded only in tying the system into an even bigger knot that finally froze completely.

Withdrawing themselves, the three materialised in the core, taking on their physical forms.

"Well," Daniel said, looking on the bright side. "At least he can't get into an even bigger mess while we figure this out."

"And we must figure it out because I still remember our trip to 90,057, and that's well beyond Fortan's present time. If the system remains frozen, or if it starts and we haven't fixed the error, we won't have made that trip and..." She looked at Daniel. In Eternal terms, that particular session had been a watershed in their relationship.

"Quite," he acknowledged, redirecting his gaze to the floor when Almega raised an eyebrow.

"As if I didn't know? Just be grateful most of the others are too wrapped up in themselves to bother exploring what you two get up to."

"Most?" Alex said, mildly alarmed. All of the Eternals were free to do whatever they wanted, but living with the consequences if the others found out was usually enough to keep them from being too outlandish.

"Who do you think?" Almega replied, and nodded towards the frozen system.

"That explains a lot," Daniel commented drily. "I'm surprised he didn't crow it across all existence."

Almega conjured a chair and sat down.

"If he did, he wouldn't have anything over you. It would soon blow itself out. He was saving it."

"Oh great! Thanks for the warning!" Alex groaned. She looked back at the program. "Can we separate that bit out and leave him in there? Indefinitely?"

Almega shook his head.

"Tempting, but no."

"Whatever this is," Daniel mused, pacing the room, "it's affecting the lot. That suggests a glitch that is within the system as a whole, but the system is perfect. When we try to fix it from the outside, it only gets worse."

Alex picked up on his thinking.

"We can't shut it down, and even if we could, Eternals are in there and we have no idea what effect that will have on them."

"We don't know which of us was the programmer, and even if we did, the knowledge has been erased," Almega added, nodding to Daniel whose investigations had revealed that curious fact.

Rubbing his chin, Daniel paced the enclosure. Finally, he looked up.

"So… what if we traced where the glitch started and fix it from the inside?"

"And get caught like Fortan?" Alex said. "No thanks!"

"We can't leave it. It'll affect us regardless of whether we're in or out. The fact it hasn't yet suggests it cascades through the system bit by bit, minor errors building into bigger ones as the consequences ripple outwards, later sessions being re-written in light of the previous changes. It's not instantaneous, otherwise we'd already be stuck with irreconcilable memories. We're outside time, but the events we experienced are in time so eventually, within the program, they will be altered. I can't imagine the effect that will have, no matter where we are. Logical contradictions have to be resolved, so either everything resets, including us, or we cease to exist."

"Given your mood of late, I'm surprised you're not more enthusiastic regarding that last option," Almega observed drily.

"For myself is one thing, and I'm feeling less self-destructive now."

He did not add that Alex's presence had certainly helped in that regard, but Almega knew it anyway.

"But it's not fair on all the others."

Alex was mulling over her own experiences.

"Hang on. What if we went in like ghosts? Not as an avatar, still remembering who we really are, and able to influence events around us?"

"We can already see what's happening from here," Almega reminded her.

"Yes, but we can't interact within the program. In my last session I saved people who shouldn't have been saved, but I was already dead, so I've proved it can be done. What if we went in as ghosts to start with?"

"But that will also have an effect," Daniel reminded her. "The program will be flooded with tales of supernatural occurrences. If things are changing then our actions could ensure belief systems become more fixed. Having experienced the *joys* of religious pogroms, I don't care to reinforce them!"

He winced, vividly recalling that in one session it didn't seem to matter what you believed in: one religion; another; none at all – sooner or later you were a target for burning.

"Then you'll have to be subtle," Almega replied, the idea growing on him. "Influence, suggest, but no overt supernatural behaviour. You can tap into the system to identify what tweaks need to be made to put things back on track, move around without the limitations of being instantiated as a mortal within the program... the best of both worlds. An immortal ghost in the machine. I just thank whatever accident it was that meant you two were the ones outside when this happened. Can you imagine if it had been Fortan and Gracti?"

"Don't even go there!" Daniel shuddered. "The thought of being dependent on those two for rescue..."

"Or Hentric?" Alex offered.

All three shook their heads.

***

After some discussion, the battle plan (as Daniel termed it) was resolved. They would determine the earliest point at which the error manifested within the program and see if fixing it there resolved all the later issues. If it didn't, they'd move through the program, going to each point where a single, identifiable change could iterate through the system and put things back on track. Between them they'd analysed and identified what had happened to Alex on her last trip and found a way to repeat it, this time allowing them to choose whether or not they could be seen – a necessity if they were not to cause mayhem by virtue of their mere presence. Their powers in Oestragar to move, change appearance, create and relocate were also preserved, allowing them to call on a secondary program Alex created to run in parallel to provide what they required within the system without harming the main program as a whole.

"I really hope we don't have to go through the whole lot," Alex muttered as she finessed the final touches. "I'd rather do new things than repeat old journeys."

"You're a dab hand at that," Daniel observed, watching her interaction with the secondary program. "Are you sure you didn't design Omskep in the first place?"

"If I did I don't remember. Besides, you can blame this talent on my last session. Not that I could write programs in there, but this system is completely intuitive, so what I learned about computers and programming there can be applied here much more easily. It's just a question of logic and common sense."

"The problem with common sense, in my experience, is it isn't common and often doesn't make much sense. I mean, why did you put that in?"

He mentally pointed to a section of the program.

"To close the open call here," and she indicated another point. "It's not intelligent. It can only do what it's told, so if I don't close it the handle will hang around waiting, picking up every other instruction. Eventually, something will trigger it and there'll be hell to pay."

He raised his eyebrow at her terminology.

"You know what I mean. Now leave me alone so I can check it."

Shaking his head, he strolled over to Almega who was exploring the main program.

"I think I've identified the first point where the error starts to creep in, and it's long before Fortan's session. How do you feel about Ancient Greece?"

"I remember what it felt like to get a spear in the chest at Thermopylae. I can live without going through that again!"

"You and your obsession with war. Why don't you try a little peace and quiet every now and then?"

"Because extreme circumstances bring out both the best and the worst in people. It's the quickest way to learn, albeit the endings tend to be a little abrupt."

"Well, you'll be pleased to know it's after that, at the height of the Greek Classical Age in the third year of the 92nd Olympiad."

"Wonderful. I get to see the Parthenon before it blew up."

"And I get to see Socrates talking in the *Agora*," Alex added, having finished her checking.

"Just listen. No making suggestions," Almega warned, wagging his finger.

"As if I would!" When he continued to glare at her she added, "Seriously! It's a pity Phil wasn't real. He'd have loved this."

"Perhaps," Daniel allowed, "although in my experience it's rarely a good thing to meet your heroes. They tend to have clay feet."

"Speaking from experience?"

"Leonidas had the most dreadful halitosis. I wonder his wife could bear to be near him."

"In the absence of dental hygienists, I doubt he was the only one. I'm ready," she added. "Do we leave a part of ourselves anchored here?"

"It won't be the same as a usual session, but probably a good idea. Being aware of both what is happening inside and outside the program, you can exit quickly should you need to and witness the effect of your decisions while you're inside. Might encourage you to be a little more circumspect."

"Why are you looking at me?" Alex complained while Daniel smothered a grin.

"You have been known to... what is the phrase? Ah yes, dive in where angels fear to tread."

"It's rush in, and Pope was referring to fools. You will, at least, concede I'm not a fool?"

"In this situation, we can all be fools," Daniel returned ruefully. "We'll need to tread very carefully if we're to navigate this one. Normally, we don't know the consequences, have little power and we're constrained by the program. Now..."

"No swanning around like all-powerful deities. I get it. So, what do we have to do?"

Almega was focused on Omskep.

"I'm still working on that. It's not entirely clear what the turning point was, only that originally the oligarchy of the Five Thousand was ended in that year, but in the new program, they're still in power ten years later. They passed pretty much all the same laws so far as I can tell, since the Five Thousand were the leading voices anyway and dominated the Athenian Assembly, but one minor alteration to one apparently insignificant law would be all it takes to cause mayhem hundreds or even thousands of years down the line. We can focus on putting that event straight since it's the most obvious one, but that may not be what has to be changed. It could be, and probably is, some minor thing that doesn't look important in and of itself, but in the grand scheme of things turns out to be the key. You may need to make a person stay a day longer or leave a day earlier, sit somewhere else, use a different phrasing... Argh! How can we know what changed and when? There are literally billions of variables!"

Daniel rested a calming hand on Almega's shoulder and drew on his lessons from his last session.

"The Five Thousand were those who were allowed to vote in Athens after the Council of the Four Hundred was overthrown by Theremenes in 411 BC," he said, sounding more like a school teacher than his immortal self. "Theremenes worked with Alcibiades to bring about the defeat of the Peloponnesian fleet at Cyzicus that allowed money to flow into Athenian coffers from the Black Sea. That extra revenue allowed the Athenians to restore their traditional democracy... such as it was." When Alex gave him a curious look he added, "You should know this if you were a history teacher. Citizens only and no women, amongst other requirements."

"I did modern history when I was teaching. Primarily 1832 to 1948."

"That's not history!" he blurted, his last training session still dominant in his memory.

"It was in 2017. Classical Studies was covered by another member of staff. And not allowing women to vote was hardly unusual. They still didn't have the vote in your last session, and I doubt you marched with the suffragists."

"Beth talked of them. I think she supported them, though not the suffragettes, but given the consequences for my position if it were ever found out, she kept that relatively quiet. We discussed it, in private. She firmly believed the day would come, and I remember thinking that provided it was women like Beth who were voting, it wouldn't be a terrible thing, especially given some of the idiot men I'd encountered."

Alex nodded approvingly.

"How progressive of you. For the time period, I mean. Mind you, I remember reading about you in the archives. You were an unusual teacher."

"On more than one occasion the headmaster accused me of being too soft on the boys, but I got good results and the parents liked me, so he couldn't do much about it."

Almega looked from one to the other and cleared his throat.

"Not that I wish to interrupt this charming bout of ego-boosting, but the program?"

"Well," Daniel mused, shifting gear with ease, "given it was the success of the Athenian fleet that toppled them: either they didn't win a big enough victory; didn't get enough cash; the Athenians didn't get up the gumption to overthrow the oligarchy, or the oligarchs wouldn't let go of the reins. That's a lot to get through even to fix the obvious."

"I can simplify it slightly," Almega offered after making a quick check. "According to the program, they still win a major victory at Cyzicus."

"So, it's the cash or the people," he mused, stroking his beard. He heard Alex giggling and looked up sharply.

"Sorry," she said, raising her hand. "I just can't get used to you with a beard. I've known you so long without one, and seeing you do that... Don't get me wrong, I think it really suits you."

"I'm glad it meets with your approval, because I have no intention of removing it, for the time being at least."

Almega snapped his fingers to garner their attention.

"Can you two remain on topic? We need to get on. There may be no linear time here, but the program itself has it as a necessary feature to enable it to run, and the errors are accumulating. The sooner you get started, the sooner we can find the trigger and move on."

"Right, ready when you are," Daniel said, straightening.

"Same here," Alex nodded, taking a position beside him.

The secondary program was activated and the Alex and Daniel in the room seemed to grow fainter.

"Are you in?" Almega asked.

"Oh yes. Right in the heart of Ancient Athens," Alex replied, but she sounded perplexed.

"What's the matter?"

"Everything's moving really slowly. I mean really slowly," she repeated, stretching the words. "Is that how the problem manifests?"

Almega chuckled. "No. It's how *you* manifest. Don't forget, as an Eternal you experience time outside the program, and we're running quite a bit faster, relatively speaking. It's just a translation problem. Normally you're in there as an avatar, so you automatically slow down, now you're going to have to do it consciously."

Alex snapped her fingers.

"Of course, I forgot!" There was a pause and then she grinned. "That's better!"

"Where are you planning on going first?"

"I think we'd best just look around and get the lay of the land," Daniel provided, taking in his surroundings. "You keep investigating at your end, we'll see if we can identify the characters."

"How about Alcibiades or Theremenes?" Alex suggested.

"Neither are in Athens. Alcibiades was a nasty piece of work, out exclusively for himself. He worked for the Athenians, the Spartans, even the Persians. Think Fortan with no morals whatsoever. He and Theremenes are with the fleet."

"So why are we here? Surely we should be with them?"

"I didn't set a location for you. Did either of you choose Athens?" Almega interjected.

"I was curious about Socrates, but I didn't choose a location consciously," Alex provided.

"You were the one who said we were going to Ancient Athens when this started," Daniel pointed out. "That may have driven my focus, but I didn't consciously make the choice. I thought you did it."

Almega observed the system.

"And yet you've already had an effect. So whatever it is you need to do is probably where you are."

"What kind of effect?" Daniel asked.

"The Five Thousand oligarchy now ends after two years."

"What? We haven't done anything! How could it have changed?"

"Perhaps it's something we're going to do?" Alex suggested. "We're outside of time, this is in time... Perhaps our thoughts about our future actions have an effect?"

Almega interfaced with the secondary program and the two faint versions of Daniel and Alex in Omskep became more solid.

"What happened?" Daniel asked, looking around him.

"I pulled you out," Almega replied. "If your thoughts alone can have consequences, we need to consider our plan of action rather more carefully before we begin."

"When do the Five Thousand finish their rule now?" Alex asked.

Almega checked the program.

"Back to ten years, which suggests there was something you were thinking of doing in there that had an effect, but now you haven't done it..."

"If I were mortal, I'd be getting a headache right about now," Alex commented, searching her memory to see if she could identify anything she might have done had they remained in the program. Finally, she shook her head. "Too many thoughts. I've no idea if any of them was the trigger."

"Same here," Daniel admitted. "It seems we had better keep a very tight rein on our mental musings and not act on anything unless we check it first."

"We can't check every step!" Alex cried.

With some thought they worked to add an extra feature to the secondary program. This would act like a targeting device. It would monitor their actions, whether committed or merely thought about, and with the final ideal solution placed as their eventual aim, allow them to move in on it as they went, calculating solutions for each of their actions before they committed them. Alex called it GPS for time travellers, terminology Daniel had to think about for a moment before he got the reference.

"You've been lost in the Edwardian age for far too long," she commented. "You need to get with the times!"

"You say this when we're about to step into a period before electricity?"

"Actually, there's some suggestion they were aware of electro-plating. May have even used it to attach fragments of gold to certain items."

She grinned at Daniel, pleased she could provide some historical data of which he was apparently unaware.

"And probably considered it alchemy or magic," he replied. "If we find a light switch in the Parthenon I'll believe they've got it. Ready?"

"Ready."

Once again Almega initiated the secondary program and Alex and Daniel entered Ancient Athens.

Chapter 3

"This is going to be impossible," Alex groaned as they passed down another side street bustling with people.

For three hours within the program they'd been looking around, trying to identify anyone or anything that might be the key to changing the outcome.

"When we first came here, there was something at least one of us was thinking of doing that made a difference," Daniel observed, looking around thoughtfully at the myriad faces, as though the key to their problem would present itself.

Facing forward once more he found himself nose to nose with a man who walked through him before Daniel had the chance to move out of the way.

"Dammit, I hate this!"

Alex was floating above the throng to avoid such encounters as well as to see more, and he joined her. Brushing himself down he gave a glare to the man, who was continuing on his way through the crowds, unaware of what had happened. With a shake of his head Daniel continued.

"The second time that thought didn't enter either of our heads, and consequently nothing changed. All of which begs the question: what were we thinking the first time we weren't thinking the second?" He turned to his companion to find he was alone. "Alex? Where are you?" He floated back, locating Alex at a bakery. "You can't be hungry?"

"More curious. And you must admit, it does look delicious."

He looked around, taking in the stores selling fish, game, fresh figs, grapes and other fruit, cheese, honey-based sweets and, of course, amphora full of wine from across the Aegean.

"Limited but good. The land doesn't lend itself to farming and the Greeks made a virtue of necessity. Large meals were considered inappropriate and some of the ancient writers blamed their enemies' defeat on their excessive diets. However, given a café isn't an option and men and women did not dine together, we can't indulge even if we were solid."

"You got to taste all this when you did your training here. I never got around to this period," Alex sighed, mentally adding it to the list of 'training to complete' in her head, albeit she added the rider that it would probably be better to do it as a man.

"Be grateful you didn't do the Spartan diet." He shuddered. "Melas Zomos, also known as black broth. Boiled pigs' blood and meat, salt and vinegar. I'd kill just to get away from it. In fairness, it was the diet of the soldier more than the women."

"And given all men in Spartan society were soldiers, that means it was the man's diet." Alex gagged. "I'm just glad our problem could be traced to Athens rather than somewhere in Sparta. Given the choice I'd become vegetarian, and from what I remember there was no choice. Still, if we're going to be here for a while sorting this out, it would be good to attend a symposium and try some of this."

Almega's voice interrupted them.

"And that's exactly what you should do. When you thought of that the time line changed. Instead of ten years we're down to less than a year more than the original."

"Which means we need to become solid," Alex said practically, looking around for somewhere they could change.

"And you need to become solidly male," Daniel added. "No women at a symposium." Off Alex's look he added, "Don't blame me. Blame the times."

"Once we're done with all this I vote you do some training in a matriarchal society, just so you can find out what it's like to be a second-class citizen. This time without an understanding husband," she added, referring to their swapped sex training session.

She pointed beyond the city limits to a grove of trees that would afford them some privacy to change, as well as allowing them to walk into town like any other citizen rather than appearing in the middle of it.

"Do I have to wear the beard?" Alex asked once they'd transformed, both wearing the bodies of educated, wealthy Ancient Greek males.

"No, but if you don't want to get the attention of some of the older men you'd best be in your late twenties or early thirties."

"Or I could already be taken." She winked at him and then aged her appearance to late twenties.

"Just friends, I think, for this encounter. Now, names..."

Almega's voice filled their ears.

"Alex can be Alexios, so no problem there. Daniel, it's up to you. Iason or Demetrios?"

Off Alex's frown at the first one Daniel explained.

"No J in Ancient Greek. Jason."

She snapped her fingers. "Of course, Ο Ιασονας και οι Αργοναυτες."

He winced. "Your Ancient Greek is appalling. Between now and the symposium it might be an idea to download it?"

Alex concentrated for a moment, then offered her corrected version of Jason and the Argonauts.

"Better? I'm just glad that no matter what language we speak in here, we hear each other in our own language. Outside training, I think better in the original."

She dusted herself down, adjusting her clothing in keeping with her new, male body.

"What name are you going with?"

"I think Demetrios. As good as any and easy to remember," he replied. "What are we? Visiting merchants? Philosophers? Playwrights?"

"All three?" Alex grinned. "I'll be the new playwright, come to Athens to learn from the greats, you be a merchant who's made his money and is now exploring philosophical issues, also on the lookout for inspiration."

Daniel could see the advantages.

"It would give us a backstory that might get us through the right door. I could be funding you. Where are we from? We can't be local. Athens is big by ancient standards but too small for a wealthy merchant not to be known."

"Pella or Pergamon?" Almega suggested. "Both were cultural centres and a good distance away. Pella had good trade links by sea, Pergamon by land for the spice trade."

"Pergamon is in what became Turkey," Daniel added, once again drawing on his teaching, "so could explain our interest in what's happening with the Persians. Pella was in Macedonia."

"In that case Pergamon sounds like the better bet," Alex offered. "It's far enough away we're less likely to encounter anyone who's been there, and that means we don't have to know the entire city layout or invent a relationship with someone. It would also explain any accent in our speech."

"Pergamon it is, then. A spice trader," he mused, rubbing his hand over his longer and thicker beard. "Cinnamon, cardamom, ginger, pepper... If I have some samples it might give us an in."

He held out his hand while mentally calling on the secondary program, and a leather bag appeared with a rope tie that doubled as its carrying strap. Carefully opening it he identified the various spices packed inside, each in their own linen wraps, so he'd not look surprised later.

Alex took a deep breath, the assorted scents wafting on the breeze.

"OK, now I *am* hungry!"

Repacking his bag Daniel rose to his feet.

"Then we'd best be off. Almega, any idea where we should be heading?"

"The market you were in earlier would make sense. Where else would a merchant be? Check your purse. I added some coins to it, else no one will believe you're remotely successful."

"Good point, and only part-time merchant," Daniel corrected, identifying the purse and its contents now attached to a belt around his waist. He straightened and slung the larger bag over his shoulder. "Otherwise I'd be expected to have slaves and that would be a nuisance." He placed his hand on his chest. "I am now seeking philosophical enlightenment," he intoned gravely, raising his chin until Alex's snorts of laughter brought him down to earth. "You'd best not do that while we're at the symposium. A struggling playwright should not mock his benefactor."

"Then his benefactor needs to stop acting like an idiot. C'mon. Now we've got bodies my stomach's growling."

***

It took a while, but in due course their slightly over-loud discussions on matters philosophical and trade related attracted attention. When Almega alerted them that a group of young men who were not too subtly dogging their footsteps were their best bet, Alex raised the stakes.

"And do you not think any man who borrows money from another is his slave?"

Daniel quickly caught on – one of the advantages of having worked together so many times, albeit unwittingly during the trainings.

"The way you speak, I assume you are arguing slavery is in and of itself unjust," he said, "yet surely you agree some slavery is just? If a man be immoral he deserves his state. If he borrow from another with no intention of repayment, he is immoral and thus his slavery is entirely justified."

"But the intention to repay may well be there, just not the means," Alex returned, quietly indicating the group who were now closing on them.

He gave a subtle nod, aware of their audience.

"If we judge by intention then all could claim good intent. How would we know? And if we don't know, can any of us be just when we enslave another?"

"So by your argument, since we can never truly be said to know a person's intent, whenever we pass judgement on another we are unjust," she returned, keeping up the momentum. "Then it would follow all of us should be slaves, for surely we have all misjudged intent on numerous occasions and thus been immoral which, by your own argument, justifies slavery. However, we can also argue that all men, being honest, can admit there have been times when they were younger when they claimed an intent they did not truly have. A child may do such things because they do not know better, as may one who is not wise enough to see the consequences of their actions. You say they, too, are immoral for falsely claiming an intention and thus should be enslaved. Once again, this makes all men slaves."

In Omskep Alex turned to Daniel.

"Blimey this stuff is dry! Hope we don't have to keep it up much longer!"

"I think we've snared our targets. Just a little more should do it," he assured her.

Back in Athens, Daniel laughed.

"Then all of us would be free for a slave requires a master. If all are slaves there are no masters, therefore none are slaves."

"And we are all masters?" Alex smiled.

"I think you will find the argument works equally the other way," a young man interrupted, bowing to them both. "If all are masters then none are."

"Indeed," Daniel replied. "If there is to be balance, there must be slave and master, for the one demands the other."

"And why not let all be free?" Alex returned. "Masters, yes, but masters of the arts, of philosophy, of rhetoric, not of men." *'Or women'*, she added to herself.

"And we clearly have a master of rhetoric here," the young man replied, smiling at Alex.

"Merely a struggling playwright," Alex returned. "Alexios of Pergamon."

"To my regret I must confess I have never heard of you... yet," the man replied. "'Though I little doubt that will change. My name is Galenos. I overheard your discussion. You are obviously well versed in the philosophical arts."

"Merely practising. I am Demetrios, also of Pergamon. A humble merchant and your servant, sir."

"What brings you to our fair city from so far?" Galenos replied, taking Daniel's measure.

"My companion and I heard that Athens is the city of artists and philosophers. We both wish to improve our skills, but we have only just arrived and truly we should be seeking lodging for the night. I fear we became distracted."

He made a show of looking around in the hope of identifying temporary accommodation.

"No need. My friends and I," and here Galenos indicated the young men with him, "were heading to a wealthy friend's house for a symposium. Once our discussions are concluded I doubt any will be in a state to go home, and Miltiades has room and to spare."

"You do not know us, sir," Daniel insisted while Almega told him they'd hit the jackpot. "Why would you invite strangers to dine with you? Besides, Miltiades may not wish our presence."

"Strangers may be messengers of the Gods. You are clearly not pirates as you insisted on paying for the goods you bought," and he indicated the bread and fruit Daniel had haggled for with the street vendors, "and I heard you say you had spices for sale. Bring those with you and I have no doubt Miltiades would consider you a welcome guest indeed. With the war our trade has suffered, and while the sea lanes are now open again it will take time for shipments to pass through. I know I speak for all of us when I say your spices would be welcome at the table."

"Have you been watching us?" Alex asked, stepping up to stand beside Daniel. "I warn you, if you are thinking of stealing from us we are both capable of defending ourselves. While you outnumber us and so would likely be victorious, we are neither of us incapable and you would not escape unharmed."

"Alexios, you do us a disservice, I assure you. We were indeed watching as you are new to the city and we were as wary of you as you are of us, but once we heard your discussion we knew you would be welcome and I, for one, would like to hear more. Please, come dine with us? Miltiades' house is but a short walk from here."

Daniel and Alex feigned reluctance as the others added their entreaties until they finally accepted the invitation. Galenos introduced his two companions, Aetios and Timon and together the group headed through the city streets until they reached a more upmarket area towards the outskirts of the town. Finally, they reached a large house and when the slave answered the door Galenos led the way inside.

Miltiades was gracious in his welcome to his unexpected guests, but his courtesy turned to delight when Daniel insisted he had to pay for their entertainment and lodging and offered his spices. When Miltiades said it was too much Daniel dismissed it, explaining he had more en route and since he had been made aware how much the city craved his goods he knew he would more than recoup any loss. Besides, he argued, he hoped Miltiades would speak well of him to others and so increase his reputation.

Having sampled Daniel's offerings, Miltiades handed them to his slaves with instructions that the cook use them freely in the evening meal.

"I will have no problem recommending your wares, sir," Miltiades assured him. "They taste fresher than many I have sampled since before the war. Perhaps even then. As for your reputation, that will depend on the quality of our discussion. Galenos tells me he overheard you discussing the merits of slavery. I am an old man and have had many slaves. A number have earned their freedom and I have no doubt my present slaves will do the same. They stay with me because they know I am a fair master. Do you not approve?"

Daniel raised his hands in a placating gesture.

"It was not slavery as such we were discussing, more the rightness or wrongness of who is taken as a slave."

Miltiades nodded, satisfied his way of life wasn't being impugned by his unexpected guests.

"A suitable starting point for our symposium," he declared.

He led the way to the dining room where a number of couches were arranged around the walls, each with its own small table on which slaves were placing starters and filling the shallow-bowled kylix with wine.

Daniel leaned down to Alex.

"Watch the wine," he whispered. "Not as strong as ours but not strained either. The dregs can choke."

"Noted," Alex whispered back while she watched Galenos and Aetios take their positions on the couches. Satisfied she knew what she was doing she followed suit and before too long the meal was in full swing.

A selection of snacks including chestnuts, flatbread, cheese, a dip made from fish, fruit and honey cakes and a steady stream of wine provided by the slaves began the proceedings and Alex began to feel frustrated that their real purpose in coming here seemed to be slipping away from them. The food was basic yet good, but it seemed to be distracting them. When she opened her mouth with the intention of beginning the discussion Daniel's phantom form in Omskep quickly stopped her.

"The meal has to be finished before the symposium can begin," he explained. "Eventually Miltiades will signal it by pouring a libation to Dionysius and, unless they decide to draw lots, he'll be the master of the feast, determining the strength of our wine. There'll still be food left to soak up our drinking, but the main feast will be over and we'll be able to concentrate on the discussion. It won't be much longer. Enjoy the food and relax!"

Alex sighed. She knew he was right, but still...

"I know, I know. I just want to get on with it. It feels like we're getting side-tracked."

"You were the one complaining you were hungry," Daniel reminded her.

"Yes, and now I'm not," she retorted. "And eating like this just feels uncomfortable. I feel like I want to stand up and walk around just to let the food move down a bit!"

Daniel drew her attention back to the room where Miltiades had risen to offer the libation. As predicted it was to Dionysius, a God with whom Timon, in particular, seemed to feel a strong affiliation. A slave settled in the corner and began playing what, to Alex's ear, seemed quite discordant notes. Back in Omskep Daniel hastened to reassure her.

"It's a different scale to the one you're used to. Don't worry, we're not required to listen to it. It's to ensure there's no painful silence while people gather their thoughts. Just think of him like the background noise in a coffee shop."

Almega cocked his head, listening to the slave's playing as he watched the program.

"Not bad," he said after a few moments. "By the standards of the time, Miltiades has found himself quite the musician."

"I'll remember to thank him," Alex muttered.

Daniel shook his head.

"Thank Miltiades, not the slave. As his master, it's Miltiades who should be complimented for his excellent taste and support for the young musician. The slave is never complimented directly by a guest unless the host encourages it."

Alex let out a loud groan but acquiesced and the two returned their focus to the symposium. The slaves removed most of the plates, leaving honey cakes and flatbread to help absorb the wine, and refilled their kylix, mixing wine and water as Miltiades directed.

The matter of intention, which Galenos introduced as their starting point (providing an extraordinarily accurate summary of the earlier marketplace discussion for Miltiades' benefit), quickly carried the debate into other realms including, much to the visitors' delight (and Alex's relief), that of politics. Timon, who had focussed almost exclusively on the drinking aspect of the symposium and was now in his cups, raised the issue.

"Intent is everything," he slurred, raising his kylix. "For example, the intention of the present rulers of Athens. Do they intend to return us to the democracy for which we are justly famous, or retain power?"

Alex noted that Miltiades was frowning, but Timon seemed completely unaware that he was stepping on tender toes.

"Come Miltiades. You are one of them. What say you?"

"I say this is not fit for discussion."

"I must confess," Alex said, mindful of the delicacy of the situation, "I have heard a great deal about Athenian democracy but being so far away Demetrios and I have only recently become aware that it exists no longer. It seemed such a remarkable thing, if you would not mind enlightening us as to what it entailed and why it is no more we would be grateful. Of course, if you cannot speak of it, we both understand..."

Miltiades sighed, lowering his brows at Timon.

"You see the trouble you have stirred up?"

"It's a fair question. If you will not tell us, tell our guests why the marvel of the world was dith... diss..." He was struggling to get his words out, the alcohol numbing his tongue. "Closed down," he said at last, replacing the offending word. "You never know," he added, in the sort of drunken whisper that can be heard across a stadium, "he may even reveal whether it's to be started up again. Wouldn't that be a wonder!" He hiccoughed and grinned, burying his face once more in his wine.

"Come now, Alexios," Daniel interjected, well aware of the path Alex was taking, "our city laughed at the notion as you well know. It was a nice experiment, but clearly not the way to run a society. Hence the Athenians wisely abandoned it."

"On the contrary," Miltiades countered, and Alex had a hard time hiding her smile that so simple a ploy had worked, "we merely decided that in a time of pestilence and war, a focused guiding voice would be more effective than the disparate suggestions of many. As you may have heard, we had a plague some years ago, then the war with the Spartans and constant encroachments by the Persians. Our people could not make up their minds as to the best way to deal with so many problems, so 30 men took over to try and provide a more targeted response, but they forgot themselves, enjoying their power too much. At that point they were overthrown and five thousand leading citizens granted the right to debate and discuss strategies and ways to resolve our problems."

"And how were the five thousand chosen?" Daniel asked, genuinely curious.

"How else?" Timon giggled, catching a slave's tunic and demanding he empty the kylix of its dregs and refill it.

"The most powerful citizens – by which, of course, I mean the wealthiest – threw out the tyrants and set themselves up to replace them. Seemed like a good idea at the time," he added, contemplating the floor thoughtfully. "Whether it still is…"

The slave looked to Miltiades who shook his head, pointing at the water jug and indicating a larger proportion be added to Timon's cup. The slave dutifully put a little wine in the kylix and topped it up with a much larger amount of water. The way he did it indicated this was not the first time they had dealt with Timon's drunken ramblings.

"Your pardon, Miltiades, if I have caused offence. I assure you I was merely curious," Daniel began but Miltiades waved his apology away.

"You have done nothing wrong. Timon will regret his behaviour in the morning, if he remembers any of it. As it happens, with the recent success of the fleet I am to attend an ekklesia tomorrow to discuss returning Athens to democracy."

"And that means?" Alex nudged. "I'm sorry, I fear I'm ill-informed on the subject."

In Omskep she looked at Daniel.

"Ekklesia?"

"Political assembly," he provided. "Honestly, for the equivalent of a god you really do need to be more aware. It's hardly an effort for us to do some research."

"I prefer to be surprised," she responded. "All your studies take the fun out of it!"

Back in the room Miltiades, unaware of the exchange, continued.

"Since it was invented in Athens, that is hardly unexpected. A wonder of the world, Athenian democracy advocates that all citizens be allowed to vote on what the city will do."

Alex pretended to choke on her wine.

"ALL citizens? You allow women to tell you what to do?!" she gasped.

Their host laughed good-naturedly.

"Of course not, don't be ridiculous. What would women know of how to run a city or conduct a war? Only men have the wit to handle such weighty subjects. No, male citizens only. Women, slaves and visitors from outside are not allowed a voice or a vote."

'Of course not,' Alex thought, focusing on her wine to hide her expression from their host.

In Omskep her phantom self was not so quiet.

"Tiny minded, arrogant, misogynistic..."

"I agree with you," Almega placated as Alex stormed around the room, apparently looking for something she could hit with impunity. "Just remember it'll be over two thousand years before enlightenment comes, and several hundred years after that before the reality of equality sinks in across the program. Miltiades is simply expressing a widely held belief of his time. In his mind, women are incapable of thinking."

"Tell me we're close to finishing this," she growled, "because if I have to listen to much more of this BS I swear I am going to hit someone."

"You're close. Miltiades is clearly one of the leading lights and his words apparently carry weight. Keep doing what you're doing and with luck everything will go back to the way it should be."

Daniel smothered a grin at Alex's simmering fury.

"Best focus back in the room, Alex. You're twitching and Galenos is starting to look worried."

Returning her attention to the room Alex pretended to swat an insect to explain the odd behaviour. Relieved, Galenos smiled and nodded, then returned his focus to the conversation.

"How does anything ever get done?" Daniel asked, filling the gap with a less contentious matter. "Surely no group so large will ever agree on anything?"

"We discuss and debate the merits of different positions and then, after careful consideration, we hold the vote. In fact, under normal circumstances the system worked well. Those who knew what was happening spoke in favour of their positions, while those who didn't understand bowed to the wisdom of their betters and voted accordingly. Unfortunately, when the Gods chose to humble Athens, even the wisest could not decide how best to respond, and that left the people confused and fearful. No decision could be made."

"And your present leaders? I gather from Timon the ones chosen were the most powerful, but does that mean they are also the wisest? I certainly concede in your case as I have had the pleasure of witnessing it for myself, but cannot power also be accrued by heredity and luck? I know that happens in Pergamon. Perhaps..." and he paused as if dealing with an internal conflict, although none such existed, "...perhaps there is wisdom in a crowd? When a large group find themselves all in agreement, either all are fools, which seems unlikely, or they have found true wisdom. The larger the group, the greater the chance of wisdom? I confess, I find the idea both confusing and interesting, although whether the citizens of Pergamon are as wise as those of Athens is something of which I have yet to be convinced."

"It is true there are few cities in the world capable of handling democracy," Aetios interjected, satisfied that on this matter he was in the right and so did not risk making a fool of himself. "It is dependent not only upon a wise populace but a courageous one, prepared to trust the people."

"Then the people of Athens were courageous indeed," Daniel averred. "Perhaps now they are not so, and that is why you are withholding the restoration of their rule?"

"Indeed," Alex said, hoping to drive the point home. "After all, there is no plague and no war. What other reason but that you now realise the bulk of the people are fools and cowards, not to be trusted with weighty decisions?" Daniel winced and Alex, realising she may have gone too far, bowed her head. "Forgive me. I think the wine must have muddied my wits."

Miltiades was silent, lost in thought. Finally, he drew breath and shook his head.

"No, your wits are not at fault. It is a fair assessment. With the threats now over, the only reason we would maintain power would be because we did not trust the people, and that reflects poorly on us." He swung his legs from the couch and stamped his feet on the tiled floor. "You have given me much to think about and I thank you for that. The assembly tomorrow is an important one and I must rest. Please, feel free to continue. The wine is plentiful, even with Timon's prodigious consumption, and my slaves will ensure you have a place to sleep. Thank you, once again, for your spices and your debate. It has been an enlightening evening. Goodnight." And with that he left the room.

"I hope I have not caused offence?" Alex queried, following Miltiades' exit.

"Not at all," Aetios smiled, pulling a grape from its bunch and popping it in his mouth. "You have given him food for thought and Miltiades likes to contemplate such things in solitude. Take it as a compliment. He usually remains until all of us are like Timon! That he felt the need to remove himself tells you the quality of debate was superior to the usual."

Daniel turned to Galenos, keen to further their cause.

"The meeting tomorrow. Is it closed or can others listen, even if they cannot speak or vote? I would appreciate the opportunity to see how Athens governs itself."

"Due to the large number the meeting is in the open, and with the presently smaller attendance there will be room, but as you are not a citizen you will not be able to get too close. Watch from a distance only. Still, it would give you the chance to witness wise men debating in a civilised manner. A far better approach than that of the barbarian races who must submit to the rule of one who attains power merely by accident of birth or through the sword. Such men often do not seek advice and consequently make mistakes, frequently at the cost of their leadership. As you say, there is greater likelihood of wisdom in a crowd, although I confess I have never heard that before. Despite your protestations there is clearly wisdom to be found in Pergamon."

"Perhaps," Daniel replied, dismissing the compliment politely.

"And you? Do you want the return of democracy?" Alex asked.

"I am not one of the five thousand, but as a citizen I would welcome the restoration of my vote."

He looked over at Timon who was now snoring on his couch. A slave carefully relieved him of his kylix and placed a throw over him.

"Even Timon will have that right," he continued thoughtfully, "although one hopes if it is restored he will refrain from the wine during the debates!"

"He does seem to have something of a drinking problem," Alex agreed.

Galenos nodded, a long suffering sigh indicating he'd had to fix the mess Timon's over-indulgence caused on more than one occasion.

"A dedicated worshipper of Dionysius, to be sure. His problem, such as it is, is that his stomach has a greater capacity than his wits, and he has never learned it is better to be a master of wine than its slave. Even the god would be content with marginally less worship, I think," he finished, ruefully.

Daniel chuckled good-naturedly at the reuse of their primary discussion, while in Omskep Alex summarised the problem.

"That's one way of describing an alcoholic."

"A rather elegant one," Daniel agreed.

"I, on the other hand, know when I am replete," Galenos continued. "I think I will follow Miltiades' example and seek my bed. When you are ready, just ask the slaves where you may rest. I will see you in the morning. Thank you. Your company has been everything I hoped it would be. I trust you have also enjoyed the evening?"

"Indeed we have," Daniel replied. "It has been most informative and the company everything I could have wished for."

He bid Galenos goodnight and then followed Alex who walked to the central courtyard from where it was possible to look up into the night sky.

"Not ready for bed, yet?"

"Not yet," she replied, keeping her voice low in case any were within earshot. "I didn't drink nearly as much as it appeared and besides, if *we* can't hold our drink there's no hope for anyone. I do like looking at the stars when there's no light pollution, though. Feels like you can reach out and touch them when they're this bright."

She sat on a stone bench, her hands braced behind her and leaned back, admiring the view. Daniel sat beside her.

"In fairness, in Oestragar we can, but I know what you mean. On still, clear nights in the trenches I used to do the same. Usually got spoiled by a Very Light that would blind you for ages, but it was a reminder of how small our fight was in cosmic terms. I used to wonder if anyone was out there and knew the stupidity of the creatures on this planet. Now I know."

"Yes and... yes," Alex agreed.

He let his eyes rove the stars for a while before drawing a deep breath.

"We'd best check in and see how we're doing."

Leaving their bodies apparently lost in contemplation of the night sky, they both switched their focus to their phantom forms in Omskep.

"So, did we change it?" Alex asked, peering over Almega's shoulder.

"It's still in flux. My guess is Miltiades is wrestling with his conscience. We'll know better when he's slept on it. Even at best case scenario there still seems to be something missing, but I can't quite nail what it is."

He swept his hand through the images that flashed before them, looking for the key.

"It vanished briefly when you said you would like to attend the debate, so I suggest you go."

"Well, there's no reason for us to wait," Daniel smiled. "We'll put our bodies down and then fast forward to when Miltiades gets up."

Almega shook his head.

"A little earlier, I think. An early morning trip to the market seems to be in order, 'though I cannot see why." He shrugged, still flicking through the files, then sat back. "Perhaps something will be triggered once you're there?"

"That or we have to hope that close enough will do," Alex replied, gazing at the program to see if she could find something Almega had missed. He levelled a look at her that spoke volumes. "Yeah, maybe not."

"While it may not be the key, we need to eliminate it by getting it back where it was. If there's still something out after that..."

He raised his hands in frustration. Alex moved to offer a comforting pat on the shoulder, before realising in her present state it would be pointless. She offered verbal support instead.

"Then we'll hang around until we find that other thing, whatever it is. If necessary we can keep going back and step in as every single citizen until they're all doing what they did originally. It'll take a while, but if we have to we can do it. For now, let's get our bodies settled, then we can jump forward."

They returned to their positions on the bench and got up, stretching to work out the stiffness from leaving them in the same position for so long. Standing they saw Miltiades' room darken as, presumably, he extinguished his lamp, and then went in search of a slave to find them a room.

The slaves were waiting dutifully on their late-night guests and within short order they had been shown to sleeping quarters by one, assuring him they were happy to share. Apparently, this was not unusual as he calmly bid them a good night. As soon as the door was shut they settled their bodies on the beds, stepped out and stepped back in just after dawn. Assuring the household they had slept well and Daniel wanted to visit the market to gauge interest for his trade before the meeting, they headed out.

Walking the uneven road Daniel stumbled and Alex grabbed him just as a loaded cart thundered past. Daniel dusted himself down, staring after the cart, the driver whipping the horses mercilessly.

"I remember him. I saw him the first time we visited and he was mistreating the animals then, too. I was sorely tempted to give him a taste of his own whip!"

Almega's voice echoed in their ears.

"Do it! That gets us down to only one week extra!"

"What? How is punching that idiot's lights out going to affect the vote?!"

"Who knows? Do it!"

With a determined stride Daniel headed after the driver, finally catching up with him when he pulled the foaming, shivering horses to a halt near the market, ready to offload his goods. When the carter raised his whip again to force the animals to back the load into a narrow side street, Daniel reached over and snatched the whip from the brute's hand. Alex stepped forward to calm the animals and stall holders offloaded their goods, while Daniel gave the man a piece of his mind.

"This is the second time I've seen you abusing your animals, but this time you nearly killed me. What is so urgent that you have to drive without thought for your animals or others using the road?"

The man tried to snatch the whip back but Daniel was a foot taller and easily kept it from his reach.

"Give that back or I'll call the soldiers!" the man demanded.

"Please, call them. I'd be delighted to enlighten them as to your behaviour. Explain yourself, sir!"

"It's 'cos he gets drunk in the evening and is always late getting to work!" someone called from the crowd that was quickly gathering.

"Nearly ran *me* down last week!" someone else added.

Apparently, the man had few friends in the market as more and more added their complaints now that a wealthy man was taking a stand.

Daniel arched an eyebrow, glaring down at the inhumane carter. The ruddy face with burst blood vessels across the cheeks and nose gave the lie to his protestations that he never touched a drop, and flushed deeper when the cries from the crowd caused his temper to escalate. Deciding to take a swing, the carter pulled back one massive fist, but Daniel had too much experience with too many different forms of fighting to be caught so easily. He neatly sidestepped, tripping the carter so he landed face first in a pile of excrement left by his own terrified horses. The crowd roared their appreciation as the carter pulled himself to his feet, wiped off the worst of the muck and then turned, teeth bared, determined to exact revenge. Again and again he swung wildly and Daniel merely avoided his blows, letting him exhaust himself. When he was satisfied his opponent was thoroughly winded, he tripped the man up again but this time pushed him onto his back and placed his sandaled foot on the man's heaving chest to hold him down.

"Keep that up and you'll be dead before you get the chance to kill your horses with overwork, and the only person to blame will be yourself. If I were you, I'd take this opportunity to change your ways, because if you continue in this vein you will kill someone and then the best you can hope for is exile. The worst will be crucifixion, and given how angry the crowd is, I suspect they would be delighted to watch you strapped down and slowly strangled."

A cheer from the crowd at Daniel's words supported his suggestion.

"Now, can I let you up, or do you wish to continue this futile engagement?"

The carter's bloodshot eyes stared up into Daniel's cool, blue ones and saw the utterly implacable determination within. He looked over to Alex who had calmed the horses but was also projecting a self-assurance that did not bode well if he didn't submit. Hungover as he was, the carter was not a fool. He raised his hands in surrender and Daniel lifted his foot and then reached down, offering the man his hand to help him up. Once he was back on his feet the carter asked for the return of his whip.

"Of course."

Taking hold of the ends of the thin, wooden stick to which the woven leather straps were attached he broke it over his knee. Alex quietly summoned a small dagger that she offered to Daniel who used it to slice the leather straps in half. Once the whip was effectively destroyed he handed it back.

"In my experience, horses respond very well to care and encouragement. If you get up early you won't have to rush here and so will have no need of this."

Once again the two men locked eyes, but the carter knew he could not beat this man in a fair fight. Perhaps he would find him later in the dark and be able to use a dagger of his own, but not now. He took the remnants of his whip and threw them aside. Collecting his money from the stall holders who had taken delivery, he pulled himself up onto the cart and, with a final look around the crowd, his gaze settling on Daniel and Alex, he flicked the reins and pulled back onto the street proper. The crowd parted to let him through, a few jeers following him. Daniel shook his head and turned to Alex to find Miltiades walking up to him.

"I have never seen fighting like that before," his host exclaimed. "You are barely breaking a sweat while your opponent is in quite a lather. Even allowing for the fool's poor health that is an achievement. I have seen him render many an opponent to a bloody pulp before now. Is that the way men fight in Pergamon?"

"Ahh, no. I learned it from someone who learned it from someone from the far east," Daniel replied awkwardly. He'd not intended his host or anyone else of note should see his fighting skills, and with a certain number of caveats that explanation was more or less true.

Miltiades nodded, happily accepting the explanation.

"It is certainly different and, in this instance, very effective. Akin to wrestling but less brute force. Once more I find I am impressed by you, Demetrios. I missed you at breakfast and wanted to say goodbye. I am to the Pnyx for the ekklesia. I think this will be a lively gathering. Galenos informed me you wished to see Athenian governance at work and I now invite you both to attend as my guests. You may not speak, but you may, perhaps, learn. That is, if you still wish to attend?"

"We do!" Alex quickly provided, "and we are most grateful."

Miltiades dismissed the thanks with a wave of his hand.

"You deserve payment. That carter has been a thorn in our sides for some time. I have no doubt he will already be purchasing a replacement for his whip, but you gave us very satisfying entertainment while you taught him a lesson. That said, I would advise you do not walk alone at night from now on. He will seek retribution and what cannot be done in daylight may easily be hidden by night."

"I confess it is tempting to give him his chance. He would be the one left in the dust, I assure you."

Miltiades regarded Daniel and nodded.

"I suspect that may well be true, yet I still caution you. He will not alert you to his presence until after he has slipped his knife between your ribs."

Daniel grunted his understanding and decided to change the subject.

"Have you made up your mind as to your position in the debate today?"

"I have," Miltiades replied as the three made their way to the open, flat area atop a hill that provided space for the Athenian assembly.

"Would it be inappropriate to ask...?" Alex began.

"It would. However, I can tell you that the people of Athens are neither cowards nor fools and neither are their leaders. Nor do I wish to treat any as if they were."

Daniel nodded and smiled. Their discussion had achieved its aim.

"Will they let you speak?" he asked.

"One of the advantages of living longer than most is that I am permitted to speak before the younger men. They will hear me, whether they wish to or not."

It took a while to reach the area and Alex and Daniel quietly removed themselves to a spot high enough to see what was happening without encroaching on the meeting itself. In groups or alone the members of the assembly came together until there was a noisy crowd gathered in the lea of the stone platform. Once all were congregated, the presiding officer banged a large stick on the ground to bring the meeting to order.

When the crowd had quieted he called out in a loud voice, "Who wishes to speak to the Popular Assembly?"

"Still using the traditional opening," Daniel noted under his breath.

"What did Miltiades' mean when he said he got to speak first because he's old? He's not that old."

Determined not to miss a thing by focussing on Omskep, and switching to their own language – which would sound like gibberish to the locals – Daniel replied.

"By our standards, or even by the standards of our last training sessions, no, but by the standards of this time? Anyone over fifty was traditionally allowed to speak first."

"If over fifty is considered old, what does that make us?" Alex chuckled, matching his speech.

A few raised eyebrows around them could be safely ignored. The Greeks called anyone who didn't speak Greek 'barbaroi' – barbarians – but Athens was a port and used enough to hearing foreign tongues, even if this was one they'd never hear again.

"Well, given we're beyond time and space, eternal. But by their terms? Perhaps prehistoric?"

She snorted.

"Literally! Look, here he comes."

Behind them a man, who had been heading for the stone to speak, overheard their conversation, stalled and blanched. He'd understood every word they'd spoken, which meant they could be only one thing. Edging through the crowd he found a position from where he could see their faces but not be seen. Given who and what he was, he could easily strip away the illusion they cast around themselves within the program and see who they really were.

"Eridar," he murmured, nodding to himself, "and Oslac, too. Good! I wondered how long before you realised something was wrong. But we need more time."

He backed away, fully aware that Eridar and Oslac could see his true nature in their present form as easily as he could see theirs. As he did so he was halted by a slave who had been searching the crowd for him. He listened as the slave spoke urgently, nodded, turned to another member of the assemblage and whispered something to him, then left the Pnyx as quickly as he could without drawing attention to himself.

Alex was listening to Miltiades' impassioned speech for the return of democracy. She smiled to herself as several of their arguments from the night before found echo in his words. The symposium had clearly had the desired effect and their arguments were now swaying the assembly. She looked over the crowd, many of whom were nodding, and saw someone hurrying away from the meeting. From this distance and with his back to her she couldn't make out who the man was, but he was certainly eager to be away. She nudged Daniel and pointed, the two sharing the same thought. 'Who would leave something as important as this?' Their unspoken question was answered when Miltiades finished and the leader of the Assembly called on Athanasios. A few around them, who apparently felt the present situation should continue, called out in support of the proposed speaker, only to express their disapproval when someone shouted that Athanasios had been forced to leave due to an accident involving a cart and his father-in-law. The crowd mumbled their displeasure when another took Athanasios' place. The new man, Zeuxis, was ill-prepared in comparison to Miltiades and obviously had not expected to be required to provide the primary argument in opposition. His hesitations while he gathered his thoughts and repetition due to lack of preparation were painful to watch in comparison to Miltiades' polished performance. It was not that Zeuxis was a poor speaker – judged by the standard of politicians Alex had listened to in her last training he was singularly impressive – it was more Miltiades was so good.

"So that's why I had to pick the fight," Daniel muttered, the pattern of interlocking events now becoming clear.

"You think it's the same man?" Alex asked, privately wondering how many carters there were in Athens.

"The fight would have made him late for his next market delivery. He was probably in a hurry and angry. A moment's inattention was all it would take. If the father-in-law was elderly he wouldn't have been able to get out of the way. It seems my prediction came true even sooner than I thought."

"It was only a question of time given the way he was behaving. Something of a miracle it hadn't happened before. So, if this Athanasios had been here...?"

"He's probably a gifted rhetorician, capable of swinging the vote. Without him we get..." He pointed to Zeuxis.

"More Cameron than Churchill," Alex nodded.

"Who?"

"Oh come on. You may not have done my training, but you know who Churchill was."

"Of course I know Churchill. Who was the other one?"

"My point, and it doesn't matter."

A cheer only they could hear made them both grin.

"You did it!" Almega's voice echoed in their heads. "The time-line's back where it was!"

Within Omskep the phantom of Alex turned to Almega.

"Does that mean we can come home now?"

"Whenever you like! That carter seems to have been the key. If you hadn't got him, even getting the democracy back on line wouldn't have made a difference. Seems he had a descendent over three thousand years in the future who made some radical changes. Now there is no such descendent."

"And has the Gordian knot around Fortan untied itself?"

Almega checked and the smile on his face faltered. "Yes and no. It's changed, certainly, but I'm not sure it's changed enough to get him out. I'll get to work on it, but I'll probably need your help."

Daniel shook his head, more aware than Almega of the social niceties that had to be observed.

"We can't leave right now. At the very least we have to congratulate Miltiades and say our goodbyes. If we don't we'll be remembered as the rude merchant and his boyfriend who stuck their oars in and then vanished without a trace. It's sure to raise questions. The minute we can get away we will. Just whatever you do, don't make it worse!"

Almega glared at Daniel's phantom.

"I never make the same mistake twice. I will examine it so I can give you a proper report once you return." He peered once more at the program. "No need to rush. I think this might take a while."

"Let's not hang around one minute longer than we have to," Alex suggested. "The longer we're here, the more chance we'll do something that'll make an even bigger mess of things."

"Such confidence," Daniel replied drily, "but I agree. The sooner we're out of here, the better. Besides, I hate wearing sandals. I keep getting stones in them."

Once the vote was cast and the ekklesia had agreed to return democracy to Athens, Daniel and Alex slowly made their way down towards Miltiades, who was in the middle of a throng of well-wishers, patting him on the back for a job well done.

"Well done indeed," Daniel agreed, bowing to their host while the crowds milled around them on their way back into town. "I have rarely seen such a thrilling meeting. Normally they are enough to send anyone to sleep."

"I fear you only got the half of it," Miltiades replied, shaking his head. "A true contest would have occurred had Athanasios spoken. That man has wit above that normally granted mortal men. I do not think my task would have been so easy, but it appears the gods favoured the return of democracy. After all," he added, turning a shrewd eye on Daniel, "it was you who stalled the carter."

"It was the same man, then?" Alex asked.

"I gather so. It may or may not please you to know he has been arrested. Nearly wounding a visitor is bad enough. Nearly killing the father-in-law of a member of the ekklesia on the same day is another matter altogether. He has crossed the line and Athanasios will not let it rest. He will seek revenge. If he doesn't he will appear weak and that would never do."

"Perhaps it's as well," Daniel replied, falling into step beside Miltiades as they headed down the hillside, Alex drawing up the rear. "There are many horses that would welcome that brute's demise. Quite a number of ordinary people, too."

"Indeed. So, now that you have seen Athenian democracy restored, what will you do? Having considered our conversation last night I'm convinced you came here to make that change. Your intervention with the carter merely guaranteed it would occur."

Miltiades paused and looked around him. Their slow progress had ensured they were now alone amongst the trees. He lowered his voice.

"And perhaps now you would be kind enough to satisfy my curiosity?"

Daniel shrugged. "If it is within my power."

"Of that I am certain. Pray tell me... which of the gods do I have the honour of addressing?"

After a shocked pause Daniel chuckled, trying to laugh it off.

"I am but a poor merchant who happened to find himself in the right place at the right time. If there has been divine intervention then I am but a vessel, not a god."

Miltiades narrowed his eyes and the look he gave reminded Daniel this man had been a successful politician for many years.

"Too many coincidences, my friend. I have lived and run my business long enough to know when I am being manipulated... and when a man is lying. I see it in your eyes." Without turning he added, "And you, Alexios, are also not what you appear. You keep quiet counsel, but I was near you when Demetrios demonstrated his fighting skills. You did not see me for I was in the shadow. You had no knife, then suddenly there was one in your hand, summoned as if by magic. Again, I beseech you. I am an old man not long for this world and I know how to keep silent on that which others should not know. Can you not satisfy an old man's wish to look upon the true face of his faith?"

"Truly, Miltiades, you misjudge us. Demetrios is a merchant. I am but a playwright, and not a very good one given no one has heard of me. We are not gods," Alex insisted.

"Last night, when you went into the garden, I could see you from my room. I watched you talking. I could not hear your words, but I saw you. At one point you sat side by side and then became like statues. No movement, no breath, no blink of an eye. It was as though you had paused in time. My eyes may be old," he added, seeing Alex about to argue, "but they see very well still. It was that as much as the quality of our debate that convinced me I had to present the case for the return of democracy to Athens. After all, who am I to argue with the gods?"

In Omskep Daniel and Alex looked at each other and at Almega. Alex voiced the question hanging in the air.

"Would it hurt?"

Almega checked the time-line.

"Apparently not. He's right he's not long for this world. He'll be dead within a year."

"A year? What killed him? He seems fit and healthy enough," Daniel replied.

"Does it matter? Looking at this, your thoughts about appearing to him as his gods don't affect the time line. He becomes a little more religious, but that's common as people of his time near their end." Almega checked the program again. "It may help you to know he worships exclusively at the temples of Athene and Apollo."

Alex nodded. She'd encountered this before.

"Cramming for their finals. Not unheard of even in the twenty-first century, and I guess we know who we are supposed to be. Let's just check there's no one hiding in the undergrowth."

She quickly ran through the point in the program to satisfy herself they were genuinely alone.

"If you are going to do this," Almega added, leaning back while Alex made her observations, "make sure you do it properly. You're gods, not teenagers."

"So far as I can tell, the Greek gods acted like spoiled teenagers most of the time," Daniel observed wryly.

Alex glanced up from her observations and gave him a wink.

"What was written about them and what they really were needn't have anything to do with each other. For the sake of the program," Almega pleaded, placing his hands in the prayer position, "act appropriately."

"All clear," Alex announced, "and don't worry. For all we don't care for the idiot, we're not going to risk Fortan getting stuck in there forever."

"Besides, if the program can't complete there's quite a bit of our memories that would become logically incoherent, not to mention impossible," Daniel added. "I'm not particularly eager to find out what happens when that combination of immovable object and irresistible force meet."

Back in front of Miltiades Alex and Daniel exchanged a look, checked their surroundings again just to make sure, then Daniel leaned forward.

"Miltiades, you have done Athens and the world a service beyond all you will ever know. If you speak of what we are about to reveal to you, all that will be destroyed. Do you agree on your word of honour to remain silent?"

"I do."

With that, Alex and Daniel morphed into the appearance of the appropriate gods. Miltiades went to fall to the ground but Alex stopped him.

"No need to kneel, Miltiades," she assured him. "You have earned your right to remain standing. We are both grateful for your service."

Keeping his eyes lowered, Miltiades fought to stop himself shaking into pieces.

"My lady Athene, my Lord Apollo. If I have been of some small service I am grateful beyond all expressing."

Alex raised his chin and smiled at him.

"You have. You may take pride in your actions today, and your wit. I have always said the men of Athens are wise beyond measure."

Well, she was supposed to be the goddess Athene. Calling them arrogant, misogynistic, narrow-minded primitives probably wouldn't go down too well, even if it was true.

"That you caught us despite our efforts only goes to prove that, but I do ask once again that you do not speak of this. Events have been set in motion that must come to pass."

"My lady, you have my word of honour as a citizen of your city," Miltiades assured her.

"That is a promise I know we can trust," Daniel averred, "and now we must be gone. I am afraid Demetrios will not be able to provide you with the spices the city craves, but others will fulfil that need. However, perhaps you will accept this," and here he summoned another bag of samples, which he handed to Miltiades, "as partial payment for your actions today and to enhance your meals until the shipments begin to arrive?"

"My lord, you do me too much honour!" Miltiades protested, but clutched the bag to his chest.

Alex glanced at Daniel, rolling her eyes. They both knew Miltiades would never allow those spices to be used, given where they came from. They'd probably be buried with him. Still, it was a small thing and nothing extraordinary or likely to attract attention.

"Goodbye Miltiades. Thank you," Alex said and vanished, Daniel following suit. However, while they had disappeared from their host's sight they remained there, watching him.

Miltiades' face was a picture. A mixture of awe and delight and so many other emotions it was impossible to catalogue them all. Alex had tears in her eyes and when Daniel gave her a look that effectively said, 'what's the matter with you?' she stepped beside him and wrapped an arm around his waist.

"Oh, come on. We gave him his dearest wish in the whole world. Look at him. He's in heaven. I feel like Santa Claus!"

"Santa Claus?" he replied, returning her grip. "Being Athene isn't good enough for you?"

"Says the guy who got to be Apollo. The lyre and the younger look were nice, but I can do without a repeat of the dirge they called music and I think I rather like the beard now. Winged sandals?"

"Probably massively inaccurate, but what the hell. It's what he was expecting to see and he recognised us, so..."

"So it's nice to be able to boost someone's spirits now and again. Why have we never taken this approach to the programs before?"

"Because the temptation to constantly interfere until the beings within the program were incapable of doing anything for themselves would be too strong?" Daniel offered thoughtfully. "Right now we're constrained by the need to ensure the program stays on track, for our own sake if not for that of Fortan. If we could have done this from the beginning, I've a feeling the program wouldn't last that long. Sooner or later one of us would lose our temper and destroy it, wipe the slate clean and start again."

Miltiades, who'd been murmuring what was presumably a prayer of some sort finally opened his eyes, turned around, took a deep breath and, still clutching the spices to his chest, made his way down the hillside and back into town.

Alex looked around, taking in the vista.

"Nice view of the Parthenon from here. Wonderful to see it all intact. I must admit, I thought all this took place over there," and she pointed to the Acropolis. "Until this trip I'd never even heard of the Pnyx."

"You and most of the world," he smiled. "Outside academics and natives, few would know the details. And it's not like this area looks particularly auspicious." He gestured around. "Who would know this, and not that," and he waved to the temples on the opposite hill, "is the real cradle of democracy?"

Grunting agreement, Alex nudged Daniel, indicating Miltiades' rapidly disappearing form, and together they followed, shadowing his steps.

"Returning to our earlier conversation..." she began, negotiating the rocky route, then she cursed herself for forgetting her present state and levitated over the uneven path, "the program has effectively wiped itself more or less clean and started again several times. The end of the dinosaurs, the acid wars, the destruction of the earth leaving humans on colony planets..."

Daniel shrugged.

"I didn't write it, so far as I'm aware, so I can't explain the reasoning behind it. I think on that score we just have to trust Omskep knows what it's doing. And why are we following Miltiades? Our job's done. Shouldn't we get back to Oestragar and see what's happening with that thorn in my side?"

Alex briefly redirected her focus on Omskep.

"Almega's still exploring, so there's no hurry," she replied. "Besides, I want to visit the Agora. You never know, Socrates might be down there." She chuckled. "Interesting, that you think of Omskep as if it's a living thing."

"Doesn't it feel like that to you?" When she gave him a confused look he continued, "Seriously, don't you ever find yourself curious?" She shook her head. "Maybe it's just because I was outside it while everyone else was engaged," he added thoughtfully. "Theoretically we choose our training, but there are times I have felt as though there was a particular time period or a particular event I had to attend. Has that never happened to you?"

"Nope. I've always felt free to go wherever and whenever I wanted. Perhaps certain events make me think I want to follow them up and see where they go from the inside, but I've never felt any compulsion."

"I wouldn't call it that, exactly. Just a nagging feeling something won't be right until I do a certain thing, be a certain person... I suppose that's why I see Omskep that way. I have all the choices possible, but I find there's always one that leaps out at me. If I ignore it the pressure builds until its irresistible."

"I never knew! I assumed you were the same as me. Not that it ever occurred to me to question it. I guess if I had I would have found out. So how did you manage while you took your..." she paused, seeking an appropriate term that wouldn't cause offence, "retreat?" she decided and looked at him to check his reaction.

"A good term for it," he assured her, having sensed her reluctance. "Why do you think I stayed in the house and avoided everyone? When I went anywhere near the others, Omskep seemed to hover behind them, demanding my attention. Staying in the house, however false the impression, seemed to give me some measure of peace."

"When all this is over and done with, that might be worth exploring. See if the others feel the same way." She looked up at the sun. "We'd best get a move on. If Socrates is down there I don't want to miss him because we dawdled."

"Haven't you learned yet that you should never meet your heroes?" he replied good-naturedly, but he allowed her to pick up the pace and lead him back into town.

"I'm not expecting a full-on Platonic dialogue, I'd just like to hear him."

"He was an ugly little pug, if I recall the statue correctly. Fat, balding, snub nosed... He wasn't going to win any beauty contests."

"Looks aren't everything," she responded, then winked. "Not that I object to your handsome features, but it's what's inside that really counts."

Daniel gave her an affectionate squeeze.

"Thanks for that... I think. I hope what's inside these features is just as worthy."

"It is," she assured him. "If it wasn't I'd never want to be near you. Why do you think I avoid Fortan? Still want to meet Socrates, though."

"Uh uh," he replied, wagging a finger. "You can see and hear, you can't meet."

They floated above the crowded Agora, catching snippets of conversation en route. In general, the elite were talking about their restored franchise, while the slaves, visiting merchants and others who were not so fortunate were carrying on as usual.

"I suppose it makes sense," Alex observed. "It doesn't affect them, so why care about it?"

"A far cry from even my last training session," Daniel returned. "Just because it didn't directly affect us didn't mean we weren't reading every newspaper and paying attention."

"In my last session people could get wound up about things happening on other continents that would never affect them. The joys of the internet. Still, it also meant people had realised all are part of the same system."

"'Any man's death diminishes me, for I am a part of mankind. Therefore, never send to know for whom the bell tolls, it tolls for thee', " he agreed. "Donne got the right of it, even so long ago."

"The playwrights of Ancient Greece did too," she reminded him. "Stories of the Trojan women and the like. It's easy to cut yourself off until it's right in your face."

"There's probably an element of practicality as well," he replied. "Worrying or talking about it doesn't change it, and there's mouths to be fed. Living in an era where the basics are covered gives you the luxury of caring about other things. Something you can't do when you're worried about simple survival."

Suddenly, Alex's attention was drawn to a small crowd, in the middle of which was a pudgy, balding man, whose bearded face and upturned nose was quite distinctive.

"I think I've spotted him," she said, urging Daniel to join her as she floated over to listen to the conversation.

The area being crowded and Daniel distracted by a conversation between two soldiers regarding battle tactics that he found intriguing (particularly in comparison to twentieth century approaches), it was a while before Alex found him and relayed what she had heard.

"I'd forgotten Socrates' aversion to democracy," she sighed, shaking her head. "So far as he's concerned the restoration is a step backwards. He's very much in favour of an elite running the state and minimal interference from the less able."

"Meritocracy," Daniel agreed. "I did warn you."

"I know. But at least I did it. Where were you?"

"Listening to the soldiers. I found it interesting that allowing for the absence of artillery with a range of miles, and arrows instead of bullets..."

"Not to mention aircraft?"

"That too. Despite all that, it's surprising how little difference there is. In hand to hand fighting, change their uniforms and I might as well be listening to my own men. The same worries, fears, thoughts about the enemy and humour."

"Bit of a difference between a javelin and sword, and a rifle and bayonet."

"Yes, but beneath that it seems soldiers are soldiers regardless of the era."

"People are people. It's all the same program and it's adaptable. Once the initial parameters are set it's just changing the content and letting the people respond accordingly. It's only when you get the odd-balls the response changes, whether they're the innovators or the tyrants."

They moved to the edge of the Agora where it was a little less crowded, enjoying the relaxed atmosphere.

"Makes you think, doesn't it?" Daniel said at last.

"About what?"

"We're always the bit players. The big parts are taken by the program. We're never the Einsteins or Newtons or even Socrates."

Alex shuddered, different images filling her mind.

"Or Stalin or Hitler or Caligula. Personally, I'm glad for it. I'd hate to have to live with those memories once we got back to Oestragar. Imagine getting home to find you'd been a serial killer and having every murder repeating in your head."

"You'd erase them. I know I would, although I doubt Fortan would care that much," Daniel returned, rolling his eyes when he recalled the source of their trip. "Speaking of, I think we'd better get back and see what Almega has found."

When he noticed Alex looking longingly around the marketplace he took her hand.

"You can always pop back another time if you want to."

"I know, but this has been a unique experience. Getting to see it from inside and outside at the same time... I rather enjoyed it."

"I know what you mean," he agreed as they returned to Omskep, "but once we've fixed this mess I doubt we'll be able to make a habit of it. Can you imagine what would happen if Gracti or Hentric had that ability?"

Alex winced.

"Now that would foul up the system beyond any repair."

"And it's not like we could keep it from them," he continued. "Once this is over, I suspect we'll have to wipe the memories of this from all of us just to keep things safe, even the formidable Almega," he grinned as the subject of his comment turned and raised an eyebrow.

"Compliments will get you nowhere," Almega replied, watching Alex summon a chair into which she flopped unceremoniously. "And don't get too comfortable, you're not done yet."

"What? I thought we fixed it?" Daniel said, leaning over Almega to look at the program.

Alex jumped to her feet and joined them, sighing when she took in the results.

"We fixed that, but there's another one." She pointed to a different section of programming and then took a closer look at Fortan's knot. "He does seem a little less stalled."

Almega nodded.

"It's moving but it's..." He cast around for the right word.

"Stuttering?" Alex offered.

"As good a description as any. I doubt the programs or even Fortan are aware of it, any more than they were aware of being stalled, but it is moving. Unfortunately, right now it's moving in the wrong direction, so it still has to be fixed."

"So where are we going this time?" Daniel asked, summoning Alex's chair and settling himself into it.

With their recent success he had little doubt they could handle whatever else came up. When Alex frowned at him he merely raised an eyebrow.

"You make comfortable chairs," he commented, stretching out.

"Closer to your time," Almega informed Daniel, ignoring the byplay. "In fact, I suspect this one is still strong in your mind."

Alex glanced at the point in the program to which Almega referred.

"No way am I doing that one as a passenger!" she exclaimed.

Almega was inclined to agree.

"I think this time being a ghost in the machine might be more appropriate."

"Which will make it harder to alter events..."

"At least the main one is still in place," Almega replied. "That might be a bit harder to pull off and, as you were saying, there are some things for which none of us want responsibility."

"One thousand, five hundred and three dead. Better than several million, but still..."

The number was familiar to Daniel who sat up straighter.

"You are joking?!"

"Do we know what we've got to do?" Alex asked.

"Not yet, but if the last trip is anything to go by I think we'll find out once you get there."

Daniel sighed, rubbing his forehead as he contemplated the task ahead.

"Where do we join her?"

"Everything seems to be fine until just before she sinks... or just after. It's not clear."

"Typical!" Daniel said. "From the warmth of the Mediterranean to the freezing waters of the north Atlantic. It's as well we'll be spirits, although as you pointed out," and he nodded to Alex, "it will be hard to change things in that state."

"It'll also be a lot harder knowing these programs only to have to watch them die," Alex commented sadly.

"Just remember they are only programs," Almega suggested. "Being separate from them will help there, but you might want to avoid getting to know any of the children. Somehow reminding yourself they're not real never works when it's kids. I suggest you pop back here if things get too personal. Focus on getting the job done."

Alex nodded. "I know but still... Why did it have to be *Titanic*?"

Chapter 4

"OK, *Titanic*. What do we know?" Almega asked as the three sat around a glass topped desk Alex had materialised within Omskep.

Illuminated on the table's surface were graphs, images and statistics, while a 3D semi-transparent representation of the ship floated above it, turning slowly. This hologram-like representation provided cutaways as Alex tapped on various sections, and could zoom in with a thought, giving highly detailed views of the interior.

Alex looked through the cutaway of the boiler rooms she was presently examining towards Daniel.

"After you. I imagine you remember it from your last training session," she reasoned.

"Vividly," he agreed, shifting in his chair. "All right. Sets sail from Southampton at noon on the 10th April, 1912. Stops at Cherbourg in France and Queenstown, later called Cobh, in Ireland to pick up passengers before setting sail across the Atlantic on the 12th."

Almega picked up the narrative.

"Has two days of clear sailing, then hits an iceberg at 11.40 pm on the evening of the 14th of April."

"Sinks at 2.20 am on the 15th with the loss of 1,503 passengers and crew including women and children," Daniel concluded, shaking his head.

"OK, those are the basic facts, but what about the rest of it?" Alex asked, unimpressed by their summary. Off their slightly blank looks she continued, "What you've described is an oversized train wreck, not *Titanic*. It was more than a ship sinking: it marked the beginning of the end of an era; a change in social attitudes; it led to changes in the law... Why do you think she captured the imagination so much that a film could be made about her nearly a century later and make more than it cost to build the ship?"

When her companions continued to look mystified she started pulling up images.

"Look. Captain Smith," and she pointed to the image of a white bearded man obviously nearing retirement, "had received numerous ice warnings during the day but ignored them, maintaining a speed of around 22 knots and holding his course when other captains in the area decided it was better to heave to because of the risk of hitting an iceberg in the dark. It's a clear, still night with no moon, so the iceberg can't be seen by the lookout Frederick Fleet until it's too late. It's not helped by the fact the iceberg has turned turtle – what they call a black or blue iceberg – so the white surface that should have made her visible isn't there. If I recall correctly, the lookouts don't have binoculars as no one could find the key to the cupboard, 'though how much difference that would have made given the conditions is debatable, and there may have been some weird optical effects that night that stopped them from seeing it before it was too late. When the warning is telephoned to the bridge, Captain Smith has gone to bed and First Officer Murdoch is in charge."

The images above the table reflected her narrative, but both Almega and Daniel were quick to realise Alex wasn't drawing from them to tell her tale, but rather creating them herself to accompany her narrative.

"He orders the ship turned to port and apparently puts her into reverse in an effort to prevent the collision, but an 882-foot-long ship can't turn on a sixpence and there wasn't enough warning, so she turns far too slowly, resulting in the iceberg scraping her starboard side under the water line. Several large holes are put in her, the steel plates buckling under the enormous pressure. Water flows into the six forward compartments, dragging the ship down by the head. The bulkheads only go up to E deck, which is ten feet above the water line, so once the water reaches there and starts overflowing the sinking is inevitable. The Department of Trade is still working from old lifeboat regulations that are based on a maximum 10,000 tons, not the actual number of passengers and crew. *Titanic* is 46,000 tons and actually has more lifeboats than the law stipulates, especially with her sixteen watertight compartments that were meant to ensure the ship herself could act as a lifeboat, even if sections were sheared off, but there aren't enough to rescue half those aboard. Thomas Andrews, who helped design her and is with her on her maiden voyage, did want to install more as did her original designer, but they were overruled as it was thought it would make the deck look too crowded. Andrews is last seen in the smoking lounge looking at a painting of Plymouth harbour and goes down with the ship."

She zoomed in on that section of the ship, allowing the others to see what she was describing. Looking at them she realised they were staring at her rather than the hologram.

"What?"

"You're not reading that or even calling on the information from Omskep. Where are you getting all this?" Daniel asked.

"You spouted on Ancient Athens, this happens to be an interest of mine," she replied. "I was a history teacher too, remember? Besides, this is the most famous wreck in history and there've been hundreds of programmes purporting to explain what actually happened."

"All of which you've apparently watched," Daniel observed.

"And that's a problem? I can shut up if you want."

"No, no," Almega returned, sitting back in his chair and folding his arms. "I'm curious to see how long you can keep this up."

Alex looked at Daniel who also waved her on, then back to Almega.

"You didn't pass comment when Daniel did this last time, so if this is some residual misogyny from Athens..." she pouted.

"Far from it," Daniel assured her. "I didn't deliver half as much information as you have so far, and it doesn't look like you're even close to stopping. I'm genuinely impressed. Seriously," he added when she remained unconvinced. "Please, carry on."

Not sure whether to be proud or insulted, Alex prepared to continue, then paused, perplexed.

"Where was I?"

"Her designers were over-ruled on the lifeboats and Thomas Andrews went down with the ship," Daniel provided.

"Right. So, Captain Smith orders passengers into the lifeboats, women and children first, around 12.30 am. Second Officer Charles Lightoller takes that to mean women and children *only*, and as a result allows lifeboats to leave less than half full if there are no women and children nearby to fill them. He even orders a bunch of male passengers and crew out of a lifeboat, threatening them with his gun. The boat finally leaves with only 17 aboard when it was designed to carry 40. That's only one of several lifeboats that are allowed to go with a fraction of the numbers they were built to carry, which adds around 500 to the loss, and many passengers refuse to believe she can sink and consequently won't get in them. All the time the Marconi operators... um..." She thought for a moment, determined not to miss a fact now if only to drive her point home, "Jack Philips and, uh..." She snapped her fingers until the name came to her, "Harold Bride, keep up the messages asking for assistance and *Titanic* is one of the first ships to send out not just the traditional CQD but the new SOS mayday call. Bride survived but Philips didn't. Up on deck the musicians keep playing to keep the passengers calm. They start with up-beat music, and some claim they were still playing ragtime at the end. Others say the last thing they heard was 'Nearer My God to Thee' or 'Songe d'Automne'. Not one survived the sinking... and before you ask, no I can't name them."

"I'd say that shows bias against musicians," Daniel grinned, but his good humour was rooted solidly in Alex's enthusiasm and knowledge.

"Oh, indeed," Almega nodded, smothering his smile with his hand.

Alex frowned at him and he cleared his throat, composing his face into a more dignified expression.

"Sorry. Carry on."

"She sinks in under three hours. The *SS Californian*, commanded by Captain Stanley Lord, is closest to her but doesn't respond to her mayday rockets and his Marconi officer is asleep. In the later investigations, Lord maintains it was another ship that his crew saw, not the *Titanic*, but Lord never recovers from the accusations that he failed in his duty. The *SS Carpathia* does respond, but she's too far away and by the time she arrives all that's left alive are those in the lifeboats, and not all of them. Most of those in the water would have died of cardiac arrest within fifteen to thirty minutes due to the extreme cold. Others are killed jumping from the ship or as a result of falling debris, including the funnels. Amongst the dead are some of the wealthiest people on the planet at the time, including John Jacob Astor and Benjamin Guggenheim. Isador and Ira Straus, owners of Macy's department store, stay aboard together and are last seen sitting on loungers on the deck. J.P. Morgan, owner of the White Star Line, cancelled his trip at the last minute, claiming sickness. That he is found perfectly healthy by journalists after the disaster is one of the arguments used by conspiracy theorists who claim the sinking was an insurance fraud and it wasn't *Titanic* but *Olympic* that went down. That doesn't stand up to examination when you consider *Titanic's* loss nearly destroyed Morgan's International Mercantile Marine which finally had to apply for bankruptcy protection in 1915. It was only the demands of the First World War that saved them. More likely, Morgan was taking the opportunity for some extracurricular activities away from his wife. When the full scale of the disaster is known, the percentage of steerage passengers who died in comparison to first class causes quite a stir. Six hundred and ninety-six crew, including Captain Smith and First Officer Murdoch, and five hundred and twenty-eight Third or Steerage-class perish, compared to one hundred and twenty-three First-Class and one hundred and sixty-seven Second-Class. Part of the problem is *Titanic* had metal grills to keep the classes separate in accordance with US immigration requirements, and in the rush to wake First and Second-Class passengers the stewards forget to unlock the grills, leaving steerage trapped below with a very confusing route to get up to the decks where the lifeboats were stored. Also, some stewards may have refused to open the gates until the First and Second-Class had got off. Anyway, by the time any do get up top, the lifeboats are already gone. Oh, I forgot!" she interrupted herself, "while Lightoller is threatening men with his gun, other officers, including Murdoch, are allowing men aboard lifeboats if there are no women or children nearby."

"That's considerate of them," Daniel commented drily.

"This allows Sir Cosmo and Lucy, Lady Duff-Gordon to escape together, although Sir Cosmo never lives down the shame of surviving. Another survivor is J. Bruce Ismay, Chairman and Managing Director of White Star Line. If the films are to be believed, he snuck aboard a lifeboat like a coward, but in fact it seems he did help load and lower lifeboats, only going aboard one that was already being lowered when it was clear no one else was around to do so and after being ordered to get in by Murdoch. Still, he's another one who never recovers from the damage to his reputation. That's fuelled by negative press from

William Randolph Hearst who couldn't stand him and seems to have been determined to make the most of the opportunity. Lightoller survives aboard Collapsible B, which is upside down having washed free of the ship as she went down, and while his behaviour that night is questionable, he does use the subsequent inquiries to push changes in the law including a provision for lifeboats based on numbers aboard rather than tonnage, and instituting twenty-four hour manned wireless communications. Oh, and he answers the call to sail his yacht as one of the little ships that rescues the men from Dunkirk in 1940, so I guess he redeemed himself in the end."

Finally, Alex paused and drew a deep breath. She turned to Daniel, daring him to make a comment.

"What? Don't tell me you've run out?"

"Not quite," she crowed, delighted he'd fallen for her trap. "At the investigations in the US and UK they decide the ship sank in one piece, but when she's found in 1985 it turns out she broke in two around the third funnel. The bow went down in a see-saw motion, planing down, plateauing, then planing down again for two miles, reaching about twenty-five miles an hour before ploughing into the seabed at an angle, staying upright and still recognisably *Titanic*."

Again, the images shifted to match Alex's description, decks and pieces ripping off as the bow plunged.

"The stern, which bobs around for a bit after the bow breaks free, turns and sinks, probably spinning several times on the way down before landing a third of a mile from the bow. It implodes as it drops due to the pressures on pockets of trapped air, and that then rushes out doing more damage. It's made worse when it hits the bottom, with decks pancaking down, so it's almost unrecognisable."

"So we don't want to be in the stern when she goes down," Daniel commented, looking at the grotesque mess that was now before him.

"I'd say we don't want to be *aboard* when she goes down," Alex clarified. "If we have to explore the wreck I suggest we wait until she settles first. Ideally, I'd rather we didn't even have to do that. While the vast majority were topside, a few would have been below, and drowning wasn't the only thing to kill them. She's two miles down and the pressure down there is over 6,500 pounds per square inch. That's enough to crush hand and foot bones and cavities such as skull, chest and abdomen if there's any air in them. Not to mention metal, glass, wood and everything else flying around, ripping you to shreds. Anyone trapped in an air-pocket and somehow still alive as she went down had a gruesome end. Personally, I don't care to stumble across someone in that state. They may be programs, but still..."

"Quite."

"One more thing I remember... She had a fire in one of the coal bunkers that raged for about ten days, being finally put out on the 13th. Coal fires weren't that unusual, but several suggested this one warped the bulkhead, making it more susceptible to failure when hit by freezing-cold water and the pressure of the water accumulating on the other side."

"Which means we probably want to avoid the coal bunkers and boiler rooms too, if we can. Although judging by the look on your face that's one of the places you want to check out first, right?"

"C'mon, it's like the JFK assassination. Finally, we can see where the smoking gun is actually located."

"Or you could just look at the program?" Daniel suggested. "It's not like we're limited in Oestragar."

"Two problems with that. One, we know the program isn't running correctly at the moment, so what it says right now caused the sinking and what actually caused it may not be the same thing; two, if, due to the programming errors, Fortan somehow becomes aware of what's happening to him, I don't want him to be able to accuse us of leaving him there one instant longer than is necessary. It'll make him even more impossible than he is already." She paused and then added, "and three, exploring it first-hand is much more interesting than looking at a program. I wouldn't do this as an avatar, but in our present state?"

"One of us must have, or will do once we get this sorted, else why have it part of the program?" Daniel mused. "I confess I'm not over-eager for the first-hand experience myself. While I applaud your empirical approach, I'm not sure interesting is the word I'd use. Terrifying might be a better description, but you're right we need to get in there to see what's going on, and with your knowledge I'd say we've a good chance of identifying the problem, whatever it is. Are we any closer to figuring out what went wrong?"

"Right now, I've several theories regarding what went wrong with the voyage," Almega replied, bowing to Alex, "but as to what went wrong time wise, I'm still not sure. As I said before, the event, whatever it is, seems to straddle the sinking and I think it starts in Southampton, so it looks like you'd better join her there and keep alert."

"Anything happen in Southampton you're aware of?" Daniel asked, happy to let Alex lead the way this time. He'd also just remembered something but decided he could keep that to himself.

She mulled for a second and then said, "*Titanic* almost collided with the *SS City of New York*, which was pulled towards her as she set off. It's said a few considered that a bad omen and left her at Cherbourg or Queenstown as a result, although they may have just been using *Titanic* as a ferry to those ports. If they did change their plans, then on this occasion their premonition was accurate."

"A coincidence, but a rather ominous one, I admit."

He took a deep breath, stood up and held out his hand. "Shall we?"

The look on his face gave Alex pause. "Daniel, is there something else I should know about? You seem... uncomfortable."

"Perhaps. We'll see when we get there."

With that ambiguous comment he gestured again for her to join him.

Confused, but aware there was nothing that could physically hurt them no matter what, Alex shrugged and took his hand. Within moments their physical presence was absent from Omskep, leaving their phantom selves in situ. Almega settled in front of the main readouts to follow their progress.

***

"She certainly is impressive," Alex commented as they floated invisibly over the ship.

"She was the largest moving man-made object ever built," Daniel agreed, "and while later years would produce objects far larger, I'm not sure they were always so graceful."

"See the fourth stack?" Alex pointed. "Absolutely fake. Only three are needed for the boilers. The fourth one was used for cargo space. It was added to make her appear more powerful than she was." Daniel was scanning the huge crowds that filled the dock. "See anything?"

"Lots, but nothing that leaps out at me. It's not like the thing or person will have a massive arrow over their head saying, 'here I am'."

"It really does look like the films. I'm half expecting to see Rose and that arse of a fiancé of hers turn up."

"Who?" he replied, still scanning the crowds.

"Hollywood movie. Don't worry about it. I doubt we'll want to watch it after this trip."

She floated next to him, scanning for anything that might give them a clue. People were hugging each other goodbye, some were giving their friends hearty slaps on the back for their good fortune. Crew and dockworkers mingled with the passengers guiding and helping, directing each class to the appropriate gangplank, supervising loading, checking tickets and keeping things moving. Amongst steerage there seemed to be quite a number who didn't speak English.

"That probably didn't help when it came to it," Alex commented. "The stewards could have yelled 'I've opened the gate' and half of them wouldn't have understood."

She was watching a man with a hand crank film camera who was already aboard the ship, filming what was happening, when she noticed Daniel stiffen suddenly. She turned and saw he was staring at the queue for second class.

"Daniel? You OK?"

"Beth!" he whispered.

Instantly, Alex was on high alert.

"Beth? As in your wife in your last training? She was on *Titanic*?"

"She can't... She never said."

He swooped down to watch as she shuffled with the queue towards the crewmember checking tickets.

"No! Beth, don't! Get away from here!"

He moved in, instinctively, determined to stop her by any means, when Alex swept in front of him.

"Daniel, stop!" Alex grabbed his shoulders, forcing him to look at her. "Daniel! She can't have stayed aboard because she married you, so there's no need for you to interfere. Either she's seeing someone off or she gets off at Cherbourg or Queenstown. Very worst case, she survives the sinking and returns from America."

"What if she's the problem?" he replied, still staring at Beth who was looking up at the huge ship with a smile on her face, clearly delighted with the idea of the journey ahead. "What if her getting on is what shouldn't be happening? I've got to stop her!"

"Almega, need some help here!" Alex cried, still holding Daniel back. He tried to get around her but she remained stubbornly in his way. "Is Beth the reason we're here? Do we need to stop her getting aboard?"

"No. According to your program, Alex, Beth is not the problem. Daniel, calm down. She's a program and she married you, so something gets her off the ship or she survives the sinking. Either way, she'll be fine."

"Passenger lists!" Daniel cried. "Is she on the passenger lists?"

Almega quickly pulled up the lists. "What was her maiden name?"

"Williams. Elizabeth Williams."

A few moments of silence followed, then Almega informed them she wasn't on any of the passenger lists.

"But she's here. I'm looking at her!"

"Maybe she was travelling under another name?" Almega offered.

"Maybe that isn't Beth," Alex reasoned. "The program often doubles up on appearance when there's no danger of the people meeting."

"I know my wife, and that is Beth!" Daniel growled, jabbing a finger in the woman's direction.

"All right, that's enough," Alex replied and forced the two of them out of the program.

Standing with Daniel in Omskep she was tempted to slap him. Instead, she did the next best thing.

"Eridar!" He stopped struggling and stared at her. "Yes, Eridar. Remember him? You're not Daniel any more than I'm Alex."

She morphed into her energy state, hovering in front of him.

"We are NOT program. We're Eternals who have avatars within the program. She's a program. She was your avatar's wife In. The. Program!" She punctuated each word to drive it home. "We've a job to do and we can't do it if you're like this. We've got two days before she sets off across the Atlantic – plenty of time to figure this out and get her off if she is your avatar's future wife – but I need you with me on this. It's too big a job to do alone."

She returned to her shape as Alex, laying a hand on his cheek.

"I know that last session did a number on you, and I won't force you to take erasure, even if it would solve this very quickly, but you've got to put things in perspective. Daniel – your character – was in love with her. Eridar can't be."

She led him to a summoned chair and sat him down, calling a second for herself.

"You knew something about this before we left. I think it's time you filled us in."

He sighed and rubbed his face, finally resting his elbows on his knees, hands clenched together. Alex sat back and waited, knowing pushing him would achieve nothing. Almega, too, merely turned in his seat and remained silent. After what felt like an interminable silence, Daniel spoke.

"Beth never said, but if the subject of *Titanic* came up she always pulled away. We met in July and the investigations were still all over the newspapers. In 1912 it was the main event. All the hints leading to war became background if they were noted at all, but the investigations kept *Titanic* alive. I remember meeting Beth for tea one afternoon when the US investigations were being reported in the papers. I started to read it aloud and she asked me to stop. When I failed to notice how upset she was becoming and carried on anyway, she got up and left. It was as close to a fight as we ever got."

"Could she have had a twin you were unaware of?" Alex asked.

"If she did there was never any hint of it. She had no other family I'm aware of and none turned up to our wedding."

"If that was her," Alex began.

The look from Daniel was loud and clear. In his mind there was no doubt whatsoever.

"OK, we saw Beth using a Second-Class ticket. That was far from cheap, so how could she afford it? What did she do for a living when you met her?"

"She came to the school looking for any job and ended up helping matron and the housekeeper. She was thrifty with money – considerably better than I, truth be told – so she was a welcome addition to the school. She more than paid for herself within a year, so the headmaster kept her on. By that time, we were pretty much set on getting engaged, so Mr Pitlock knew he'd soon have the extra hand without added expense as her accommodations would be freed when she married me."

"Of course," Alex sighed.

Once more she promised herself after this was over she'd be taking training at a time when women were accepted on their own merits.

Noting her expression Daniel rolled his eyes.

"Alex, you choose to represent yourself as a female. You could be male if you wanted. It's not like any of us are forced to express a particular sex."

"True, but the longer I do it, the more I appreciate the female perspective. You should try it. Anyway, we're getting off topic. If she had no particular skills or training, and she had no wealthy relatives...?"

He shook his head.

"Again, not that I'm aware of."

"Then that leaves the question of how she could afford the ticket. Might she have been travelling with someone?"

"She was alone in the queue."

"So perhaps meeting them later?"

He shrugged. He was as bewildered as Alex, if not more so.

"All right, so now we have two mysteries to solve: what's put this part of the program's history out of joint and how; and what happened with Beth. I've no doubt we can figure them out, but it will take both of us. Can you handle this, or do I need to leave you here and take Almega along instead?"

At that suggestion Daniel stiffened, his chin jutting out at the implied insult.

"I will manage, thank you," he replied, his opinion of her suggestion apparent in his clipped tones.

"You can't spend all your time watching Beth. We'll keep an eye on her, but she's not the main event, as it were. Almega checked and we know she'll be OK, so no spying on her twenty-four hours a day."

"I do not spy!"

"Then no hovering over her. We've got to check out the whole ship, not just the areas she's in. We've got over two thousand people we need to investigate, a massive ship and only four days within the program to do it."

"I understand."

She reached out to him, consciously imitating his earlier gesture.

"Together, right?"

After taking a moment to pull himself together he nodded and took her hand, the two re-entering the program.

"All right, I'm going to check if that fire story is real and if it was considered a problem. It shouldn't take long and then I'll do a recce of the lower decks. Why don't you follow Beth and see where she ends up so you can pop in on her later, then go up top and work your way down? We can meet in the middle, so to speak. She's not due to pull out yet, so we have time to get our bearings before the incident with the *New York*."

As she turned a thought occurred to her.

"You can't show yourself to her or talk to her, remember? Anything you do could affect the program and make things worse."

"Worse? The ship's going to sink killing more than half aboard. How could it be worse?"

She cocked her head to the side.

"You have to ask?"

"All right," he sighed, "I'll stay invisible."

She raised an eyebrow.

"And inaudible," he added. "Satisfied?"

"Almega, if he even thinks of doing anything that could compromise the program, you yank him out and alert me."

"Of course," came Almega's voice.

"I'm not used to being ordered around!" Daniel admonished her.

"Sure you are. You were a captain, not a Field Marshal; a teacher not the headmaster," her voice took on a teasing note, "and a husband, not the wife!"

She winked, then paused, softening her tone.

"Daniel, I'm not trying to be mean. I'm trying to protect all of us. I don't think you'd do anything deliberately to cause trouble, but when we're emotionally involved it's easy to make mistakes and not realise they **are** mistakes until it's too late. If it was my parents from my last session on board, I'd expect no less from you. Hell, Almega tells me I rescued kids who should have died. If you'd been watching over me, or Almega had realised what was happening and pulled me out, whatever consequences that action has would not be realised." She lowered her head. "I'm afraid we're going to have to fix that and, to be honest, I don't want to be the one to do it, so I'm hoping you'll be there for me then, just as I'm here for you now."

"I'm not sure that's something I would find easy either," he admitted.

"We'll work it out when we get there. Let's focus on one problem at a time." With forced brightness she said, "So, you take the high road and I'll take the low road?"

"And I'll be on C deck afore ye," he finished, returning her pasted-on smile with an equally fake one of his own. "This is going to get a lot harder, isn't it?"

"It's looking that way, but let's wait and see. You never know, fixing this one may be the key. Everything could reset and we'll be back to our usual existence."

They both rolled their eyes at that suggestion.

"Yeah, like we're going to get that lucky. All right, I'm off to the coal bunkers. You'd best chase after Beth. Look after yourself and if it gets too much, yell out. I'll be right there for you."

"Thanks."

Daniel swept down to follow Beth's retreating figure as she entered the ship. Alex watched him for a moment, then descended through the decks and bulkheads until she reached the coal bunkers. There, as she'd reported, it was clear the stokers were dealing with a fire, but it was equally clear they didn't regard this as a major event. The top coals had been moved to another bunker and the coal that had already caught was being moved out of the bunker that was burning and fed into the boilers. The bulkhead was hot but not red hot, and while the stokers were sweating from the heat and the exertion, their actions weren't frenzied or in any way indicated major concern. Clearly this was not the first time they'd encountered such an event and doubtless all felt it would not be the last. Determining to revisit later to check if anything had changed by the time the fire was extinguished, Alex made her way to the orlop – which on *Titanic* was the second to lowest deck, the tank top being right at the bottom. Occasionally she dipped down into the tank top, always moving forward and weaving across the deck with particular focus on the starboard side. Cargo and baggage rooms filled with everything from shipping boxes and suitcases, to large trunks and cars were passed until she reached the prow. There she moved below the keel to check the ship's external integrity. Despite the murky Southampton dock-water she could see through it to the sides – an advantage of the way she was interacting with the program. Nothing was out of order. Any suggestions this was another ship that had suffered severe damage and been repaired went out the window. Just to make absolutely certain, she floated up the side until she reached the name. There was no indication the word 'Olympic' had ever been there.

"Well, that's that theory shot out of the water," she muttered to herself before descending once again, this time pausing at G deck.

Near the bow she found the squash court and the mail room. Standing in the latter she looked at the ladders opposite, one leading to the upper decks, the other to the orlop, and shook her head.

"Ten out of ten for trying to get the mail through, guys," she said to herself. "Minus several thousand for trying it when the ship's sinking. You didn't have a hope!"

She swept past the coal bunkers and boiler casings, heading for the stern and found the refrigeration units storing the meats, vegetables, dairy products, fruits and more that would be needed for the voyage. The massive, sealed areas explained the air pockets that exploded in the stern when the ship went down. The sustenance was still being loaded and Alex found herself in awe of the sheer amount of food being delivered.

"They certainly were well fed when they died," she commented, shaking her head.

Floating up through Number 5 hatch she found herself in the midst of the toilet and bath facilities on F deck. Moving forward once more she saw some crew quarters for engineers and Third-Class stewards, then came across the kennels. She sighed, knowing of the twelve dogs and numerous other animals (including the ship's cat, hens, roosters and some cockerels) only three of the dogs would survive, in all cases because their wealthy owners refused to be parted from them and took them on board the under-filled lifeboats. The rest of the dogs would be seen running along the deck as the ship was sinking and would be killed in the panic or freeze in the water. One would be found clutched by its owner, both dead, several days after the sinking. She knelt before one of the animals, a King Charles Spaniel, that couldn't see her but did seem to sense something was there.

"Sorry old feller," she whispered. "I wish I could help you. No one deserved this, but you didn't even get a say in the matter."

Rising she looked around. Right next to the kennels was one of the bakeries, the enticing smells filling the area.

"Now that's plain mean!" She turned back to the dogs. "Hope you get given some of that!"

Passing through bulkheads to the Third-Class dining rooms, she next encountered the Turkish Baths with their steam, hot, temperate and cool rooms. While she knew, intellectually, that all this existed aboard the ship, seeing it was something else. She'd not been to a Turkish Bath in any of her trainings and it was tempting to enjoy the opulent surroundings, but she shook her head, determined to finish her exploration as efficiently as possible so she could check on Daniel.

"Later," she promised herself.

Beyond that and further forward was the salt-water swimming pool and then Third-Class cabins. These were small but clean and the fact that, unlike other ships of her time, Third-Class were not expected to bring their own rations but could count on being fed as part of their ticket, meant the rooms were tidier than was probably usual. Knowing she was nearing the squash court again she floated up Number 2 hatch to E deck.

This was Second and First-Class with a few Third-Class squeezed into the smaller spaces. Alex had thought the ship was laid out strictly on a deck by deck division: First-Class on this deck, Second on that deck and so on, so it surprised her to find First and Second-Class passengers practically next door to each other and Third-Class on the same deck, albeit the latter were separated from the wealthier classes by grills. Still, given the limited space it made sense to pack smaller quarters into every inch available to maximise profits. She peered into one or two First-Class rooms. Not as impressive as those above, she knew, but positively palatial even in comparison to her experiences in the 21st century. Towards the stern she found the musician's accommodations. A few of them were in there, chatting and stowing their belongings, having only joined the ship when she docked in Southampton. One was tuning up.

"You will do yourselves proud, guys," she murmured and bowed her head.

She watched them for a few moments, then moved on. The last thing she needed was to really get to know people who would not survive.

Once more in the stern she ascended again through Number 5 hatch to D deck. This was Second and First-Class and the luxuriousness of the ship was starting to show in the quality of the décor. On the starboard side was the hospital where Third-Class passengers were already being checked for lice and infectious diseases. To port were shops for the butcher and baker, and amidships she encountered the main First-Class dining area, which spread across the full width of available space. Beyond that was the reception room and the bottom of the grand staircase. She paused there for a moment, looking up towards the glass dome. Moving further forward there were some First-Class cabins. These weren't at the top end of the scale, but in comparison to Third-Class they were quite impressive with sinks, carpets and far more space. Floating outside she looked up.

"Nearly there," she muttered and headed up to C deck. "Now, Daniel, where are you I wonder?"

***

Daniel had followed Beth aboard to her E deck room, which was close to the Second-Class entrance. He smiled as she unpacked, recognising patterns from when they were married. 'Blouses or shirts out first, because people notice the top before they notice the bottom', she'd told him. 'Hang them up as soon as you can. Fold your trousers over the clothes hanger to keep the wrinkles out. Same with my skirts and dresses. Underwear last because no one should see that except those who know you... intimately.' That last comment had earned her a kiss, he remembered, and the rest of the unpacking on their honeymoon had been forced to wait.

She was singing to herself as she worked. He had heard her humming occasionally when they were married, but even in church she'd avoided singing – a source of sadness for him as he suspected she had a good voice. Now he realised he was right. While she was keeping the tone low, her voice was crystal clear and every note was hit squarely. If she was this good when she wasn't even trying, why had she avoided singing so assiduously when he'd known her?

Lost in his memories he almost didn't notice her heading for the door.

"Now where are you going, all dressed up like that?" he mused.

It was possible she was going to explore the ship, but somehow he doubted that. He followed her along the gangway towards the stern until finally she stopped by a room from whence emerged the sound of someone practising music. Checking the corridor briefly she cleared her throat and then knocked politely. A man answered the door.

"Hey, Beth. He's been waiting for you. Glad you're here at last. I was starting to fear he would pine away!"

At that moment another man pushed forward.

"Beth! You made it!" he cried before pulling her in for a kiss.

"Beth?" Daniel gasped. "You were dating one of the musicians aboard *Titanic*?!"

***

By the time Alex tracked him down, Daniel had been staring over the rail for nearly an hour.

"I thought we were meeting on C deck?" she commented, settling beside him. "How's Beth?"

He shrugged, still apparently fascinated by the way the light glinted off the small waves and the flights of seagulls swooping and calling to each other.

Sensing something had changed but not wanting to push, Alex merely stood beside him.

"She's getting ready to leave. I've not seen anything so far that sets off any alarms. You?"

He shook his head but remained tight-lipped. She turned to face him.

"All right, you can tell me or Almega can. Which will it be?"

Realising he had no choice, Daniel relented.

"Beth was dating one of the musicians. He gave her the ticket."

"Not that it matters, but which one?"

"William Brailey, the pianist, although presumably he didn't hoick that thing out at the end. He was a professor of music, so one assumes he had other instruments he could play."

"So we don't know her real last name, but maybe we now know how she got her made up one?" she suggested. He begrudgingly conceded that point. She nudged him. "Hey, she married you, not him, so something obviously happens over the next few days."

"You mean apart from him drowning?"

"Apart from that, yeah."

"It's stupid, I know. I just thought I was special to her." He paused, shaking his head. "That came out wrong."

"Daniel, you are special, and you clearly were to Beth, but you must have realised she had a life before she met you?"

"We never really discussed it. I've been standing here thinking about it, and only now do I realise how much I didn't know about her. It's as though the person I thought I knew and the real person have nothing to do with each other."

"I suspect that's true of most relationships. We've all got things we're not proud of, or which hurt too much to share. I doubt you shared every little detail of your life."

"This is hardly a little detail," he returned rather huffily.

"When she shut down on you, did you ask her? Did you show her you cared and wanted to be there for her?"

"It was 1912. Men didn't do that."

"There's your answer."

The sudden deafening noise of the ship's massive steam whistles announcing *Titanic's* departure made both of them jump.

"No danger of missing that one," Alex commented when the blast finally ended.

From their position above the wheel house they had an excellent view forward, but Alex decided to float above the ship to follow events from the widest possible position. Through their phantom selves in Oestragar they could continue their observations while maintaining distant positions. They watched as *Titanic* slowly began to pull away from the dock and make her way out to sea. As she neared the turning Alex drew Daniel's attention to the *SS City of New York*.

"She's starting to strain her moorings," Alex commented.

"What's causing this?"

"The sheer bulk of *Titanic* as she turns is pulling *New York* towards her. Smith will see what's happening and start up the port engines to wash her away before they hit, but it gets pretty close."

A series of loud reports announced the snapping of the hawsers, separating *New York* from her mooring. The two watched from their different positions as a tugboat fought to keep *New York* away from *Titanic*. Alex scanned the ship and noticed the man with the hand-cranked camera following the events carefully. She swept down to see what he was capturing on film. The man was clearly enthusiastic, delighted to be able to record the near collision as it unfolded, and it struck Alex that no such film had ever been found. She wondered what else the man might have recorded and whether the film would have made a difference to the investigations if it had been recovered after the disaster.

"Whatever you were thinking just then," Almega announced, "is part of the problem. Everything just went haywire for a moment."

"It's the cameraman!" she declared, delighted they'd found part of the solution so quickly. "Who was he?"

Almega did a quick search.

"William Harbeck, second class passenger, travelling with a woman who is not his wife. She's a Parisian model by the name of Henriette Yvois. His wife lives in Ohio with their two sons. Looks like he was hired by White Star to record the maiden voyage. He was supposed to disembark as they neared New York harbour to record her arrival. Neither he nor his girlfriend survived the sinking."

Daniel, alerted to the discovery, appeared beside Alex.

"It's not this that makes the difference," he commented, watching as the *New York* drew closer. "This was reported in the papers at the time, otherwise you couldn't have known it before we started this trip."

"I agree," Alex returned, then leaned towards him and added in a conspiratorial manner, "but what else might he have recorded while aboard a ship stuffed to the gunwales with the rich and powerful?"

She and Daniel shared a look and then Alex called on Almega.

"Is that what happens? Does he record something he shouldn't have?"

"He may have," Almega answered vaguely, "but I can't determine what it might have been. It's likely whatever he filmed was only known to a small group of people who disseminated the information without revealing its source. That makes it a little hard to track. I can only suggest you keep a close eye on him for the rest of the trip to see what he might have recorded."

"Does it matter?" Daniel interrupted. "The main thing is it seems that while originally his film was lost, in the new version it wasn't, just hidden. All we have to do is find the film and then make sure it stays lost."

"But if we don't know who or what he filmed, we may not find who grabbed the film. After all, if it was a discussion between politicians, one group might have grabbed it; a discussion between industrialists, another. An invention might be grabbed by either," Alex reasoned. "It might even have floated free and been picked up by someone from one of the ships that came out to collect bodies after the event. That's far too many options to check."

"I doubt there's an original invention on board we don't already know about," Daniel said.

"But the plans for one?"

"Ahh. There you may have a point. So, we must spend the rest of the voyage watching this chap like a hawk. I hope he gets around a bit."

"Unfortunately, according to the records he spent a lot of his time watching his girlfriend playing solitaire," Almega put in. "Not exactly thrilling."

Alex turned to Daniel.

"Shifts?"

He nodded.

"Shifts."

***

It took an hour to return *New York* to her moorings and make it safe for *Titanic* to leave Southampton. The Eternals followed Harbeck while he filmed the events and then turned his lens on the passengers and crew strolling about on the promenades. Most seemed happy to be filmed, smiling and waving or nodding at the camera. Some merely noted it and carried on as if it wasn't there. One or two frowned and changed their route to avoid him. The Third-Class seemed happier to be recorded than First and Second, and quite a few simply failed to notice him.

"Probably never seen a cameraman before," Daniel observed. "They're still very new."

"So new it's called a kinematograph rather than a movie camera," Alex agreed.

"He's getting some good shots. Rather a shame the film was lost."

Alex frowned, her eyes flickering around as she mulled something over in her head.

"I know that look. You've realised something."

"I'd make a lousy poker player," she agreed. "It's just occurred to me that while the film was lost to history, it's still in the program. What he's recording right now would be accessible via Omskep... In theory at least."

"I'm checking through the program for you, now," Almega provided. "It's hard to track, though. One piece of code looks much like another. It's only when he's actively using it that it comes to the forefront and there are lots of other things going on at the same time. Narrowing it down will take a while."

"Do you need some help?" Alex asked, shifting her focus to Omskep.

He gave her phantom form a quelling look.

"I've been working with this for longer than I care to remember. I know Omskep better than I know myself. Your secondary program was innovative, and I doubt I could have created that as fast as you did, but here I will manage. Just keep an eye on him. The feedback from the secondary program while you two are watching him helps me narrow my search area."

"The active streams we're interacting with light up like a Christmas tree," she agreed.

"Yes, but since the streams include everyone and everything aboard *Titanic* that could possibly affect your perceptions, that's still a fair amount of data. Don't worry, I'll whittle it down. Now shoo!"

Chuckling, she returned to Daniel who was standing behind Harbeck so he could see whatever the camera captured. At that moment Harbeck stopped cranking, covered the lens, folded the tripod and hoisted the camera onto his shoulder. The Eternals followed him as he went inside and spoke to a man Almega identified as Chief Officer Henry Wilde. Wilde escorted Harbeck to the wheel house and thence to the Bridge where he was greeted by Captain Smith. While clearly not entirely happy at having Harbeck filming on the Bridge, Smith was nothing if not courteous, allowing the cameraman to record the ship's passage as seen by her commanding officers.

"Is there anything he might be capturing in here that was solely the property of White Star Line?" Daniel asked. "Something useful to a competitor?"

Alex shook her head. "In many ways, *Titanic* was incredibly old fashioned. The Cunard lines had the most advanced stuff at the time. White Star focused on luxury rather than speed, and speed is what usually leads to innovations. All this," and she gestured around the Bridge, "is well known."

Harbeck finished his filming, covered the lens once more, then asked Captain Smith if it would be all right for him to come back when New York was in sight. Smith suggested he'd get a better picture from the forward deck as there would be a lot of staff moving in and out as they neared their destination, and there was nowhere he could position his equipment where he wouldn't be in the way of someone.

"We certainly don't want to put our passengers at risk for the sake of a good picture," Smith explained politely.

"And you don't want him anywhere near you if it's humanly possible to avoid," Daniel added.

"I didn't realise you were so empathetic," Alex smiled.

"Hardly. I've seen that look on officers before, usually when dealing with journalists or politicians. I can guarantee that once Harbeck is out of ear shot, Smith will take Wilde to task for allowing the man up here in the first place and will order him to ensure no one else lets him on the Bridge ever again."

"Which means there's no danger of him recording what happens here after they hit the iceberg. Pity, it would have been useful material, if it had survived."

"With the low light in here at that time of night, it would be too dark to film anyway. Now where's he off to?"

They followed their quarry down to one of the dining salons where he filmed briefly, but the frowns from the passengers made it clear he was now crossing a line they were not prepared to tolerate. A few summoned crew to express their displeasure and they, in turn, walked over to firmly request he desist. After trying to argue his point as the official representative of White Star, tasked with recording all aspects of the voyage, he conceded defeat, covered the lens and headed to his room. Once he'd deposited the camera he went in search of his girlfriend. Finding her, appropriately enough, in the Café Parisien, he ordered a drink and settled down.

"He's in for the long haul," Alex observed.

"Hmm. Toss you for it?"

She shook her head.

"I'll do the first shift. You go see if you can find Beth. I know you've been itching to look for her since we left Southampton."

Daniel smiled. There were definite advantages to working with someone who knew him so well.

"You're quite right. Thanks."

Vanishing from the ship he returned to Omskep and moved to look over Almega's shoulder.

"Any joy with the film?"

Almega shook his head.

"Not yet, and now he's not using it, it's no longer in the forefront of the program."

"In that case, could you see if you can find Beth? I could search the entire ship..."

"But this would be a lot quicker, I know. I marked her when you first encountered her so we could keep an eye no matter what. Right now, she's in the First-Class Reception on D deck. It's just forward of the main dining area on the starboard side."

"First-Class? What's she doing there?"

"I think you'd best go look for yourself," Almega replied enigmatically.

With a frown, Daniel relocated himself by the Grand Staircase, then followed the sounds of a piano playing. As he entered the Reception Room, the musicians switched to a very familiar tune, Moonlight Bay, but the voice that accompanied them was what made him stumble and then hurry around the corner. There was Beth, leaning against the piano, singing her heart out. He'd heard her hum the tune on numerous occasions, which was why it was so familiar, but hearing her singing with the support of the quintet was a unique experience. He quickly found a spot where he could listen and watch without risking being sat on or walked through.

When the song was done Daniel applauded, but he was the only one. The rest of the 'audience' simply carried on drinking and talking. Beth leaned over the piano and said something to Brailey who grinned and nodded. A few seconds later, a tune Daniel associated more with Al Jolson began, 'That Haunting Melody', and Beth hammed it up as if she was at a music hall. While a couple of the patrons looked less than impressed, most seemed to appreciate

Beth's take on the song and actually paid attention. Other songs followed and before long Daniel realised they were performing the equivalent of the top 20 for 1912. A few older music-hall pieces were thrown in for good measure, including 'Burlington Bertie'. Beth asked for and was given a gentleman's top hat for the performance and it was clear this wasn't the first time she'd performed the song.

"And you were a music hall singer," Daniel sighed, shaking his head. "I didn't know you at all, did I?"

After an hour of playing, the musicians took a break, Beth returning the gentleman's top hat and giving the old boy a kiss by way of a thank you. The gentleman seemed delighted, although his wife looked rather sour. Alex appeared beside Daniel and gave him a nudge.

"I heard the performance through Omskep and came down to see it first-hand. She's quite something, isn't she?"

"She's so different to when I knew her," Daniel replied. "I always felt there was more to her, but she was so... proper. Never would have dreamt of doing anything like this."

"Oh, she probably dreamed it, all right, just didn't do it. Perhaps the sinking is what changes her? It would have major psychological consequences for anyone caught up in it, but to survive the sinking and lose a man she's... obviously very fond of..."

She trailed off.

Daniel followed her gaze and from their unique perspective they could see Brailey and Beth had found a dark corner and were sharing a fairly passionate kiss. They broke apart as soon as a guest neared them, making it look as if they'd been discussing something before grabbing a drink.

"If they're seen by senior crew there'll be hell to pay," Daniel growled.

"And you never tried to sneak a kiss when she was at the school?"

He stared at her in horror.

"Of course not! It was completely inappropriate, and Beth would never allow it!"

"Ah, so you wanted to, she just wouldn't let you? Maybe what happens here is why."

He lowered his head and nodded. She had a point.

"I wish I'd known this Beth. In many ways she's more like you."

"I'll take that as a compliment."

"As it was meant to be." He cleared his throat. "How come you're here? Shouldn't you be watching 'the great director'?"

Side by side they followed their quarry to the staircase.

"He and his girlfriend went back to their room and, from what I saw before I beat a hasty retreat, they will be in there for at least an hour. I nipped into Omskep and helped Almega put a monitor on their door. The second it opens, we'll be alerted. After all, with a hand-cranked camera he's hardly going to be creating the world's first porno."

Daniel glanced down the stairs to the clock on E Deck, noting the time.

"Just gone a quarter to four. She's due in Cherbourg at six thirty. Harbeck will be up ready to film that arrival, I've no doubt, but that still gives us around a couple of hours to kill, as it were."

He waved at Brailey and Beth who were headed towards their rooms, laughing and smiling.

"I'm not sure I care to follow them. It looks like this is turning into the love boat."

Alex smothered a grin. When Daniel gave her a questioning look she explained.

"There was a TV series called that when I was a child in my last training, but I don't think the makers would have been allowed to take it that far. I do see your point, though. Once we know where they're going we can put a monitor on that door too. I doubt they'll be long."

"Oh ye of little faith," he growled, 'though he was quietly pleased at her assessment.

"Not a comment on his prowess," she returned, much to his annoyance, "more a recognition that they'll be the entertainment once the ship leaves tonight and they'll need to eat before then. They can't eat and perform at the same time... for the diners," she added when he glanced at her sharply.

The couple paused at Beth's quarters, glancing around before indulging in another kiss. Daniel looked away, uncomfortable at seeing his future wife engaging in such activities with another man.

"She hasn't met you, yet. Speaking for myself, every time I met you in a program I was blown away. Anyone I'd met up to that point tended to pale into insignificance."

"Really?" Daniel smiled, his chest puffing out with pride, then deflated as Beth finally got the key in the door, despite Brailey's attempts to distract her, and the couple stumbled inside.

"Really," she reassured him. "I'll be right back."

She vanished for a few moments, then returned.

"I've put the notification on the door. Where do you want to go while we're waiting?"

He shrugged, glancing at the closed door from whence emanated the sound of giggling and low voices.

"We could go to Omskep and skip forward, or walk the promenades, admire the view off the bow...?"

'Anywhere but here listening to that,' he added to himself.

"Ha! We could do that scene from 'Titanic', standing on the railings. Not that anyone would have allowed that to happen in real life."

He looked at her curiously.

"What **are** you talking about?"

"Since it's going to keep coming up... Call on Omskep and download the film 'Titanic'. You'll see."

Daniel stilled as he watched the film to which she referred, able to get through it in seconds. When he'd finished he grunted.

"They got a lot of it right, and I see what you mean, but perhaps we should save that until she heads out across the Atlantic. I must say, Rose's fiancé in that film was a, um..."

"Arrogant, abusive, misogynistic piece of shit?" she suggested.

"As you say. I can only hope we don't meet anyone like that over the course of the voyage."

"I'm afraid such characters weren't unknown in 1912, but let's keep our fingers crossed. We've got quite a bit of time to spend aboard. How about we just skip forward while we can?"

Transferring to Omskep, they took the opportunity to check on Almega's progress.

"It will move faster if you're watching him," he agreed when they explained their intentions. "but I haven't quite nailed his filming yet." He scanned the program. "Here's the point where they leave their quarters. Nice little addition. When this is through you can explain to me how you did that."

Alex shrugged.

"It just seems obvious to me."

"But how did you know which door was theirs? There are literally thousands aboard this ship."

"I don't know," she admitted. "I kinda look at the program, overlay the visual and where the two match, bingo."

Almega frowned and then sat back. "Show me," he said, gesturing to the interface.

Alex overlaid the image of one of the corridors over the section of programming that dealt with it.

"Kinda like 'The Matrix'," she offered.

Daniel rolled his eyes.

"You and your, what's the correct term? Oh yes, pop culture references."

"You and your nineteenth century mannerisms," she returned. "We're both still working through our last training, and you've had longer than I have to shake it off. Plus, I spent longer in my time than you did in yours. You can't slough off nearly 40 years of training in the equivalent of a few days. Besides, I happen to enjoy films, what's wrong with that? Lincoln enjoyed the theatre."

"And was shot in one."

"Yeah, well there's no danger of that."

A steward started to walk down the corridor and Alex pointed.

"See what I mean? It's easier when something is moving as it stands out more."

Almega's eyes widened as an idea took root.

"Like the hand-crank on that camera of his! Let me just..."

His hands flew over the controls, scrolling back to when Harbeck was filming on the Bridge. Most of the people were holding still, more accustomed to the stills cameras of the time that required it, so the tell-tale, repetitive movement of the hand-crank stood out. Almega targeted that piece of programming, correlated it with the other examples he had and let out a cry of triumph.

"Yes! Got it! That's brilliant! So obvious when you look at it that way."

"You were too close to the problem. I can't easily read the program, so I came up with my own way of interacting with it. Didn't know if it would work, of course, but it was worth a shot."

"This changes everything! I can target every moment he's recording!"

He scanned through, pulling up various sections.

"Here, here, here... it's all right in front of us!"

"There goes my trip to the Turkish baths," Alex sighed. "Should've kept my mouth shut."

"Can you do the same for Beth? Find out if she gets off?" Daniel asked eagerly.

Using the same trick, Almega overlaid Beth's time in her room when she first arrived, identified her sub-routine through cross referencing, then scanned through the rest of the program.

"According to this, she gets off at Queenstown," he said at last.

Daniel breathed a sigh of relief.

"Thank you," he muttered.

"Of course, we still don't know why," Almega added. "From what I saw before, she was intending to complete the entire voyage. I'm not going through the whole lot doing this to nail down every single living thing aboard *Titanic* to see who she talks to, but at least you can skip the sections where she's alone and focus on when major events are happening... or at least more significant ones."

"How about we split?" Alex asked.

Still galled she wouldn't get to spend more time on the ship, she decided the best way to take her mind off it was to concentrate on practical matters.

"You go through Beth's program, I'll stick with Harbeck, and if I'm still at it once you figure out Beth's situation and she's off the ship, you can come and help me."

"It's a pity we can't nail down the film itself," Daniel said. "If we did we could simply follow it and watch it later..."

"We can watch it now," Almega interrupted.

"Eh?"

"Harbeck had ten thousand feet of film with him, or at least that's what was claimed for in the insurance settlement after the sinking. He can't put all ten thousand in the camera at the same time, so he has to swap out the exposed film on a fairly regular basis. That means mucking about with the camera. Thanks to Alex I could nail down when he was using it, but also when it was being moved around a lot in a single location. He swapped out the films in his cabin, and that seems to have been where the cans were when the ship sank. Given whatever was in the camera would have been beyond rescue, that leaves the ones in the cans waiting to be processed upon their arrival in New York. And they're... all..." he scrolled through the program, "...here," he finished. "So let's take a look."

"I'll grab the popcorn," Alex offered.

***

Alex had insisted that if they were to watch these films they had to do so in appropriate surroundings, thus she created a film theatre, replete with Wurlitzer, gold accented columns and plush seating.

"Bit cramped, isn't it?" Daniel commented as he settled his six-foot two-inch frame.

He winked as they all knew they could adjust their size with a thought. Instead, Alex swept away a square of seats and provided foot rests.

"Anything else, your lordship?"

"A drink would be nice, but I can manage that," he replied as a cup of tea appeared in his hand.

"Not exactly typical cinema fare," she pointed out, materialising a beaker of pop, complete with straw.

He raised his cup in salute.

"Not exactly a typical cinema. Shall we?"

The lights dimmed and the film started playing.

***

The black and white figures moved slightly jerkily across the screen, a consequence of the hand-cranked method of filming, but the image was remarkably sharp, and while it was clear Harbeck was expecting to be able to do some editing before it was shown publicly, a narrative was already apparent.

"He really captured that near collision with the *SS New York*, didn't he?" Daniel observed.

"Hmm, 'though a bit more of the passenger's reactions would have helped. Not that it's really possible with only one camera." The scene changed. "Ahh, and now we see the happy passengers, reassuring us they're all ok."

"Despite being four feet from disaster," Daniel agreed. "Captain Smith looking stern and in command. Even there you can see he's not thrilled at being filmed."

"Where's this bit? Oh, Café Parisien. Did you know, by the way," she added, taking a mouthful of drink, "that the waiters in there were all Italian?"

Daniel shrugged. "They're foreign. That's all the average Brit would have noticed in 1912. French waiters aren't as deferential to their customers and the First-Class passengers would expect nothing less. Ahh, First-Class dining with and without customers. He must go back when it's practically empty to get this shot."

She nodded, adjusting her sight to accommodate for the film quality.

"A bit dark. Hardly surprising most of the filming is outside. Those cameras simply couldn't cope unless they had bright sunlight. Which, of course, limits the places he could film."

"So, the chances are whatever we're looking for was filmed on one of the promenades," Almega interjected. The other two looked at him. "What? I'm here too, you know!"

"Could also be a very well-lit room," Alex suggested.

They continued to watch, the film ending with well-dressed people strolling the Second-Class promenade deck. Alex leaned back, shaking her head.

"I didn't see anything especially noteworthy. Did you?"

"I think we need to watch it again, this time paying attention only to what's happening in the background. Whatever he caught wouldn't have been front and centre because if it wasn't supposed to be captured on film, the ones doing it can't have realised he was there or didn't think they were in shot."

All agreed with Daniel and, with a wave of her hand, Alex rewound the film and started it again.

"You know, when you're watching the background there's a lot more going on," Daniel said after they'd been watching for a while. "This is going to take several viewings."

"Something else just occurred to me," Alex said through a mouthful of popcorn. She cleared it and continued. "We know he can't film below decks because it's too dark, but he would have wanted to show that aspect as well, perhaps in programmes to go with the film in the theatres. Might he have had a stills camera with a flash as well as the movie camera? If so, what we're looking for could be on there."

As Daniel groaned at the thought of even more stuff to go through, Almega connected with Omskep and went through the files.

After a few moments he said, "You will doubtless be delighted to learn that while Harbeck did have a stills camera, he didn't use it much. Mostly it seems to have been back-up for just the situation you mentioned. I've pulled the photographs..."

He waved his hand and the primary film was replaced by, at most, fifteen photographs.

"Doubtless he would have taken more, had events not prevented him."

They decided to take 5 photographs each and examine them in detail. By the end they all agreed that while the photographs were interesting, and a *Titanic* 'buff' (as Alex termed them) would be thrilled to have the access they had, there really wasn't anything of obvious import to any of them.

"Which means we're back to the film. How about we do the same as with the photos? Split it up and each concentrate on one section?" Daniel suggested.

In agreement, the theatre was replaced by three separate viewing booths at right angles to each other, so none would be distracted by what was happening on the other screens.

It took a while and repeated viewings before Alex suddenly was heard to say, "Hang on. What's that?"

The other two paused as Alex re-ran the section.

"I think I've got something here. Take a look."

A screen appeared in front of all of them, the film projected on it and blown up to a massive degree.

"I zoomed in on the backgrounds to make it easier, and then I noticed that."

She pointed to a mirror in which the heads of two people were reflected.

"Now the guy on the right is Major Archibald Butt, military aide to President Taft. My question is, who's the guy he's talking to?"

"And, of more interest, what are they talking about?" Daniel added. "Where is this?"

"First-Class reading room," Alex provided. "The camera seems to be behind a partition and out of sight of those two, so they probably thought themselves safe until..."

At that moment Butt looked up, saw the camera reflected in the mirror, and urged his companion to join him outside, away from the prying lens.

"Whatever they were discussing, they didn't want it recorded."

Daniel had called up all the information he could about Major Butt.

"Now here's an interesting thing: this memorial letter penned by President Taft after he heard of Major Butt's death aboard *Titanic*. There's one line that stands out. Taft says, and I quote, 'His character was a simple one, in the sense that he was incapable of intrigue or insincerity.'"

"Another stupid officer, then," Alex dismissed.

"But that's just it. Speaking as a recently ex-military man, that doesn't make any sense. He was a Major, which means he had some talent – Americans didn't buy commissions for the second sons of wealthy families, the way it happened in England. Even if they did, a rank of Major still has to be earned. Secondly, if the man was such a dunderhead, why was he Military Aide to Taft and, before him, Roosevelt? Roosevelt was a military man himself, and a fair one if the records are to be believed. He was also an intelligent President, so he wouldn't hire an idiot to advise him. Anyone who was as lacking in guile as this suggests would be a liability in government. You would have to be careful what you said around him for fear it was spread, yet Roosevelt and Taft considered him a close friend. Close enough for family in Taft's case. Butt must have been able to keep his mouth shut and know the difference between what could and could not be shared and with whom. Finally, why write something like that in a memorial to someone you admire? As Alex's comment clearly demonstrated, it would be interpreted as saying the man was thick. Dutiful, yes, but stupid nevertheless. It's practically an insult..."

Alex was quick to catch on.

"Unless it was deliberately put there to deceive people who thought Butt was engaged in something illicit, like espionage."

"Exactly! I think we need to listen in on that conversation. When was this scene filmed?"

Alex shrugged.

"There aren't any dates. Harbeck didn't use a clapperboard to record when or where things took place, but judging by what came before it, it's definitely after they left Queenstown, so they're en route across the Atlantic. The reading room is on A deck, port side and there's plenty of light, so given they're heading south-west I'd say it's late morning or very early in the afternoon. But which day... There you've got me. Not the 11th as they left at 1.30

pm and there's other footage before this at sea in good light, including footage off the stern with no sign of land. That leaves 12th, 13th or 14th."

"We're sure this is linear?" Daniel queried.

"Has to be. He doesn't have the facilities to swap film while it's being exposed, even if he wanted to, and there's no reason to. All editing can be done once they arrive in New York. I'm sure Almega put them together in the right order."

Alex grinned over at Almega who nodded.

"Triple checked. The cans of film were numbered, presumably so he could keep track... And they were dated!" he exclaimed, pulling up the relevant material.

After scanning through the films from after Queenstown he found the section.

"Narrowed it a little bit. This is either the 13th or 14th."

"Did this section contain the end of the film?" Alex asked.

Almega checked. "Yes, there's a blank run-off at the end."

"Then I'd lay odds it's the Saturday."

"Why do you say that?" Daniel asked.

"Because there's a scene after this towards sunset and then what looks like Second-Class promenaders dressed to the nines in the morning. The only reason Second-Class would be dressed that well in the morning would be if they'd been to a church service, and we know there was one at 10.30 on the 14th. That means he swapped the film out just after church on Sunday, ergo this must have been filmed Saturday afternoon."

Daniel gave her an admiring look.

"You should have joined the police force in your last session."

"Trying to track where my pupils found their essays taught me a lot about detective work. The lazy ones would combine stuff they found on line, then pass it all off as their own. Unfortunately, the differences in the quality and style of writing gave the game away, and after that it was just a question of tracking down the source so you could get them for plagiarism. Thankfully, they never tried it more than once in my classes."

"I can believe it. All right, Saturday from say 10 am to 1 pm we need to be in the reading room. That still leaves finding out what happened to Beth. We know she got off, which is a relief, but not why. I'd like to find that one out, if you don't mind. Maybe then I'll be able to make sense of the differences between the woman I married and the woman we've seen on board."

"I think that's a good idea. Besides, I'm as intrigued as you, and it won't take long. Everything has to happen between leaving Cherbourg and arriving at Queenstown, so from 8 pm on the 10th to 11.30 am on the 11th."

"Your reasoning?"

"We know where she is around 4 pm. Give them an hour or so to finish up, then they've got to eat. The ship arrives at Cherbourg at 6.30. The time when she's going to have most interaction with the other passengers is once the evening performance starts, and there's no point in doing that until everyone is ready to eat. Unless she has a major flare up with Brailey, which looks unlikely at the moment, the most likely cause of her departure is something to do with another passenger."

"Or, as I said earlier, she and Brailey are caught in flagrante delicto by a senior crew member."

"Would that be enough to get only her thrown off the ship and not him?" Alex queried.

"He's part of the ship's entertainment..."

"So's she."

"But, as you have repeatedly pointed out, women are treated differently in 1912."

"I still think it's going to happen later. Tell you what, you keep an eye on her from after they leave her cabin to the beginning of the evening dinner. That gives me some time to check on the coal fire and track down Major Butt...

Honestly, if I were him I'd want to change my name or my rank. Sounds like something out of 'Catch 22'. Anyway, at the very least I can search his room and see if there's anything in there that might give us a hint as to what he was up to. I might even catch him meeting our unknown guest."

"He was in B-38," Almega provided helpfully. "Forward, port side."

"I swear, Almega, sometimes I think you're psychic," she grinned.

"Merely experienced. You might as well go back to when Beth leaves her room. Nothing's going to happen before then."

"Right," Daniel nodded.

Once again they left their phantom forms in Omskep and returned to the ship. Alex instantly floated down towards the coal bunkers while Daniel followed Beth and Brailey to the Second-Class dining area.

Chapter 5

While Alex and Daniel were investigating their respective areas aboard *Titanic*, Almega was doing some investigations of his own. They'd focused their attentions on the change itself rather than how that change lead to Fortan getting stuck so many centuries later. Now they had a course of action and a possible source of the trouble, he decided to look ahead and see what was going on in the altered timeline. This was done merely out of curiosity. Once it was fixed, the altered timeline would no longer exist and what he discovered would become academic at best, but it was intriguing and not something he could do under normal circumstances. Being who he was, Almega never got to experience the doubt and uncertainty provided to the other Eternals in their training sessions. Under normal circumstances that fact never bothered him, but recent events had developed a curious streak in him he wanted to indulge. After all, he'd probably never get another chance once this was all over.

That she sank was still a fixed point which, while incredibly depressing, was something of a relief – the consequences if she didn't would be astronomical given who was aboard. However, when he realised the consequences if they didn't solve this one, Almega found himself staring at the program in horror.

Very aware of the phantoms behind him, he made sure his body language didn't communicate his discovery. As calmly as he could he followed the paths of the new program, becoming more and more disturbed by what he found. If this was what curiosity led to, he was no longer sure he wanted it. He glanced over his shoulder and saw the phantoms were still just that, obviously focused on whatever they were experiencing within the program, but he knew now that he would have to speak to Alex without Daniel being aware of the interaction. He could keep it to himself, of course, and for a while he contemplated that option, waging an internal war. If Daniel found out and discovered Almega knew and didn't tell him, the results would be catastrophic. If he told Alex then eventually Daniel *would* find out, given their unique relationship. On the other hand, if Daniel found out some other way and Alex wasn't prepared, Almega would have no ally when the inevitable explosion occurred, and a second experience of the fury that particular Eternal could unleash when he felt betrayed was more than he cared to handle. The fact Daniel was already dealing with revelations regarding his ex-wife would not help matters, although it might give him the moment of privacy he required.

With that thought in mind he continued his investigations.

***

The fire wasn't out, but it was much more under control, and a careful examination of the soot-stained bulkhead showed it had never reached the temperatures required to do it any severe damage. The firemen continued their work, happy the situation was being dealt with and singing songs to keep their stoking of the boilers uniform, not too little and not too much. The tunes were catchy with a steady beat and the men had settled into a rhythm they could keep up for hours at a time. Alex was reminded that hardly any of them would survive the wreck but they would keep the boilers going to provide light and power to the Marconi wireless until the last possible minute. The ship certainly didn't founder for lack of courage. Unfortunately, it was looking more and more like a deadly concatenation of human error and natural conditions had led to the ship's demise. If it hadn't been such a mild winter, allowing icebergs to move into the shipping lanes; if the ice warnings had been heeded and the ship had paused in the night or taken the longer, more southerly course; if the iceberg they'd struck had been the normal, white variety that could be seen in the dark, instead of a black berg that had turned turtle and was effectively invisible; if the sea hadn't been a mill pond, or the moon been out so the iceberg could have been seen sooner; if the ship had been going more slowly so there was time for it to shift course or even if they'd hit the iceberg head on; if the designers hadn't been over-ruled on the additional lifeboats or had been able to get the bulkheads above E deck; if the *Californian* had kept a Marconi watch through the night or responded to the flares... So many seemingly minor issues. A change in any one of those would have ameliorated the disaster. The whole lot together was a match made in hell.

Depressed but satisfied with her explorations, Alex made her way up to B deck to check out Major Archibald Butt's cabin. One advantage of her present state was that even if he did walk in he wouldn't see her, and while he might wonder why his paperwork was out, he'd probably blame a curious maid or steward. That would be bad news for whoever he targeted, so Alex was going to do her best not to leave such obvious clues, but it wasn't like he'd live long enough to make good on any threats he might make.

She shook her head.

"Alex, you are turning into a cold-hearted bitch," she muttered.

Arriving at B-38 she floated inside. The Major was nowhere to be seen. Understandable. The amenities aboard *Titanic* meant there were plenty of places to go for entertainment outside, making the cabins – even one as comfortable as this – of more use as a bedroom than a place to lounge during the day. She looked around, trying to work out where the Major might have placed private paperwork he did not care to share. After checking the dressing table drawers and those under the wardrobe without success, she gazed around the cabin and noticed his carry-on baggage. Glancing over her shoulder to make sure the door was locked, she manipulated the program to lift it from under the bed and then open the suitcase.

On the top were spare items of clothing, small or personal enough for it not to matter if they were left in the bag. Aware a military man would notice if his stuff was not neat and tidy when he returned to it, Alex was careful to levitate the whole en masse so it could be replaced easily and with no apparent disturbance. Beneath that was a manila folder. Alex grinned to herself, quickly extracting the contents. It was the work of a moment to realise this is what she'd been after.

"Almega," she called out.

After a short pause she heard the Eternal's voice.

"I take it you've found something?"

"I have. Can you zoom in on where I'm at and grab the files? I don't want them to be out when the Major returns."

After a few moments and with Alex's help to focus the secondary program on the stuff she wanted, the files had been copied ready for detailed viewing. She quickly put the originals back in their folder and in the bag, placed the clothing on top, re-closed the suitcase and levitated it under the bed, and all not a moment too soon as a key in the door alerted her to the arrival of the room's occupant or, at best, his servant. She waited and saw the Major walk in and go straight to the suitcase.

"Almega, he may be adding something more. Can you...?"

"Already pulling it up. I've added it to the rest."

"Excellent."

She watched the Major for a few moments, but it was clear that after stowing his paperwork he was now dealing with some basic domestics, including grabbing a clean shirt. Being a rather pudgy man, getting up and down the endless stairs in *Titanic* would have quickly worked up a sweat. While he finished she continued her conversation with Almega.

"I'll let Daniel know I'm checking some files and then pop back to Omskep. The less time wasted in the program, the better."

"I agree, but I am growing tired of staying in here, so I'll meet you outside. I feel the need for some fresh air."

"Oh come on, Almega. You no more need air than I do!"

"A change of scenery, then. Indulge me. You've got the entire ocean at your disposal."

"Will do. Where's Daniel?"

"Second-Class dining. You were right, they needed to grab something to eat before the evening performance."

"Ha! I should have laid a bet! Be there in a tic."

She re-materialised by Daniel who was standing with his arms folded, leaning against some wooden panelling in the dining hall.

"Everything all right?" she asked.

"His repartee leaves something to be desired, but apart from that..."

"I *may* have found something. I'm just going to nip back to Omskep to check it out. Almega's getting a bit of cabin fever from being stuck in there watching us so we'll be outside, but I shan't be long. Will you be OK for a bit?"

"Nothing's going to happen in the next few minutes. Wish it would. This is sending me to sleep!"

"I've no doubt we'll have more excitement than we know what to do with before too long. I'll let you know what we find."

He waved her off.

"Take your time."

She left the ship, her phantom form solidifying inside Omskep. After a brief glance around she relocated outside.

Almega had materialised a rather lovely garden through which he was now strolling and Alex quickly popped over.

"Very nice," she commented. "Based on something?"

He shook his head. "My own creation. I'm not so desk bound I can't imagine things for myself, you know."

His rather snippy tone took her by surprise.

"Almega? Is everything all right?"

He handed over the files.

"You'd best read these."

She quickly flipped through the paperwork, releasing a grunt at the end. "About what I was expecting. Business never let the threat of war get in the way of making money." She looked up at him. "But that's not what's got you upset."

"Always the most perceptive. I never could hide anything from you."

"But you can hide it from Daniel. At least, I assume that's the real reason you asked me to meet you out here?"

"Psychic, too, apparently," he chuckled.

He materialised a bench and sat down, indicating she should join him. After a few moments he sighed.

"Curiosity. It killed the cat, apparently, and it's proving a dangerous trait in an Eternal."

Taking in his expression she decided to cut straight to the point.

"What have you done?"

"I wanted to explore the consequences if we didn't resolve this particular conundrum."

"A moot point, given we have to resolve it if we're to free Fortan."

"Daniel may not think Fortan is worth it," Almega observed.

"In all honesty I don't think he's doing this for Fortan so much as for everyone else," Alex returned. "If it was only him trapped in there and no one else would be harmed by leaving him, I've no doubt Daniel would have been perfectly happy to put that section of the program in a box, put a ribbon on it and a sign saying, 'Do not open until Xmas."

"We don't have Christmas in Oestragar."

"Exactly."

"Ahh. Well, when he discovers what I have learned, he may consider that a viable option once more."

Alex leaned back, settling in for a long explanation.

"I've read the records. What are the consequences?"

"The United States supports German armament in the lead up to World War 1."

"Hardly unusual. As I recall, they were still selling oil to the Nazis after Pearl Harbour."

Almega nodded. While it didn't make sense, facts were facts.

"Harbeck doesn't make it, but the film is found and used as blackmail material. When President Taft realises the Major's negotiations are available to the highest bidder, he turns to the one person whom he trusts with the information. Someone who knew the Major well."

"Theodore Roosevelt," Alex grunted, starting to see where this was going.

"Exactly. While the two of them try to outwit those who would blacken America's name in the international arena, the election comes up. Originally, Taft and Roosevelt split the Republican vote. Now they have common cause..."

"Wilson is beaten and Roosevelt regains the Presidency?"

"As you say."

"And Roosevelt was much more in favour of a standing army because of his background."

"Indeed. The people are still keen to stay out of European affairs, but Roosevelt, learning the film had been acquired by an antagonistic party..."

"Who?"

"The Democrats. They were going to use it to show a friend of the sitting President was in cahoots with the

Germans and up to no good. So, Roosevelt gets the drop on them – I believe that is the phrase?" Alex nodded and he continued, "and releases the details ahead of them, together with reports of the efforts by various parties, including the Democrats, to blackmail the government. He uses this to prove the Germans have been manipulating American foreign policy."

"I bet that went down like a lead balloon."

"As a result, German Americans are incarcerated and America enters the war in 1915, after the sinking of the *Lusitania*."

Alex nodded. "Which was when Roosevelt originally argued America should get involved."

"A sizeable army is ready by May, 1916 and joins the Allied offensive on Germany."

Alex's eyes widened as the implications sank in.

"Ohhh shit!"

Almega raised his eyebrows at her unusual language but agreed with her assessment.

"That would mean the war's over before Passchendaele and the Russian Revolution never gets going."

"There are definite advantages in our present situation to your having studied history in your last training."

"Does World War II even happen?"

Almega shook his head.

"The League of Nations has teeth the original did not, Roosevelt made sure of it, adding clauses that constrained Wilson, who succeeded him, to keep America involved and active. In addition, the early entry of the Americans meant they were at the Battle of Fromelles in July 1916. Amongst others they were up against the 16th Bavarian Reserve Regiment. One of those killed in that regiment, as a direct result of American assistance, was a Lance Corporal messenger. He was hit by an American shell on the 20th of July."

"Oh, you have got to be kidding me? They killed Hitler?"

"Um hmm. So while there were plenty of others who chafed at Germany's status after World War I, the unifying force wasn't there."

"What about in Italy? Mussolini?"

Almega snorted his derision at that notion.

"Apart from the fact even his own people weren't conned by that self-aggrandizing popinjay..."

"You sound like Daniel!" Alex grinned.

"He's rubbing off on me. Anyway, the second Il Duce tries to expand Italy's power into Abyssinia, the League of Nations put their foot down and stop him. He dies an embittered old man on Elba. His choice. He felt he was the natural heir to Napoleon."

"Still suffering from delusions of adequacy then? Well, so far it's sounding great. World War One ends early, World War two never happens. OK, the space race is going to be massively delayed, but that's a small price for stopping the holocaust."

"Which is probably the point Daniel will blow a gasket and I'll have to take cover but hear me out. Unfortunately, without the pressure of German aggression to distract the allies, Japan is dealt with quickly in its empire building efforts and the much stronger League of Nations sends in a massive force to put a stop to it almost before it starts."

"All still good, and once more the League is shown to have the teeth it should have had originally," Alex commented, waiting for the inevitable 'but'. Almega didn't disappoint.

"But without the need to put an end to the war in the Pacific, the Manhattan Project isn't begun until the late 1950's and without the Cold War there's not the pressure or funding to finish it quickly. It's finally completed in the mid 70's and by the time of your last training, highly developed nuclear weapons exist across the globe, and since no one has fired one in anger, no one knows how truly devastating they are, or the long-term consequences. Plenty of academic papers warn of the risks these things pose, but no one really believes it, particularly not politicians."

"I can see where this is going," Alex sighed. "Is there anything left of the earth once the inevitable global thermonuclear war kicks off?"

"Not much. What starts as a skirmish in the Middle East quickly escalates and within a week there's nothing left. The subsequent nuclear winter kills off pretty much anything that wasn't caught in the initial bombings and it takes over a thousand years for humanity, or what's left of it, to recover, not to mention the planet. They're practically blasted back to the stone age."

"Einstein said he didn't know what World War Three would be fought with, but World War Four would be done with sticks and stones."

"Einstein never leaves Europe, and his pacifist ideology isn't readily accepted. He writes numerous papers on the consequences of the deployment of nuclear weapons, but no one cares. He becomes a laughing stock and dies a little-known professor in Heidelberg."

Alex leaned back and rubbed her face.

"So short term positive easily outweighed by longer term disaster."

She leant forward, elbows on her knees and blew a breath between her fingers that were pressed to her lips as if in prayer.

"When Daniel hears the first bit he's going to go berserk. We have to put it right, but when he finds out..."

"Which is why I wanted to meet you out here. One dose of Daniel on the rampage was quite enough, thank you. If anyone can keep him on an even keel and make him listen to the rest of the story, it's you. And at least this way I'll have someone with me in the trench when the howitzers open up."

"Oh, gee, thanks!"

She sat up straight, took a deep breath and squared her shoulders.

"Ok, so do we know who the Major was meeting?"

"I did a little digging. I'm not entirely sure but I think this is the man you're looking for."

He handed over another file and Alex quickly scanned it. After a few moments she frowned.

"Is it just me, or does this guy's report make him sound like a serial killer?"

"Could be."

"Wonderful. The Harold Shipley of 1912 aboard *Titanic*. This just keeps getting better and better. All right, I'd best get back before Daniel notices I'm gone. I suggest we keep this," and she waved her hand to indicate the conversation they'd just had, "to ourselves. No need to tell him if we don't have to, and in this case stopping global catastrophe within the program more than justifies maintaining the original time line, even if we didn't have to bail out Fortan."

"Not to mention your own memories..."

"There is that." She stood up. "Time to go and see what happened to Beth, then listen in on that conversation." She paused and added, "Um, when we do get that film, what do we do with it?"

"I suggest what probably originally happened. Make sure it's in the cabin and let it be sunk with the ship. Just to be absolutely certain, it might be an idea to crack the can so the water can get in there and thoroughly ruin it."

She nodded and vanished. Almega sat for a few moments contemplating the peace of his created garden.

"Have to come back here when this is all over," he muttered to himself. "I could use more relaxation in my existence."

***

Alex re-materialised a few minutes after she'd departed, partly to get past the boring process of watching two lovers eat, and partly to ensure Daniel had no reason to suspect a longer delay.

"Have they reached dessert yet?"

"Yes, but they're in no hurry to eat it. I've been watching them for what seems like hours and I'm starting to feel nauseous. Would you mind taking over until things kick off?"

"Sure. Oh, Almega thinks he may have found the bloke the Major was talking to." She summoned the file and handed it over for Daniel to scan.

"'Dr Ernest Moraweck'," he read aloud. "'ENT, living in Kentucky', like Butt – which probably explains how they knew each other. 'German parentage, travelled frequently to Vienna and Berlin'." Daniel's eyebrows raised. "Seems like a perfect candidate for a little undercover work."

"Keep reading," she advised. "It's about to get very interesting."

"'Some suspicion as to what he was up to as he befriended elderly women and, when they died, got mentioned in their wills. Had been visiting Germany because a family contested his right to a villa in Freiburg owned by wealthy widow Magdalena Hasse who died in his house!' Blimey, if he was going to do a Doctor Crippen he really should have learned from that one's mistake and not done it in his own front room! 'Left $50-75,000 in his will...'" He let out a low whistle. "That's quite a chunk of change in 1912, even for a doctor. 'Investigations had been started but were stopped once he was reported dead. Body never found'. Do we know he drowned?"

"In the original time line, probably. In the new one it seems he didn't and used the film and other proof of his clandestine activities to blackmail the President."

"But if he was a murderer the President could have simply organised a show trial and had him executed."

"Only if he could guarantee he'd be able to get his hands on all incriminating materials without the fact he'd just executed a man without due process finding its way to the press. Doctor Moraweck was careful to keep the location of the film and the other incriminating evidence secret while handing over just enough to prove he had it. The film on its own wouldn't have been enough since it's silent, but it is proof his other material is real, and that's what gets the Presidents worried. It's as well he died in the original sinking because he's a right pain in the butt this time around."

"Pun intended?"

"Ouch! No! I think this trip is getting to me. Can we fast forward a bit? Whatever causes the problem clearly isn't here. I mean, look at them!"

"I have been," Daniel intoned dully.

"If Brailey has his way she won't be leaving her room, let alone the ship. Ergo, something has to happen with someone else that forces her to disembark. I'm guessing it's a First-Class passenger, probably a woman."

He turned to look her full on, arms folded.

"All right, Sherlock Holmes, explain that reasoning to me."

"She intends to sail all the way to New York. Brailey has bought her ticket and she's repaying him by working her passage as entertainment. So long as she and Brailey aren't caught making out in a corridor, senior crew won't care. And if they do catch them, Brailey is equally likely to be thrown off, or at least be formally reprimanded. Something like that would have been remembered, and there's no record of it. After watching her performance I'd say Third and Second-Class would love her, but it's a different matter for the women in First-Class. Did you see the look that bloke's wife gave her?"

"Which bloke?"

"The one who loaned her the top hat for 'Burlington Bertie'. That woman was not happy her husband was clearly enamoured with Beth, and it showed. No disrespect to Beth, but she's a music hall act, not opera. Thus, she is seen as below the standards required by first class. As popular as she is amongst the men, the women aren't going to tolerate her. She's a threat because their husbands like her and she's fun – a reminder of what they cannot have, certainly not in public. They'd have to lower their standards to accept her and not one of them will do that..."

She paused and thought for a moment.

"Actually, Margaret Brown probably would, but she's in a league of her own. She wasn't born into money and she doesn't seem to be a snob, and the one thing I've noticed about these rich women is that the vast majority are snobs of the first water."

Beth and Brailey had finally finished their meal and were heading to their rooms to get ready for the evening's entertainment. The Eternals followed along behind, Alex still talking.

"No man from any class is going to want to get rid of her. She's too much fun and, frankly, too good looking. That leaves the officers and the women. I've explained the officers, Third-Class have no power, so that leaves the upper classes and Brailey only entertains in the First-Class areas. She won't sing publicly without accompaniment, ergo, it's a First-Class woman who causes the trouble."

"As unpleasant as this thought is, isn't it possible her attractiveness could entice a First-Class male to try and have his way with her? She would reject him, of course, and getting her thrown off could be his revenge, especially if the rejection is public."

Alex considered for a moment.

"OK, I admit that one hadn't occurred to me, but so far we've never seen her and Brailey more than a few feet from each other unless they're in their quarters."

"Not always then," Daniel winced.

"Right, sorry. Anyway, if any passenger tried to have his way with her, I imagine Brailey would be in like a shot to defend her. Again, they'd both get into trouble and it would be noted. No record so it didn't happen."

"I wasn't even aware there was a singer aboard *Titanic*," Daniel offered.

"Nor I, but if she gets off at Queenstown because of a First-Class complaint, White Star wouldn't want to advertise she was ever there in the first place. No one would talk about it and it's hardly a priority in the aftermath of the disaster, hence the lady vanishes!"

The couple had reached their respective rooms and gone in to change.

"Will they go straight to the Reception Room, do you think, or wander around for a bit?" Alex wondered aloud.

"They'd need to be ready in case any passengers request music from the songbooks they've been given. Quite a repertoire covering classical and popular. I will admit, they're a talented bunch."

"Only the best for *Titanic*," she agreed. "Hardly any point in jumping ahead now. Might as well listen to them." Off Daniel's long-suffering expression she added, "Think of it as a free night's entertainment on the world's most expensive ship."

"We can't even grab a drink."

"Well, we could if we stepped into someone temporarily."

"Maybe once this bit is over. If I step into one of the gentlemen and forget myself, I'm liable to do something I'll regret."

"How *are* you doing?" she asked solicitously. "You've been holding up remarkably well after your initial meltdown, but this must be difficult for you."

"I won't say it's been easy, but knowing she will get off has helped," he admitted. "Seeing this version of her... I wish we'd both lived long enough for me to discover her other talents. I've a feeling our child might have helped bring them out, but we'll never know. I suppose it's some kind of..." He fumbled for the right word. "Gift? I get to see her one more time; find out more about her than I ever would have when I was in the training."

Brailey stepped out of his room and walked forward to knock on Beth's door. A call from within informed him she was not yet ready and he'd have to wait. Brailey leaned against the door, adjusting his cuffs.

"Of course, it would be even better without him," Daniel added, jerking his thumb at Brailey.

"I don't know. If he wasn't here you might be tempted to interact with her, and you can't do that, so it may be he's a blessing in disguise."

He grunted but didn't disagree with her.

"Have you checked on that doctor fellow... Moraweck?"

"We know he was a Second-Class passenger, but we don't know his cabin number, so unless we stumble across him by accident, we've more chance of tracking him down if we simply wait until he meets with Butt, assuming it was him."

"He does seem a very likely candidate, albeit a rather unpleasant one."

"You ever met a nice serial killer?"

"Tch, tch, circumstantial evidence. While his behaviour is rather suspicious, he could just have been remarkably unlucky."

"I think the widows who met him may have been the unlucky ones. Ahh, Beth's ready."

The door opened to reveal Beth in a beaded dress that was quite stunning. Daniel couldn't hide the smile as he admired her, Beth turning in place to give Brailey a look.

"I bought it especially for this trip," she informed her boyfriend. "Will it do?"

"You look amazing, honey," Brailey assured her. "No one will be able to take their eyes off you."

"That's what we're afraid of," Alex murmured as the two headed off, their observers in tow.

×*×

Beth's performance forced Alex to apologise.

"All right, she can sing opera. I really am impressed. You got a good one there, Daniel."

He nodded, a hint of tears in his eyes.

"Nothing here that could possibly cause offence to the passengers. Look, even the Captain approves."

He gestured towards Smith who was en route to the First-Class dining area and had paused to listen to Beth's performance. When she finished and took her bows the Captain strolled over, said something to her and then took her hand to bestow a kiss. Beth blushed and smiled at the praise.

"Maybe not yet. I suspect the tone may change as the evening wears on. Opera won't go down so well by ten and then they might roll out the more fun stuff. If anything's going to cause trouble, that'll be it."

They hung around, enjoying the show while keeping an eye open for problems. Just past ten, as Alex had predicted, the tone of the music changed and Beth was giving some rousing renditions of music hall favourites, several of which encouraged audience participation, at least in the choruses.

"Uh oh," Alex said, nudging Daniel. "Someone isn't happy at all."

She pointed to a woman who was scowling at her husband who apparently only had eyes for Beth. Finally, she poked him quite forcefully, making him turn. Some words were exchanged, the woman making it clear she wished to leave and the husband making it equally clear he was enjoying the show and wished to stay. With a huff the lady stood up and then waited, apparently thinking her husband would realise he'd crossed a line and correct himself. Unfortunately, her husband – who'd been enjoying a rather good wine – completely missed her signals.

"Oh, you're going straight to hell for that one," Alex observed.

The woman, now in a fury, looked around and spotted Murdoch, who was presently off duty and enjoying the show. She marched over to him and Daniel, unwilling to let his future wife be maligned, popped over to hear what she had to say.

"Madam, I assure you she is a woman of excellent repute. White Star Line would not engage someone who was not. In fact, she has a fiancé here aboard ship."

"Nonsense! Have you not been watching? She's leering at the men like a cheap whore. I demand you have her removed from the ship."

Alex could see Daniel's face turn stormy and quickly popped over to run interference.

"I'm sure this is a misunderstanding, and Miss Beth's performances have proved very popular both in London and aboard ship. She's quite the up and coming star."

"Quite the up and coming harlot, you mean! Look at the way the men are looking at her. Every one of them is undressing her with their eyes. If you don't remove her I will speak to Mr Ismay, and if he doesn't remove her I will speak to my MP when I return to England and tell him White Star encourages lewd behaviour amongst its passengers! We'll see what that does to your reputation!"

In a huff the woman turned to sweep out. Daniel, by now incandescent with rage, stepped on her dress, applying more than enough phantom pressure to hold it in place. The ripping sound was sufficiently loud to stop several in their tracks. The woman turned to Murdoch, who was the nearest person to her, and slapped him.

"How dare you! I will have the cost of this dress taken out of your wages, and given how much you earn that will leave you penniless for at least a year!"

"Madam, I assure you, I had nothing to do with it!" Murdoch insisted, utterly bewildered.

"Don't be ridiculous. It could only be you. If you're going to lie, at least be convincing about it."

The woman's rant was making Daniel's fury blaze and Alex quickly grabbed his arm.

"What are you doing?! We want Beth off the ship and it looks like this bitch is going to do that for us. No reason to make it any worse for everyone else!"

"She called Beth a whore!"

"Which we both know isn't true. Her marriage is probably falling apart and she's blaming everyone but herself. Look, you go watch over Beth because any minute now she's going to be really upset. I'll watch the witch."

She pushed him towards Beth and quickly hurried after the woman whose strutting walk showed she was not finished. Sure enough, the woman headed straight back into the dining area, making a beeline for a table where J. Bruce Ismay, Chairman of White Star Lines, was entertaining some guests.

"Mr Ismay, I wish to speak to you if you don't mind."

Ismay looked up with a frown.

"Clearly, madam, you are upset, but can it wait? As you can see, I'm still talking to my guests."

"Now, if you please!"

Her strident tones made Alex wince. Few would be able to ignore this woman when she was on the rampage. Ismay politely excused himself, encouraging the woman to move away to minimise the disturbance to the others at his table.

"How may I help you?" he asked courteously.

"You have a cheap whore entertaining aboard this ship. I demand she be removed at once!"

Ismay stared at her. To his knowledge there was no one among the staff who would fit her description.

"White Star Lines does not engage anyone whose reputation is in question. To whom are you referring?"

"That... that female presently screeching in the reception area."

Ismay frowned, hearing Beth's clear voice through the doors.

"Do you mean Miss Beth? I assure you she is a fine, upstanding woman of impeccable credentials. We engaged her at the request of her fiancé and because she has a wide range of musical talents. I recall she was singing opera when I came in. She, as with all the musicians aboard *Titanic*, only performs pieces requested by passengers and the repertoire has been thoroughly vetted to ensure it causes no offence."

"I find her offensive! The men only have eyes for her and she is blatantly encouraging their moral turpitude."

"I'm sure there's been a misunderstanding..."

"That is what one of your officers said before he tore my dress!"

Ismay, who had been looking around to see if there was a steward nearby who might help him remove the woman, paused and stared at her, stunned.

"I beg your pardon?"

"You heard me. That officer in there deliberately stepped on my dress and tore it. Do you have any idea how much this dress cost?! I demand restitution from White Star Line and I expect you to remove that woman from the ship forthwith."

Seeing there was no reasoning with her, Ismay sought a way out.

"I will speak to the officer, but I cannot ask Miss Beth to leave until we reach Queenstown."

"That will be acceptable, provided she does not sing anymore."

She stood, chin up, eyes boring into Ismay, clearly waiting for him to act on his promises. Realising he had no choice, Ismay summoned a senior steward and asked him to fetch Miss Beth as soon as she finished her song.

"Don't wait for her to finish," the woman called after the steward. "The sooner that howling is stopped, the better!"

Alex had an overwhelming desire to empty several glasses of port over the woman's ivory dress and then throw her overboard but, as torturous as this was, ultimately it would be for the best. A few minutes later Beth entered the dining room, obviously confused, Daniel following her.

"Ah, Miss Beth. Sorry to have to call you in here, but we've had a complaint."

"A complaint? What about?"

"Don't play the innocent!" the woman screeched. "You know perfectly well what this is about, the way you've been flaunting yourself and encouraging the men to behave disgracefully! You ought to be ashamed of yourself!"

Beth was completely at a loss.

"I'm terribly sorry, I wasn't aware..."

"Oh, don't lie! You know the effect you're having on the gentlemen in there. Even my dear husband has been caught by your wicked behaviour."

"Wicked? Mr Ismay, I assure you..."

"I'm afraid I've been asked to have you removed from the ship," Ismay said gently.

"Removed? But I've been booked all the way to New York. I'm sure this is simply some misunderstanding. Perhaps if I speak to this lady's husband..."

"You will do no such thing!" the woman interrupted. "It will only make the situation worse. Mr Ismay, if you do not remove her I will make sure White Star's name is blackened on all the social calendars. I assure you I have the ear of ladies whose husbands carry considerable weight."

Ismay carefully took Beth's elbow and led her to one side, keeping his voice low so the woman wouldn't hear him.

"I'm sorry Beth, there's nothing I can do. If I don't put you off at Queenstown she's going to cause more trouble than we can handle. You do understand? We can get you a position on another ship, I'm sure, just not this one."

"But I've done nothing wrong!" Beth cried, tears leaking down her cheeks. "And Ted and I are going to get married. We needed this trip to raise the money. I gave up my home and everything. I've nowhere to stay."

Daniel turned to Alex with a frown.

"Ted?"

"His middle name was Theodore. He went by the name Ted."

"Ahh."

Ismay continued trying to ease Beth's distress.

"I know, and I am truly sorry. I'll make sure it's all sorted out when we get back. Please don't make a scene. I know you've been wronged, but unfortunately I have to listen to our First-Class passengers."

"I think," Beth said, wiping the tears from her eyes and fixing Ismay with a fierce look, "that if you ask the rest of the First-Class passengers you'll find I've been a welcome break... especially those married to women like that!"

"I'm sure you are, but it's only one trip. I promise you I'll make it up to both you and Ted once we get back from New York."

He reached into his pocket and pulled out his wallet, extracting a five-pound note.

"Look, this will cover you for the trip, all right? Put it away and don't let her see I've given it to you. It'll keep you going with food, rent and what-not until we return."

"Mr Ismay..." Beth began, trying to return his money, but he pushed it away.

"Shh, don't worry about it. Put it up your sleeve or something. Now go to your cabin and pack your stuff. We arrive in Queenstown at 11.30 tomorrow morning."

He pulled out his pocket watch and checked the time.

"The band will be finished for the evening shortly, so I suggest you make the most of it and enjoy yourselves aboard *Titanic* tonight. Go on."

He ushered her towards the door. Beth turned to the woman as if she was going to say something and Ismay subtly shook his head.

Mustering her dignity, Beth straightened and said, "I'm sorry, Mr Ismay, if my performances have not been up to the standard expected of the White Star Line or have caused offence. I will pack my belongings and leave, as you request, as soon as we dock in Queenstown."

"Thank you," he replied, watching Beth leave the dining room before turning to the woman. "Is that satisfactory?"

"It is. Now I would like you to speak to your officer about my damaged dress. I do expect to be fully compensated."

Ismay sighed. His expression, although tightly controlled, made it clear he would like to be anywhere but dealing with this woman right now.

"Of course, if you could point out the officer?" He indicated she should precede him to the reception room. Pausing at his table and in a low voice he said, "I shan't be long, but perhaps we should retire to the smoking room? I will join you once I've dealt with this unpleasantness."

"I should say so!" one of the men returned. "Anything to get away from that old harridan!"

"Damned shame," another opined, placing his napkin on the table before rising. "I was enjoying that young woman's singing. I'll miss her on the rest of the journey. Still, when women get like that there isn't much you can do."

"Quite. If you will excuse me, I will meet you shortly."

Alex turned to Daniel, placing a gentle hand on his arm.

"Keep reminding yourself that cow just saved Beth's life."

"I know," he replied, his face still thunderous, "but I can't help hoping..."

"Don't say it!" Alex interrupted. "I know exactly what you're thinking and if she is a victim you'll regret it. Even a bitch like that doesn't deserve it."

Daniel growled his dissent but held his tongue.

"Now, I think Beth and Brailey may be a bit tied up for the rest of the evening, and as much as you may wish to offer it, she can't cry on your shoulder yet," she continued, giving his arm a squeeze. "Let's keep an eye on them to make sure Brailey doesn't do anything he's going to regret, then we can fast forward to tomorrow and see her off at Queenstown. At least then we'll know she's safe."

***

Brailey was, predictably, furious, and offered to leave with Beth at Queenstown. Beth talked him down, arguing that they needed the money and they shouldn't both suffer because of one woman's evil streak. Once they were in the Second-Class section where there was no danger of being seen, Beth showed him the money Ismay had given her, assuring him she would be fine until his return.

"It's only a couple of weeks, Ted, then we can be together."

"Yeah, but there was so much I wanted to show you in New York."

"We can do that on another trip. I'm sure there'll be plenty of them."

"So long as that bitch isn't aboard!" he grumbled.

"Well, if she likes White Star, maybe after you get back we should talk to Cunard?"

"Maybe," he allowed. "This is just so bloody unfair!"

"Yes, it is, but I think we can survive two weeks. Come on. Mr Ismay suggested we make the most of the ship for our last night, and I intend to do just that. Who knows if I'll ever get another chance?"

They strolled the decks, Brailey offering Beth his jacket to ward off the night chill, and even managed to sneak a quick stroll along the First-Class promenade, thanks to an officer who had been informed what had happened and quietly let them pass.

"Sorry to hear you'll be leaving us, Miss Beth," he said, bowing over her hand.

"Me too, but I'm sure there'll be other chances."

"Mr Murdoch had some fine words about that woman, I can tell you. She's certainly not made any friends aboard this ship. You, on the other hand... Well, I think it's safe to say you will be missed."

"Thank you."

"Go along, the pair of you. I'll keep an eye out. Not that any of the First-Class passengers are likely to be using the promenade at this time of night. Don't be too long and keep the noise down, just in case."

"We will!"

Together the lovers quickly moved along the deck, taking in the view. Before too long they returned, the night air now chilly enough to make them seek the warmth inside. Daniel and Alex watched over them as they did a quick tour, the staff – having learned what had happened – allowing them access to most areas provided there were no First-Class passengers present. At gone midnight that meant they effectively had the run of the ship, allowing them to ooh and ahh over the facilities. Eventually they made their way back to Beth's room, disappearing inside and leaving their invisible guards to return to Omskep.

"Do I want to know whether that... that..." Daniel began, trying to find an appropriate term for the woman who had caused Beth such misery.

"Perhaps," Almega replied. "The important thing is, it achieved the desired outcome. I put a watch on the door and they don't re-emerge until 8.30 am. They'll then grab some breakfast before Brailey helps Beth get her stuff together ready to disembark. It may interest you to learn that the woman will discover her husband was having an affair and changed his will before the voyage, leaving all his worldly belongings to his mistress and their unborn child. By the time she gets home, the cause of Beth's distress will be worse off than Beth is right now."

"Justice!" Daniel growled gleefully.

"Trying to be charitable – and I admit it's not easy – that's probably why she was so vindictive," Alex said thoughtfully. "She knew her marriage was on the rocks and was lashing out at perceived threats."

"She'd have had more chance of keeping him if she hadn't been such a harpy," Daniel insisted.

"True, but when people are afraid they don't always see the best option. Anyway, enough of that, so... back to the ship for around 9 am?"

"Or jump straight to the 13th so we can get this over with," Daniel replied, but his tone was less than enthusiastic.

"Nah, I think you need to see Beth off properly," Alex smiled, seeing the light return to Daniel's eyes at her words.

He faded out with a grin and Almega nodded to Alex.

"That was kind of you," he observed.

"I *am* kind! Besides, given what's ahead, every pleasant memory is worth collecting."

"And you care about him..."

"I care about everyone... even Fortan, 'though I admit that is a struggle sometimes. But Daniel is probably the easiest to get along with. He's... different to the others."

"At some point you can explain that to me."

"If I ever figure it out for myself," she remarked, and stepped back into the program.

***

Beth's departure was a cause of manfully suppressed distress amongst many of the First-Class male passengers, although the looks of relief on some of their wives' faces was proof that if that particular woman had not sent her packing, one of the others would have.

"So many miserable marriages," Daniel observed.

"That's what happens when you marry for money or power," Alex agreed. "At least you know that for you and Beth it was nothing like that."

"You'd need the money or the power," he agreed. "We had neither."

Alex nodded approvingly when more than one surreptitiously pressed notes into Beth's hand, thanking her for the entertainment she'd given them.

"Looks like she'll be fine until she meets you."

"A small gesture for them, given how much they're worth, but it would have meant the world to Beth," he agreed. "She's probably better off now than she would have been had she completed the voyage... assuming they'd made it to New York and back. I did wonder how she survived until she joined the school. That fiver Ismay gave her would have lasted two weeks, but not much more, especially since she has to get back to England."

"A much-needed cushion," she agreed. "When the news comes that Brailey's dead that's going to be devastating for her."

"Certainly explains a lot about her behaviour when I first met her. Excuse me."

Daniel floated down to the boat that was ferrying passengers to and from the ship, Queenstown harbour being too small to handle *Titanic's* bulk. He quietly leaned down and pressed an invisible kiss to Beth's cheek, which was wet with tears. Beth frowned, pressing her fingers to the spot, having felt something she couldn't explain.

"Goodbye, my darling," Daniel whispered. "I'll see you soon. Have patience with the fool history teacher at Herabridge. He loves you more than he can express."

Beth cocked her head to one side, a curious expression on her face.

"Where on earth is Herabridge?" she muttered.

Realising he was revealing too much, Daniel quickly returned to the ship. Alex, having overheard the exchange, merely nodded to him.

"That explains how she found you," she commented.

"Sorry. I shouldn't have done that."

"I doubt there's any harm done," Alex assured him.

"None at all," Almega confirmed. "You've merely ensured things play out as they should."

Daniel grunted and headed over to the other side of the ship, Alex watching him quietly.

***

Once *Titanic* was out on the open sea, she sought him out.

"How are you?"

"Happier, now I know she's safe."

"Ready to jump forward to Saturday?"

"Hmm. Let's get this over with."

The two faded back into Omskep, then jumped ahead to 10 a.m. on Saturday. Quickly making their way to the reading room on A deck, just off the First-Class lounge, they awaited developments. The well-lit room resembled a London club, albeit less smoky and used by both men and women. A few men were sitting around, reading everything from books to work related papers, while several women were penning messages that would be delivered to the mail room for posting once they reached New York. While not as silent as a library, the area had a similar atmosphere. At 10.45 Major Butt entered, looking around before settling himself near the door with a book he'd brought with him. At just gone 11, Harbeck entered with his camera, looking around and nodding to himself, satisfied the light was sufficient to enable filming. He positioned himself in a space just around the corner, near the windows, his camera tripod allowing him to sweep the room smoothly. He had started filming when the door opened to admit Moraweck.

"Seems Almega was right," Daniel observed.

"Don't sound so surprised," Almega replied, causing Alex to grin. "You're not the only one who can do research, you know."

Moraweck quickly scanned the room and then walked to Major Butt who marked his place and stood up.

"Ahh, Doctor, so good of you to join me," Butt said in a soft voice, extending his hand.

Moraweck shook it, still gazing around the room.

"I'm only Second-Class," he said, his tone equally low, "are you certain no one will mind?"

"You are my guest," Butt assured him. "Besides, this won't take long."

The repetitive noise of the hand-cranked camera caused Moraweck to look around, seeking the source, but as Harbeck was around the corner he was out of sight. Butt, picking up on his guest's nervousness, looked up and saw Harbeck's reflection in the mirror above the fireplace.

"But perhaps we had best take this outside. We don't want to disturb the other patrons."

He nodded subtly to the mirror. Moraweck glanced over, saw the camera, blanched and quickly followed the Major outside, Daniel and Alex floating beside them.

Checking around to make certain they could not be overheard, Butt began the negotiations.

"What news?"

"His Imperial and Royal Majesty wishes to convey his pleasure at your country's offer of support."

"Glad to hear the Kaiser recognises a good deal when he hears one," Butt replied, obviously less than impressed by the pompous title.

"Quite," Moraweck returned, slightly uncomfortable, "But as you know he abhors delay. He is eager to improve his naval forces and feels the United States could provide the ship-building resources he requires. The British navy's prominence at sea is a source of much disquiet in Imperial circles and he is certain America is equally desirous Britain be prevented from total domination."

"America is little concerned with Britain's focus. Most of it seems to be on Africa, and that is not within our purview. However, business is business, and our shipping magnates are eager to negotiate a deal to provide you with the ships you require."

Moraweck let his eyes rove the promenade.

"This ship might as well be a battleship, given its size. Could America provide military pieces as impressive as this?"

"I would remind you that the owner of White Star Line is an American, J. P. Morgan," Butt returned, a hint of steel in his voice at the implied insult. "The safety features and specifications for this ship are easily accessible. Employ them in your battleships and dreadnoughts and they will never sink."

"What about submarines? While his majesty does not entirely approve of submarine warfare, he does appreciate their advantages."

"The first successful attack by a submarine was done by Americans, as far back as the Civil War. America can provide all the Kaiser could require. The question, however, is what is he prepared to pay for?"

"That will depend on how much America will charge."

"The President also seeks some reassurance these ships will not be used against America herself."

Moraweck waved off the query.

"His Majesty's focus is entirely on expanding Imperial influence in Africa. He is sure America agrees Britain has too many holdings overseas that she can only maintain due to her navy. Some... redressing of the balance of power would be in both our interests, don't you think?"

"As you say."

Moraweck looked around again, then leaned forward.

"His Imperial Majesty Franz Joseph may also wish to engage America's resources, should this arrangement prove successful."

"Really? Given Austria's landlocked I can't see why she would need a navy."

"You forget, the Austro-Hungarian Empire includes Croatia on the Adriatic. Austria has as much need of ships as Germany."

"Indeed? Then I'm sure America can provide all the ships required by both countries. Now, do you have an initial proposal? Are you empowered to negotiate a contract? Once we reach New York I can speak to Washington and we can begin as soon as the ink is dry."

Moraweck withdrew a document from his coat and handed it over. Butt opened it, glanced down the page and let out a low whistle.

"I think the President will be very pleased with this arrangement, as will the American ship-builders. I will have to confirm it with him, of course." He tucked the envelope into his jacket.

"Of course. However, his Imperial Majesty asks that you take this as a final offer, non-negotiable. I think you will agree it is quite generous, but he expects the modifications including double hulls and separate compartments with centrally controlled watertight doors to be included as standard. In return, I believe America would be given preferential trade opportunities within the German and Austro-Hungarian Empires. That would open major markets for American businesses."

"That's a tune I've no doubt the President will be delighted to hear. In fact, hoping that would be part of the negotiations, he empowered me to give you this."

Butt handed over a document of his own. Moraweck scanned it, nodding.

"I think this is a trade deal all countries will find satisfactory," he said at last, pocketing the document. "Do you have a means to convey our agreement using the ship's telegraph?"

"A way has been prepared," Butt assured him. "I'll compose the message and get it off before the end of the day. It's the weekend, so the final decision won't be taken until Monday, but that shouldn't be an issue. By the time we arrive in New York, all the paperwork should be waiting for you."

The two men shook hands and went their separate ways, the Eternals watching their departure before Daniel turned to Alex.

"I know they're not at war yet, but surely America could see there was no way Germany would keep its promises?"

"I think your last training may have coloured your view of Germany at the time. Besides, *Titanic's* fate will prove all those fancy features still won't create an unsinkable ship, and business is business."

"Moraweck will be taking that paperwork back to his cabin. He won't want to walk around with it. I'll follow him and see if I can grab it without him knowing."

"And I'll go back and check on Harbeck. That film must run out fairly soon and I'll make sure we get the right can."

Daniel followed Moraweck to E-78. There he watched as the doctor slid the note into an anatomy book whose heavy, hard back covers had been slightly hollowed for just such an occasion. He re-attached the pastedown so that it secured the document as well as hiding its presence, then placed the book on his dressing table along with some others.

Daniel nodded approvingly.

"Hidden in plain sight. And who would think it unusual that a doctor has textbooks?"

When Moraweck left, Daniel extracted the document from the plain envelope then, as this left a hollow space in the boards, replaced it with a page of nursery rhymes and re-secured the pastedown.

"Let's see how much blackmail you can manage with those."

Dropping down to the boilers he slipped the paperwork into the blaze. That done he focused on Alex, materialising beside her as she stood in Harbeck's cabin.

Harbeck himself was sitting at a table, swapping film. He'd placed a cloth over the table lamp to keep the light low and sat with his back to it while he performed the task, his shadow covering the camera. The used film already sealed away, he was fitting the fresh film spools into place within his wood and brass camera. Once the door to the camera was shut and latched, Harbeck checked the lens cap was secure and then cranked the camera to roll on the film so the unexposed parts were ready behind the lens.

"I remember changing ordinary camera films under a blanket," Alex said. "Must be a lot harder when you have to thread it through a film camera without getting fingerprints all over it."

"The bits with fingerprints are on the run-off," Daniel replied, "so it doesn't matter. About four feet of film either end is useless, but it does mean you can change it in low light rather than pitch blackness."

Alex raised her eyebrows, surprised at the efficiency of such an early camera.

"Easier than I thought."

Harbeck finished his cranking and turned on the light, making a note on the can with the used film before storing it with the others. Collecting his stills camera, he left his cabin, locking it carefully behind him. Alex turned to Daniel.

"You know, we can solve this one very easily. Just open the can right now and expose the film. He won't know, neither would anyone else until they tried to develop it and we'd know everything was sorted."

"We still need to make sure it's here in case future divers find this room, or at least the contents of it..." Daniel replied, visualizing the destruction of the stern Alex had shown them before this trip began. "Almega, are these films ever found?"

"Someone spots them as small, unidentified objects after they scan the entire shipwreck, but by the time anyone comes down to double check, the encroaching sand dunes have buried them. There are 6 cans spotted. How many are there with you now?"

"Six," Alex confirmed. "OK, we'll expose it anyway, just to be safe, then keep an eye open until she sinks to make sure none are stolen from the room. For all we know, it isn't Moraweck who steals it, he just ends up the beneficiary."

"Five instead of six wouldn't cause a problem, would it?" Daniel asked.

Alex shrugged. "Butterfly effect. You never know the consequences of any change."

"In that case, what about the file I just took from Moraweck's room and burned?"

"Books would rot away faster than metal," Almega returned. "By the time they find *Titanic* the first time it would already be gone, and in the original time line there's no evidence it ever existed, so I can only assume it either went down with the ship, was washed away, or no one noticed it had any significance and it was trashed."

Alex was already prising the lid off the film can when they heard a key in the lock. Afraid Harbeck was coming back, she quickly relocated the film with the others and waited. When the door opened both Alex and Daniel stared in shock.

"Fortan?!"

The man entering the room paused, cocking his head as if he heard something, then carried on, quickly locating the film. He pulled a replacement can from a specially designed pocket inside his coat, copied the writing on the original, then slipped the replacement into place. With a final look around he exited, followed swiftly by the Eternals who were torn between astonishment and fury. Aware he might somehow be able to detect their presence, they kept back, close enough not to lose him, not so close as to risk being sensed. He quickly made his way up to D deck, went through the dining room (which was presently being prepared for the lunchtime session) and the reception room, then along a corridor and into a cross gangway before arriving at D-38. There he put the film in one of the drawers beneath the wardrobe, placing clothing on top to hide it. Clearly satisfied with his work he walked out again.

"I'm following him!" Daniel asserted, heading out.

"Almega! We need an explanation!"

***

"There's no one associated with D-38 so far as I can tell," Almega insisted, looking again through the available records, "but that doesn't mean there wasn't someone in there. Perhaps someone who happens to look like Fortan?"

"Might he have done a past training in *Titanic*?" Alex asked.

Almega checked his files, coming up empty.

"He's more or less ignored the first half of the twentieth century for training. He only picks up when the wars are over and big business starts controlling everything."

"Sounds like the Fortan we all know and love," Alex said, sarcasm riddling her tone.

"But it can't be," Almega insisted. "He's never been there and he's trapped, so he's not going anywhere for the foreseeable."

"Perhaps we've fixed the problem, or will do, and that releases him to play games with us?"

"It's definitely Fortan," Daniel's phantom said, joining the conversation. "I'm with him now. It's his way of behaving, his mannerisms, everything."

"Almega is a dead ringer for Phil, my colleague from my last training, but it wasn't him. The program may have simply used Fortan as a model for this character."

"I tell you this is no copy," Daniel insisted, fists clenching. "If he's been playing with us all this time I swear I'll kill him!"

"No, you won't," Alex replied.

"Just try and stop me!" he glared at her.

"I won't have to," she returned calmly. "As you discovered while I was in my last training, we can't even kill ourselves, so you've no hope of killing another Eternal." She turned to Almega. "He is truly stuck, right? I mean, we didn't miss something and he's sneaking out when we're not looking?"

Almega rolled his eyes but checked the section of the program where Fortan appeared to be trapped.

"Still there, still juddering and..." he popped out, then popped back in again, "his primary is still in his quarters. Hasn't moved a millimetre."

"If his primary is here and his training version is trapped in the program, that can't be him on *Titanic*," Alex said, shaking her head.

"And I tell you, it's him. Come and take a look for yourself!" Daniel insisted.

Alex joined him aboard the ship, watching the man who looked like Fortan playing poker with some other passengers. She looked over his shoulder at his hand, then waited to see what he would do. Fortan folded, smiling at the other men.

"Too rich for my blood, I'm afraid," he said, tucking his cards into the deck.

"But he had three of a kind," Alex said as the others finished playing and revealed the winning hand was two pairs.

Daniel nodded. "He's setting them up. Over the next couple of hands he'll win back most of what he just lost, but not so much as to make the others realise he's cheating. He'll probably string them along until tomorrow night, then he'll take them for everything they have."

"But what's the point? If he goes down with the ship..."

Daniel raised an eyebrow at Alex's apparent innocence.

"Do you really think he's going to do that? He'll get what he wants, then make sure he's on Murdoch's side so he can hop into a lifeboat. Or maybe with Lowe. Anywhere but near Lightoller's area. He knows what's going to happen and he knows how to get away. This **is** Fortan."

"How can it be? His primary is in his quarters, his avatar is in the program centuries ahead... How can he be in two places at the same time?"

"Why not? We are," and the phantom Daniel tapped her on the shoulder in Omskep, while he winked at her aboard *Titanic*.

"Then we should be able to sense him, but we can't. And he should be able to see us."

She stepped in front of Fortan, standing in the middle of the gaming table.

"Fortan? Fortan! You can see me, right? Hello?"

She waved a hand to gain his attention, then slapped her hands together right in front of his nose. Fortan didn't even blink, dealing the cards as it was his turn and very subtly dealing some of his own from the bottom of the deck.

"Ooh, I hate cheats!"

"I propose we give him a taste of his own medicine," Daniel suggested. "After all, we can use the secondary program to change the cards being dealt."

A smile blossomed on Alex's face. "Right! Almega? Are we clear?"

"Go ahead. There's no effect on the rest of the program."

Fortan won the next hand, just, and the dealership passed around the table. In agreement, Alex and Daniel manipulated the cards so that Fortan got a full house while the other players each got four of a kind. Convinced he had the best hand, Fortan went almost all in, only to find himself swamped. Astonished and disbelieving he frowned at the dealer.

"I say, old man. That was an unusual hand you just dealt. You did shuffle them properly?"

The dealer frowned at Fortan as he collected the cards and nudged them back into the pack.

"If I'd been trying to cheat, I would have made sure *I* had the best hand, not Mr Maloney." He handed the cards on. "Mr Bishop, I believe it's your turn to deal."

The next hand proved mediocre for all. Fortan won, but the pot was small. When it finally came back to him he shuffled and then began to deal, again pulling some of his own from the bottom of the deck. Daniel ensured those cards were utterly useless to him. When he opened his hand Fortan struggled to hide his confusion.

"Everything all right?" Bishop asked him.

"Yes, fine. I must be getting tired. Having a hard time focusing on the cards."

He laid the dire hand on the table, releasing a convincing yawn.

"I fold and I think, gentlemen, I will call it a night. Perhaps I could meet you again tomorrow evening?"

Maloney patted the significant pile of coins and notes in front of him.

"Always happy to play with a man who's prepared to lose. I'll give you a chance to win some of it back. I won't make any promises you will, mind."

The others agreed and Fortan bid them goodnight.

Walking out onto the Second-Class promenade he paced, his hands going through the motions he had employed when base dealing. Everything in his experience told him he had performed his tricks flawlessly, so how had he lost? With a frown he looked back at the other players. Behind him Daniel chuckled.

"That'll teach you, you double dealing piece of..."

"Daniel!" Alex cried, effectively silencing him while she pointed to a bulkhead.

The glowing outline of a door was beginning to form, fading into existence before their eyes.

"Almega, can you see what we're seeing?"

Almega's hands swept over the program, trying to identify whatever it was Alex was referring to, but nothing appeared to be wrong.

"What am I looking for?"

"Daniel? Can you see it?"

Daniel walked up to the outline, reaching out to touch it. In that moment, while they were both distracted, the man who looked like Fortan seemed to split in two. One version continued to pace the deck, racking his brains to figure out what had gone wrong. The other looked up, saw Daniel and Alex and bolted. Alex caught the movement from the corner of her eye and spun around.

"Daniel, it **was** Fortan. He was hiding!"

Daniel, who'd been about to touch the glowing outline, turned and the door promptly vanished. He looked back, realised the bulkhead was now blank, felt it to double check, then took off after Alex who was chasing Fortan. Weaving up and down, through the decks and over the ship, Fortan proved wily. Inside Omskep, Alex and Daniel agreed to split and catch him in the middle. When Fortan dropped, Alex went after him while Daniel floated above, waiting for him to return. As he did so another door appeared, this time in the air. It opened and before Daniel could stop him Fortan had shot through it and the door closed and vanished again.

Alex, who was close on his heels, stalled and stared at the empty space.

"What the hell was that?!"

Daniel was shaking his head, bewildered.

"Almega, you must have picked that up?"

"I have no idea what you're talking about," Almega replied. "Everything looks perfectly normal from here."

She turned to Daniel. "Are we going stark, staring mad?"

"Both together, seeing the same thing at the same time? I shouldn't think so," he replied.

"If he can do that..." Her eyes widened. "The film!"

Swift as an arrow she shot down to the ship, through the deck plates and bulkheads until she reached D-38. Inside she opened the drawer, pulled out the film can, yanked it open, unspooled the film and shoved it under the cabin light, making sure every part had been exposed.

"That's more or less fixed it," Almega declared, clearly delighted as Alex quickly rolled the film back into place and put it in its canister. "There's still something slightly awry, but I can't nail it down."

"I'm on my way."

She solidified in Omskep, calling on Daniel to join her. Before he could finish materialising, Alex had marched over to Almega's work area and asked him to step aside so she could examine it for herself. Daniel joined her, looking over her shoulder.

"Anything?" he asked.

"Nothing. According to this, whatever we just saw didn't happen."

"But that's impossible!"

"Ahh, can someone explain to me what's going on?" Almega asked.

"Look for yourself," Alex offered, stepping aside so Daniel could check the program.

He stared at it for a few moments, then pulled back, shaking his head.

"We didn't dream it, so where is it?"

"Could Fortan have developed a secondary program like ours that only he has access to?"

"Hello?! I'm still standing here!" Almega interrupted. "Kindly explain what happened."

"We saw a door," Alex provided. "It first appeared in a bulkhead by the second-class promenade. It disappeared and the Fortan we were following split into two. One was human, the other was apparently our Fortan. We went after him and he disappeared through another door that opened in the sky."

"But that's..."

"Impossible!" they all said together.

"We know," Alex continued, "but that's what happened. I'm going to go check Fortan's quarters. See if I can find the source of the program."

She vanished, Daniel blinking out almost immediately after to follow her. Almega, feeling somewhat left out, was going to do the same then stopped. If Fortan was somehow manipulating the program, leaving Omskep unguarded might not be the best move. He decided to stay where he was. Alex and Daniel were perfectly capable of checking without his aid.

When they returned they announced they could find nothing, both of them radiating frustration and confusion. Alex was talking aloud, trying to work out what was happening.

"When I stood in front of him he couldn't see me. When he split into two, the card player still couldn't see me, but the other one could..."

"Which suggests Fortan was in there but perhaps in his subconscious mind?" Daniel offered. "Maybe not even paying attention... a bit like when we're on the ship and dealing with something we become completely unaware of ourselves in here."

"So he was what? Entertaining himself inside that card-sharp?"

Daniel shrugged, as devoid of ideas as Alex.

"Almega, have we done with *Titanic* now? Is it all sorted?" she asked.

Almega looked at the program, shaking his head.

"Still something... it's minor. So small it doesn't cause an issue for centuries, but it's still not right."

"Argh! I want to focus on what's going on with Fortan! This fine-tuning is going to drive me up the wall!" Alex moaned. "Can you at least identify when this minor alteration takes place?"

"Sometime during the sinking, and it's something to do with Moraweck, from what I can tell."

"Oh great! And here I thought we'd avoided that bit."

"Then let's get to it," Daniel replied, practically. "At least we know who we have to watch."

"Where is he at 11.40 on the 14th?" Alex asked.

"In his quarters, asleep."

"I'll monitor him," Daniel offered. "Why don't you keep an eye on Fortan... or whoever that bloke is who looks like him? No doubt he's wringing every last penny out of his targets."

As one they faded from Omskep, Daniel materialising in Moraweck's cabin while Alex did a quick check of Fortan's and then headed off to the Second-Class smoking room.

When Alex arrived, it was to find the Fortan lookalike was already there and apparently doing moderately well. She glanced at the clock on the wall. Nearly 11.39. Already the engines had been put to all stop. Any second now...

A slight sensation, so subtle Alex only felt it because she was paying attention, and then it was gone. She could understand why for ages no one believed anything serious could have happened: it was decidedly anti-climactic. The mortal wound the ship had taken was invisible to all but those right on top of it. Mentally Alex plotted what was happening. Boiler Rooms 5 and 6 were already starting to flood, the watertight doors were closing and the firemen were rushing to get through them before they became trapped. The card players carried on, oblivious to the panic several decks below and hundreds of feet ahead of them.

As another hand was dealt one of the players, different from the previous night, drew on his cigar and then cocked his head, listening.

"I say, that's odd. The engines seem to have stopped."

The others paused, then the dealer, Maloney, shrugged.

"Probably nothing. Your bet, I believe?"

A few minutes later there was a cry and someone entered with a large chunk of *Titanic's* assassin.

"Hey! Anyone need ice in their drinks?"

The players turned in their seats to gaze at the speaker.

"What on earth have you got there?" Bishop asked.

"We just glanced an iceberg. This was all over the deck."

A few others walked in with similar prizes. Laughing and joking, the men tossed the ice between them, heading for the promenade.

"Shut the door! You're making it damned cold in here!" Bishop shouted.

"Bloody fools," Maloney sighed.

They returned to their game. Fortan glanced at the clock but continued playing. The engines restarted.

"Whatever it was, they seem to have sorted it," the cigar smoker commented.

"You know, don't you?" Alex muttered, staring into Fortan's face. "Even if it's only subconscious, even if it's not you but the Fortan inside you, you know. You've an hour to clean up and make it to a lifeboat if you want to be sure to get off."

Bishop raised his glass, signalling a steward that he needed a drink.

"Anyone else fancy a refill?" he asked.

While the other's demurred, Fortan nodded and emptied his glass.

"Probably a good idea. It's a chilly night," he smiled. "Thank you."

Alex looked at the clock again. Ten to midnight. Over a million gallons of water had already entered the ship. A few minutes later the engines stopped, and Alex knew they'd never work again. The players carried on until a loud noise made several jump. Fortan, Alex noticed, didn't even blink.

"Oh yes, you know," she asserted.

"What the devil is that?" Maloney asked

Someone walked in from the promenade.

"Hey, they're venting steam!"

"Odd. Surely they need all they can get to keep moving?" Cigar Smoker commented.

"Except she isn't moving," Bishop observed. "Haven't you noticed? We're dead in the water."

"Perhaps that's why they're venting? Wouldn't want the pressure to build too much while they're dealing with whatever it is... Ahh, I bet five."

A steward walked in, clearing his throat loudly.

"Gentlemen, could I have your attention please? The Captain asks that you all collect your life-jackets and assemble on deck."

"What on earth for?" asked Cigar Smoker.

"Merely a precaution. I'm sure it's nothing serious, but the captain does insist."

"I'm not going out there just to satisfy some whim of the captain. It's freezing!"

"Perhaps we should indulge the request, at least halfway," Fortan said. "May I suggest we collect our life-jackets and then continue the game?"

"Oh, very well. It was a lousy hand anyway," Cigar Smoker replied. "I fold."

"And I," Fortan added, tucking his cards into the deck. "I will return shortly."

The other two players settled the hand between them, then headed for their cabins. Before too long all had returned, placing their life-jackets by their seats. Fortan had also brought his coat, which he folded and placed under his chair. A bulge in the folds showed the film can was hidden inside.

"Right," Fortan smiled. "Whose turn to deal?"

Alex wondered how Daniel was getting on.

***

The loud thumping on the door would have been enough to wake the dead, Daniel thought as Moraweck roused himself to answer it.

"Begging your pardon, sir, but the captain asks that all passengers dress warmly and assemble on deck with their life-jackets."

The steward closed the door and moved on, knocking on the next cabin door to repeat the message. Moraweck frowned and then cocked his head.

"Engines have stopped," he muttered.

He checked his pocket watch. It was gone midnight. That seemed to decide him. He dressed quickly, pulled on his coat and life-jacket, grabbed the text book and stepped outside, Daniel on his heels.

Moving along the corridor and up the stairs, Moraweck came out near the First-Class dining hall, running into a few confused passengers who were wandering about, complaining at being woken in the middle of the night. He continued ascending until he heard the ship's band. They were playing in the First-Class lounge and Moraweck was wondering what he was supposed to do when a steward opened the door.

"Come in, sir. All welcome while we sort out the life-boats."

"Life-boats?" Moraweck returned, startled.

"Only a precaution while the engineers are working. We have the ship's designer aboard, Mr Andrews, so I've no doubt all will be fixed shortly, but until then the captain wants everyone ready. No doubt if you do end up in a life-boat you'll be back before dawn when we'll make you a nice, First-Class breakfast to make up for your trouble."

Frowning, Moraweck nodded and entered the lounge. He walked through to the promenade, watching officers and seamen preparing to lower the life-boats.

"Andrews is involved *and* they're getting ready to lower the life-boats? I think this is more serious than they're telling us," he muttered to himself.

Passing through to the reading room he turned aside from the doors, withdrew the book and tore at the pastedown. Extracting the envelope, he tucked it into his pocket, then abandoned the book on a table.

***

Nearly 45 minutes after the iceberg, Bishop frowned at his drink.

"Um, is it just me, or is this ship... tilting?"

He indicated his drink, which was now angled more to the starboard side. There being a natural pause in the game, the players stepped outside to take a look, Fortan remaining at the table. When they came back, the chill steaming off their clothes, he looked up curiously.

"Well?"

"Damned odd," Maloney said, re-seating himself. "But with that steam venting you can't hear yourself think out there.

"How about we up the ante?" Fortan suggested. "If there is something seriously wrong, this may be our last chance."

The others laughed at the very idea there could be a genuine problem, but happily accepted his suggestion.

"Not much time left if you want to get off," Alex commented, watching Fortan's expression.

Cigar Smoker was dealing so she left the cards to fall as they may. Fortan would win or lose based on skill, although she had little doubt from now on he had every intention of winning. She glanced at the clock. She knew that the mayday calls were being sent out by Bride and

Philips and the crew were swinging out the life-boats, ready to lower them.

***

Daniel watched Moraweck as he waited in the First-Class lounge. The band were playing ragtime to keep the crowds from suspecting there was any significant issue, but he could already see the starboard list and he wasn't the only one. Moraweck was starting to look decidedly uncomfortable and he walked up to one of the stewards.

"We will be able to get off in the life-boats should it get to that point, yes?"

"Women and children will be taken off first, but after that the gentlemen can leave. I doubt it will get that far. Would you like a drink?"

Moraweck nodded, ordering a brandy.

"I'd have a double if I were you," Daniel said, watching Moraweck nervously nursing his drink. "You're going to need it."

***

"Not wanting to alarm anyone, but I get the distinct impression something is seriously awry," Cigar Smoker commented as his drink's tilt became more pronounced, this time towards the bow. "Perhaps we should follow the captain's advice?"

"Let's finish this round," Fortan demurred. "It seems I'm finally on a roll. You wouldn't deny me my chance to recoup my money, would you?"

With a shrug, Cigar Smoker dealt the cards. Alex saw Fortan glance at the clock. It was 1.15 am.

***

The arrival of a bevy of stokers, surging up the grand staircase half an hour ago had startled the passengers, finally alerting them there was a genuine problem, but still they were reluctant to get aboard the life-boats. Daniel shook his head. Only an idiot could be unaware of the serious drop in the ship's bow by this point. It wouldn't be much longer before the water started lapping over the top of it. Why on earth didn't they get in the life-boats?

"Is the ship going to sink, daddy?" a child asked.

"No darling. Remember? I told you how safe *Titanic* was."

"But she's tilting and they're putting people in the boats."

"Then it'll be an adventure, won't it? When we get to New York you can tell everyone how you got in a life-boat in the middle of the Atlantic. Not too many get to do that!"

The father gave his child a hug and looked up at his wife, nodding towards the life-boats that were being filled.

"I do think you should get into one of them, darling, just in case."

"Only if you're coming with us," his wife replied fearfully.

"Women and children first. Don't worry, once you're all off they'll let us get on, but you need to get into the life-boats nice and quickly so we can join you."

"And you will follow us?"

"The second they let me. Don't worry, my dear, I won't be far behind."

He urged her to the life-boat, helping her aboard and giving his daughter a last hug before handing her over.

"Daddy will see you very soon," he assured them, then stepped back to allow another woman aboard.

Daniel lowered his head. It was clear the man suspected this was goodbye, but he hadn't given up yet. It wouldn't be long, though. He looked over at Moraweck who was eagerly seeking a berth and being rejected at all points. The difference between his increasingly panicked efforts and the stoicism of the father were marked. Daniel had seen it before during his last training and, looking around the deck, he could identify the same mix of emotions as existed just before they went over the top. Some fearful, some resigned, some determined, some filled with courage and focus, some terrified and trying to hide shaking hands. Before long there'd be a lot more of the last, and that's when it would get really ugly.

***

"Hey! I just met one of the stewards. He says there's water up to E deck!" cried a young man from the doorway.

Another walked in and confirmed the claim.

"You can see it if you look down the staircase! This ship's sinking!"

"Impossible!" Cigar Smoker exclaimed, putting in his bid.

"Perhaps we ought to make this round our last? Just in case?" Fortan offered.

Over the last few hands he'd accumulated a considerable sum, more than recouping the money he'd lost setting this up and most of it down to skill once Alex realised how he was cheating and put a stop to it. He would have amassed far more without her interference, and the fact was clearly galling to him, but at a loss to explain it he'd changed gear and proved a truly adept player... or the Fortan inside him was.

"Good idea. Not sure I can afford another after this anyway," Maloney said, eyeing Fortan's pile. "Your luck certainly seems to have changed.

"About time, don't you think? I've been losing to you gentlemen for most of the trip."

Bishop collected the cards and started to shuffle.

"Up the ante again, gentlemen? If we're to go out, we might as well do it with a bang."

All agreed and the cards were dealt.

At 1.30 a man rushed into the smoking lounge.

"The water's over the bow!"

Fortan collected his considerable pot and bowed to the other players.

"Gentlemen, it has been a pleasure, but I think, perhaps, it's time we abandoned our game."

He quickly downed the large glass of whiskey he'd been nursing and put on his coat and life-jacket.

"Much good will all that money do you," Maloney grumbled, following suit. "Unless you have a life-boat hidden in that coat."

Fortan merely smiled and exited, heading for the port side of the ship. Given that was the way she was now listing, the others headed starboard. Alex followed, nodding to herself.

"You're heading for Boxhall's life-boat number 2," she muttered, realising it was the only one he had a chance of getting on.

With only 17 aboard out of a possible 40, and Boxhall himself one of them, it was the perfect target, but she couldn't remember any Second-Class passengers being aboard, which meant this could be the slight difference Almega was worried about.

"It's definitely to do with Moraweck," Almega said in answer to her query. "The film can Fortan has is useless now it's been exposed."

Alex watched Fortan calmly climb aboard the life-boat and smile at the other passengers. Most were First-Class women, but three children, two mothers and a father from Third-Class were also there, as well as some stewards and another member of the deck crew. Fortan volunteered himself for one of the oars and they pulled away from the ship. Alex wondered how much longer she'd have to wait before the real Fortan stepped out again.

***

The loud report of guns had driven back the panicking passengers as Lightoller maintained his women and children only policy. Moraweck was now desperately seeking any way off the ship, announcing to all who could hear that he was a doctor and therefore of potential use. One of the women heard his cry and looked at the others in the life-boat she was about to enter. Some minor injuries caused by the crush and clumsy negotiation of the listing deck were in evidence.

"Perhaps you should take my place?" she suggested, sadly. She knew this would spell her own doom, but a doctor might keep others alive.

Daniel, alerted to the risk, whispered in a crewman's ear.

"Doctors not needed. Women and children must be saved," he urged. "There are no life-threatening injuries aboard."

"Women and children first, sir!" the crewman insisted, pulling the woman forward and helping her onto the life-boat.

A few more whispered reminders and other men pushed their wives or other women forward, forcing Moraweck back. Finally, the officer ordered the boat lowered, leaving Moraweck on the ship.

"That was it!" Almega cried. "Moraweck has to go down with the ship. Keep him from getting aboard any of the remaining life-boats."

"Right!"

Daniel followed Moraweck, whispering counters to all his pleas. While a part of him hated condemning a man to a watery grave, each time a woman or a child took his place he felt justified. For a short while Moraweck thought he might still have a chance as Captain Smith, Thomas Andrews and Chief Officer Wilde called out to the life-boats to return to collect more passengers, but it soon became obvious none had any intention of answering the call. Fear, Daniel knew, made people do things they would later regret. In this case, fear their life-boats would be swamped by the increasing number of people in the water, crying out against the cold. It wouldn't be until most were dead that some boats would return, but by then it would be too late. At last there were no life-boats left and the ship had minutes to live. Moraweck gripped a railing, desperately trying to hold on as the ship's tilt increased to the point where some slipped from the deck into the water. By now the ship's band, which had assembled on the boat deck, had given up even on their more soothing pieces, designed to keep people calm rather than energise. The tilt was too severe to allow them to do anything but hold on. Now it was a matter of deciding whether to jump, fall or sink with the ship. Daniel looked at Brailey. The man had acquitted himself bravely and Daniel was pleased to know Beth had picked someone who deserved her love.

The lights were starting to flicker, warning that the water was reaching the last boiler rooms and would soon take out any remaining power. The fear radiating off the crowds in the stern was palpable and Daniel wanted to be anywhere but where he was, surrounded by terrified civilians, the remaining women and children sobbing and clinging to the men or each other. Some men tried to gather together deckchairs to provide a floating oasis once the ship disappeared, but the list was now so acute the deckchairs slipped away down the promenade. With a crash the forward funnel collapsed and fell into the sea, crushing any below it. More screams and cries of fear followed. People lost their grip and slid down the deck, crying out as they splashed into the freezing waters. The second funnel followed the first, the propellers now high in the air. Surrounded by well over a thousand terrified people, all of whom knew every breath could be their last, Daniel found himself shaking. The groaning cries of the ship reached a crescendo as the lights flickered and died, the angle now so steep as to be intolerable. A wrenching, booming, tearing sound filled the air and the stern crashed back into the horizontal, the last two funnels collapsing into the sea, crushing more below them. After the shock, for a moment people breathed again, believing the stern might still stay afloat and provide the life-raft so desperately needed, but the hope was short-lived. *Titanic's* stern tilted heavily to port, tossing off many of those still clinging to her, and rose up. Daniel floated above, watching as people were flung from the deck or clung on, staring ahead as the water rushed up to meet them. With a final cacophonous bellow, the stern plunged and vanished beneath the water. Loud explosions could be heard echoing up from the depths and huge billows of air swiftly followed, marking the collapse of the remaining air pockets. The freezing night was filled with the cries of the dying, calling for the life-boats to return and save them. Water churned as people swam about, looking for something, anything that could get them out of the deadly water. Women begged that someone save their children even if they, themselves, could not be rescued. Men without life-vests grabbed those who did have them, dragging them down. A child, whose mother had put him on her chest to keep him out of the water, shook her, begging her to wake up. Finally, his little body shaking uncontrollably, the little boy lay down, his face by his dead mother's. His shivering stopped as he wrapped his arms around her neck, and soon he'd joined her in death.

Tears pouring down his cheeks, Daniel kept watch from above until Moraweck's ungainly efforts to swim to a life-boat slowed and then stopped altogether. Floating down he gazed into eyes that were now fixed in a glassy stare. Moraweck was dead.

Satisfied he'd done as requested and knowing there was nothing he could do for those few still hanging on to life, Daniel quickly identified Alex's location and went to her. Together they watched over Fortan's boat until, just after 4 a.m., it was picked up by *Carpathia*.

"He chose his boat well," Alex observed. "One of the last to leave but the first to be collected."

The passengers were soon aboard and being offered blankets and hot drinks. Fortan gratefully accepted both, then moved away from the others. As soon as he was out of sight he split once more. The real man continued to sup his drink, thanking everything he could think of for his rescue. Fortan dusted himself down, gave a little salute to his 'host' and turned...

...To find Alex and Daniel both standing there, arms folded.

"You've got some explaining to do!" Daniel bellowed.

"Oh, I don't think so," Fortan replied calmly. "Not yet, at least. But don't worry. All will become clear, you just have to figure it out. Besides, how can I explain anything if I'm still trapped?" He paused and then added, "Oh, and don't worry about the program. That gentleman was actually one of the stewards masquerading as a Second-Class passenger. He was meant to be rescued."

A door opened behind him, light spilling out of it. Alex and Daniel flew forward, trying to catch him. With a grin, he stepped backwards and the door vanished, leaving the Eternals to fly straight through *Carpathia's* bulkhead and out the other side.

"Where did he go?" Alex cried, looking around her.

"Somewhere we couldn't follow," Daniel replied and vanished.

Alex took one last look as more survivors were helped aboard *Carpathia* and then returned to Omskep. Daniel was nowhere in sight.

Chapter 6

"Where is he?" Alex asked as soon as she materialised in Omskep.

Almega, buried in his research, merely shrugged.

"He was barely here before he disappeared. I'm afraid he wasn't so kind as to give me a forwarding address."

Alex was about to vanish when his words registered.

"Have you been doing some sneaky trainings without our knowledge?" she asked. "That's a very twentieth century turn of phrase you've got there."

"If I'm to keep on top of this, I have to study," he replied, his hands weaving their intricate dance within the program. "I've reached the twentieth century. By the time you get back from wherever you have to go next I'll probably be at the fiftieth." He turned and smiled. "I'm getting faster the more I do."

"Uh huh. I can name some students who would have killed for such study skills." She frowned. "Come to think of it, when I was an undergrad I was one of them."

She watched him race through another fifty years and then shook herself. His speed was almost mesmerising.

"All right, I'm going to go find him. I'll keep the link open so you can track us down when you need us, just... knock before entering? He wasn't in a good place when we left."

"Understood."

Alex's first stop was at Fortan's quarters but, finding Fortan alone and apparently undamaged, she headed for Daniel's cottage.

The door was open – Daniel's sign that he was willing to accept visitors. A holdover, she suspected, from his time at Oxford where 'showing oak' by opening the outer door but keeping the inner one closed of the two-door rooms was the way to announce to fellow students you were in and happy to see people. She went inside. There she found Daniel at his desk, staring at the picture of Beth and surrounded by several more photographs and other media. These he'd obviously grabbed from the program, as they showed her performing aboard *Titanic* and they were in colour.

"I thought I'd find you at Fortan's, beating seven bells out of him," she commented by way of greeting.

"The thought did cross my mind," he replied, his tone flat, "but there's no point. He's still trapped, and if I'm going to tear him a new one I'd like him to be aware of it."

She settled into her usual spot.

"Did you know Moraweck would be one of the last on board?"

Still fixated on the images, he kept his back to her.

"No, but I figured Fortan would get off safely. Made sense."

"Which is why you left him to me. Daniel..."

Her words were stalled when she heard the tell-tale sound of a choked breath.

"She could have been one of them," he got out, fighting to keep his emotions in check and failing miserably. "I know they're only programs but..." He put the photograph down, his hands visibly shaking.

"But she wasn't," Alex reminded him, leaving the double meaning implicit. To Daniel, Beth was more than another program.

Swiftly stepping over to wrap her arms around his shuddering shoulders, she tried to move him away from the thought that was tormenting him.

"The bitch got her off, and she was safe and warm in a bed in Queenstown when the ship went down."

"I was watching. There was a woman..." He swallowed thickly. "She'd tried to protect her child, but..." He slammed a fist down onto the arm of his chair. "Sorry!" he said, sniffing loudly. He scrubbed his hands across his face and wiped his eyes brusquely. "I should be stronger than this."

"Says who? That was one of those most traumatic things I've ever witnessed. If you *weren't* upset by it I'd be worried."

"I've seen death before, many times," he tried to argue. "In my last training I saw young men torn apart. You'd have thought if anything could get me used to it, that would."

"But that was the death of soldiers who knew what they were getting into, and it still hurt. This was women and children and men who thought they were going to a new life in America. It's completely different."

"They're programs!" he cried. "They shouldn't affect me this way."

"It doesn't matter. You can rationalise all you want, what you saw was..."

She paused, her own emotions rising to the surface as her mind echoed with the screams and gasps of the dying.

"I can't even find words to describe it."

She knelt beside him, one arm still wrapped around him as he bowed over his knees, drawing in deep, shuddering breaths. In their energy forms they might not need breath, but when using a human body, even in Oestragar, it was possible for them to demonstrate all the emotional responses of humans. If he moved to his true form she'd still witness his energy pulsating, changing colour and jagged edged – a sure sign of emotional turmoil and harder for other Eternals to defend against. That he stayed in this form even now was almost certainly to spare her the full power of his feelings, and she was glad for it. Given her own emotions were fragile she doubted she'd be able to cope.

"I'm just very grateful you spared me that horror," she said, gently rubbing his back. "If we slept I'm certain I'd be having nightmares."

He drew a deep breath and sat up, turning concerned, red-rimmed eyes on her.

"How about you? Are you all right?"

She rested back on her heels. That was typical of Daniel, to worry about her when he'd borne the brunt of it. It was why she was so fond of him.

"Honestly? For the first time in my existence I'm seriously thinking about taking erasure." Her eyes were sparkling with unshed tears and her voice was growing thicker. "I knew about it, read about it... but to witness it first hand and not be able to do anything about it. Programs they may be, but that was more real than anything I've experienced. I felt so helpless. Knowing everything in advance just made it worse."

She paused and looked at him, taking in his worried expression.

"I saw you, watching over them... I wanted to help but I was afraid if I did, that would be the moment Fortan would slip away from us."

"I didn't want you there," he returned vehemently. "No one should see that if they don't have to. And you were quite right to stay with Fortan. I just wish I could make sense of it."

Whether he was referring to the disaster or their fellow Eternal's behaviour was unclear. She decided to go with the less emotionally charged option. If nothing else, it would bring them back to an even keel.

"He seemed to be implying there was something we should know. That we were missing something obvious."

Satisfied he no longer needed physical support, she rocked backwards and stood up, retaking her seat on the couch.

"Almega's checking the system to determine our next move. He's getting so good at this he's probably already found it."

She went to contact Almega but a touch on her arm stopped her. Daniel shook his head.

"I think we need a little longer. Let's let him come to us."

In agreement she acquiesced and leaned back.

"At least Fortan didn't queer the pitch by saving someone who wasn't meant to be saved," she commented.

"Hmm."

"I wonder if his host won all that cash originally, or if that was Fortan looking at the other hands and telling him how to bet?"

"Wouldn't put it past him, but Fortan did seem convinced it wasn't going to be a problem," Daniel replied, starting to put away the material he'd gathered on Beth.

Watching him, Alex could see he was simultaneously burying his feelings and regaining his control. Moving to the practical was a sure way to help both of them file their feelings to be dealt with at another time.

"Whoever he was, that bloke's going to wonder why he has a film can in his coat. I can't see anyone of that time period being interested in stealing it, which means Fortan was in control of him at that point."

"Clearly it doesn't contain anything of any consequence," he agreed. "Even if he had the desire to get it developed – which I doubt given the cost and lack of availability in 1912 – any surviving contents don't cause any problems. If they did, we'd have known about it."

He carefully placed a stand on the mantelpiece. On it, a 3D projection of Beth performing on *Titanic* awaited activation.

"If I were him, when I found it I think I'd toss it over the side."

Daniel turned and looked at her curiously.

"Why?"

"Think about it. You've just escaped a wreck by a miracle, you're amongst those few others who also survived and you realise you have a film you don't remember collecting, which is obviously not something you're supposed to have. You're gonna think you're going nuts, or at least were very drunk, and you certainly don't want to be caught with the evidence. You can't hand it over without people asking how you came to have it in the first place. You're out at sea... It would be easy to drop it over the side and pretend it was never there."

"Which is exactly what he did," Almega said, walking in. "Thought I'd find you here and I didn't want to pop in without asking. I hope I'm still welcome?"

"Why wouldn't you be?" Daniel asked, waving to the settee for Almega to take a seat. He collected the black and white photograph of Beth from his desk and hung it gently back in its place, missing the look Alex and Almega exchanged.

Settling himself beside Alex, Almega continued.

"The man you say Fortan was... inhabiting? He was a Mr John Ellis from Southampton, married with four children. Interestingly, he returned to England, went back to sea and a few months after *Titanic*, jumped ship while docked in the US and was never heard of again. He may have felt he no longer needed to work, given the money he found in his pockets, and decided to start a new life in America. After that I've no means of tracing him. He may have changed his name, but he doesn't affect the timelines so far as I can tell..." He shrugged. "History seems to have absorbed him."

Alex exhaled. "That's a relief. I think I've had my fill of 1912."

Daniel nodded his agreement but said nothing.

"Then you may be pleased to hear that Fortan is no longer juddering. He's not flowing smoothly, mind you – he still pauses from time to time – but he is moving forward, and the path seems more in line with the original direction. Not one hundred percent, admittedly, and there's still some fixing to do, but it's a definite improvement."

"Good." She materialised a mug of tea, the chill of the Atlantic still dogging her memory even though she never physically felt it. "As much as he annoys me, I don't wish him ill, and we will have to get him out eventually, if only to find out what he's playing at."

"I really don't think it's him." When Alex opened her mouth to protest he raised his hand. "No, hear me out. I've checked in every way possible. I was watching every piece of programming when Fortan disappeared the second time. None of what you experienced registered at all."

"Well we saw it; talked to him... It definitely happened," Alex said. "Maybe it's been put somewhere else. Hidden in the part where Fortan is at the moment, for example. Given the problems that's going through you'd have a hard time telling if it was proper code or not."

"Oh, it's proper code, and with no extras. It's not the code that's wrong there, just Omskep struggling to run it, but that seems to be as a direct result of whatever has gone wrong before it. Almost like Omskep's suffering from the equivalent of a severe bout of indigestion."

"How can it? We're outside time, including Omskep," Alex frowned.

"Yes, well... sort of. We're more outside entropy, if that makes any sense, and that's the usual way of measuring time within the program, but for us to have experiences we can recall or even hold this conversation there has to be something which might as well be time, it simply doesn't touch upon us or Oestragar. Duration without effect."

"Yet Omskep's got 'indigestion'," Daniel said, putting finger quotes around the word, "and in our minds there's change..."

"I can't explain Omskep, but if anything, you're becoming more organised rather than more disorganised. The more training and experience, the more understanding."

Both Daniel and Alex levelled looks at him, expressing clearly that they were having a little trouble with that idea.

"OK, more for you two. The others... maybe not so much. You've always been the odd ones out amongst the Eternals. The others remain more or less fixed, but you alter with your experiences."

"That's probably because we're the only two who always reject erasure," Alex suggested.

Almega nodded.

"Almost certainly. You can't develop or change if you keep resetting yourself. Speaking of... do you...?"

"No!" both Alex and Daniel replied instantly.

"As bad as it was... I can't bear the thought of losing any of what I learned about Beth," Daniel added.

"To me it seems disrespectful somehow. I know that sounds odd," she added off Almega's look. "Put it down to Oslac being Oslac."

"The explanation for everything," Almega smiled.

"Getting back to Fortan..." Daniel said, drawing the conversation around to its starting point as he settled back into his chair, "If what we saw isn't registering where he's trapped or where he turns up, maybe it's at the very beginning of the program? With space, time and matter so condensed at the start, but all the future potential wrapped in the code, you could lose just about anything in there and unpicking it would be a complete nightmare."

Almega grunted his agreement. "I thought of that, but as you say, it's a mess so practically impossible to search. I *am* trying. He might also have a secondary program but not in his quarters. I'm not about to search Oestragar to try and find it. Infinity takes a while to go through," he finished with a wry smile.

"Which means that for now we have to play the game by his rules," Daniel growled. "But you said you didn't think it was Fortan, which begs the obvious question: who else could it be?"

"I don't know, but with all due respect to our, um, friend... I don't think he's capable of something like this."

"Now there I **do** agree with you," Daniel replied firmly. "Arrogant, conceited, sneaky, yes, but super intelligent enough to pull off something like this? No."

"So, someone pretending to be Fortan to throw us off the trail? Someone so good they can hide their true identity from us? None of the others are that smart. **You're** not even that smart," Alex said, looking at Almega. "No disrespect."

"None taken, and I agree with you, which makes it all the more puzzling. I'll keep monitoring. Hopefully something will come up that will give us a clue."

Silence fell as each was lost in their own thoughts and Almega quietly observed the pair.

"How are you two?"

"I think we'll be all right," Daniel replied, looking to Alex for confirmation. She offered a tight smile of agreement. "It was different to when we experience things like that in training. When you come back from those sessions they become... more like a dream or nightmare that you can safely ignore most of the time. This one was rather more... upfront."

Alex nodded.

"While obviously we don't have the same problems as the programs and it's easier for us to move on, that one is definitely going to linger. I can compartmentalise it so it doesn't have the same effect, but the memory is... vivid."

"Very," Daniel agreed.

"It would have hit you harder, Beth being involved..." Almega began.

"Yes, but knowing she got off safely, that she and I would meet and have our time... That's definitely helped. And Alex has her usual way of easing my mind."

"I have?" she asked in confusion. "I just listened."

"Sometimes that's all it takes," Almega observed, but he was frowning. "Always the same with you two. You're solid as a rock when together; far more likely to... oh, what is that term I read? Oh yes! 'Lose the plot' when apart."

"Probably from so many training sessions where we had to rely on each other without knowing who we really are. Gives you an insight into each other's psyche."

"It's the fact you do rely on each other, no matter where you come from, your backgrounds or any reasons provided by the program to split you apart. A few of the others tried it and their results weren't nearly so positive. Fortan called you two 'the old married couple'," Almega revealed.

"One more reason to rip him a new one when we finally get him out of there," Daniel growled, "as if I didn't have enough to last the duration already."

Alex considered the issue, then dismissed it.

"We've always got on, for as long as I can remember. I certainly never had to work on it," she said, raising a questioning eyebrow at Daniel.

"Nor I," he admitted. "And we do fight from time to time," he defended.

"And neither of us has had a problem with you," Alex said.

"Well, apart from after my last training, but everyone got it then, including Alex."

"Nice to know I wasn't alone. I did wonder..." Almega said.

"If the door's closed, stay out," Daniel suggested.

"I'll remember that, 'though hopefully you'll never have one that bad again."

He smiled and then looked around taking in the new decorations quietly. When the silence continued a little too long, Alex and Daniel exchanged looks.

"Um, Almega, not that you aren't welcome, but why did you drop by?" Daniel asked. "I assume it wasn't to check out my choice in décor."

"Oh! Sorry!" he replied, refocusing his attention. "I thought you might like to know I've found the next problem, but if you want to take a break to recover..."

"Well, we could have, but now you've said that we don't have a lot of choice, do we?" Alex sighed.

She glanced over at Daniel. Their recent experiences were still in both their minds, but she knew now was not the time to address them. If they were still pressing when this session was over, they could reassess the situation. She had the feeling that dealing with his last training session the slow way had taught Daniel myriad coping mechanisms, and when he returned her look with a firm nod and smile of reassurance, she knew they'd be all right.

Almega observed the exchange and gave a chagrined nod.

"Next time I'll give you a pause before telling you. If there is a next time," he added quickly before settling into a briefing mode. "It's in 2654 so not too far from your last session... relatively speaking. After the Great Melt, anyway."

"Landscape's a bit different, then," Daniel said.

"Indeed. And humans have started colonies off world," Almega continued.

"That took longer than I thought it would," Alex returned thoughtfully. "After that rush in the twentieth century everything slowed down to a crawl. It was only the risks posed by the Great Melt that put funding back into space exploration."

"Necessity being the mother of invention," Almega agreed.

"Or just a mother," Daniel muttered, his tone indicating he'd had more than his fair share of finding hacks to get around urgent problems. "Sorry! Carry on."

Almega considered Daniel's expression thoughtfully, but let it pass and continued his narrative.

"All right, by this time there are data forests all over the planet. That's restored the atmosphere and, combined with increased focus on renewable energy sources, reduced global warming..."

"...Given a home to a wealth of animals that were dying out with the reduced land mass," Alex added, "although not as many as might have been. Pine forests are far from ideal."

"But very fast growing, which is what they needed. Of course, wood boring or other damaging creatures were effectively obliterated," Daniel added.

"In my last training we had what were called 'computer viruses'. Who knew in the future the woodpecker, beaver and termite would become bigger threats to data storage?"

Almega decided to step in before they became too distracted.

"Quite. Anyway, from what I can tell your target is central North America, a place called New Uruk, Montana."

Daniel thought for a moment, going through his memory to drag up the relevant information. He could have called on Omskep, but he prided himself on his ability to recall details of the relevant history.

"Wasn't that one of the new towns created in Flathead National Forest?" When Almega nodded he added thoughtfully, "With all that data storage it made sense they'd need somewhere for the human component, even with robots doing most of the work. That was one of the first data forests, as I recall. Ended up joining with about nine others to form MIW Data Storage Services."

"New Uruk?" Alex said, pronouncing the name carefully. "A bit Babylonian."

"They created a whole raft of towns there with names based around the Epic of Gilgamesh. According to the story, Gilgamesh predated the flood and he and Enkidu chopped down the trees in the Great Cedar Forest, so town names include Humbaba, Enkidu, Gilgamesh, Ishtar and Shamash. Slightly ironic, but Humbaba protected the trees, so that's the hub town. That we're going to New Uruk suggests the problem starts on the outskirts and spreads before the other towns realise what's happening."

"Towns might be giving them more credit than they deserve," Almega said. "The human populations are small, so that should make things marginally easier. They're only there for monitoring and to do things the machines aren't programmed for. The robots plant replacements, inject DNA storage, extract and deliver data to the network, perform basic arboriculture, that sort of thing. Humans step in when the machines don't know what to do. They've even got machines to fix machines. There are also outposts in the forest manned by one or two at most and they move around depending on where they're needed."

"That's a massive area. I hope you're not expecting us to cover all of it?" Alex said.

"No, the problem's definitely centred in New Uruk. Oh, the locals call it something that sounds more like Newark, but with an extra diphthong."

"Given Newark is several feet below water by that point, I suppose there's no risk of confusion," Alex conceded. "Do we know what the problem is, yet?"

Almega shook his head.

"Still working on that, but once you're on the ground the secondary program should be able to home in on it."

"Naturally. Wouldn't do to give us all the information before we set out," Daniel grumbled.

"I'm doing my best! You forget how many lines of code there are for a single ant, let alone anything larger, and in this one we have the added problem of them storing their own data in the tree DNA, and that's also been incorporated into the program. Every line of code for every tree has their computer data wrapped in it as well. Add in the optical readers, underground fibre-optic networks, birds, insects, humans, animals, soil, air particles..."

Alex raised her hand to forestall the potentially interminable list.

"All right, all right. We get it. At least we're landlocked this time. After the last one I don't want to see water on that scale ever again." She finished her tea. "Let's go."

***

Once again they returned to Omskep, if only because having all their senses as well as thought to hand in both Oestragar and within the program maximised communication efficiency.

"I'll be watching for the slightest hint of whoever that is masquerading as Fortan. If you see him or those doors you mentioned, let me know. I've doubled up on the secondary program. Now as well as your 'GPS' as you called it, I've got one looking for the slightest change anywhere; not just in your present location and ahead to Fortan but backwards too. The tiniest alteration should show up."

"Excellent," Daniel said. "With any luck we'll finally be able to nail him down and get some answers."

The two faded from Omskep, their phantom forms maintaining the contact while their other selves appeared in the middle of a dense pine forest.

Alex took a deep breath and let it out with a whoosh.

"It must have rained last night," she observed. "Hmm, reminds me of my last training." When Daniel looked at her curiously, she added, "There was a line of pine trees between the main building and the car park."

"I take it by your time staff weren't living in, then?"

"The only person who still had permanent accommodation within the school grounds was the principal, and he was part of a dying breed. By my last training, principals moved from school to school to develop their careers."

"Rather than staying put and developing the school," Daniel commented, his tone sour. He pointed ahead. "I see the outskirts of the town."

They stepped onto what passed for the main street and Alex looked around.

"Small is an understatement."

A post office that doubled as a stationer, food store including grocer, butcher, bakery and fishmonger, hardware store, and a coffee shop that doubled as a bar were the sum total of shopping places lining the street. After that there was a large building that dominated the area.

"That must be central operations," Alex commented.

"Uh hmm." Daniel agreed. "Robot repairs, delivery of data, maintenance, central control for the robot workforce... There'll also be a nursery out back for the seedlings ready to be planted when old trees die or succumb to the elements, and a backup data area, probably in the basement. Any trees they know are nearing their end will have their data harvested ready for injection into new trees."

Alex smiled. As usual, Daniel had done his prep work. The fact she preferred to just dive in and wing it gave them something to talk about.

"How do they know when to replace them?"

"Trees talk to each other, and the system monitors those conversations," he returned, knowing Alex's preferences and happy to be teacher once more. "When one is dying it sends out a message to those around it who withdraw their support. That gives the robots the alert and they prepare for substitution. They download the data, uproot the old tree and plant the replacement, giving it what it needs until it can establish communication with those around it, who'll then take over the sharing of resources. The old tree is put through a data wash so nothing stored in its DNA can be read and then it's placed ready for use in buildings, furniture or whatever's needed. Nothing's wasted."

"It seems losing several million hectares of real-estate can have a positive outcome."

"And there's lots of money to be made from planting trees now," Daniel pointed out.

"Of course," Alex replied in a droll tone. "So much more important than when all they were doing was providing air to breathe."

"Question is..." Daniel said, looking around, "where do we start? Almega?"

"Whatever happens hasn't happened yet, so the secondary program can't get a fix. The scene is being set, however, so I suggest you listen in on a few conversations and see if anything comes up."

"Ahh, the scientific approach, then?"

"Your sarcasm is getting worse, you know," Daniel observed.

"What can I say? Being sent on wild goose chases brings out the best in me." She winked at him and headed towards the coffee shop. "Anyway, sarcasm is the highest form of intelligence."

"And the lowest form of wit," he finished, following her. "Why the coffee shop?"

"Why not? As good a place as any to start. Listen in on a few conversations, get a handle on some of the key players in the area, check out the politics..." She passed through the door. "Of course, all that requires customers."

Daniel arrived beside her and gazed around the empty shop. Even the barista was missing.

"Apparently, not a coffee drinking fraternity."

"Or too busy. What time is it?"

"Just gone 10," Almega supplied. "They've probably grabbed their morning coffee and gone to work. I suggest you return at lunchtime. For now, perhaps central operations would be worth checking out?"

As they moved towards the large building, a robotic 'dog', the size of an Irish Wolfhound, trotted past them. In a harness on its back it was carrying nearly twenty recyclable coffee cups. Alex watched it, shaking her head.

"The future is a weird place... relative to where I was last, I mean. I guess we now know why the coffee shop was empty."

"A different approach to take-out," Daniel agreed. "One would think it would make more sense to have vending machines in the plant."

"Ahh, but nothing beats a fresh, barista-made coffee," Alex opined. "Could use one of those myself." An instant later a similar coffee cup appeared in her hand and she took a large gulp. "Just as I remember it."

"Given it came out of your imagination, that's hardly a surprise."

"Tell me the secondary program isn't going to become your personal vending machine!" Almega grumbled.

"That's for when we need something instantiated within the program. This little creation was all my own work, so you needn't worry," Alex assured him.

She turned to offer Daniel one, only to find him nursing a cup already.

"Anything you can do..." he said with a grin.

Before long they were at the entrance to the large building. Walking through the door they looked around and Alex spotted a map. Together they examined it, Daniel deciding to check out the nursery first while Alex would investigate distribution.

***

With her mind still filled with memories of the 20th and 21st centuries (plus their brief sojourn in Ancient Greece), distribution was a little overwhelming. Robot dogs were being loaded up with sturdy saplings by machines that lifted the readied trees off a conveyor belt and attached them to harnesses on the dogs. Two dogs and one android would then head out to plant the trees the dog carried, the second dog being loaded with mulch, water and poles to support the saplings until they could stand on their own. Four humans watched over the activities from computer consoles. Looking through the open roller-door at the back of the room, Alex could see driverless electric vehicles waiting to ferry their cargo closer to the planting sites, after which the dogs and support androids would, she assumed, dismount and continue on foot.

"Need another walker over here," one of the men shouted, pointing to two already laden dogs. Within moments an android had arrived ready to go, and the trio joined the others outside.

On the other side, returning dogs and androids were checked, their data detailing what they'd been doing and where they'd been quickly downloaded. Any excess muck was cleaned off and then they went to a holding area to await their next assignment. Alex noted a few moved to the back and plugged themselves in, suggesting they'd been out for some time. These had apparently been doing maintenance on the forest, testing, measuring, tending and otherwise keeping an eye on the status of the trees in their care.

As she watched, two larger versions of the dogs, the size of small horses and bearing humans, trotted into the loading bay and the riders quickly dismounted. With their data tablets in their hands they went to the computer consoles to download their updates and chat to the resident humans. A whirring, buzzing sound heralded the arrival of a small number of drones who settled onto a specially designed platform, plugging themselves in to download data and to recharge.

Alex peered over the shoulders of the humans to look at the data readouts. Soil quality, the status of the trees, the size and signal quality of the underground networks, moisture content, weather reports... everything was being monitored. A computer map that filled one wall with red, amber and green markers gave an overview of the area the complex covered, allowing patterns to be detected quickly. At present there were a few small amber points to which appropriate robots were being sent, one red point that, she gathered, was a tree that was dying and needed to be replaced, and the rest was a reassuring green. So far as she could tell, based on the wall display and the relaxed atmosphere, everything was as it should be.

"Hey Daniel? Everything looks fine here. Pretty amazing really. How are things with you?"

"So far, so good," he returned. "This is quite a setup."

***

Daniel looked out across the massive greenhouse. Row upon row of soil areas stretched out before him, running from bare soil waiting for plants, right the way up to saplings ready to be added to the forest. Sensors in the soil and tags inserted into the trees once they were large enough fed back data. Androids walked the rows, watering, adding nutrients, clipping, planting, re-potting and adjusting local lighting levels to create the most balanced, healthy trees he'd ever seen. In the middle of the nursery there was a large central computer around eight feet tall and four feet in diameter. It had work stations in each side manned by the only humans in the area, and fed back the data alerting the humans and machines to any problems the moment they arose. The ceiling, forty feet above, was presently open as it was a warm, sunny day, but looking at it more closely he could see there were panels that could provide the illusion of same even when thunderstorms raged outside. A thin membrane across the open roof ensured no unwanted insects or birds could come in and damage the young trees. A gentle breeze provided by giant, slow moving fans kept the warehouse at the optimum temperature for growth, moving the air around to keep everything fresh.

The trees seemed to be growing at an accelerated rate, making Daniel suspect they had been genetically modified to suit this particular purpose. Going to the far end where the ready-to-go saplings were located, Daniel watched the androids collecting samples from each plant. They fed those into a machine which broke down the samples, encoded data that was constantly streaming into the machine with the resultant DNA, then expelled the sample for the android to take back to the plant and inject. Once that was done, connectors were attached to the roots that were then plugged into a temporary network. As each tree connected with the network and proved it had assimilated the DNA coding, it was gently removed, complete with its connectors, and taken to a holding area where it was provided with nutrients and reconnected until such time as it was ready to be planted outside. Nearby, the other end of the conveyor belt Alex saw in distribution was constantly moving, ready for its next load, and Daniel noted the wall it passed through was actually two large doors that could be opened when something larger needed access – such as when the central computer had been delivered. Daniel knew every tree had at least one back up and, in some cases, two or three, depending on the value placed on the data. The trees holding the same data were digitally marked to ensure they were never planted too close to each other, so if a freak storm wrecked part of the forest, other parts could take up the slack without loss to the data stream.

The sheer bulk of data one tree represented was daunting, and Daniel called on Omskep to find out where all the information was coming from to justify such a massive resource. 64K resolution films and images in 2 and 3D coming in from media companies and ordinary users explained some of it. Hospitals now had detailed, fully interactive holographic versions of their patients that recorded every change in their status, providing a massive library that could be accessed to identify emerging problems and provide archive material for research purposes. Most of the trees were for static, long term storage, but experiments had allowed others to be adapted to provide short term and regularly updated access. Unfortunately, the constant rewriting of DNA inside those plants meant their lives were considerably shorter than that of the others. Most of that task, therefore, was still done by standard server farms, stored several meters below the earth's surface and cooled by solar panel powered refrigeration, which meant they could be located in deserts rather than damaging the newly restored polar ice caps. The heat they gave off was also converted to energy and, augmented by the solar panels, helped to keep the server farms running. Every person on the planet seemed to have their own tree (plus backup) to cover archived personal data, which was updated from the server farms every ten years or at death, while people in positions of influence, such as government leaders and other powerful individuals, got several backups just in case.

Looking at the trees it was impossible to tell which person was connected to which tree, but the software that handled the encryption recorded everything so the network could maintain the records correctly without anyone being the wiser as to what information was where. Daniel knew that other data forests across the globe ensured that even if a nuclear weapon went off, devastating one of them, the data would be saved in another and which forest the updates went to first was constantly moving so no one forest was the primary archive. Unless the entire planet exploded it was hard to see how such a system could fail, and even then there were off-world backups. With so much redundancy built in, the history of the human race would surely be preserved somewhere until the end of the universe. Daniel was starting to see why Almega was struggling to find the source of their problem. That he managed at all was nothing short of a miracle and Daniel's respect for the Eternal grew. Yes, the encoding was different, but someone clever (and whoever was causing their problems was certainly that) could hide their own code using the computing power within this part of the program, allowing Omskep to encode the whole and thus cover their tracks.

"Almega, old man, I doff my hat to you," he said. "How you're finding anything in the data streams is beyond me."

"Nice to know my skills are appreciated. And less of the old, if you don't mind. Appearances to the contrary, we're all the same age."

Alex appeared beside Daniel to take a look at the nursery for herself.

"A little salute to me, too? I created the secondary program, don't forget, and it's monitoring all this."

"Still don't know how you did that," Almega said, "but you definitely deserve credit for it."

"Thanks. Not sure about that myself. All I can say is it felt right, which isn't much use to man nor beast. Anyway, the more important question is: is it telling us what we need to know yet?"

"You're in the right place, but the source is no clearer than it was when you went in. To be fair, you've barely been there an hour. Give me a *little* time. So far it's been your thoughts that have helped identify the issue, so I suggest you start thinking and we'll see if that triggers anything."

Daniel looked around, taking in all the activity around them.

"There's so much that could go wrong. Where do you start?"

Alex was inclined to agree.

"But nothing that could devastate the entire system, and I think that's what we're looking for. A few damaged trees would be nothing given the back-ups, unless it was the same data being targeted?" When Almega didn't respond she moved on. "So, if it's not that, what's left?"

"The trees themselves? These ones have been genetically modified to grow faster..."

"Is that a recent innovation?"

Daniel shook his head.

"They've been using them for a while, now, and there have been no problems."

"But something's changed, or is changing. A virus in the data? Perhaps someone found a way to hack the storage encoding?"

Again, no response from Almega.

"There are fail-safes. Any hint of malicious code and the whole lot is dumped. Heuristic analysis has reached levels of accuracy you could only dream of in your last training," Daniel supplied.

"Listen to you! The man from the Edwardian era spouting on computing!"

"I would remind you that was only my last training. I was a programmer in the 92nd century a few trainings back, with an interest in the history of computing."

"But as this never happened, you have no idea what goes wrong now," Alex sighed.

"Sadly, no. If I did, it wouldn't be a problem."

"Which means all we can do is listen, watch and wait." Alex growled in frustration. "What about checking upstairs? There aren't many humans down here and machines can only do what they're told. That suggests the rogue element is probably human."

"And equally probably Fortan, or whoever it is that looks like him," Daniel agreed. He paused and then raised his eyes heavenward. "Come on, Almega! We must have hit something!"

"Your Fortan doesn't show up, so if it *is* him, the secondary program won't find him until you figure out who he's occupying at the moment. As for your other suggestions, nearly all caused a buzz, but nothing I can nail down."

"Argh! Come on," Alex said, jabbing a finger upwards and across, pointing at the rest of the building before flying off.

Daniel watched for a moment, somewhat put out by the abrupt order, but he recognised the frustration behind it. He was feeling the same way. Rather than remonstrate he followed her and together they ascended through the floors until they reached the laboratory where Daniel stopped, leaving Alex to continue to administration.

***

It was amazing how little had changed when it came to paperwork Alex mused as she looked around the room full of desks with men and women working at their computers. Each cubicle had a clear screen around it, and a low background hum indicated the administrators relied more on speech recognition than manual typewriting skills. Entering one of the cubicles Alex listened as a woman dictated a letter regarding the delivery of fertiliser. The increased volume within the cubicle suggested the clear screens were noise dampeners, allowing the administrators to speak in their normal voices without disturbing those around them. Moving to another desk she found a man engaged in a video call with someone from Paris, while a third revealed someone who preferred to take a more old-fashioned approach and was typing at phenomenal speed. Once again there was no sense of impending disaster, no tension in the voices, and the water-cooler gossip was just that: gossip, containing nothing enlightening or exciting.

"Admin's a bust. Having any more luck where you are?" she asked Daniel through Omskep.

"If I was I'm not sure I'd recognise it," he admitted. "One lab looks much the same as any other to me, and I can't see anyone in a panic."

"One of you must have seen something, anything that might be the problem," Almega said. "According to the secondary program you're right on top of it."

"I've seen nothing," Daniel replied.

"The most exciting thing I've seen is one dead tree being replaced. Hardly news," Alex agreed.

"That one's raising a flag. Check it out!"

The pair returned to distribution. Alex pointed to the map where the flashing red marker had now been joined by several others across the board.

"That was quick!" Alex frowned. "From one to..." she counted, "Twenty-six!"

"Thirty-two," Daniel corrected, pointing to another clump in the bottom left. "Thirty-seven... OK, **now** they're worried."

The atmosphere in the room was changing as fast as the display. The crew at the computer consoles were going through the data, desperately trying to find the source. The conveyor belt was delivering trees as fast as possible, dogs and walkers being loaded up with increasing speed, but it was obvious they wouldn't be able to keep up with the forest deterioration.

"What's causing this?" Alex asked, and the two Eternals moved to the computers to check the readouts.

"All those trees are dying?" Daniel queried, his bewilderment causing his voice to rise in pitch.

"And at the same time? This is crazy. Why should everything be fine one minute then suddenly we've got tree Armageddon?"

Daniel stepped back, considering the problem.

"The trees have been modified to increase growth rate," he said, speaking his thought processes aloud, "and trees used for regular updates have a much shorter life-span."

"So could these trees be getting unanticipated updates?"

"Wouldn't affect them all this fast," he countered, watching the board.

Alex was pacing, trying to fit the pieces together.

"If they've modified the trees to make them grow faster, that means they've been playing with the DNA..."

"And the data storage is also encoded on the DNA..." Daniel continued.

"Which suggests someone's added something to the storage codes that directly attacks the tree DNA..." she returned, the two bouncing off each other like some frenzied tennis match.

"The storage coding is encrypted, so no one would realise a suicide key had been added, and as it's not strictly part of the primary code, it wouldn't be checked…"

"And with the whole lot connected, not only are the newly planted trees going down, but as the old ones are accessed across the network, they're getting the new data and also being triggered."

Almega interrupted.

"Two things. First, the entire data archive is backed up across the globe once every twenty-four hours, which means you have less than thirteen hours to stop them."

"If it updates to the rest of the world, every tree on the planet will soon be infected," Alex said, her eyes flicking across the board as more and more red flags appeared.

"And because they use the same trees with the same encryption software so the whole world can access the data, it's easy to spread the virus."

Daniel, too, was watching the board, shaking his head as the shift from green to red spread at a disturbing speed.

"If they don't figure it out in time, there won't be a tree left standing of this type anywhere on earth."

"Right, so that's your primary," Almega interjected. "But secondly, there's someone out of place. Can't quite nail down who, yet, but as you meet the crew I'll be able to check them against the system and see who isn't where they should be."

"Definitely second. Stopping this before it wipes out the entire forest has to be our priority," Alex replied. Turning to Daniel she asked, "How can we make them turn it off? If they stop the access and updates, the rest of the forest will be fine provided the code is cleaned."

Based on his own experiences, Daniel was inclined to agree.

"There has to be a distribution hub that connects this building to the optical fibre network that serves the trees. If we can find that and disable it, that'll give us a bit of time to figure something out."

"We also need to disable the connection to the rest of MIW. Right now the problem's here in New Uruk. Once it gets to Humbaba it'll distribute it to all the outlying towns and that'll be it."

"I'll look for the one to the forest. Since it runs underground it's probably in the basement. You look for the one to head office," Daniel said and headed off.

Alex looked around, then called on Almega.

"I need to see the network connections to this building. Can you do that?"

"One moment... Try that," he said.

Alex now saw the complex not as a building, but as a schematic, and this made it easy for her to identify the network links.

"Daniel!" she called out. "I've found your connection."

He reappeared beside her, seeing the building as she did.

"I confess, that didn't even occur to me. Nicely done. Um, I suggest that since cutting the connections might be a little obvious, we need to short them."

In agreement they each set off. Moments later the cries of the workers confirmed their work was a success.

"This does pose a slight problem," Daniel observed, watching the pandemonium. "They no longer have internet access, and since everything is done in the cloud, they can't find the solution themselves."

"Knew there was a reason I always preferred software that ran from my computer," Alex said. "Their helpers are useless as well," she added, pointing to the robots, which were now silent and still, deprived of their network-based instructions.

"I think it's time some remarkably prescient programmer and an expert DNA specialist arrived to fix the problem."

"That would be you and me, right?"

"Right."

***

Daniel and Alex moved into the forest to change and, since they'd need credibility, Alex created two horse-sized 'dogs', both as their method of transportation and to establish they had the ability to work without the network. All the time she was humming, with a large and rather silly grin on her face.

"What is that tune?" Daniel asked at last.

"Oh come on! 'Here we come... to save the day!'," she sang. He stared at her. "Sorry! Couldn't help myself."

"Try," he suggested dourly.

"Something wrong with me being in a good mood?"

"More... inappropriate. If we don't fix this..."

"Which we will," she asserted.

"But if we don't," he continued.

"I have complete faith in our abilities. Besides, we have to. We have no choice, therefore, we will." She took in his gloomy expression. "Hey, I'm happy. We've figured this one out, we'll soon be finished and, best of all, no sign of Fortan!"

"No sign yet," he reminded her. "I haven't dismissed the idea he's behind this. Just because we haven't seen him doesn't mean he's not here. And remember, Almega said someone wasn't where they should be. It may turn out that's the person who caused the trouble in the first place... or the person in their place did it, and how much do you want to bet that's where we'll find Fortan?"

"Way to put the dampers on a girl's mood!"

"As I said, inappropriate."

"Look, you deal with your problems by getting angry. I deal with them by making jokes. Of the two I'd say my approach was at least less destructive."

"You're sounding like Hentric."

"Low blow," she returned and stuck her tongue out at him.

"And now you're just being childish."

"What's the point of living for eternity if you can't be a child once in a while? Not all the time," she conceded, thinking of Hentric's tendency to play the fool at any opportunity, "but every now and then..."

Daniel was checking the saddlebags and decided to change the subject.

"Portable DNA reader, top of the line computer independent of the network, ID passes... What else do we need?"

"Well, if I knew who and what I was, that would help," she returned.

He pulled out her ID, read it and handed it over.

"You are Dr Alex Biscombe, a retired IT whizz. And I'm..." He checked his ID. "Hmm, apparently I'm Dr Daniel Lafayette, specialist in DNA programming also retired. We must have made a mint when we were working," he mused.

"Nice we get to keep our own names. Thanks Almega!"

"My pleasure," Almega returned.

"Any danger the real people might queer the pitch once this is fixed?"

"I don't think so. For one thing your characters are an amalgam of real people. There's no Lafayette or Biscombe who exactly matches your profiles, 'though there are several people you could be. Also, there's no record of this happening originally, so whatever is done here can never get out. You've stopped the problem going beyond New Uruk, so now it's a matter of keeping the fact there ever was a problem from escaping. If you do that, your existence has to be erased as part of it."

"That may be easier said than done," Daniel replied. "Even if we can get those within the complex to believe us and keep shtum, that still leaves everyone else."

"There is no one else. Literally everyone works either in the complex or is entirely dependent on it. There's no reason those few working in the town should ever know about this if you move quickly."

Daniel remained unconvinced.

"Ignore him. He's on a downer at the moment," Alex said. "Anything else for us?"

"I've got a download waiting so you can get familiar with your characters and their skills. Ready?"

"And waiting," Alex replied.

The two paused while they accessed and memorised the data and then Daniel nodded and quickly mounted. Alex, being shorter, made a couple of attempts before standing, hands on hips, staring at her mount.

"Oh for crying out loud! Can't you, I dunno, get down a bit so I can mount?"

The robot obediently lowered itself so she could reach the stirrup.

"That was easy," she muttered and swung into the saddle. Looking at Daniel she added, "Good to see your mood's improved, but you can wipe that smile off your face."

"It's not like you have to be that height," he pointed out, still grinning at her clumsy technique.

"I know, but I got used to this body in my last training and I haven't had time to adjust. Besides, this is the right height for Alex Biscombe." She looked down. There were no reins or, for that matter, a mane. "What do we hold onto?"

"First, you don't use reins to hold on. You use them to add gentle guidance. Second, these don't need guidance from legs or reins as they're voice controlled – as you just discovered – although they do have sensors to pick up leg pressure for seasoned riders, and a tap on the right or left of the withers," and he pointed to the spot, "replaces the reins. And if you are feeling nervous..."

He reached back and pressed a button just behind his right leg on the saddle. Cushioned, curved braces emerged and locked themselves around his thighs.

"They release with a press of the button or with a verbal command," he explained. "Release." The braces retracted.

Alex pressed the button and watched the braces fix her firmly in place. "How come you know all this and I don't?"

"Apparently, Dr Lafayette is a real horse-rider in his spare time and uses these when going around data forests. It was in my character brief."

"I'm grateful they don't use real horses for this stuff – it's been centuries since I went riding – on the other hand, real horses wouldn't have the limitations these usually have when the network is down, so why do they use them?"

"Network outages are practically unheard of as you well know, so that's hardly an issue, but I think the bigger reason is the ground is incredibly uneven. A horse risks a broken leg in a place like this, especially going at speed, and it can't use ultrasonic probes to check the ground is solid before it puts its hoof down. These can. Top speed, forty-five miles an hour, even over rough terrain, which is faster than any horse could ever achieve." He indicated the road. "Shall we?"

"After you."

"Take me to New Uruk main complex," Daniel ordered. His mount promptly set off.

"Follow that horse!" Alex said and her mount pulled in behind Daniel.

With a gentle kick she got alongside and together they trotted towards the town outskirts. Once there they slowed to a walk, checking the shops. So far, so good.

"Can't be on the same network," Alex observed.

"The complex would need a huge data feed and it has to be secure," Daniel agreed.

Alex pointed ahead where a worker from the complex had emerged and was headed to the post office at a run.

"Woah!" Daniel said, stopping both his mount and the runner. "What's up? You seem to be in a bit of a panic."

"Network's down. Everything's gone haywire. Gotta call Head Office," the runner got out between pants.

"I'm a specialist network engineer," Alex offered, pulling out her ID and handing it to the man. "Before you let Head Office know something's gone wrong, maybe I could take a look? As you can see, we don't need a network to make our equipment work." She patted the neck of her steed. "If you don't want us, that's fine, but we're here and willing to work if you'd like us to."

"What about your friend?" the runner asked.

"Oh, I'm pretty good with networks, too, but I work in DNA encoding," Daniel replied, handing over his ID as well.

The runner was torn, looking between the post office, the riders and the complex. Finally he sighed, apparently surrendering to the inevitable.

"You might as well come to the barn, but it'll be up to my boss whether or not you can work on the equipment."

"Makes sense. He'll want to check us out, and quite right too," Daniel smiled. He could be very charming when he wanted to be and Alex noticed he was racking up the charm offensive even as they headed to the complex.

No one in there stood a chance.

***

"And you were just wandering around and happened to pick up on our signal breakdown?"

The boss, Mr Harris, was making it clear by his tone that he didn't believe a word of it. He handed back their ID badges, his eyes narrowed as he awaited their explanations.

"Networks are my specialty," Alex supplied. "Fibre-optic connections are fast, but even using Alon they're still fragile, and given the speed your trees grow, the matching underground root systems could put a great deal of stress on the optical fibres and crack them. I was scanning the underground network checking for signal resistance when I saw your signal switch off. That's when I told Daniel and he suggested we come over to see if you needed any help."

In Omskep Daniel turned to Alex.

"Alon?"

"Aluminium oxynitride, aka transparent aluminium. Been around since the 21st century, but it was expensive to make then. Now it's more common than standard glass and a lot stronger. Used for all data networks because of that, but still subject to damage with large root systems. That was in *my* brief," she supplied.

Back in the program Daniel smiled at Harris.

"As for me, MIW was the first of the data forests," Daniel explained, "and you've done much of the DNA development work that's now commonplace across the planet. I was interested to find out if there were any long-term consequences or DNA degradation, which is why I was sampling. All the DNA I'm interested in is contained in the needles," he added, summoning to his pocket and then showing Harris a small box of labelled fir needles.

"Your data was safe. Besides, I couldn't read the data packets even if I wanted to. Without the key, the encoding's too strong." He popped the box back in his pocket.

Harris still looked unconvinced. Daniel, who'd played more than his fair share of poker games, decided to go for broke.

"Look, we're here and happy to use our network independent equipment to help, but we're just as happy to carry on our own studies. I was getting some interesting readings before Alex interrupted me."

"What kind of interesting readings?" Harris asked.

"Your trees, or at least some of them, seem to be ageing prematurely. Any idea why that might be so?"

"Nice carrot," Alex commented in Omskep.

His phantom form winked at her. After what felt like an interminable pause by Harris, he upped the ante.

"If you think we're up to something, you can stay with us at all times, or bring in some people who know what they're doing with DNA and IT to watch us. Whatever you decide, can we make this quick? I want to continue my investigations and things like that are a bit time sensitive, especially when the changes are happening so fast."

"All right," Harris said at last. "Trask, go get Emile and Harding. They can watch over these two and help if needed. Oh, and you'd better call in the workers from the outlying areas. Looks like it'll be all hands on deck for this one." He turned back to his guests. "Guess we'd better start in distribution."

***

Harris pointed to the giant screen.

"It's not being updated at the moment, but the last reading showed this."

Even though he'd already seen the damage, Daniel managed to look surprised and let out a low whistle.

"This is a bigger problem than I thought. How fast did this develop?"

"From start to the network cut-off? Less than an hour."

Daniel's shocked expression earned a chuckle from Alex in Omskep.

"You're bucking for an Oscar with this performance," she said.

"Care to join in?" he replied, somewhat testily.

"Just waiting for my cue."

Harris continued. "We were trying to get the replacements out, but with the network down the workers don't function. Once the outlying crews come back in we should have enough people to start the process."

"Better wait until I test the replacements," Daniel suggested. "If there's a problem out there, there might be a problem in here. We don't want to make it worse by planting sick trees."

"Sick? They're healthier than I am!" Harris complained.

"Even so, if you don't mind I'd like to do some random sampling, just in case. We can start with the ones that were about to go." He patted his briefcase. "I've got the tester in here. I doubt your equipment works right now."

"Which leaves me," Alex said while Daniel set off to find somewhere to work. "We don't know what killed the network. Could be physical or could be malicious code."

"It was a short," Harris replied, hands on hips. "I've got people working on fixing it right now."

"To the forest?"

"And to Head Office."

Alex cocked her head.

"Two shorts, at the same time, isolating you completely? Are you sure it's not malicious?"

"And then you two conveniently show up." Harris said, narrowing his eyes at her.

"All right. I can understand your hostility." She sat down. "I'll just sit here and mind my own business."

Harris looked over her head as Trask arrived with two others in tow.

"Harding," he called. The young woman trotted over. "Ms Theresa Harding, this is Dr Alex Biscombe. She and her friend over there were taking in the sights of our data forest when they detected the network outage."

Alex stood and offered her hand. Harding regarded it suspiciously.

"She's the one out of place!" Almega crowed.

"And might she have caused the problem?" Alex returned.

"Could be. Worth keeping an eye on, anyway."

"I don't suppose you know who should be in her place?"

"Not yet."

"No. Of course not. That would make it easy," Alex grumbled.

In distribution her hand hovered while Harding stood with her arms at her sides, refusing to return the handshake. Alex dropped her arm.

"Oh for crying out loud! You know what? I'm going into town to grab a coffee. If you need my help, you'll know where to find me." She got up and headed for the exit.

In Omskep Daniel stared at her.

"What are you doing?"

"We can't have the network up before you find the problem. If I'm in there helping, they're going to realise I'm stalling. If I go to the coffee shop I can make it look like I'm working on my computer, come back here and invisibly stop any attempts they make to restore the system, giving you enough time to finish your analysis. I can also watch Madam Miserable here and see if she's doing something sneaky on the side."

"Smart plan." In distribution he said, "OK, Alex. If they get over their paranoia they can come and get you."

He turned to the man Harris had brought over to be introduced.

"Dr Daniel Lafayette, this is Dr Claude Emile, our resident DNA expert," Harris said. "Dr Emile, Dr Lafayette detected advanced ageing processes in one of our trees."

"More than one, actually," Daniel corrected as he and Emile shook hands. "Dr Emile, I hope you'll let me help you, but if you don't want me to, I'm sure there's space in the coffee shop for two."

Emile shook his head.

"Frankly, I'll take whatever help I can get," he said.

"Good. In that case I suggest we first check the trees that were about to be sent out. If they're all right, once the workers arrive they can begin planting while we check the rest."

He contemplated the doors between distribution and the nursery.

"Can those be opened? If none of the other units are having the same problems, we can take it whatever is causing the trouble here is somewhere in these sections and it'll be quicker if you don't have to go the long way 'round or climb on the conveyor belt."

Emile was happy to oblige and made his way over to the door panel.

"Right now the air flow system is stalled, so opening the doors would at least add some more breeze, and it's a warm enough day it won't hurt the younger trees."

He tapped a code into the panel. While the network was down, power was not and the simple control promptly opened the huge doors, giving a view from distribution straight into the nursery. Daniel asked for a desk and some chairs, which were quickly provided, and then settled down where he could see both rooms.

Emile returned and watched as Daniel set up his computer and then pulled out the DNA reader.

"That your analysis equipment?" Emile asked, his eyes wide as he took in the machines. "That must be top of the line. I've never seen one of those in action."

"I test them for companies as well as using the best for myself. Any errors and this piece of kit will spot it, and in a fraction of the time required by most of what's out there."

He smiled up at Emile who, while eager to see the machine in action, was also revealing in his body language the stress occasioned by the looming disaster.

"Don't worry, I'm sure between us we can figure this out and get everything running smoothly again."

"I hope so. What we saw before the network went down was terrifying. I dread to think what it looks like now."

Daniel handed Emile a sampler with which he collected DNA from one of the trees that was waiting by the wall in distribution. Daniel popped it in the machine and set the program running.

"I've never heard of you," Emile said, by way of filling the time.

"Hardly surprising," Daniel replied. "I don't work for any company and I never wanted any publicity, so I did my research in private and released it to the universities to chivvy them along when I thought they were moving too slowly. Ahh, results are in," he added, relieved he wouldn't have to lie any more for the time being. "And we do have a problem. Look!"

"A suicide gene?! How the hell did that get in there? Everything's checked at every stage to stop computer viruses and malicious code."

"But this isn't part of the filtered data stream, it's specifically targeted at the tree DNA, and since such programming is shaped by the individual tree and will always have subtle differences, it's not scanned. Let's check the trees in the nursery. If they've all got it, you'll have to junk the lot and start again."

"Right!"

Emile left at a run and Daniel sampled another tree to check whether this was across the board or just a select few. By the time Emile came back, the machine had confirmed the new tree was in the same state as the previous one.

Harris was watching over them when Trask ran in.

"How's it going with the network?" Harris asked.

"A bust so far. Every time we think we've nailed it, it goes down again. I think we may have to call in that other woman to take a crack at it. Maybe it *is* a virus, but we can't see it."

Harris nodded.

"She's at the coffee shop. Go get her," he ordered.

Trask ran out. In Omskep, Daniel turned to Alex.

"Your grand entrance is coming up," he advised her.

"Nuts. And I'd finally got my coffee. Talk about slow service!"

"Bring one for me?"

"Will do."

Emile stood beside Daniel, holding out the samples. When Daniel didn't respond Emile tapped him on the shoulder.

"Dr Lafayette? From the nursery," he explained. "One at the start, one just before they're given their data and sent in here."

Daniel returned to the room and looked up at Emile, taking the samples.

"Sorry. I was distracted."

He loaded the youngest sample first. The machine announced it was clear.

"That bodes well," he commented, putting the second sample in. That, too, came back clear.

When they saw the results, both men looked at the machine in the nursery that provided the data encoded

DNA. It was the last point where code was introduced to the saplings. Emile didn't need any prompting. He picked up the clean sample, ran to the nursery machine and popped it in, then cursed.

"Without the network, the machine doesn't work."

"Then I guess we have to wait for Alex to return," Daniel replied calmly, "but I suspect we may have found the source. Question is, where could the code have come from?"

Harris paced, thinking through the question.

"The code that feeds the machine is checked at every point. There's no way a virus could have got past all the checks before it arrives here at New Uruk, but that machine doesn't run an anti-virus. It's just an encoder, combining clean data with tree DNA."

"But it is a computer, which means it can be hacked," Daniel pointed out.

"But only by someone here at New Uruk. You'd have to physically access the machine..." His eyes widened at the implications. "Oh shit!"

Harris turned and ran off.

"It appears," Daniel said, leaning back in his chair and watching Emile carefully, "that you have a saboteur."

Emile's face showed shock, anger and confusion, but not guilt.

"But who? And why? Everyone depends on the data farms. You could sabotage your own material and not know you're doing it, so why would someone take that risk?"

"Excellent question," Daniel allowed.

Alex strolled in bearing two coffees.

"Figured you might want one," she grinned, holding out his.

"And you'd be right," he replied, taking it. "We think we've identified the source, but without the network we can't test it." He pointed to the machine. "Think you can fix it so we can get a short data packet in here without also sending to the entire forest? I suggest blocking any other outward communications until we nail down what's happening. We can't take the risk of corrupted data being uploaded across the planet."

Harris, who had returned and heard that last remark, paled visibly.

"We can block outgoing communications using the firewall. It'll be quicker than disconnecting all the computers. But I would like our robots working again. I think we may need them."

"So long as they're on your side?" Alex asked.

"You think...? Surely no one could..." He swallowed and then shook his head. "No, there was nothing wrong with them when the network went down, and there's been no hint of rogue programming in them."

Alex picked up her briefcase and set it down on the desk next to Daniel's.

"But it has happened before?"

"Nothing major. Usually a glitch that makes them stumble around, walk into walls, that sort of thing. We wipe the memory, reinstall and they're good as new."

"Tell you what, I'll check the robot program anyway, but first," and she tapped on her computer, "let's get you that data packet. I can send one from this straight to your machine. Would that be enough to test?"

Emile nodded. "Any data would do, but the machine encodes only when it reaches a minimum of 1 zettabyte of information. Anything less would be a waste."

"One zettabyte coming up," she said, and set to work.

With a little help from Almega she got a data packet of the right size, then she pulled out the encoder's data cable from the wall socket, checked the connection, quietly summoned an adapter to her bag through the secondary program, and linked the two computers together. Sitting down she sent the data packet and then waited. In under thirty seconds the encoder's readout indicated it was ready for DNA and Emile popped in the sample. Once the data had been encoded with the tree DNA and the result delivered for injection back into the tree, Emile brought it over to Daniel's machine and they tested it.

"It **is** that machine!" Emile crowed when the result of the previously clean sample now included the suicide gene.

"Let me work on this for a bit. I think I can track down the dirty code and fix it for you," Alex said. "Meantime, I suggest you try to figure out who did it."

"What about the network?" Harris asked.

"You don't want that back up until we know the system's clean," she advised.

She gazed at her computer for a moment, tapping her lips, then looked up at the wall display. The amount of red was disturbing.

"Hmm, I'll have to do more than clean the encoder. I'm also going to have to add a filter program that can fix the trees already out there and block the malicious code from spreading. I can't turn the clock back on the infected trees so they will all have to be replaced sooner rather than later, but if I remove the genetic error they'll recover enough to give you time to do that." She looked up. "By that I mean they'll die in the next few months rather than the next few days. It's the best I can do unless someone around here has access to the fountain of youth." She started tapping away. "Keep me plied with coffee and I think it'll take an hour, two tops."

Harding, who had come over when she saw Alex return, raised her eyebrows.

"You're *that* good? We couldn't even *find* the problem with the network, much less fix it."

"Did you know where to look?" Alex replied, coldly.

"Alex is the best in the business," Daniel told Harding, seeking to calm the outburst he could see on her lips. "Even if her people skills sometimes leave something to be desired."

Alex snorted her opinion but carried on with her work. Daniel lowered his voice, murmuring in Harding's ear.

"Between you and me, I think she dreams in machine code. She wrote all the program on that computer of hers and they work faster than any I've seen."

"But they're not available to the rest of us," Harding commented sourly, "meaning we have to call on the likes of you when things go wrong. And how much are you planning on charging us for this *service*?"

Alex frowned, still focussing on her work but with one ear on the conversation.

"We came here to help, not make a profit," she said. "All I require is coffee. Daniel?"

"Same here. I assure you, Ms Harding, we're not here to profit from your misfortune, nor did we have anything to do with it. I'm just glad we happened to be around."

"As for my program," Alex added, looking up, "they're a little complicated for general use and I've never bothered to tidy the interface because it makes sense to me." She turned back to her computer. "Maybe I'll fix that one day, but not today."

In Omskep Daniel grinned at Alex.

"Now who's bucking for the Oscar?"

"If I fix it too fast they'll think I caused the problem in the first place. Too slow and we won't get it done before the system back-up is due."

"And the interface?"

"The front end looks more in keeping with this time period, but underneath it's 92nd century, as is the hardware under the hood. Now we know what and where the problem is, this set-up will be able to fix it easily. Nothing from this time could do it. This is **very** advanced programming, way beyond anything the locals could have come up with."

"Fortan!" Daniel growled.

"I'd bet the house on it, but I don't think he's in Harding. She's a miserable bitch with a burr up her backside, but I can't see any evidence of Fortan in her, beyond a superiority complex a mile wide. Hardly a unique identifier. Why don't you help the others and keep an eye out for him? If you can get Harding to go with you that'll help. She'll want to know all about this kit and I can't tell her anything. Not to mention having her hovering over me like a vulture at a kill is unsettling, to say the least!"

Back in the distribution room Daniel tapped Harding on the shoulder.

"Care to show me where the network I/O's are? I'm not Alex, but years of working with her has taught me a lot. Perhaps between us we can fix it."

He packed up his computer briefcase and waited politely. Harding frowned at Alex, still not entirely convinced, but Daniel's suggestion made sense and they would need the network restored as soon as the code had been cleaned.

"Don't forget the firewall," Alex called after them. "Don't turn on anything until that's blocking all communications. We need to make sure we're not going to infect anyone else!"

"I'll do that now," Harris said and set off.

Alex settled down to her work. *'Fortan, or whoever you are,'* she thought to herself, *'when I get my hands on you... Oh, what's the use?'* She shook her head, knowing full well there was little anyone could do if an Eternal couldn't control themselves. *'Your explanation had better be phenomenally good!'*

***

Once Harris confirmed the firewall was blocking all communications in and out of the complex, Daniel set to work. Without Alex's interference it was an easy matter to restore the network, but realising, as Alex had pointed out, that fixing it too quickly would call into question their honesty, he used his own 92nd century training to run around the program, confusing Harding who was desperately trying to keep up with him.

"I don't understand what you're doing!" she lamented. "Is there a virus or not?"

"There was, but it was a well-hidden little troublemaker," he replied, successfully smothering a grin. He tapped a button, made a show of checking the screen and tapping in more code, then gave a firm nod. "Try it now."

A few moments later there was a yell of delight from upstairs.

"Network's back on!"

Harding was leaning over trying to figure out what he was doing, and Daniel blanked the screen before packing up.

"Right, shall we see how Dr Biscombe is doing?"

"None of that made any sense," Harding complained. "I think you made that all up!"

"And yet the network is working again and Alex is fixing your code. Your lack of faith in our abilities despite overwhelming evidence to the contrary is becoming a little wearing," Daniel returned. "Just because you didn't understand it, doesn't mean it can't be understood." He stood up, towering over her and indicated the door. "After you."

Harding scowled but led the way and together they headed back to distribution.

***

"You managed to get rid of the network gremlin then?" Alex said by way of greeting.

"A troublesome little blighter, but it is no more," he replied with a smile. "How are you doing?"

"I think we're nearly there, at least for that," and she jerked her head at the offending piece of equipment. Tapping a button, she sent the cleaned code to the machine. "Grab a sample and try it now."

Emile, who hadn't moved far from Alex's side, gleefully set off to collect a sample from the nursery while Alex prepared another major data transfer to satisfy the machine's enormous appetite. The machine was flashing its demand for DNA by the time Emile came back. Daniel, who had set up his machine beside Alex, stopped him.

"Hold on. Let's make absolutely sure that's clean before we put it in."

"I got it from the nursery," Emile insisted.

"I know, but while we're pretty certain the problem is in that machine, we haven't checked every tree in the nursery, so allow me my own paranoia?"

Emile nodded and handed it over. Once Daniel was satisfied, it was popped into the machine and then returned with the encoded data. Daniel ran the test on the new sample and, after a few seconds, grinned.

"All clear!" he declared.

Alex took a breath, stretched her back and then settled down again.

"Right, now for the rest of the network and a quick check on your robots. I'll do that first so you've got some helpers. I suggest you trash those trees," and she pointed to the ones that had suffered at the hands of the infected encoder. "No point in planting them when we know they've got a massively reduced life cycle already. Get some new ones ready. Once the network is on there's going to be a lot of backdated data waiting to be encoded, not to mention getting started on transferring the data from the trees out there." She jerked her head towards the forest. "I'll see if I can add a timer to your readout so you know which ones need swapping out first."

Quickly, people set to, removing the bad trees and readying clean ones for when the machine's external network connection was restored. Daniel relaxed knowing, from a brief glance, that Alex had already completed the work and was now stalling to maintain the pretence.

"How much longer?" Harris muttered through gritted teeth.

"This was a very clever piece of code," Daniel answered, partly by way of distraction, partly to get Harris thinking about who might be the culprit. "Know anyone in New Uruk with the sort of innovative computer skills needed to pull this one off?"

"I'd have to check through the personnel records," Harris replied. "Which I can't do until the network's restored. It's all in the cloud."

"Your robots are clear," Alex interrupted. "Turning them back on now."

A whirring noise and the robots began to reactivate, but as they were still awaiting instructions they merely stood where they were.

"What do you want them to do?"

Harris leaned down, his answer muttered under his breath so only Alex and Daniel could hear him.

"The outlying crews will be here any moment. When they are in the building I want the robots set to guard duty. No one's to leave until we find who's behind this."

In Omskep, Alex turned to Daniel.

"If it is Fortan..."

"We know it has to be," Daniel replied. "As you said, that coding was far beyond their capabilities."

"Then whoever he's occupying wasn't aware of what they were doing when they were doing it. That means whoever it is will get into trouble for something they didn't actually do. That could seriously damage the time line."

"She has a point," Almega agreed. "Right now you've almost got things back on track, but how you resolve that problem and whether you can shift Harding will determine whether this is completely fixed."

"Also, how they explain to Head Office the sudden network failure," Daniel added.

Back in distribution Daniel decided to take the bull by the horns.

"And assuming they're kind enough to admit to their actions, what are you going to do then? Hand them over to the authorities and admit you suffered a major security breach? How *are* shares trading in MIW at the moment? Think they'll stay there once this gets out?"

Harris rubbed his forehead, his confusion and fear for the complex coming to the surface.

"Well what the hell else can I do? I can't let them continue to work here. What if they do it again and this time you're not around?"

Alex sensed it was her turn to wade in.

"I've added some new security to your systems. Trust me, no one will be able to repeat that performance. To be fair, your encoder was an accident waiting to happen. It had no internal protection whatsoever. I assume that's the case in all the centres, so that's something you need to address. Anyway, this one's armed to the teeth. Any attempt to hack it physically from within the building will be shut down so fast it'll make the hacker's head spin."

She neglected to point out that the level of hacking used originally could have passed through every contemporary security system, including the top end version she'd just installed. Fortan would be leaving once they found him, she was certain, and that meant the problem wouldn't be repeated. She levelled a look at Harris.

"However, this does highlight a major problem with your approach. This hack worked because you only use one type of tree. That makes for an easy target and, frankly, isn't that great for the environment either. I suggest you use this as a timely warning. Add some different trees into the mix. Make it harder for hackers and better for the forest. What you're doing here can be done with any type of tree. You use these because they grow fast, but they're still short lived for long term storage. Sycamore, oak, elm, beech and all the other deciduous trees live longer and add the sort of biodiversity that's good for the forest and the planet. Imagine how much data you could store in a redwood! I'm not saying replace the lot," she added quickly when she saw Harris preparing to argue. "Just add a few and try it out. It'll take a long time to grow those ones, 'though you can probably alter the DNA to make them grow a lot faster than they do at the moment, but a redwood would hold thousands of times more data for a lot longer than those things."

"You could make it a symbol to start with," Daniel suggested. "Plant some cedars in keeping with the Babylonian myth your towns are based on. No one need be the wiser that you're also using them for storage."

Harris paused, considering the idea.

"Head Office will never approve," he countered at last.

"Which is why you don't tell them," Alex said. "This time it was a deliberate human attack. What if some disease appears that focuses on these trees?"

"Like Dutch Elm disease in the 20th century," Daniel added helpfully.

"Exactly. Think how much data you risk losing putting all your eggs in one basket. But mix things up a bit and the data could be shifted to different tree types and stay secure."

"You have a point," Harris allowed. He turned to Emile. "Do you think you could speed up the growth of some other varieties?"

"I'd love to. I've been trying to get Head Office to allow me to do that for ages, but all they see is the profit margin. Short term the deciduous trees would be more expensive, but long term they'd be a lot cheaper, and as we store in the trunks rather than in the leaves, there'd be no loss of data and they could store much more. We'll have to admit we've lost some trees this time around, so we could probably hide their purchase in amongst the paperwork for the replacements."

"And how are we going to explain all this without giving the game away?" Harris sighed.

"Landslip after the rain last night?" Alex suggested.

"Robot run amuck?" Daniel put in.

"Bad stock?" Emile offered.

"Or all of the above," Harris finished thoughtfully.

The subtle noise of electric vehicles followed by booted feet announced the arrival of the outlying workers. Harris turned to Alex.

"I meant what I said about the robot guards."

"You've got it," she replied, sending the order.

Immediately, the androids and dogs went to the doors. Once the workers were in, they closed the doors and stood in front of them.

"Thought it better to keep them inside," she said in response to Harris's confused expression. "A robot army surrounding the building might make your locals sit up and take notice."

He acknowledged the sense of that precaution and then gave the order that all staff from the rest of the building were to join them in distribution.

Some arrived by the stairs, others via elevators. While the team was congregating Alex and Daniel watched, looking for a familiar face – or an unfamiliar one whose hidden persona might be clear to them if he deigned to permit it. As the crowd adjusted to the space Daniel spotted him.

"Check out your two o'clock," he advised Alex in Omskep.

She turned and saw a young man whose outline – visible only to the Eternals – showed he had a stowaway. It seemed right now Fortan was in direct control rather than hidden in the subconscious, and thus was visible. He was ducking behind some other workers, trying to stay out of sight and get to the door. Alex turned to Harris.

"I think I know who caused your problems," she told him quietly. "Look at that man over there."

"Which one?" Harris muttered back.

"The one trying to sneak to the door without being spotted. Hang on."

She turned to her computer, located the nearest door guard to Fortan and gave it some new instructions. When he tried to get past, the android grasped him tightly around the wrist and refused to let go. Being considerably heavier and stronger than the average human, the android had the advantage, but given who they were dealing with, Alex sent a second to grasp Fortan's other wrist and hold him in place. Daniel quietly moved around the building's outer walls until he reached their quarry and smiled at him.

"Won't be a moment," he assured him. "We don't want anyone leaving until Harris has had his say."

Fortan peered thoughtfully at Daniel, then shrugged and stopped struggling.

In Omskep, Daniel relayed Fortan's identity to Almega so he could keep an eye on him. After a quick check Almega let out a cheer.

"He's the last part!" he yelled. "He needs to become part of their IT staff."

"After what he did?!" Daniel returned in astonishment. "They're more likely to nail him to one of their trees than promote him!"

"Then you'll just have to change their minds. Once he's there and everything's working again, your job will be done."

"All right," he sighed and returned to distribution. "This is going to be a hard sell!" he muttered.

"Ladies and gentlemen," Harris called, his voice loud enough to be heard above the susurrations of the crowd, effectively bringing silence in the room. "As you're aware, we've had some problems." He took a deep breath. "I'm going to be completely honest with you... We had a virus."

Gasps greeted his revelation. Cries of "Impossible!" and "How?" filled the air.

"If this gets back to HQ you know as well as I do that they'll be all over us like flies on a cow pat. That will be bad for everyone; from me right the way down to Chloe who works the checkout in the store. They could close us down and, if they aren't completely satisfied with their investigations, they'll fire all of us and replace us with new staff."

Once again the room filled with mutterings, and this time the tone was angry. Harris raised his hands to bring silence.

"We've seen it happen before. We know it's a possibility. So, as we've fixed the problem and security has been tightened so it never happens again, with your approval I propose an alternative explanation: a combination of bad stock, bad weather, and an issue with the robots. We've had such minor foul ups before, it's just this time they happened together. All of this did happen, so if any of you are feeling uncomfortable you can reassure yourselves you're not lying. All I'm asking for is a little economy with the truth. Now, if anyone has a problem with that, speak up." He waited. One hand went up. "Yes?"

"Can we be sure the new security will stop another attack?" someone called out.

"Alex? I'll leave that one to you," Harris said, stepping back.

Alex looked out across the crowd – a sea of worried faces.

"You don't know me, but I can tell you I'm the best in the business when it comes to IT. What I've done to secure your system..." She chuckled. "Well, let's just say my bosses wouldn't be too pleased I used such high-level security for something like this. But what you do here matters and I wanted to give you the best security possible. Could it be hacked? Not from outside. The network security stops anything like that dead in its tracks, and if something did get through that would be everyone's problem, not just yours. From inside? I suppose it's possible there's some child prodigy amongst you or due on the horizon who might have the ability in time, but not now. No one can give you a one hundred percent guarantee, but I'm going to stick my neck out and say I can give you ninety-nine percent. Is that good enough?"

"Can't ask for more," someone replied and there was a general chorus of agreement.

"In return, can you do myself and my DNA expert friend over there a favour? Pretend we weren't here. You think you've got trouble? You have no idea the chaos that will ensue if anyone finds out we've been using our skills outside."

"How do we know you didn't cause the problem in the first place?" another asked.

Alex rolled her eyes. Some people just didn't *want* to be helped!

Harris stepped forward, keen to nip this in the bud.

"We've found the hacker," he assured the crowd, "and it wasn't either of these two. That they were in the area and willing to help without charge is a miracle, I admit, but if all they want in return is to be forgotten, I can manage that. How about the rest of you?"

"If you don't tell I won't," the original speaker yelled good naturedly. Several others expressed similar sentiments while a few added their thanks.

Alex waved off the thanks and sat down. Harris looked over the crowd.

"Anyone else?" When no one had anything to add he continued. "All right. Now, because of this mess we're seriously behind. I propose we work together to get this sorted. The network will be turned on again shortly. When that happens I've no doubt we'll be inundated with calls asking what happened. Please stick with what I just told you. Consistency is the key. If anyone hears anything different, we'll have inspectors down here in a matter of hours. Do I have your agreement?" The noises of support were loud. "Right, admin? Would you please handle the communications? Remember, bad stock, bad weather, some minor problems with a couple of the robots which led to a network outage. Tell them we're back now and concentrating on catching up. Procurement, please liaise with Dr Emile so we can get replacement stock. After that, Dr Emile, if you could discuss your ideas with the lab?"

"I'd be happy to, sir," Emile replied, a huge smile on his face.

"Excellent. Peripatetic staff, I suggest you avail yourselves of the cafeteria while we get the new trees ready for distribution. We'll need your help to augment the robot staff if we're to fix this in a timely manner. Don't worry, I'll foot the bill for this coffee break and we'll call you when we're ready. Stay in the building, please. When we're ready we don't want to have to go looking for you! Nursery and distribution staff, you know what we're dealing with. Get to it and be as fast and efficient as possible. Oh, and there'll be a bonus for everyone if we manage to pull this off." Sotto voce he added to Alex, "It'll cost me a small fortune, but it'll be worth it!"

Happily, the crews made their way to the cafeteria while the resident staff went to their respective stations.

Daniel turned to Fortan.

"If you want to keep your job, be honest. This is going to be a tough sell as it is," he rumbled.

The body containing Fortan nodded as Alex and Harris walked over.

"Mason, isn't it?" Harris asked.

"Yes, sir."

"Did you plant the virus in the encoder?"

"I did."

Taken aback by the lad's brazen approach, Harris had to pause a moment before he asked his next question.

"What did you hope to achieve?" he said at last.

'Mason' looked at Alex and Daniel, then turned his steady gaze on Harris.

"To prove the system wasn't safe and, yes, to get noticed. I've been out there for nearly three years. I have the IT skills but Ms Harding wouldn't give me the time of day. I tried every other route, sent memos, tried to see you, but no one was listening. I could see a disaster just waiting to happen and it scared the hell out of me. I figured if I caused it, at least I could fix it and then maybe you'd listen to me."

"Are you expecting a promotion?!" Harris asked in astonishment.

"No. I'm hoping you'll realise I'm wasted out there and give me a chance to work with IT. I *am* good," he added, the emphasis clearly for Alex and Daniel's benefit, "and I'm capable of much more. All I wanted was a chance to work on the systems: make them safer; see if they could be improved; make the robots more adaptable. Ms Harding wouldn't let me anywhere near them and no one was listening. Have you any idea what it felt like being out there, knowing the risks we were running, trying to do the right thing the official way and being ignored?"

"The curse of Cassandra," Daniel nodded. "To have the gift of true prophecy and not be believed. I suppose we should be grateful you waited three years." He turned to Harris. "If I could see disaster looming and no one would listen, I'm not sure I'd be as patient."

"I know I wouldn't! In fact, I wasn't," Alex added. "It's not the ideal way, but when needs must. But the damage you nearly caused! If we hadn't been here…"

"I had planned to be here when it all kicked off and be able to help. I tried, but Ms Harding saw me hanging around this morning and ordered me out. She and I don't get on."

"Ms Harding seems to have a problem getting on with everyone," Alex agreed, levelling a look at Harding.

Harris turned to Harding for an explanation.

"Well? Is what he says true?"

"I did order him out this morning, but I had no idea he'd planted a virus!" Harding replied. "If I had known I'd've fired him on the spot!"

"Hardly your job, Ms Harding, but then that's never stopped you in the past, has it?" Harris grabbed a work tablet and called up the personnel files. "According to his documents, Mason here is an ideal candidate for IT. Why didn't you take him?"

"I felt he was too young and too unstable," Harding defended herself. "A few years in the field seemed a good way to calm him down, so I had a word with distribution and got them to take him on."

Alex shook her head, seeing through Harding's claims immediately.

"I think he was too good, and you were frightened of losing your job."

"You do seem to have a problem with anyone who knows more than you do," Daniel agreed. "Look at the way you treated us."

Harding was furious, but in the face of Daniel's calmly raised eyebrow there was little she could say. Harris was looking the young man over.

"Well, the instability seems to have been proved, but that can be put down to age, I think. Also, perhaps, not thinking through the consequences? You could have lost all these people their jobs, not just Ms Harding."

"Yeah. Didn't think of that one," 'Mason' replied, bowing his head. "I am sorry. It was never meant to go this far. When I saw what had happened I headed back immediately to fix it, but when I arrived and saw these two…" He nodded at Alex and Daniel, "I figured at best they were from Head Office, at worst they were Federal… or higher. It all got out of hand so fast and all I could think was I needed to get out of here."

Harris cocked his head. "Why didn't you tell Head Office about your concerns? Or the newspapers?"

"I knew that would get everyone into trouble and I didn't want that. I just needed to make someone listen to me before it was too late!"

"Hmm."

Harris looked Mason over. The young man seemed genuinely distraught. Harding, on the other hand, had cooled her temper and now looked like the cat who'd got the cream, convinced Mason would be fired and she'd never have to deal with him again.

"I take it you two will be off as soon as this is finished?" he asked Daniel and Alex.

Alex nodded. "We can't hang around. Our real jobs are calling and Mason is right. We're a bit above Federal."

"High enough that if I looked you up I wouldn't find anyone matching those names?" Harris asked.

"Yeah. Sorry. We have orders, too."

"Seems to me," Daniel said, "that this young man made a mistake, but he did it with the best of intentions. He tried the official channels but being blocked at every turn he was left with no choice if he was to stop a disaster. All right, he nearly caused one, but that wasn't his intent. He planned to fix it."

"Unfortunately," Alex interrupted, "I don't think he could have. Your coding is good, Mr Mason, but you left an open call that allowed it to run amuck. In effect, it rewrote itself and became rather more powerful than you intended. I barely managed to fix it. If it wasn't for the fact I did something similar when I was your age I wouldn't have known what to do with it. In fact, it was a similar mistake that brought me to the attention of my present employers." She turned to Harris. "He's got talent, Mr Harris, and lots of it. It would be easy to fire him, but if you employ him where he should be, he could get the message out officially to the rest of MIW and help secure the system so this can never happen again. That would win New Uruk a lot of points and make sure no one else suffered such a disaster."

Harding looked like she was about to burst a blood vessel. Harris, on the other hand, had a look in his eye that indicated he could see an opportunity to turn this disaster into a PR triumph.

"Ms Harding, I have a proposal. Alex, Daniel, can you keep Mason here while I discuss this with Ms Harding alone?"

"Of course," Daniel nodded.

Once Harris and Harding were engaged on the other side of the room, Alex turned fuming eyes on 'Mason'.

"Fortan, what are you playing at? Have you any idea the trouble you could have caused?"

"Not really," he smiled. "I knew you'd pick up on it. Almega's very good and that secondary program you wrote is a stroke of genius, I must admit. They've lost a few trees, but the outcome, in the end, is actually very positive. Better security, greater bio-diversity. Perfect! Of course, it was going to happen anyway, but no one knows where the idea to diversify originally came from. It just happened in this year, as did greater security for the encoders. Now we have the source."

"Why you... if you weren't in some innocent's body..." Daniel growled.

"Oh come on! You can't hurt me here and you can't hurt me anywhere else. I'll be gone again soon, but Mason *is* a very clever young man with outstanding IT skills. It's why I picked him. I merely tweaked his disgruntlement so he went further and wrote a better virus – one I knew you'd be able to fix. Nice job explaining it, by the way."

"I figured you weren't going to hang around and there's no way Mason could unpick that code. Do you know how far ahead I had to go to find that fix?!" Alex replied.

"Yes, but you did it." He glanced over at Harris and Harding who were having a heated discussion. "We don't have much longer, so I'll make this quick."

He drew a deep breath and then paused. Alex and Daniel caught wisps of conversation, so faint it was only their nature as Eternals that permitted them to hear it at all.

"They have to know!" Fortan said as though responding to some point of argument. "We're so close, it won't make any difference now. All right," he added after a short pause, "but they have to have something!"

He turned to Alex and Daniel and squared his shoulders.

"First of all, I'm not Fortan, or at least, not *your* Fortan. That won't make sense now, but it will in time. In a very real sense, I'm not here at all. I'm just another program. It's the only way I could get in here and work on getting you out. We're trying everything we can, but fixing a stable doorway to allow you to leave when the system is breaking down is... well, difficult! We're working just as fast as we can and we're nearly there. A little longer and it'll all make sense, I promise. Meantime..."

Fortan and Mason separated, the young man looking slightly dazed once the Eternal had stepped out.

"It's all right, I've slightly manipulated the program. He'll be OK again after I leave."

A door appeared behind him and Daniel immediately moved towards it. Fortan stepped in front, raising his hand.

"Woah there! That one isn't for you. Even if you tried you couldn't pass through. If you could we wouldn't be in this mess. Trust me, when your door appears, you'll know it's the one. Oh, and when you do get Fortan and the others out, be nice to him. He's had a terrible time being stuck in there and it really isn't his fault. I just couldn't have him running around while I was interacting with the system. You wouldn't believe the programming errors that would cause!"

He stepped backwards into the door, partially vanishing, then reappeared.

"Oh, and you needn't worry about the other trees in the nursery. They're all clear. See you soon, my friends!" and with that he vanished through the doorway which faded from their view.

Mason shook himself and stared at the androids holding him.

"Look, I know I was out of line, but is this really necessary? I'm not going to run. Where would I go? Not to mention," he added, looking over Alex's shoulder, "it looks like my career prospects here might be looking up at last."

Alex looked over and saw Harris and Harding were returning, Harris looking rather pleased with himself, Harding irritated but resigned.

"You've fixed it!" Almega cried. "Mason will replace Harding within the year. Harris helps her join another company that isn't quite so cutting edge where she does well, so everyone's happy. You can come home."

"Right," Alex nodded vaguely and gave the androids the order to release Mason.

She was still in shock from Fortan's words and, looking at Daniel, she could see he felt the same. She was also confused. Almega seemed unaware of what had just happened. She wanted to ask Daniel what was going on but he frowned and shook his head. Now wasn't the time.

"All right, Mason. Ms Harding and I have had a long talk and she's going to let you try out in IT. This isn't a free pass," he added when Mason nearly cheered. "You will be watched. You pull another stunt like that and I'll have you sent to a maximum-security prison for the rest of your natural life. Is that clear?"

"As crystal," Mason replied.

"You will answer to me. Ms Harding will be your supervisor and I will get her reports, but you and I will meet every week without fail, when you can update me on what's happening and any other glitches you've found. Part of your remit will be to look for any other security issues and bring them to me immediately. You will do nothing, I repeat, **nothing** until you've cleared it with me. Got it?"

"Got it," Mason nodded, then added, "and thank you. I know I don't really deserve it after causing this much trouble, but I promise I won't do anything like this again. I don't know why I did it this time. It just kinda happened."

"Let's hope nothing else 'kinda happens'," Harris said, the threat underlying his words clear. "Ms Harding, would you care to escort our wayward genius to somewhere he can make a positive contribution to fixing this mess?"

"Yes, sir."

Together, Harding and Mason headed towards IT, Harris watching them go.

"He's going to have a hard time – frankly he might have found jail easier – but if he's tough enough to survive he may be the answer to a prayer."

He turned to see Alex and Daniel staring at each other.

"Hey, are you two OK?"

"Yeah. Ah… Look, I think you'll find Mason more than up to fixing the rest of the system. He just needs to reboot the androids with standard protocols. We have to leave," Alex replied.

"Sorry to see you go. Thank you. I know we weren't too welcoming when you arrived, but I hope you can forgive us?"

"Not a problem," Daniel replied, eager to get this over with. "We'll just pack up and get out of your way."

"You're sure Mason can fix the rest?"

"I've a feeling he's going to be one of your best workers," Daniel replied. "Just give him a little time."

***

With all their stuff packed up, Alex and Daniel took to their mounts, getting a couple of miles from the town and deep amongst the trees before they felt it safe to dematerialise, leaving nothing but a depression in the earth.

Back in Omskep they turned as one to Almega.

"Any joy with Mason?" Daniel asked.

"Beyond the fact he will be their lead programmer within five years? No. No sign of Fortan. No sign of the door. Nothing. Can't even find any evidence of it in the rest of the program."

Again, Alex and Daniel stared at each other. How did he not know what had happened? Oblivious to their confusion, Almega continued.

"You've done a fine job. Quickly, too. I'll check Fortan and see how he's doing, and if he's still not clear I'll find out where you have to go next."

"Yeah. Um, do us a favour, Almega? Don't rush this one. Daniel and I need to, ah, decompress a bit."

"Really?" Almega was surprised and turned to look at them properly. "This wasn't nearly as stressful as the last one."

"No, and if you'd given us a breather after the last one we wouldn't need the time now," Daniel replied testily, then took a calming breath. "Just... give us some down time. We'll let you know when we're ready."

Almega frowned but nodded.

"Very well. I'll wait for your call. Just don't leave it too long. If there is a problem we will need to fix it before it moves too far forward."

"We know," Alex replied as the two vanished from Omskep.

Chapter 7

Sitting in Daniel's front room, Alex found herself at a loss. Not only had the rug been pulled out from under her feet, the floor and ground had been taken away with it.

"What just happened?" she asked at last.

He stared ahead, equally at sea and casting around for any purchase.

"Almega seems completely unaware of what's going on," he said, deciding to give his attention to something that seemed relatively solid. "And Fortan? He said he's a program! Well, in there at least."

"But a program Almega can't see. And when he said about the door…"

"You know what this means?" Daniel murmured, reluctant to speak it aloud.

Alex nodded. Taking a deep breath, she said the words neither of them wanted to admit.

"Oestragar is a program too."

"And we're avatars from a higher level," he added, placing his hand over his eyes, as if blinding himself to the sight might make it go away.

Alex collapsed back in her seat, shaking her head.

"Is it possible?" she said at last.

Daniel squeezed his eyes, dropping his hand back to the arm of his chair.

"I don't know. I mean, if this is the same as when we go into the program, we wouldn't know we were avatars until we returned."

"Certainly would explain a lot," she mused. "Our relationship, the differences between our approach and that of the others, Almega's inability to pick up on Fortan or the doors..."

"He said the system was breaking down," Daniel mused thoughtfully.

"Yeah, well we knew that!"

"No... I don't think he meant here. I think he meant wherever he is."

"So are you saying what we're seeing happening to Omskep here, is just symptomatic of what's happening there?"

Daniel nodded, still struggling with the revelation.

"If that's the case," Alex continued, "why are we running around trying to fix things? If it's a program within a program, the simplest solution would be to delete the whole thing and start again."

"But if they did that we'd lose our memories of everything we've done, wouldn't we?" He locked questioning eyes on Alex, unable to comprehend the consequences. "If deleting it makes us lose our experiences and they've decided not to, then it looks like they're trying to preserve everything we've experienced *and* get us out."

"Considerate of them," Alex muttered, then paused. "Or... in order to fix whatever's happening there, they need us to retain our memories of here?" She shook her head. "I'm confused."

"Given how many trainings we've done since we've been here, that would be a lot to lose."

"Yeah," Alex sighed. The thought was far from pleasant.

There was a pause as the two privately mulled over their new status. Finally Daniel drew a deep breath.

"That Fortan... he seemed rather nicer than his namesake here," he observed. "And he's not using that avatar. The Fortan we know, if the other one's to be believed, is just a program, set in his ways."

"They all are, even Almega. Aw nuts!"

Daniel looked up, trying to determine the source of her outburst.

"It's just... I like Almega," she explained. "Next to you, he's the nicest Eternal around. He's not just a program. He's a friend."

"We make friends when we're doing our training," he pointed out.

"I know," she whined, "but now I know he's a program it's going to be really hard to..."

"We can't let him know," Daniel interrupted. "We can't let any of them know. Hentric, Gracti, Accron, Paxto, Bregar, Zorpan..." He trailed off, knowing Alex could fill in the missing names. "All programs. We can no more let them know than we could have told Miltiades or Beth or Harris or any of them. If we're struggling with it, can you imagine what it would do to them?"

Alex started to giggle, then laugh out loud.

"What's so funny?" he frowned.

"Fortan. The one here, I mean. Can you imagine his reaction if he found out he was 'only' a program, given how he talks about them?"

"Oh," he said as a grin started to spread across his face. "I see what you mean."

He started to chuckle. Before long, both were laughing out loud as they imagined Fortan's arrogance being completely undermined by the discovery of his true state.

"All those times he had a go at us for caring about the program!" Alex got out between gasps.

"And when he lectured us on what it meant to be a 'proper Eternal'?" Daniel, too, was now struggling to get his words out, tears of laughter falling down his face.

"And you getting so mad at him..."

"Can you blame me? When I came back from that last training, he told me I ought to be ashamed of myself, and that no Eternal worth their name would ever allow themselves to get into such a state over things that don't really exist."

"Which means, by his reasoning, we shouldn't ever listen to a word he says ever again!" Alex just managed to finish the sentence before she completely lost the ability to speak and ended up thumping the arm of her chair.

There was a hint of hysteria in their response, but there was also genuine humour. The emotional landslide that had been building since Alex returned from her training finally destabilised and collapsed, leaving the two Eternals in thrall to that most liberating of emotions: laughter.

***

Outside, Almega heard them. He'd come by to make sure they were all right, their behaviour being unusual enough to give him cause to worry. Hearing their humour restored (although what could be *that* amusing was beyond him) reassured him they would be all right. To further ensure that, he decided he would take on a task he'd been hesitant to approach. It wasn't something he wanted to do, but he felt he owed it to them.

He returned to Omskep and found Alex's last training. He knew eight of the children should have died in that plane crash and if he was to ensure everything was put right, the discrepancy had to be addressed. In addition, any memories of Alex's post-mortem actions needed to be removed. He felt sure the others would be occupied for a while, and it would be no matter for him to come back within seconds of departing. For his first ever trip, this was a baptism of fire, but Alex and Daniel were his friends, and he had no intention of putting either of them through the misery of what had to be done.

Steeling himself, he stepped into the program. They'd faced *Titanic*, he could face this.

***

By the time they'd finished going through all the moments Fortan had unknowingly denigrated himself, both Alex and Daniel were hugging aching sides.

"Oh, that felt good," Alex said at last.

Daniel pulled out a handkerchief and wiped his tears, still chuckling.

"Um hmm. Of course, now we have to figure out what happens next."

"I don't think there's anything *we* have to do," Alex returned. "So far as I can tell, it's all in the hands of the other Fortan."

"He said we'd know our door when it appears. I guess that means it'll look different to the one he uses, but I'm wondering what will happen to our avatar selves when we leave?"

"Carry on, I suppose. We can't die or vanish like in the ordinary program."

"You know, this may solve the problem we were talking about before," Daniel said, rubbing his beard. "We won't have to wipe *our* memories, but when we leave it would be an easy thing to wipe those of our avatars and Almega. That way no one here would know what's been happening while the others were in trainings."

"Would make it easier for everyone," Alex agreed.

Daniel opened his mouth to speak, then paused as another niggling and elusive matter resolved into a sharp point.

"I've had a thought... Fortan said he kept our Fortan trapped because of the programming errors that would occur if both of them were moving around at the same time, and since Fortan is moving in the program, albeit slowly, I take it he means moving around in Oestragar."

"Uh huh."

"And the others are also trapped, keeping them out of the way."

"Your point?"

"I think that was deliberate. We're both avatars from the higher level, so we're not a problem, but why isn't Almega an issue?"

"Maybe it *is* just Fortan, given his higher version was visiting, and the others are merely a coincidence?"

"Hmm. Perhaps," he allowed.

After some consideration he dismissed his concerns – at least for the moment. Alex was probably right, and if she wasn't they'd find out eventually.

"Ready for the next one?" he asked.

"Not yet. Frankly, right now I could murder a cuppa. Let's just relax for a bit, then we can go back. Almega isn't a stupid program, even if he is one. I need to be better prepared to deal with him or he's going to realise something is wrong."

***

If this was a fraction of what they felt dealing with over one thousand five hundred dead, Almega was happy to leave them alone for the next millennia, and Fortan would just have to suffer. Still shaking, he switched to his energy state to better deal with his experiences. How did Daniel manage what he had seen in World War One without taking erasure? In fact, how did either of them cope? Almega had a greater insight into those two Eternals than he'd ever imagined possible for him.

His first thought was to erase the memories so he could move on, but then he paused. He'd had to do it. If he hadn't, the rest of the program would have been damaged. That he'd left it this long was a concern, but a quick check of Omskep showed that somehow it had adjusted to the corrected input and what was left to fix was minor and something he suspected Alex and Daniel wouldn't mind doing. If he erased these memories he'd be no better than Fortan or Gracti or any of the others who habitually took their training and then erased anything painful or uncomfortable, and while Almega didn't feel he was better than anyone else, he certainly didn't care to feel less either. Besides, those children – programs though they may be – deserved to be remembered. Omskep had created them as part of its program and surely there was a reason. The program wasn't random. If he'd learned one thing since this whole debacle had begun, it was that actions had consequences. If a choice was made differently, everything subsequent to that choice also changed. If it didn't then the established rules of science within the program, based on cause and effect, would be meaningless, and that way lay utter chaos. While some of the results were horrific, others were truly wonderful and it occurred to him that this was the natural consequence of a well written and structured program.

Daniel's questions after he returned from his last training battered at Almega's mind. Where did the program come from? Who wrote it? How was it here at all? How were any of them there? He could better understand Daniel's confusion, but he had no more answers now than he had then. Omskep **was**. They **were**. It was simply the nature of existence. He was grateful they had something to do, because otherwise he couldn't imagine what would happen – a bored Eternal would be destructive at best, at worst they'd go insane – but how this convenient solution came about was beyond him.

He returned to his physical form and took a deep breath. No, he would not erase what he had seen and done. It was terrible, but it was also necessary. Saving programs that should not have been saved assuredly damaged or prevented lives later. Of course, it was equally true that saving those lives would have meant others could have been born and some good things come about, but ultimately he was left with a bottom line: allow the program change to remain unchecked and the Eternals would suffer, and that he could not allow.

Taking a leaf out of Daniel and Alex's book, he compartmentalised his experience so he could deal with it in stages when he was ready. Now all he required was a detailed analysis of the next trip so that, when they were ready, he could send them properly prepared to deal with it. His experience had certainly given him a greater understanding of their frustrations and, if he could make this last trip easier, he was determined to do so. He set to work.

***

"I suppose we'd best get back to Omskep and find out what Almega has in store for us," Alex said, finishing her tea. "If nothing else it'll distract us until Fortan and whoever's helping him can get the door ready so we can leave."

Daniel swept his hand across the table and their crockery vanished.

"Hmm. You know, after spending so long here, there's a part of me that will miss all this" he admitted.

"I guess it's all relative. Spending less than a hundred years within the program feels like it matters until you return to Oestragar. Spending a few millennia here will doubtless feel like nothing once we reach whatever the next place is called. We know Fortan is there, and possibly easier to get along with. I wonder what the others are like?"

Daniel paused and contemplated her question.

"Assuming we're not special – and I don't think either of us are so arrogant as to think we are – I suspect more like us. That is, easier to get along with, not so opinionated or silly…"

"Fortan may disagree with you on the first point, Gracti and Hentric on the second," Alex chuckled.

"We all have our prejudices," he conceded, "but I think the reasoning is sound."

She stood up, straightening her clothes.

"I wonder how long we've been here?" she mused.

He raised a questioning eyebrow.

"Not in terms of here, I mean there. And I know there's no real temporal passage in the normal sense, but if experiences are to be had in anything like a sane order, they must have duration the same as us. Not to mention Fortan said they were working on getting us out, which also suggests events take place in order and thus in something recognisably akin to time. So how long, in their terms, have we been absent?"

"If it's anywhere like here, they can skip time in the lower program." He frowned. "Though apparently not at the moment."

"Weird, isn't it? I mean, it's bad enough we've got a problem here, but now we know there's a higher level and even *they've* got errors, it does make you wonder what could be causing it."

"Hmm. Well," he continued, easing himself out of his chair, "we're not going to find out while we're here. Come on, the sooner we get back to Almega, the sooner we can crack on with the next one and, hopefully, find out what's going on."

Together they dematerialised, heading for Omskep.

***

"Ahh, there you are," Almega smiled as the two appeared. "How are you feeling?"

"A bit more together," Daniel admitted. "Have you found our next stop?"

Alex merely looked at Almega. It was surprisingly easy to forget he was a program, which was a relief. Turning, Almega caught her scrutiny and looked down at himself.

"Is there a problem with my attire?"

She shook herself. *'He must not know'* echoed in her head.

"No, sorry. I was miles away."

"Really?"

Alex had the distinct impression Almega was looking at someone else while gazing at her. It was a disturbing sensation. She dismissed it, deciding she was seeing things now she knew Almega was a program.

"Anyway, as Daniel said, we're here and ready to go. What's next?"

"A rather easier trip and I managed to find exactly what you have to fix, so this should be a quick in and out."

Daniel blinked in astonishment.

"What brought about this remarkable change in approach?"

"Not having anything else to do," Almega replied pragmatically. "Plus, we're nearly at the end of this and things are almost back to normal, so it was easier to see what was happening and where the key differences were."

"Not that I'm in a hurry, but don't we have to sort out the mess I made as well?" Alex pointed out. "That would have ramifications that would put a major spanner in the works."

"Not a problem. Those mistakes have been fixed."

"When?"

Almega focused on his workspace, not looking either of them in the eye.

"I checked while I was waiting for you. There was an avalanche shortly after you left. Turns out the ones who died were caught up in it. It rushed in the back of the fuselage and that was that."

"Really?" Alex queried. It seemed unlikely they would be that fortunate.

"Really," he replied, turning to face her. "The hypothermia suffered by the remaining survivors also effectively nullified the consequences of your actions. They seem to think they hallucinated it all, which is convenient." When Alex still looked incredulous, he smiled. "Honestly, it's sorted. You can check for yourself if you don't believe me." He gestured to Omskep.

"Ah, no, thank you. If I did that, I'd know which ones didn't make it, and I'd rather remain ignorant. I taught most of them and I'd prefer to remember them alive."

"As you wish," he returned blandly, although he was relieved by her decision. If she looked too closely, she might spot his intervention. "Anyway, that leaves one last trip. It's to 3047." When the two continued to wait, Almega added, "Twenty years after the Emergency Education Act?"

"Bugger!" Daniel swore. "The Education Experiment."

"Precisely."

"OK, I never did that training," Alex admitted. "Care to fill me in?"

"Neither did I," Daniel admitted, "but I studied it after I came back from my last training." When Alex looked at him curiously, he added, "I wanted to see what happened to my chosen profession."

Almega took up the narration.

"By 3027, education across the world was in crisis. With the state taking over all aspects of primary as well as secondary human socialisation, teachers were using every trick in the book to meet targets."

"I remember those all too well." Alex commented, rolling her eyes.

"And, of course, they couldn't, so more and more left teaching and the state-hired replacements were typically short term, not to mention they were simply not that good at it. It wasn't a vocation for them, so they gave up a lot quicker."

"Don't blame them," she said, thinking of all the times she'd considered quitting.

"Strikes, demands for wage increases and a reduction in class sizes, student and parental complaints... In the end, several countries, including your old one, decided to take human teachers out of the system. Artificial intelligence developments meant it was possible for students to be trained entirely by computers, so the new system required students to spend eight hours a day at VR terminals where they registered with their education codes, while two-way cameras and random genetic sampling throughout the day via their interaction equipment ensured no cheating. Virtual schools had long since removed the need for physical ones, and now they introduced virtual teachers. Real teachers provided the original content, but then computer analysis determined best practice and virtual teachers were introduced instead. These could be reprogrammed with the latest educational approach and could respond to feedback in an instant. They could also cope with marking loads well beyond those possible by any human, expanding the class sizes to astonishing levels while still allowing one to one attention."

"Sounds perfect," Alex said, although her tone indicated she was less than impressed. "What went wrong?"

"The pressure on all to achieve the highest grades, lack of jobs even when they did, and a loss of the human element, which also led to a lack of creativity. You know that in experiments, when animals in a lab where offered a wire frame 'mother' who offered food, and a furry version that didn't, the animals went to the furry version until hunger forced them, temporarily, to the other one?"

When Alex nodded but looked confused, Almega continued.

"The same thing happened with the students. While the AI did a good job mimicking human teachers, Omskep is so far beyond humans in its programming that the human versions could sense the difference, albeit subconsciously, and didn't respond as well. They never found an efficient fix for that, and since daydreaming is hardly a full-time career option, they didn't care. The point was to get the students through with the highest grades as efficiently as possible. Time wasting and lack of attention was heavily penalised, and since it was a controlled VR environment, anything that might encourage that could be removed instantly. The top 1% went on to advanced training that did still include the human element, but the vast majority did their schooling and university from home in virtual environments."

"The change that brought back human teachers for the individual support and helped reinvigorate the creative side was eventually instigated by... oh, what was his name?" Daniel tapped his forehead, trying to dredge up the name from the depths of memory. "Teskar Malpinie in... 3089?"

"Very good!" Almega nodded. "I believe the correct phrase is 'gold star'?"

"And a tick," Daniel grinned.

"How?" Alex asked, perplexed. "I mean, how did he change it when the new system cost less, was endlessly adaptable and totally under the control of government?"

"That was the key," Almega replied. "It was realised that a properly educated populace needs to be able to think independently. Being totally under government control is fine so long as you have an honest and open government that welcomes opposition."

"Even the 19th century politician Disraeli said, 'a government is only as good as its opposition," Daniel added.

"Exactly. As business control became ubiquitous, government as a benign and independent organisation – there to support the people and protect the state – changed. It started with lobbyists in your last training," and he nodded to Alex, "but by the latter half of the twenty seventh century that had got completely out of hand and most governments were run by corporations, covertly or overtly, which, in the end, meant they were run to maximise the profit in corporate pockets."

"To the detriment of the poor, who couldn't afford their products and were effectively disenfranchised," Daniel added.

"Nothing new there, then," Alex sighed. "It's always got me. I remember a TV writer in my last training said something along the lines of 'you can only drive one car at a time, sleep in one bed, eat one meal, so why do you need all the extra cash?' But what we had was a tiny number at the top with more money than they could spend in several lifetimes, and the bulk of the Earth's population at the bottom starving and struggling for the most basic of things, like clean water and food. People should contribute to society, yes, but keeping the vast majority struggling to make ends meet no matter how hard they tried didn't strike me as the best utilisation of human capital."

Daniel folded his arms, his recent training with all its prejudices coming to the fore.

"Don't tell me you became a Marxist in your last training?"

She snorted her disdain of that suggestion.

"Don't be ridiculous. That didn't work either! I'm not saying it's not OK for people to work hard and deserve what they get, but after a certain point you can't even invest the money in your own business to develop it. All you're doing is making more money. I found it kind of sad. Even by my last training there was enough innovation and technology to give the whole of the earth's population a decent standard of living, but it was concentrated in a tiny area that won the geo-political lottery, and an even smaller percentage of the population. I know that changed eventually, but it took them so long!"

Almega cleared his throat.

"Yes, well you can debate the rightness and wrongness of capitalism some other time. I suggest looking at some of the alternatives that appeared before they finally figured it out. There are worse systems. Meantime, you have a job to do."

"And what is that, pray tell?" Daniel asked good-naturedly. "Don't tell me Teskar doesn't make it."

"That's exactly what I'm telling you. For one thing, he doesn't meet his guiding light because the man was killed by a car in 3047, so your first job is to stop that. Next, running a simulation with that fix, I found he doesn't rediscover him in 3058."

"That would be after he's incarcerated for teaching without a licence." Daniel added.

"They really did lose the plot, didn't they?" Alex groaned.

"One more effort by government to keep control – presented as ensuring the high standards of a noble profession, of course."

"Qualifications I get. Experience I get. But needing a licence on top of both of those to be allowed to do what you can't help doing? Nope. That one passes me by. Plus, it would effectively stop parents from being able to give their kids the most basic socialisation, since that's also a form of teaching."

"Hence the state taking it over," Almega agreed. "So, you must first visit 3047 and keep his guide from getting knocked down and killed, then go to 3058 and help him remember his guide and track him down. And you'll have to be quick about it as the man's dying."

"It'll be interesting to hear this guide," Daniel mused. "Teskar's speeches in the 3060s made him sound like the most amazing man ever."

"What were you saying about never meeting your heroes?" Alex asked.

"Yes, but on this occasion I might make an exception. Someone certainly lit a fire under Teskar, so whoever that was, I'd like to hear them."

"Do we know his name?"

Almega shook his head. "Teskar only ever referred to him as Mentor."

"Taken straight out of The Odyssey. Mentor was guide to Odysseus and his son, Telemarchus," Daniel clarified. "In other words, no use to us whatsoever."

"That's going to make it a tad hard to track him down," Alex pointed out. "Surely the system will have a record? We just have to find it and follow it."

"One man amongst billions and he completely obliterated his existence in the paperwork? Good luck with that!"

"Then we know he must have access to the government records departments and have excellent IT skills," she reasoned.

Daniel shook his head. "Still not near enough."

"Trace his program backwards from the moment of the crash?" Alex offered.

"I can do that once you find him, if we still need to. He had no ID on him when he was killed and was dismissed as a...um..." Almega hesitated, trying to remember the right term within the program.

"John Doe?" Alex suggested.

"That's it! Anyway, I can put you on the street where the accident happened. All you have to do is look out for someone who isn't paying attention when crossing that street."

"Oh, is that all? Like that doesn't happen hundreds of times a day even in my last training?" Alex groaned.

"Then speed yourselves up while you're observing. That will effectively slow down events enough you can intervene."

"Should've done that on *Titanic*, but the other way," Daniel grunted. "Would have saved me having to watch Beth and Brailey for what felt like hours."

"You already run faster than the program, so keeping your actual time experience within it should be easy. As I recall, Alex did it on the first trip by mistake. Slowing yourselves down to the level you're talking about, Daniel, would be a much tougher option."

Alex nodded. "I'd forgotten about that. Right, any limitations on what we can do?"

"Nothing overtly 'god-like' would help," came the sardonic response.

"And you complained about *my* sarcasm!" Alex said, jabbing a finger in Daniel's direction.

"And now you see why. It's contagious," he retorted, winking at her.

Together they dematerialised from Omskep and appeared on a city street on a fairly standard work-day afternoon. Due to their time difference, everything appeared to be in slow motion, giving them a chance to observe carefully.

"And, once again, people are people. The cars are different, the modern buildings, the clothes, but they still don't talk to each other and are always in a hurry to get somewhere. At least they're looking where they're going, not peering at a phone screen."

"I think you'll find they're doing both," Daniel replied, looking around. "Those glasses they're wearing allow them to see overlays as well as the route ahead."

"OK, so most of them aren't staring at their screens," she corrected.

"Most of them are wearing contact lenses that do the same job. The ones wearing glasses can't cope with the lenses."

"Oh great. Don't people just talk to each other in the street anymore?"

"Did they do that in your last training before mobile phones appeared?"

She thought for a moment and then had to admit they didn't.

"See anyone?" she asked after a while.

"Not yet," he admitted. "We can eliminate the women. While Teskar never gave a proper name for Mentor, he always referred to his guide as 'him', so unless there was a deliberate attempt to dissemble I think we can take it for granted the guide was male."

"What are we going to do when we spot him?"

"I applaud your optimism. Well, we could summon up a local breeze to deflect him..."

"Which, if strong enough to do that, might send him tumbling straight into the advancing car," Alex pointed out. "Or someone else," she added.

"Then perhaps we need to be visible so we can 'accidentally' walk into him and distract him long enough for the car to pass?"

"Right. Almega? Do we know where exactly on this street the accident happened?"

"About six metres to your right," he replied.

The Eternals headed to that spot until Almega declared, "That's it. You're right on it."

"I'll take this side, you take that side," Daniel suggested and Alex crossed the road, passing through several cars as she did so. Both now sought out somewhere they could appear from that wouldn't lead to questions from passers-by, but the combination of security cameras and flat fronted buildings precluded that.

"Another option crossed off the list," Alex concluded at last. "How about we mentally nudge someone to walk into him when we see him?"

"I think I've found him!" Daniel cried and pointed.

Walking along Alex's side of the street was an older man who, while occasionally glancing around, was clearly more interested in the book he was reading than the street.

"How do you know it's him?" Alex asked.

"Books are a rarity in this time. Most rely on electronic versions, so the fact he's got a real one marks him out. Besides, look what he's reading!"

Alex peered at the cover. It was Homer's Odyssey.

"Bingo!"

She looked around. A car had just made a screeching turn into the street, and even with the Eternal's time-dilated perceptions it was apparent the driver had his foot to the floor.

"He must be doing at least sixty!" Alex cried. "What is he? A bank robber?!"

"Who cares? The point is you've got to stop Mentor from crossing the street!"

Alex quickly assessed the nearby pedestrians and identified a target. The woman had hurried across the road ahead of the lunatic driver and was nearing Mentor, who was about to step onto the road. Alex leaned over and alerted the woman to Mentor's risk. The woman, who'd apparently been complaining about the driver to a friend she was in contact with through her lenses, suddenly refocused, saw the problem, reached out and stopped Mentor in his tracks. Alex slowed her personal time enough to hear the conversation.

"Watch out!" the woman shouted.

Mentor, still buried in his book, looked up as the woman's arm reached across his chest, banging the book from his hands and tossing it into the road.

"What the...?"

The car flew along the road, tearing up the book as it passed.

"My book!" Mentor yelled.

"That could have been your head!" the woman returned. "I'm sorry, but I saw you were about to step out into the road, and that madman wouldn't have been able to stop in time."

Mentor stared at his destroyed book a moment longer, then turned to the woman.

"No, you're quite right. Thank you. I think you just saved my life!"

"You're welcome. Are you OK?" she asked solicitously when it became clear Mentor was shaking.

"I will be fine. A bit of a shock, that's all. Thank you, again."

Looking both ways carefully, he made sure all was clear before quickly rescuing what was left of his book and returning to the safety of the pavement. There he regarded the torn pages and shattered spine sadly, before heading for a paper recycling bin and depositing it. With a last look after the wrecking vehicle, which had long since departed sight, he shook his head and turned to retrace his steps.

"Probably heading back to see if he can get another copy," Daniel mused, coming up alongside Alex.

Alex hummed vaguely and then returned to her real time, reaching into the recycling bin to tear a few pages from the tome.

"What are you doing?" Daniel asked, matching her time.

"We need something to remind Teskar to find Mentor. I have a feeling this may be just the thing."

"Good thought," Almega agreed, "and well done. That's the first bit sorted. Ready for the second?"

"If it's as easy as this? Absolutely!"

Almega relocated them to 3058 and a stretch of wasteland outside the busy city centre they'd just vacated. Walking along the gravel and dust road leading to the wasteland was a dejected young man. His clothing suggested a manual worker and a poor one at that. His hair was ill-kempt and he kept sweeping the over-long fringe from his face in an irritated fashion. He kicked a stone as he walked, a picture of dejection.

"That's Teskar. At least, I'm pretty sure it's him," Daniel provided. "Looks a bit of a mess compared to later images, but that's understandable, given what he's been through." When she frowned Daniel added, "Jail and then the sort of jobs they don't even allocate to robots. Make-work for ex-offenders."

"All that because he taught without a licence?"

"And the fact the boy he was helping, a young lad named Gaius Trentham, committed suicide."

"I find it hard to believe Teskar drove him to that."

"He didn't. In fact, I think Teskar actually stalled his suicide for a while. Trentham was unusually bright and from a wealthy background, but his parents seemed to treat him more like a trophy than a son: something to be shown off when guests were around and otherwise given the psychological equivalent of being stuffed in a cupboard. Having someone paying attention, encouraging his talents and actively involved in his struggles kept him on an even keel for a while, but then his parents decided to move and enrol him in a school famous for academic cramming that he didn't want to attend. Even chose his courses for him with a view to which ones would guarantee the highest income. Those mostly dealt with finance and law, but Gaius was actually a musician and a poet. He couldn't talk to Teskar about it and he decided he'd had enough. He killed himself about a month after they moved and when they went through his stuff they found out about Teskar. They called the authorities and said their son's suicide was his fault."

"Of course. Couldn't possibly be anything to do with them. How do you know he was a musician and poet?"

"After his parents died and Teskar was gaining notice, someone went through Trentham's education transcripts and found his work. Remarkably good for one so young. Still a little rough around the edges, of course, but if I'd had a son that gifted I certainly wouldn't have forced him to become an accountant."

"Or a lawyer?"

"Corporate law is where the money is, and that would have been a living hell for someone like Gaius."

"Mentor's taken up residence in the old warehouse to your left," Almega provided, effectively putting them back on track.

Alex looked up and saw the warehouse to which Almega referred. Moving swiftly towards it, she let the pages from Mentor's wrecked book separate and flutter from her fingers, using the secondary program to add a bit of breeze to carry them into Teskar's path.

Teskar paused, picked up the page that had just been caught under his boot, and examined it. He then looked around and, seeing a few more sheets, followed the trail towards the warehouse. Meanwhile, Daniel had floated inside and located Mentor's hidden library, albeit most of the books were now in boxes, which was curious. The man himself was flat on his back on a thin mattress atop a low bunk, and it was apparent he had not long left. The sunken eyes, yellowing face, thin body, laboured breathing and shaking hands were features Daniel had seen on more than one occasion. Quietly, he released the lock on the door and allowed it to swing open. As Teskar entered the warehouse Daniel also summoned a breeze and the door's rusting hinges complained loudly. When he heard Teskar mounting the stairs he returned to Alex.

"He's found him," he asserted in reply to her questioning look.

"Almega, does that fix it?" Alex asked.

"It does. You're clear to come home. Unless you want to listen in on that conversation? It is, after all, the one that got Teskar set on his crusade."

Daniel turned to Alex.

"What do you think?" he asked.

"After all you've told me about Teskar, I think I'd like to hear what was said. On the other hand, given Mentor's dying it does seem a little... indelicate?"

"Neither of them will know we're there. For all we know, Mentor's not that good and Teskar made it up himself, but if he's half as good as Teskar claimed..."

"You're desperate to listen in, aren't you?" Alex smiled.

Daniel's head rocked on his shoulders in a way that said, 'I don't want to admit it, but yes!'

"Come on, then, or we'll be too late."

Together, they went back into the warehouse.

Teskar was sitting on the floor in front of Mentor's bunk, and it was apparent they'd already moved to the core of the discussion.

"What happened?" Teskar asked.

Mentor took a breath, staring through the dirty windows of the warehouse. He seemed a little more alert than when Daniel had looked in on him. Having company had enlivened the old man, albeit briefly.

"We forgot," he said at last. "We lost our way. The dream was forgotten."

"What dream?"

"The ideal. The form if you will. We forgot what education was about. We thought it was a tool to be used."

"Isn't it?"

Mentor chuckled and turned to look directly at Teskar while the Eternals quietly found somewhere to listen and observe.

"No, but that never stopped anyone. So they carried on, thinking there should be a purpose, an aim, a practical application. There had to be a piece of paper or a pay cheque at the end of it to justify its use. We were made to believe that without that we ought to be ashamed of ourselves. Whenever we did anything, we were not simply praised for the doing itself, but asked how we were going to use it. Like Gaius. He wrote a moving poem that he put to music and the first question was 'Are you going to sell it?' When he pointed out he did it for pleasure, for himself, because it had to be done — because the characters, the words, the music wouldn't get out of his head — still people asked, 'Why not sell it?'"

Teskar nodded. "I remember. He told me he didn't want to and that he liked it as it was, without the sort of refinement needed to make it commercially viable."

"Yes, and then they dismissed it as consequently worthless. He could have argued he enjoyed it; others enjoyed it; that it was fun, but that, too, would have been dismissed, because fun doesn't pay the bills, so fun is wrong. We are told — indirectly through censure and dismissal — that we should be ashamed of producing or doing something for no other reason than that we enjoy it, and we are ashamed. So ashamed that we justify everything we do, and we either hide or deny the creation of anything for free. We've forgotten the sheer, glorious joy of creation for its own sake. And once we forgot that – once we were made ashamed of doing anything that had no financial reward – education had to fall in line. It had to be rationalised. Streamlined. Goal orientated."

"I don't understand..." Alex began, although she was already being drawn in by Mentor's mellifluous tones.

Daniel placed a finger to his lips, indicating she should simply listen. Nodding, she returned her attention to Mentor who continued, unaware of his impromptu audience.

"We forgot it's the arena. It shakes, builds, and gives the tools by which we may achieve great things. We forgot there doesn't *have* to be a job at the end of it; that failure and learning how to recover and profit from that failure is as important an experience as success if we're to become whole people. At that point everything that had no immediate, quantifiable advantage, or proved too difficult, was removed. We only kept those subjects we could justify without shame: engineering; computing; architecture; the absolute basics of language for written communication, and maths – but only the applied stuff – and we simplified to ensure best results. But that meant we had to forget Euclid. We had to forget Aristotle and Plato as they were deemed too hard, and in the end we even forgot Einstein."

Teskar frowned.

"But doesn't that make sense? I mean, what's the point of studying something you can't use?"

"There's every reason," Mentor replied, his tone rising as his passion for his cause came to the fore. "We are *not* machines. Human beings are, above all, imaginative. It's that imagination, often growing out of failure or disaster, which has helped us to survive. It shows us how to invent, build, and advance. But if you don't allow the imagination free rein; if you box it up and dismiss it as no longer required, then it dies, and with it dies every hope we ever had."

Teskar was slightly taken aback by Mentor's vehemence, but his recent experiences and the state-sanctioned 'brain-washing' he'd endured as a result were hard to kill.

"But people keep going," he replied, determined to argue the case. "They can survive without imagination."

"No," Mentor insisted, "they can't. Not for long anyway. For a while, perhaps. Then the mind becomes like a field planted with the same crop year after year. The crop falters as the soil becomes less fertile. It takes time, long enough that we forget why it happens. We don't see the connection. We see crime, hopelessness and fear, but not the true reason for it. You walk the streets and look into people's eyes. There's nothing there. They're hollow; two-dimensional. They fill their lives with worry and fear because there's nothing else left."

He paused and looked carefully at Teskar. When the young man began to fidget uncomfortably he continued.

"When was the last time you simply sat and thought about something?"

"I can't remember," Teskar shrugged. "I'm not sure I ever did."

"And now?"

"Maybe. I don't know. I see things and I want to understand, want to make it better, but I don't know where to start."

Mentor nodded and smiled.

"You just started. You wonder. The beginning of all wisdom lies in wonder. How do you think the first philosophers worked out the nature of their universe? They wondered. They wanted to know how and why."

"But they got it wrong!" Teskar cried, his frustration with the clash between what he'd been taught and Mentor's words boiling over.

"Doesn't matter," he replied calmly, "it was a start. And there you go again. As though we should be ashamed of making mistakes. Don't you see? We're stumbling in a darkness which we illuminate little by little with the light of our discoveries. Every now and then we strike a spark so bright we run on ahead of it, thinking we can see the way. There's nothing wrong with that, but sooner or later you'll fall. Sooner or later you'll have to stop and light up the world around you. And better if you do. Imagine if we just kept running in the darkness, never stumbling, never pausing, just running on and on. We'd never see anything. We'd learn a tiny fraction of what there is. A great ocean of darkness around and behind us. Ignorant, because we never made a mistake and had to pause to look around again."

Alex looked over at Daniel who was riveted, his eyes shining with delight. On this occasion the hero had lived up to the hype and her fellow Eternal was obviously thrilled. She had to admit, she could see why.

Mentor continued.

"Have you any idea how many great discoveries occurred because of a mistake? A window is left open, a culture exposed and we have penicillin. A strange stone is left on a photographic plate and we discover radioactivity. A man sits in a bath he's filled too full and cries eureka as the water overflows. A mistake can be as often an opportunity as a dead end. We don't want to be wrong, but be grateful we're not always right. The sparks that fly off when we drop the torch of knowledge can light other paths we didn't even know were there. All we need is the courage and imagination to explore them."

He paused, taking a few deep breaths. It was apparent he was using every ounce of his quickly waning strength to get his point across, and he wasn't done yet.

"What question does a child ask most until we stop them?"

Teskar shrugged.

"I don't know."

"Listen to them. The single most important question on any child's lips is 'why?'. Why is the sky blue and the sea green and the sand yellow? Why do I have to do something I don't like instead of something I do? Why are snails slow and elephants big? Why? But we've knocked that out of them. Somewhere along the line some fool, fed up with hearing that question, made it illegal. He decided it caused too much trouble, and he banned it. And we've been paying the price ever since. The crops are poorer. People don't think, don't read, don't wonder. And without wonder we're lost in the darkness. A little bit dies every day and we only notice it when the results twenty or thirty years down the line come up lousy. And then what do we do? Do we encourage music and art and philosophy? No. We tell them to work harder. We pay more for less. We work longer hours but produce less in substance. And then we wonder why we're dissatisfied. We want, but we don't know *what* we want. We know our lives are empty but we don't know how to fill them. So we fill them with more work, more emptiness. Video casts, films, computer games, and news feeds that tell us nothing. We sit back after watching some special effects spectacular, and twenty minutes later we've forgotten what it was about. There was no depth of plot, no meaningful story, no honest character development. Nothing that might contribute to our understanding of ourselves or the world in which we exist. It was pure distraction. We think we can survive with such vacuity, but we can't. We think we can fill it with quantity instead of quality, but we're like sieves. We can subject ourselves to never-ending streams of images and sounds, but we need substance else it all falls through. We need someone to give us back our dreams, or, more importantly, the means to dream our own. Real education gives us the tools with which we can dream, and dream something worthwhile. Not just things, or jobs, but life itself."

He paused, shifting himself on his bunk. Teskar went to help him, but Mentor waved him away, struggling with some inner demon only he could see. He gazed at Teskar, shaking his head.

"How can I make you understand?" he said at last. "You think it's enough to do and to be able to look back years later, hold up a piece of paper and say 'See, I got my qualification. I passed.' Anyone can pass if you give them the answers and tell them this answer should go there and that one somewhere else. The question is, do they know WHY it should go there and not somewhere else? Education isn't a cipher to be worked out, but that's what it's become. We're not just ashamed, we've become lazy. The mind is a muscle: when you stop using it, it grows weak. But everyone stopped using their minds a long time ago, and because everyone became weak at the same moment we hardly noticed. Then we found old books harder to read. Students of eighteen complained they couldn't manage texts our parents read when they were eight. So we simplified them. We're as much to blame as anyone. We acquiesced and let them take the easy route. We wanted good reports because our jobs depended on them, and no teacher would get a good report if the students had to work harder in their class than anywhere else, and often for a poorer result. The education department, the parents, the students, our bosses... they all complained if a student failed, so we made sure they didn't. And in doing that we forgot that above all education should be abrasive. Like anything worthwhile it must be worked at, and that work will be hard because it's new and doesn't always fit with our perceptions. We simplified, made everything black and white so it was easier to understand, and instead of pulling everyone up to the same level, we dragged everyone down. Someone said education to the very highest degree should be open to all, and in one breath we condemned everyone. We bowed before the screams of those who yelled elitist whenever it was suggested that not everyone could achieve the highest qualifications, and then were forced to drop the standards when reality intruded upon ideality. And those who were capable learned nothing, and those who weren't got a piece of paper that meant nothing, because life isn't laid out like a test in a school, and that's all they'd been taught to deal with."

Even Alex was nodding now. She'd seen the beginning of this in her last training and the realisation was uncomfortable, but the truth of it couldn't be denied.

"That's when they threw out those subjects that weren't quantifiable. At least then the tests meant they knew something of use to their chosen professions. That was the trade-off. Giving up our right not to be perfect meant we also had to give up our imagination, spontaneity and dreams in favour of something of use, something practical and measurable."

Teskar was staring at the dusty floorboards, his brain still fighting the paradigm shift Mentor was evoking. Trying to hold on to his re-training he fought back.

"You say we forgot Aristotle and Plato, but the AI teachers said the Great Researchers were following in their footsteps."

"We remember *what* they wrote, and *that* they wrote, but not *why* they wrote. And don't forget, Socrates didn't write a thing."

Teskar nodded, convinced Mentor had fallen into a trap.

"And we'd know nothing of him if it wasn't for Plato."

Mentor turned blazing eyes on him.

"Do you think a person makes no difference unless they write some great treatise? Do you think a life is so easily swallowed up by history? Would Plato have written so much if it hadn't been for his teacher who wrote nothing, but ignited the fire of knowledge and wonder? And would Aristotle have done so much had that torch not been passed on to him by Plato?"

"But not every teacher is a Socrates or a Plato!" Teskar replied desperately

"Of course not. If they were we wouldn't remember Socrates or Plato or any of the others. Who admires one patch of water in a sea? That doesn't mean we wouldn't appreciate that same water in a desert, nor does it mean the sea isn't of value in itself. The problem was that because not everyone has the gift; because great teachers are born and not made; because lighting a torch in someone's mind can't be immediately quantified, we didn't encourage them. We believed the fire could be passed on through electronic texts and videos and AI-controlled virtual schools."

"Can't it?"

Alex was thinking the same thing, so she was intrigued to hear Mentor's response to that one.

"Sometimes, yes, but only when the kindling is there and ready to crackle into life. The thing about a great teacher is that they can kindle wood that is sodden with neglect, rotted from inattention and dispersed with carelessness. It's hard. It's very hard. You have to give of yourself to light that fire, and every student whose soul you set ablaze with wonder needs some of you to get started. You give the spark, you fan it gently into life. You have to move carefully or you'll smother it and they'll not try again. Eventually, you have to know the point at which you can blow on it with force and instead of putting it out you'll fan it to a roar. But no one teaches you how to do that. No one can! You have to be able to feel it; see it in their eyes. You must sense the very beginning of the excitement that will course through their soul and explode in their mind. It's easy to see once the torch has caught. Easy to smother or starve beforehand."

Nice words, but... Teskar took the counter-argument that was on her lips.

"But people like Einstein were said to have been terrible in school. They didn't need great teachers."

"Some are born with the fire. Thank God! But those are the ones who you now see flying through the system seemingly without effort. They're gifted and lucky. What about people like you? What about the millions who need the spark? Why should they be denied? Why should real learning be reserved only for those born with the gift who would do well no matter the circumstances because they're driven? And you know, even the driven need help and encouragement sometimes. Look at Gaius. You thought he had everything going for him, and you couldn't understand why he killed himself. But he'd become an exam passing machine. He got A's because everyone expected him to. No one ever noticed the real him. They saw the performance and not the performer, and no one saw his fire was eating him alive until it had run out of fuel. Only when his grades dropped did anyone raise an eyebrow but even then they didn't care about him. If he'd suddenly started producing A's again everyone would have patted him on the back and left him alone, never wondering why he'd faltered or how he'd managed to recover. It's all about results. It's about machines fulfilling a function. Dreams are forbidden. Wondering is forbidden. Stepping outside the system and refusing to follow the pattern is forbidden. And anyone who creates something or looks for solutions merely because they want to... anyone who does that is to be pitied. 'Fool', we say, 'Fancy doing something for nothing'. But it isn't for nothing. It's for a reason far more real than any piece of paper or note of credit."

Again Mentor was forced to pause, drawing breath into straining lungs, but he was on a roll now and he was determined to finish.

"You think money is worth anything? You think it has a value in itself? Of course not. Money is another means to an end: with it you eat; without it you starve. But in itself it cannot feed a starving child or clothe a freezing man. But an original idea... A spark of creativity... Now *there's* something remarkable. It whirls you around in its arms, reaches out with filigree fingers and touches your soul, spreading a miracle of wonder through the length and breadth of its owner. And then, if we're lucky, that person will not just live a better life for that thought, but hand it to others, like a precious living jewel that glimmers in their eyes. Education is the greatest cure-all of them all. It cures ignorance, and ignorance has killed and maimed and tortured and destroyed more living creatures than any single thing on Earth."

His voice, which had been rising and animated, now fell to a hush. He was almost out of time. He had only one more thing left to say.

"When Pandora shut the box one voice was trapped inside, crying out to be freed. Prometheus had seen what was to come and prepared for it. When she opened the box again she released hope into the world. It's all we have, and it's carried by people like you. You must infect the world with hope, Teskar. Wherever you see the tinder in people's hearts and minds you must touch your soul to the kindling and catch them alight. Give of yourself 'til you have nothing left to give, and then give some more. Give 'til you weep with exhaustion. Whenever you lose hope, give some more, and hope will return to you as you see that blaze of the mind reflected in one more pair of eyes and one more voice. You may never write anything that will be remembered. No statue will be raised to you, nor books written about you. By the standards of an Earth which judges by material things you *will* be a failure. That is the price we pay." Exhausted, Mentor fell back on his bunk and whispered, "Believe me, it *is* worth it."

Alex raised her head to see Daniel looking over at her, his eyes bright with the very fire Mentor had been talking about. Alex wasn't sure she had any of that left. Her last training had taken every ounce of it and she had ended up going through the motions, just as Mentor had said, doing it as best she could without the original drive that had made her take the job in the first place. She had succumbed to a ritualistic approach, dotting the appropriate i's and crossing the t's as the job required. There was no time for the extras that made learning fun. Everything had but one focus: the exam. Until her short-lived job as college curator, she'd not felt the zeal that had driven her into teaching for some time. Mentor might have been dying, but he had more passion and energy for teaching than she'd felt in the last ten years of her previous training session. She was reminded of Socrates' claim that he was merely a midwife for ideas. That was what she'd wanted to be. Someone who enthused, encouraged and supported young minds to help them find whatever they had inside them, and then helped them find the courage to run with it. When did that part of her die?

Mentor closed his eyes, releasing a long sigh. For a man near his end, he'd said a lot.

"I must rest now."

Teskar took a deep breath, nodded to himself and stood up. His bearing reflected the change Mentor's words had wrought. Instead of the shuffling, slouched despondency that had marked his walk towards this place, he now stood tall. Even his fringe seemed to have realised it would no longer be permitted to be a nuisance and stayed out of his face. Daniel could almost see him mentally picking up the sword and shield and preparing to do battle. He had a hard fight ahead of him, but now the change, which would come, would come from him.

"Is this the last box?" Teskar indicated the small cardboard box that contained the last of Mentor's books.

"Yes."

"I still don't understand why you want to give them to me."

Mentor chuckled, the sound cut short by a coughing fit that racked his body before he could speak again.

"After all I've just said?"

"But they're your books. They're your life."

He shook his head, his eyes still closed.

"Not anymore. They're yours now. Use them well and protect them. You understand what they're really worth."

Teskar nodded. "Can I come back tomorrow?"

"You have more important things to do now than look after an old man. It's time to move on."

"But you'll need me."

"No, I won't."

Teskar stared and Alex could see the moment the meaning behind Mentor's words dawned. His voice, when he found it, cracked as he spoke.

"Do you... do you need any help?"

"Thank you, but this I can do alone."

Alex turned questioning eyes on Daniel.

"Where's Teskar going to take all these?"

"He's got a squat in a basement closer to the city. The building's mostly empty and the city planners want to have it condemned so they can raise another high-rent apartment block, but it's an old building and its listed status means they're having to fight not just the squatters, but the paperwork. Teskar's one of the reasons the building survived. In his down time, what little he had, he worked on restoring it. He also managed to encourage the others to help, and that drew the attention of a few philanthropists and architecture aficionados who helped to defend their work. In the end, the building will be saved, the squatters will be granted the right to remain because of the work they put in to preserve it, and Teskar's library, which eventually covers two floors, won't be discovered until he, himself, reveals it once his cause takes root. After he dies, the building becomes a museum with the books preserved in situ, but reprints are faithfully reproduced every year. He makes reading physical books popular again. Not that people quit with the electronic versions, but just about everyone has a physical copy of the Odyssey in their house, even if they never read it."

Alex thought back to her experience of that book. She'd read it and the Iliad because they were such important pieces of classical literature, shaping nearly every book that had been written since, but it had been a struggle.

"Not the most exciting of tomes," she admitted. "I must admit, when I read it I wanted to slap Odysseus for being such a wuss. All he does at the start is cry a river."

"That's just the Greek way of the time. Any emotion had to be experienced to the fullest. Passion was everything. No stiff upper lip for them!"

"Speaking of passion... That really was some speech. I wish Socrates had managed something like that when we were in Athens."

"I'm sure there were many discussions between Teskar and Mentor when they first met that weren't nearly so inspiring."

He gestured towards the old man who was drawing painful breaths that laboured in his chest.

"I think Mentor used everything he had left for that one."

"Should we stay?"

"I will. He said he could handle it on his own and he won't know I'm here, but his passing deserves to be noted. I never cared to let men die alone if it could be helped, but that's just me. You can go if you want."

"No, I'll stay too. Keep you company, at least."

***

When they returned to Omskep their mood was mixed. On the one hand they had witnessed the sad and lonely passing of an extraordinary man. On the other, his words were still ringing in their ears.

Almega looked up and smiled.

"You've done it. Everything's back to normal. Which, of course, means I now have to head over to Fortan's to be there when he comes out. I suspect his mood may not be pacific."

"To say the least," Daniel agreed. "I would come with you, but I think I'd only make it worse."

"And I've just had enough. Sorry, Almega, but you're on your own. Unless you desperately want me there?"

"No, you're fine. You've earned a break. Time to reflect on what's happened and, I suppose, decide on your next training."

Alex and Daniel looked at each other. That consideration hadn't entered either of their minds since this had begun, and since the program-Fortan's comments, it had ceased to be an option. Now came the thought that they might have to face one more training before they left.

"We'll think about it," Alex said, "but I feel like we've had the equivalent of several trainings all in one and I'm certainly not in a hurry to ship out again."

She turned to Daniel to gauge his views on the matter, even though she was fairly certain she already knew his answer. He didn't disappoint.

"I'm with you. It's not like I was in a hurry anyway, but after this...? No, I'm more than happy to take a break."

"Very well. I'll see you both later, assuming Fortan doesn't find a way to delete an Eternal!"

"Uh, Almega? You need to be careful," Alex said. "Fortan can't learn of this ability we now have."

"I believe I will be able to void his access," Almega assured her.

"Really?"

"Last time he tried that, I bombarded him with every program anyone had ever had. I have to study them in order to know when to be ready for their return. I think I gave him as close to a headache as any of us can experience in Oestragar." He chuckled. "I doubt he'll ever want to go through that again."

With a wink he vanished, leaving Alex and Daniel feeling deflated. They looked around, wondering what to do. It was Alex who finally expressed their feelings.

"Anti-climax, much?"

"Not that I was expecting a fanfare or streamers, but it does feel a little flat," Daniel agreed.

Towered over by Omskep, they were illuminated by flashes of images and surrounded by a background hum filled with hints of sounds, but to the casual observer, nothing seemed to have changed.

"Everything we went through, everything we did... and now we've nothing to show for it except that the system is running smoothly again."

He leaned against one of the walls and gazed at the pulsing, ever-changing mass.

"Still, I suppose that's the point. If you could tell we'd done anything that would be proof we'd failed."

Alex walked over and mirrored his position.

"Do we wait here? Go back to your place? Mine?" She shook her head. "No, definitely not mine. A good place to leave this," and she indicated her projected body, "for training, but not much use for anything else."

"I confess, I'm at a loss."

"Then perhaps it's time to move on," a voice suggested, and Fortan, or at least the program version of him, appeared in the room.

Daniel rocked forward to land squarely on his feet and folded his arms, levelling a look at their visitor that would have left your average squaddie shaking in his boots.

"And how do you propose we do that? I see no door, and if we simply walk out I think our absence might be noticed."

"By this lot?" Fortan replied, totally unaffected by Daniel's show of rank. "I doubt it. Far too self-obsessed."

"Your avatar being the most egotistical of the lot," Daniel agreed.

"Yeah. Sorry about that. In my defence, that's only in this universe. There are many out there where my avatar self is positively affable."

Alex summoned a chair and sat down, hard.

"There are other universes that have a level like this?"

"An infinite number," Fortan beamed. "Every alternative, every possible choice, everything that can be imagined exists somewhere."

"Parallel universes," Alex breathed. "In my last training the idea was mooted, both in fiction and by scientists and philosophers."

"Yeah, well, even the lowest program have to come up with the truth once in a while," Fortan conceded.

"I see where our Fortan got his attitude towards the program from," Daniel observed, cocking an eyebrow.

"Hardly. I love 'em! Without them, our lives would be boring indeed. But even you have to admit their perceptions are, of necessity, limited."

Daniel conceded the point with a reluctant nod.

"So how do we move on?" Alex asked practically. "And, even allowing for the self-absorption of our fellow Eternals on this plane, they would notice, so what happens to our existence here?"

"In answer to your first question..."

He waved a hand and an open door appeared in Omskep. It was impossible to see what was on the other side but positioned as it was it looked as though they'd be walking straight into Omskep itself.

"You just walk through. Your avatars will remain here, your true selves will arrive at the other side. We'll also take the liberty, if you don't mind, of erasing the secondary program and your avatars' knowledge of what happened over the past few trips. As you pointed out, if the others learned they could do that, your program would be in chaos. Frankly, with everything else we've got to deal with, coming back to fix this a second time would be annoying."

"Annoying," Daniel repeated, his tone deadpan.

Given what they'd just been through, that seemed as dismissive as someone calling an atomic explosion an insect fart.

"When considered in terms of all the possible worlds that coexist from our perspective," Fortan clarified.

"Hmm." Daniel's eyes widened as a thought occurred to him. "Hang on! You've been getting in our way all through this! You were on *Titanic* and in the data centre..." He gave Fortan a hard stare. "If you're on our side, why have you been trying to stop us?"

"I was in Athens, too," Fortan happily informed them. "I was in Athanasios, the man you saw leaving the debate."

"And he would have argued against Miltiades and wrecked everything we worked for!" Alex cried.

"He did, originally. I was in him to stop that, but your actions rendered it unnecessary. Similarly with *Titanic*. I'd taken the film to ensure it was lost, not to preserve it. You dealt with the real problem, which was Moraweck. I was, in fact, trying to fix the problems too, but you moved so fast you rendered my efforts redundant."

He bowed and gave them a rueful shrug.

"I should've just trusted you'd fix it without any help, but we've been friends for so long I couldn't simply stand back and watch. The others wanted to give you a hand too, but... too many cooks, as they say. And once you'd found ways to solve the problems, they went off to use those to address our own issues."

"And the data centre?" Daniel pushed.

"Ahh, that was a little different. Originally, the damage was caused by a terrorist organisation who released a virus across the planet a week after your intervention, and it was even more severe, affecting all the data forests simultaneously. We looked at attacking the terrorists directly, but they had so many splinter groups with back-up viruses ready to pounce, that simply wasn't going to work. Then we tried stopping the programmer, but all he did was tweak a legitimate program that was needed, and it was such a small change any number of halfway decent hackers could do it. Stop one and another did it and then another. Finally we decided the best solution would be if I stepped into the lad and caused a small scale local problem we knew you could fix. That way, the safeguards you would put in place as a consequence would spread out across the network before the terrorists' program had a chance to wreck everything. As a result of your added protections, Alex, they found their efforts completely ineffective. Nothing happened and so nothing showed up in the program. That was the real issue, but as you couldn't be in a dozen different places at once we thought this would be the best way of resolving it. In effect, we were working together, you just didn't know it!"

He rocked on his feet, obviously delighted with the result. When neither Alex nor Daniel looked convinced or eager to leave, Fortan deflated and cocked his head.

"I really have been trying to help, although I realise it doesn't look like that from your perspective." At their continued frowns he sighed, "Are you coming, or do you want to stay here indefinitely?"

"This is for real, right?" Alex asked. "You're not just our Fortan playing a trick on us so he can make a laughing stock of us for the foreseeable?"

"Sounds more like one of Hentric's jokes," Daniel growled.

"This place really did do a number on you two, didn't it?" Fortan said, his eyes widening as he realised the depth of their distrust. "Not sure what I can do to reassure you. Until you leave these avatars behind you can't recover your other memories. There simply isn't the storage in these," and he indicated their present selves. "Look at it this way: when you leave the program and return to Oestragar, you get a flood of memories and you remember who you really are. When you leave Oestragar and return to Anqueria, the same thing will happen, just on a larger scale. Until you're there I doubt there's anything I could say that would convince you."

"Why didn't you just yank us out and delete this program?" Alex asked. "If this is just one tiny program amongst an infinite number, deleting it would have been the simpler option, surely?"

"Two problems with that. One, with the way the system's misbehaving on our level we weren't sure what knock-on effect there might be on the rest of the system. Could be nothing, could be disastrous."

"Same reasoning we had when it came to our program," Daniel admitted.

"Precisely. Also, two, we wanted to be absolutely certain you'd retain your memories. Apart from the fact you've done a lot since you've been in here and it would be a pity to erase all that, there's a simple moral requirement. We couldn't erase your memories without your permission."

"Nice to know," Alex said, exchanging a look with Daniel.

"And you've learned some things while doing this that have proved useful for fixing things at our level," Fortan finished. "Taking those away we'd only have to put 'em back again, and then you'd be angry we took them away in the first place."

"And now we finally get the truth," Daniel said.

"Never denied we had a problem," Fortan pointed out. "The minute it was felt safe to tell you anything I gave you all I could. We couldn't tell you anything before we were nearly ready to bring you back. Imagine having that knowledge when you made your trip to, oh, I dunno, the 17th century?"

Alex thought for a bit.

"That was about twelve trainings ago!" she cried when she'd worked it out.

"Exactly."

Daniel shuddered.

"Point made. What about Almega's memories? He went through this with us."

"As he pointed out, he can block others from accessing his memory. Just as well given how much he knows. Almega's... a little different. You'll understand when you come home. Let's just say he's not an avatar, but he's not just a program, either."

"Really?" Alex said, hope rising. "So we're not leaving him behind?"

"You are and you aren't," Fortan replied. "Sorry, I can't be more specific. If I say more and you decide to stay here it could cause trouble. I've probably already said too much."

"You mean we do still have a choice?" Daniel asked.

Fortan was stunned by the question.

"Of course you have a choice! We could certainly use your help as there's only ten of us including you two, but I'm not going to force you. Let's face it, I couldn't even if I wanted to!"

Alex was walking around the door, trying to see through it without committing herself. She reached out and Fortan stopped her.

"Uh uh. The door would read that as you want to go home and would pull you through, leaving your avatar behind, and with Daniel here that could be a little confusing. I suggest if you're ready to go, go together, that way your avatars can be cleanly wiped. If you go piecemeal it could traumatise the avatar that sees the other one pass through. I don't think we need to deal with that."

"This avatar has suffered more than its fair share of trauma, thank you very much," Daniel said, stepping up beside Alex.

Now he'd admitted openly he was an avatar, his decision was effectively made. They couldn't stay here with that knowledge, and the thought of erasing it left a sour taste in his mouth. He turned to her and held out his hand.

"Ready?"

Alex looked once again at Fortan, who was smiling and nodding, then at Daniel.

"You're sure we can trust this?"

"No, but I'm willing to give it a go. Worst case scenario: this is a joke and we'll just have to live with it, but as most of this will have to be erased I don't think that's going to be a problem. We'll just carry on as we always have and no one the wiser. Best case: there's an infinite number of universes with every alternative possible we have yet to explore, and a new world from which to do it. If we're truly Eternals we can't be destroyed, and if it turns out we're programs then I'd rather put an end to this farce now and stop existing in a lie. I'm prepared to take the risk. How about you? Are you willing?"

She hesitated for a moment, but Daniel's firm gaze and open palm beckoned. She released a sigh and placed her hand in his.

"As I'll ever be. I suppose it's better to know the truth, but if we walk through that and I find myself waking up back in Herabridge with a stack of papers to mark, I'm holding you responsible!"

Together they walked through the door.

Chapter 8

Alex felt like she was drowning and being crushed, while at the same time a freezing metal ball covered in jagged spikes was spinning inside her mind, shredding it into confetti. Remembering how she'd felt when she returned to Oestragar after her last training – and after just about every training she'd ever had – she fought the instinctive panic, reminding herself of her nature as an Eternal. The feel of Daniel's fingers closing tightly around hers reassured her she wasn't the only one struggling.

Suddenly a voice, wonderfully familiar, echoed in the darkness.

"That's it. Nearly there. Just a little more. You've been gone a long time so it'll take a bit longer to fully integrate your true self and your new memories. Just listen to my voice, relax, and it'll come."

"Almega?"

Her voice was so quiet she wasn't certain she'd spoken the name aloud. The voice chuckled. Apparently, she had.

"Let's get you back before we start conversations. Remember, none of the feelings you're having right now are real. It's just the way your mind is interpreting the information upload and integration. Once you get enough to recognise where you are, then we can celebrate."

Daniel's voice came from her left.

"How long were we gone?" he asked, his words barely above a whisper.

"And fill in those kinds of details," Almega added.

There were noises around them, indicating movement of more than one person.

"Who's here?"

"Just me and Almega," Fortan's voice reassured them. "We didn't think you'd want a crowd, 'though the others are really eager to welcome you home.

With a wince, Alex slowly opened her eyes. Almega was smiling back at her.

"There you go."

"Hey, c'mon Eridar! You're letting Oslac beat you at something. That's not like you!" Fortan said, the smile in his tone unmistakeable.

Daniel blinked a few times and frowned at him.

"I'm not that bad!" he replied.

"Oh, you so are!" Alex grinned. Her memory restored she promptly switched to energy form. Her outline pulsed, expanding and contracting in all directions and then shot out of the room.

"Good old Oslac. Has to stretch her plasma a bit before she can settle," Almega commented.

"This is going to sound strange, but do you mind if I stick with Daniel?" He followed Alex's example, turning to energy to shake off the last of his stiffness before returning to solid form.

"Can't see why not," Fortan shrugged. "No one would find it odd. In fact, given how avidly everyone's been watching your latest adventures I think they'll find it harder to stick with your real name."

"You've all been watching us?"

"I believe the phrase is 'must see' viewing," Almega confirmed. "Apart from the fact you gave us ideas on how to deal with our own problem," and here he waved to what was clearly a secondary program attached to Omskep, "it was truly entertaining. But you needn't worry," he added, seeing Daniel's stricken expression, "we know better than the avatars in Oestragar not to interfere in that form under normal circumstances."

"There's only so much trouble we care to deal with!" Fortan confirmed.

Alex's energy ball zipped back into the room and reformed into her preferred physical appearance. "That feels better! Almega, the garden looks stunning!"

"I've missed your help, but I did what I could in your absence."

"You've done a wonderful job. And now I know where your avatar got his version from."

"You know he's not really an avatar. Never did work with me, more's the pity."

"The disadvantage of being so directly connected to Omskep. Still, it allows you a freedom and access to information the rest of us don't get."

She paused and looked up at the pulsing mass.

"So much bigger here," she added thoughtfully.

"So much more it has to deal with," Almega replied. "Yours had only one universe, and it was fixed. No deviations of any kind allowed. Here everything that can be imagined is available, and all of you keep creating new alternatives to keep me busy. Makes the version of Omskep you were dealing with in Oestragar look like an abacus."

"Hmm, considering that, how on earth did you create a secondary program here?" Daniel asked.

Alex looked up sharply and he indicated the subject of his comment. She went over to examine it. A much smaller version of Omskep, about the size of a large bowling ball, was positioned next to the behemoth and she peered at it curiously.

"This isn't my program," she insisted after a while.

"As a matter of fact, it's surprisingly close," Almega returned. "The principle was good, the application here needed some refinement."

"Took us a while," Fortan added. "Gracti, Hentric, Paxto, Almega and I all had to dig in to create it, but we got there in the end. That was part of what stalled us getting you out."

Alex chuckled.

"Has Gracti seen what her avatar is like in Oestragar?"

Fortan's lips twitched as he fought his own laughter.

"She did. She was not impressed!"

"I can imagine," Daniel muttered, thinking of the studious Gracti, buried in her studies between trips and learning everything she could about wherever she was going next. The Gracti he'd known in Oestragar would have been anathema to the one in Anqueria.

"Speaking of stalled... what happened? We were only supposed to be gone for a few trips to see what it would be like to play in the second level, not stay there for millennia!"

"At first you just seemed to be enjoying yourselves and it made sense to let you carry on," Almega explained. "Then the first hints that something was going awry with Omskep started and we focused on that, hoping to fix it before your return."

Fortan took up the explanation.

"It wasn't too bad at first and we carried on, deciding between us it was probably best to leave you where you were rather than risk bringing you back. Next thing we know, Omskep is creating errors all over the place and that's when we thought we had to get you back to help no matter what. Your programming skills, Oslac, are far superior to most of ours."

"Alex," she corrected automatically, "and I'm not that good."

Even Almega raised an eyebrow at that.

"Next to me, you understand more about Omskep than any of us, and I don't have that creative side that allows me to see around a problem the way you do."

"Anyway," Fortan continued, "when we tried to pull you out, the soonest moment we could get to you was your last training. Any sooner than that and we couldn't track you. You were in Oestragar so rarely and you just kept vanishing. Daniel deciding to take a pause gave us the chance to get a fix on him, and through him, you, but before we could yank him out, your program went crazy. That was when the plane crashed."

"Ahh! So that's why I ended up a ghost in the machine!"

"Uh huh. We nearly got you, but Oestragar was trying to pull you out at the same time and you got caught in between. Then Almega realised the shock of moving two levels at once might be too much so we pulled back and let Oestragar take you."

"So all those dreams I was having before the crash?"

"Was us poking around. It was a side effect. Sorry about that!" Fortan explained, looking slightly abashed.

"No harm done," she assured him.

"When we saw Oestragar was having the same problem but on a smaller scale, Gracti suggested we leave you to see if you could figure it out. The fact we still couldn't pull you out left us little choice anyway, but we knew your skills with Omskep would come to the fore if you were pressed. Almega kept watch and when he saw you'd worked out a way to interact without taking on avatars, we set to work to replicate the idea."

"And that trick you explained to my sub-self when you were dealing with *Titanic* really helped," Almega added. "Ever since then, the others have been using our version of your secondary program with that feature added to track the problems and fix them."

"It's been hard work," Fortan admitted. "Having you two back will certainly help, but the problem is on such a large scale I'm not sure we'll ever be able to get it back under control. We never know where it's going to spring up next, so we're having to go through every single possible universe trying to identify any problems before they get too big. You can imagine how long that's taking us!"

"Tell me the others aren't all stepping in as avatars at the second level?" Daniel asked worriedly.

Almega shook his head. "The problem is concentrated in the first level and in most cases it's still minor enough that the second levels haven't spotted it yet. Yours was the only universe where they did."

Fortan nodded and took up the narrative.

"So we're diving straight down to the first level and attacking the problems directly. We've refined your approach, so usually we only have to go in once. We've found there's always one key change. A nexus, if you will. Once that's addressed, everything else falls into line."

When Alex and Daniel looked curious, Almega filled in the details.

"When you went back to Ancient Greece that was a later problem. The problem you needed to address that sorted everything else out was actually in the Ubaid period of Ancient Mesopotamia. There was a woman who should have had a child. She had a miscarriage because of a dog that stole some food when she desperately needed it. She had another child later – one she wouldn't have had if the first child had lived – and that one did many of the same things his brother would have, but there were subtle differences and those accumulated over time. With a smaller population, those differences quickly add up."

"You mean if we'd sorted that, we wouldn't have had to go to *Titanic*?"

"Or any of the others," Almega agreed, "but your struggles helped us refine our approach, so it turned out to be a good thing – albeit rather more stressful."

"To put it mildly." Daniel growled.

Almega looked contrite.

"My apologies. The event in Mesopotamia was too minor for my sub-self to see at that stage. Using our Omskep combined with the secondary program we've become much better at it, which is as well given how many errors we're trying to fix. And in case you're worried, Fortan went back and fixed that earlier problem. After all, it was still a change in an unchanging program, so really it had to be corrected."

"I guess that explains how the air crash corrected itself," Alex mused.

Almega turned to his desk so he wouldn't have to look her in the eye, but, knowing him as she did, Alex spotted his change in demeanour.

"Almega? What aren't you telling me?"

"Fortan's quick fix wasn't needed for that," he admitted after a pause. "My sub-self had already stepped in and solved it."

Alex and Daniel both stared at him in shock, but it was Alex who gave voice to their feelings.

"He did what?!"

"When you two went off to deal with Fortan's, um, revelation, we realised you couldn't be asked to deal with that as well. You'd both been teachers and Alex, they were *your* students. So my sub-self went into the program and called up an avalanche that was very carefully targeted."

"But you **never** go into the program!" Daniel said, astonished Almega would have done that for them.

"Not under normal circumstances, no, but these circumstances were far from normal. I knew the real reason you took a break, although obviously I didn't share that with my sub-self, but it was clear you'd both become emotionally exhausted and this seemed a way to make things easier for you."

"But neither version of you has ever had to deal with anything like that before," Alex pointed out. "Talk about traumatising!"

"I've eased that, somewhat, more out of self-preservation than anything else. Even though my sub-self did the actual deed, the effects were echoing through Omskep and it was quite disconcerting. The memory has been relocated into a sub-routine, and if he does think to examine it at any time in the future he'll find it's considerably less vivid."

"What about you? You can't erase that sort of thing."

"No, but I can remove the associated emotions. Make it more like a record in a history book than something I experienced."

Alex wrapped her arms around Almega and gave him a hug, much to the latter's surprise.

"Thank you," she said quietly. "I know it had to be done, but I was dreading it."

"I would have done it, but I'm very glad I didn't have to," Daniel admitted. "I've enough blood on my hands. Quite a few of the soldiers I killed weren't much older than Alex's students and I hated myself every time. Even knowing later that they were programs didn't make it that much easier to recall. I won't hug you, but I do thank you." He nodded respectfully at Almega.

"It had to be done, and if it saved you from having to go through any more, it was worth it." When Alex released him, he turned back to Omskep. "Now we just have to find where and how the errors are creeping into the rest of the program and put a stop to them. Hopefully without having to engage in quite such violent acts. Sadly, even with your discoveries this isn't an easy task and it seems to be getting bigger every day."

Alex gazed thoughtfully at Omskep.

"Perhaps we're missing the point?" she said at last. When the others looked at her she continued, "I mean, perhaps there's one error that's the catalyst for all the others. If we can track that one down and fix it, all the others might fall into place."

Almega gave her an approving nod.

"You may be right. I'll see what I can find. We may, at least, be able to reduce the number of errors, although how events in one universe could have an effect in another is beyond me."

Daniel, used to picking up on Alex's ideas, was mulling over her thought carefully.

"I bet there's one link between all the affected universes," he drawled. The others stared at him. "It's obvious, isn't it?"

Alex grinned, already picking up on his line of reasoning.

"Of course! Us!"

Fortan and Almega looked at each other in shock, then both turned to Omskep and started working in a frenzy.

The other two watched them for a while until Daniel shook his head and turned to Alex.

"They're going to be lost in there for a while. Shall we reacquaint ourselves with our home?"

Together they walked out of Omskep.

***

"I see what you mean about the landscaping," Daniel commented.

They strolled through the gardens, which included everything from versions that would have been recognisable to Europeans in Daniel's last training, to jungles, mountains and roaring waterfalls crashing into picturesque grottos, desert blooms and the more fantastical examples from universes very different to the one they'd spent all their time in of late. Birds of every size and hue cavorted and sang above their heads, and as they created and then strolled through a portal into a section with lower gravity and towering flowers that would dwarf the Empire State building, a dragon bellowed greeting to all within earshot.

Alex smiled, revelling in the sight.

"I've always loved coming here. Is it wrong there's a part of me that always resents the fact I have to forget about this when I'm in training?"

Daniel looked up as a pair of magnificent birds, their red and gold plumage shimmering and flashing in the light, passed overhead. In their last training they would probably have been called phoenix, although he knew the method of propagation used by this particular breed was far less comburent.

"I miss it too, but I find I appreciate it even more when I return."

He drew a deep-breath, savouring the scents. With the added senses of his form in Anqueria, the mix was heady.

"'The kiss of the sun for pardon, the song of the birds for mirth, one is nearer God's heart in a garden than anywhere else on earth'," he quoted.

"Well, I can't speak for any all-powerful being beyond myself, but I certainly feel happiest when I come here," Alex agreed. "There's peace, balance, and everything working together for the common good. Even death has a purpose here."

"I think the peace is about to be shattered," he returned, nodding towards an equine figure that was cantering towards them.

"You can only appreciate it when you know the alternative," Alex reminded him, then turned to their visitor who trotted the last few meters and bowed. "Paxto! Good to see you!"

"And so good to see you two at last!" he replied, then turned to Daniel. "I wanted to say thank you. My avatar didn't really appreciate what you did for him, but I did. I wasn't in there when the sub-avatar died – something for which I shall remain eternally grateful – but that you cared enough to be upset by it and tried to explain what it meant to him... oh, you know what I'm trying to say!"

Daniel nodded.

"That one was tough. Even being removed from it twice over I find it still resonates. You're welcome."

"And as for the stuff you figured out to deal with the problems we're facing!" Paxto added, shaking his head in wonder. His mane blew in every direction and then settled once more. "Alex, you're a genius!"

"We may have just figured out a way to reduce the workload," Alex replied, "and this time you can thank Daniel for the idea."

"Really?! That's terrific! I must admit, if I wasn't an immortal I'd've found the recent events exhausting. We've been running around like... headless chickens?"

"You got it right," Alex laughed. "We'll be joining you shortly. We just wanted to take a pause and remind ourselves of everything we've missed."

"Well earned! I'll nip over to Omskep and see what you've discovered. Relax and enjoy yourselves."

With that he reared up in salute and vanished.

"It's a good thing Omskep can expand to accommodate however many want to be there, or it'd get very crowded very fast," Daniel observed.

"Ten Eternals are hardly going to be pressed into the walls, no matter what form they choose," she returned. "And I've no doubt Paxto will change to something more appropriate. He can't interact with Omskep half as well with hooves!"

She bent down to sniff at a flower, smiling as the familiar scent washed over her. Gently, she traced the outline of the petals which glowed in the wake of her touch.

"It's funny. I adored visiting the bluebell woods when I was in my last training. Always felt as close to heaven as I'd ever get. Never realised they were reminding me of this place. Fainter, of course, but the hint was there. Like a once vibrant photograph that's been washed out by the sun."

"Our avatar selves would find this far too intense," Daniel said, brushing his hands through the sea of blooms and leaving a path of glowing colour in his wake, "and they wouldn't be able to detect all the subtleties. They'd be overpowered by the dominant scent."

"Another advantage of being who we are," she agreed. "It's just a shame so few get to experience it."

"Yes, but if every being throughout the multiverse got to come here, it'd stop being worth the visit pretty fast!"

Alex shuddered.

"Point made."

A small insect – a cross between a tree hopper and a helicopter – alighted on Daniel's hand and he paused to watch it. Taking its time, it picked its way across his skin, then paused to perform some wing maintenance with a prehensile limb that seemed to be expressly for that purpose. That task completed it tucked the limb beneath its body and flew off.

"Did you ever do that thing of getting rid of all the exemplars of an annoying insect?" he asked.

She nodded, her memory quickly filling in the details.

"I had a mosquito the size of a hummingbird with a major attitude problem that was following me around. I told it to buzz off and leave me alone, but it wouldn't listen. Finally, I lost my temper with it and obliterated the lot."

"And then watched all the plants that depended on that species vanish?"

"Yep. I could have put the plants back and adjusted them to depend on a different means of fertilization, but that would have changed them and I didn't want to do that, so I put both of 'em back almost as fast as I'd taken them away."

"A valuable lesson."

He looked out over the limitless vista to his left, stretching towards distant mountains. Woodland dominated the view to the right and behind them lay the gardens they'd just left leading back to Omskep.

"Everything has a purpose, even the really annoying things, 'though in Oestragar I struggled to remember that."

"Um hmm. We can learn a lot even without attending training," she agreed, pausing to stroke a deer-like animal that had stepped out of the foliage. The beast nuzzled her and then trotted away.

Another beast, this time obviously a carnivore given the teeth and claws, burst out of the trees and the deer bolted. When the newcomer went to chase after it Alex stepped in and calmed it, producing a large slab of meat which it tore at happily.

"Now, now, my friend. She paused to say hello and you can't take advantage of that. At least give her a head start!"

The beast finished its snack and then lay down and rolled over onto its back. Alex bent to rub its belly, laughing when it squirmed under her ministrations and tried to lick her face. Satisfied with the attention it had received, it rolled back to its feet, shook off the dirt and then, with a last glance at the Eternals, took off after the deer. With a thought Alex relocated its target to another part of the garden.

"That's cheating!" Daniel cheerfully admonished, having sensed the change.

"I don't do it when I'm not here, I just don't care to see something I've just been talking to becoming lunch. There's plenty more and he won't be as hungry now I've fed him."

For a while they moved around the gardens, stopping to admire or interact with flora and fauna. At one point, arriving at an intricate display of miniature architecture from a creature that in their previous universe would have been considered alien or fantastical, Alex excused herself, shrank down to the size of one of the occupants and walked inside. Daniel took the chance to morph into a bird of prey and, with a few powerful beats of his wings, rose above the landscape to take it all in, enjoying the thrill of riding the air-currents. When he felt he'd given Alex enough time he swooped back down and then, instead of morphing back into his usual appearance, cocked his head, keeping a beady eye on the entrance to the miniature palace. When Alex stepped out he pecked in her direction.

Hands on hips she looked up at him.

"Daniel! Cut it out!"

"Oh, come on," the 'bird' replied, "Right now, *you're* lunch!"

"Uh huh?" She morphed shape and gazed down at him. "And what am I now?"

Slowly the 'bird' raised his eyes up from the tap, tap, tap of the massive claw, past the powerful legs and muscular neck to the velociraptor's head. It opened its mouth, showing the razor-sharp teeth and eyed him.

"Trouble?" he offered, then winked.

He morphed back into his normal form, followed quickly by Alex, the two of them laughing. Together they relocated to a lake the size of a small sea, fed by one of the waterfalls that cascaded down from an idyllic snow-capped mountain range. Nimbly, Alex ran to the edge, jumped up impossibly high, freed herself of her clothes and then dived into the water. She darted around, a human-shaped tuna, navigating the underwater world with ease as she explored and reminded herself of her old haunts. Finally she relaxed, hovering a few meters below the surface to watch the twinkling light as it poured down from the ersatz sun that provided illumination. A shoal of fish, neon blue, mauve and yellow swam up to investigate and then zipped away as a predator homed in. Alex turned a baleful eye on her would-be attacker, who wisely thought better of the move and lazily swam away.

Satisfied she'd settled, at least for the moment, Daniel joined her and together they floated, admiring the colourful fish and plants under the water as well as the view above. After a while they sensed the arrival of the other Eternals.

"As much as I'm enjoying the peace and quiet, I think we need to go say hello to the others. They seem eager," Daniel communicated to Alex, a hint of surprise in his mind-tone.

"We did something none of them have ever done," she returned, "and we accidentally figured out solutions to their problems. I guess they're curious."

They rose as one – their nature meaning there was no need to dry off – reforming their clothes as they went. Not that the other Eternals would have cared what form they took, naked or clothed, it was more habit. Once they were a foot or so above the water they floated over to the land where Gracti, Hentric, Brega, Zorpan and Accron were waiting for them.

"There you are!" Gracti yelled delightedly. She shook out her iridescent feathers – a hangover from a past training she particularly enjoyed – and nodded her greeting. "We knew you were around here somewhere."

"Just taking a few quiet moments," Daniel replied.

"Do you want us to leave you to it?" Accron asked, her form being closer to that of a puma, albeit the size of a Shetland pony. "Sorry, we didn't sense you were averse to company."

"No, no, that's fine," Alex assured her. "It's good to see you all. Better, it's good to see the real yous!"

Gracti winced.

"If I could tweak that program without causing havoc, believe me I would. What an idiot!"

"In an infinite number of universes, there has to be at least one where you're an idiot," Hentric offered in a conciliatory tone.

His present appearance was that of a bipedal, four-armed chameleon – an alien form Alex dimly recognised. She strongly suspected the fact he could move his eyes independently and keep watch on everyone while merging into the background had more to do with his choice than any fondness for the species.

"And one where I'm the class clown," he continued, then turned to Daniel. "I can't believe you got me to try and kill you!" he admonished, wagging one of his index fingers while two fists were planted firmly on his hips. The fourth arm showed an open palm as he conveyed his astonishment.

The ability to express in body language multiple emotions might also be a reason for choosing that particular form, Alex decided.

"In fairness, I don't think your alter-ego realised that's what I was trying to do."

"Another idiot. That must have been really bad to make you want that," Brega commented. She gave off the aura of a more civilised swan-like creature: elegant and quiet. "I, um, well, I know it's private, but as you've experienced things that are new to us, would it be all right to share?" She dropped her head awkwardly. "If you don't, that's fine too."

Daniel and Alex exchanged glances.

"So long as you can catch us up on what's been happening here," Alex replied easily.

Satisfied they were in agreement, the Eternals morphed to their energy states and for a few moments all of them were blended into one before pulling apart again and taking their preferred forms.

"Wow!" Zorpan breathed when they'd had a chance to digest the information. She was more also human looking, but with a hint of jellyfish. "It looked rough when we were watching, but now I know how it felt..." The edges of her form rippled with discomfort.

Accron was as close to tears as an Eternal could get.

"I agree. Thank you for sharing. That's given me a whole new insight."

Hentric, determined to lighten the atmosphere, patted Accron on the shoulder.

"Let's not forget the good bits," he advised. "You two had quite the adventures together, even before the new approach."

"If Fortan wants to share, would one of you mind obliging?" Alex asked. "Going through it all again..."

"No problem," Hentric nodded. "I'll take care of it."

"Those new approaches you've given us, though," Gracti said. "Wonderful! It's made such a difference."

"And the latest ideas?" Accron added. "Brilliant. I want to get back to Omskep and start working on them right away!"

"I'm with you there," Gracti agreed. "If you'll excuse us?"

Without waiting for a reply, Gracti and Accron vanished.

"Actually, I'm with them," Hentric admitted. "Brega?" he asked, holding out one of his hands to her, indicating the way to Omskep with another, placing a third on his stomach as he bowed and waving goodbye to Alex and Daniel with the fourth, "Would you care to accompany me?"

With a brief incline of her long neck, Bregar accepted his hand and the two vanished.

"Guess I ought to join them, leave you two in peace." Zorpan grinned.

"Not necessary. You can join us for some tea if you want. I only want to stop by my place just to remind myself what it looks like then, if Daniel's willing...?"

"Of course. Mine isn't so different from the one in Oestragar. It seems my tastes were fairly consistent, at least at the end, but it will be missing some things. While you're reminding yourself of your own stuff, I can fill in what's missing from mine."

The three Eternals vanished to their respective destinations.

***

"Quite Spartan," Zorpan commented as she looked around Alex's quarters. "Compared to what we saw of Daniel's, I mean."

"I never was good alone. I spent most of my down time with him even before this latest trip. Not that I don't appreciate my own company, it's just you can have too much of a good thing." She looked around. "I guess it is a little lacking in character."

"Or maybe too much. There seems to be no pattern here, just a little of everything. I like it," she added, keen not to be misunderstood, "I just don't get a feel of who you are in here. With Daniel's place, you get one person's take on everything, rather than an everything take on everything." She paused. "Did that even make sense?"

"Did to me! Guess I never figured out who I am," she admitted. "It's not like we're tied to any one version, unless we want to be. Any more than we're tied to any one look." She indicated Zorpan's present appearance. "I just never felt the need. If I want a particular take on something I only have to share with the others. You each have your preferences and, as we discovered in Oestragar, our avatars have more extreme versions."

Zorpan groaned, sweeping a delicate tentacle across her face.

"Poor Fortan found one world where he was evil incarnate. Really vicious and vindictive. He spent ages trying to keep it from us and then, when we found out anyway, went around apologising. To make him feel better we all went hunting until we found worlds where our avatars were... uh, unpleasant to say the least. I guess there's a bit of that in all of us. Well, except for Almega, of course, but then he's different."

"A fact for which I am extremely grateful," Alex agreed.

She focused for a moment, recreating items from her quarters in Oestragar and arranging them in the room. This time she added a simple, framed class photograph of her gifted and talented students from her last training. She didn't know – and had no desire to discover – which had lived and which had died, but in her mind they were as alive now as they had been when she'd left. After a moment she added Phil to the photograph. He was as much a part of that training as any, and more important than most. When she was finished she gave a grunt of satisfaction and then turned to Zorpan.

"Right, I think I'm done here. How about that cuppa?"
"Ready when you are!"

They vanished, reappearing outside Daniel's cottage.

To all intents and purposes it was the same as his place in Oestragar, if a little bigger. The trees in the garden were also larger and a few were from alien planets and alternative worlds he'd visited that didn't belong in such archetypical English surroundings, but somehow they still fitted in.

"Daniel? You ready to receive visitors?" Alex yelled through the open door.

"How many times do I have to tell you?" he replied, appearing in the entrance hall. "If the door's open, I'm accepting guests. Just come right in."

He headed off towards the kitchen at the back of the cottage.

"I've put the kettle on," he called back.

"Oh great! He's making it for real!" Zorpan almost cheered.

Alex looked at her, torn between surprise and amusement.

"You know, in my last training, being able to summon a fresh mug of tea whenever you wanted it would have been considered bliss!"

"Yes, but here? Do you think he'd mind if I watched?"

Daniel's laughter could be heard through the open doorway.

"Zorpan, it's tea, not alchemy! You must have made tea or something like it after returning from your training sessions?"

"No," she admitted. "Never occurred to me to try it here. I just summoned what I remembered."

He walked out, a tea tray in his hands and motioned for them to precede him into the lounge.

"I have to summon the ingredients, and the energy for the kettle, it's only the process I replicate. It's all fake, if you think about it, but I find it oddly relaxing."

He set the stuff down on a table that had been cleared for that purpose between the sofa and his desk chair. Alex settled down immediately on the sofa and helped herself. Zorpan walked the room, taking in the details added from their last sessions in Oestragar, as well as myriad items from before then.

"You know," she said at last, looking at the hologram of Beth, "seeing it in the sharing and seeing it for real are never quite the same. She had a good voice."

"She did," he agreed, "and if the sharing was the same it would take away one of the reasons for the trainings, though they still help pass the time."

"What I always find fascinating," Alex said, her mug held in both hands as she took a sip, "is that even though we can transmit the exact same experience to each other, each one of us interprets it differently, seeing different parts as being more important or more noteworthy. I did a sharing with Accron once, covering training in a world she was thinking of visiting. I thought the most important bit was how they'd developed a completely blind justice system where the accused were played by actors paid by the state so they always looked and spoke their best, and the lawyers had to stick purely to the facts without expressing any emotion. Discussing it with her later I realised she'd barely noticed that, but she had spotted the total lack of racism – something I'd simply taken for granted."

"It's Kant, isn't it?" Daniel said. "His transcendental unity of apperception."

When Zorpan looked confused he elaborated.

"Immanuel Kant, 18th century Earth philosopher. He pointed out that when we experience something we never see it as it truly is – what he called the thing in itself. Our own experiences that have shaped how we perceive the world – what we notice, what we ignore, what we consider important – they determine the experience, so perception is the unification of the thing being perceived and the perceiver's own preferences and interests. Accron hadn't had the same experiences as you, so when she witnessed the sharing she focused on different areas."

"When did you study philosophy?" Alex asked.

"I was a teacher. I studied everything I could lay my hands on. History, philosophy, psychology and sociology – such as they were then – physics, biology, mathematics... Everything is a part of history in one way or another."

"Yeah, but Kant? He's dense as lead!"

"I found Spinoza harder," Daniel grinned. "I felt like I needed a crib sheet of his axioms to follow his arguments. Kant's all right, so long as you remember in the Critique of Pure Reason he's working backwards."

Alex cocked her head, then turned to Zorpan who was equally bewildered. He elaborated.

"Most philosophers look at what is and ask what follows from that. Kant looks at what is and asks what must be in place in order for those things to be so. Once I got that, his book made much more sense."

"You mean it made any sense before?"

She blinked, seeing Daniel in a metaphorical new light.

"After all this time and I had no idea you knew all that stuff."

"It was in the sharing," he pointed out mildly.

"Give me a chance! I haven't even begun to filter it all yet."

"I did it while I was tidying up the place."

"Now you're just showing off!"

Zorpan looked from one to the other as though she were at a tennis match.

"Would you two like me to leave?"

"Not at all," Daniel assured her, chuckling. "Alex takes longer digesting shares, but once she has, she always manages to extract more than I do."

"Doesn't stop me from begrudging you your speed." Alex grunted.

"Just because we're Eternals doesn't mean we're the same," Daniel placated. "If we all did everything exactly the same we'd be mighty poor company for each other."

"Now there I have to agree with you."

"I find if I want to get a different perspective, the best person for me to talk to is Fortan," Zorpan mused. "We rarely see anything the same. After that, if I still need more insight, I run it by Hentric."

"That would certainly give you a broad analysis," Daniel conceded. "It would be hard to imagine two more different Eternals."

"I don't always agree with them, but it makes me think, and that's a good thing. I'd hate to get only one perspective on anything."

"I'm just glad the program takes care of the really nasty ones," Alex said.

"Ahh, but even those the world calls evil don't think of themselves that way," Daniel commented. "To them, everyone else is evil because they don't recognise what they think is obvious and needs to be done. Not that I'm agreeing with any of them," he quickly added when he saw Alex opening her mouth to remonstrate, "I'm just saying I never met a bad guy – or girl – who considered themselves bad, and I know I never will because if they truly thought they were wrong, they'd change. There's always a rationale that makes sense to them."

"Kinda puts a spanner in most religions, doesn't it?" Alex said.

"Hmm? Not that I have much time for them, especially given our reality, but I don't see what you're getting at."

She leaned back, her finger tapping the rim of her mug.

"Most religions that I've encountered believe in an afterlife, and they maintain the way to get there is to be good and follow the religion's prescription."

When the other two simply nodded, she continued.

"But with multiple possible worlds, and assuming a creator god who spans all those worlds, what is good for the heaven of one would be anathema to another as the prescriptions would change. So, someone considered very good and worthy in one world would be considered very bad and unworthy in another."

Daniel hedged.

"I don't know, there are some things that are generally frowned upon."

"Such as?"

"Murder? Or, to be more specific and to get me out of Hades for being a soldier, murder of innocents outside of war."

"That's the Spartans out of the afterlife," Alex pointed out, "or anyone else who believes the good of all in the society requires you either kill off or let die any who aren't physically perfect."

Daniel stared into his mug thoughtfully.

"For the Spartans it made sense. A weak link in a warrior race such as theirs could lead to the deaths of all those who depended on them."

"Now we're getting into Mill's Utilitarianism," she grinned. When Daniel raised an eyebrow she added, "Hey, my best friend in my last training was a philosopher. I'm not completely ignorant!"

"I never did any Earth training," Zorpan said, "and I was focussing more on your most recent experiences in the sharing... I guess that's an example of the Kantian perspective you were talking about. Who's Mill?"

"My turn," Alex said before Daniel could open his mouth. "John Stuart Mill was a 19th century philosopher who argued a moral theory based on the idea of the greatest happiness for the greatest number. Whatever you do, you have to think about whether your action will maximise happiness. If not, don't do it. By that theory, the Spartan infanticide of children who were not considered strong enough, maximised happiness for the state and ensured its survival."

"Mill was classically trained," Daniel added, determined to one-up her. "He refined Bentham while thinking about Epicurus."

"Show off!"

"Me?" he winked. "In any case, most of the same ideas appear on pretty much every planet with a sufficiently advanced sentient species."

Alex nodded, lost in thought. Taking this line of argument to its logical conclusion left only one option.

"I suppose, as far as the programs we encountered while we were training in Oestragar are concerned, Oestragar would be heaven," she observed.

Daniel hummed his agreement, idly stroking his beard.

"Undoubtedly, but a heaven only for those on Earth would be paltry, to say the least. It's incredible it never seemed to occur to them that if there were such a thing as heaven, it would have to accept beings from everywhere. Well," he clarified, "it certainly never occurred to me when I was in training."

"And every alternative version of them, from every possible world," Alex agreed. "Any one of them could fill a stadium just with alternative versions of themselves that are halfway decent – that's assuming you go with the idea you have to be nice to get into heaven. If you added in the less savoury versions we'd be overrun with just one person. If they'd stopped to think about it, their view of the afterlife was as geo-centric as Ptolemy's. And with less excuse, especially by the time of your last training! A god of all creation who only has humans in the afterlife? No aliens, no sentient gases or crystals – they'd be outnumbered billions... no, trillions to one by all the other beings, even if they just stuck to that universe. Add in all the others..."

"And you wanted them to share the garden!" he pointed out. "As big as it is, and with the infinite space of Anqueria in which to expand, we'd still have a crowd."

"At least we get tasters," she said, indicating Zorpan. "Most of us seem to like taking on different forms. I must confess that while this one is, admittedly, limited, I've kinda got used to it."

"I did go through a period where I wore the form of the last training," Daniel said. "Let's face it, this is one of them. I suppose I just got bored with it. It was fun for a while, but I kept having to change the house to accommodate the latest version and it got tiresome. It was all right when I was on my own because I could use my energy form, but as soon as people popped 'round I had to change and I kept banging into things or soaking them or some such."

"I bet Paxto's quarters had to be massively adapted for his latest form!" Alex giggled.

"It was." Zorpan nodded. "It's why I tend to avoid the ones that are massively different, although I've had my moments. He meets people outside."

"Exactly!" Daniel crowed. "You see my point? Unless I want to change my quarters from house to stable to fish tank to whatever, it's easier to pick a form and stick with it. Still, as you say, it's fun to see the other options out there."

"How did we get onto this subject?" Alex asked, bemused.

"Considering other perspectives," Daniel provided. "Speaking of, we probably need to get back to Omskep and see if the alternative perspective we gave them when we came home has borne any fruit."

Alex redirected her mental focus on Omskep for a few moments, then shook her head.

"To borrow from Fortan, it has and it hasn't. Yes, we were onto something; no, they haven't figured out how to use it yet."

"Then maybe we need to get over there and help them out?" Daniel suggested, downing his tea.

Alex and Zorpan looked at each other, shrugged and followed suit. Within moments the tea things were cleared away and the three had transported themselves to Omskep.

***

"Ahh, the Halsleds arrive!" Gracti cheered.

Alex looked at her companions.

"On Xtos, the Halsleds are a mounted unit known for their ability to turn up and save the day," Zorpan explained.

"Ahh, the equivalent of the cavalry."

"Which you would have known if you'd gone through the sharing," Daniel added with a grin. "Depending on your focus, of course."

"All right, all right!" She morphed into her energy form, writhing, pulsing and spinning, her coruscating surface sending out flashes across the room like a disco-ball.

"Hey! Some of us are trying to work here!" Almega yelled.

The disco-ball shot outside.

***

By the time Alex returned, major progress had been made. She threw a look at Daniel which clearly said, 'Are you satisfied, now?' and then turned to the others.

"Right. Now I'm all caught up, what have I missed?"

"Well, I can't find the first problem, if there is one, but you were half-right," Almega replied. "The link between the program that are going wrong is the training sessions. Specifically, those that were happening or took place just before we noticed the problems starting."

"We haven't visited anyone since Oestragar, and we left long before all this started, so we can't have caused any issues outside the one we noticed there. We know Almega never does any training," Daniel added, omitting the exception as that was covered by their efforts in Oestragar. "That leaves where everyone else has been as the worlds we need to focus on."

He looked to the other Eternals.

"And just because we didn't notice any problems, doesn't mean they weren't there," Accron added. "It took centuries for the problem Daniel and Alex should have addressed to turn into anything major, and that led to four trips to fix it, so I'd say we need to go back... What? Ten trips each to nail this?"

"Certainly reduces the work-load," Gracti commented, already loading up her own trainings. "Instead of searching through everything to find if there's a problem, we only have to look at the remaining seventy trips, maximum."

"And we've already addressed a few of them," Hentric nodded, "which leaves, what? Around forty? Fifty?"

"Which means we do four or five each and then we toss for the last ones," Fortan added.

"Forty-two, so you're tossing for the last six," Almega clarified. "I just checked all your past trainings and I've identified every one that has developed a glitch. You're right it doesn't go back further than ten trips – sometimes not even that many."

"That's easily manageable," Accron cheered. "What a relief! I was beginning to wonder if we'd ever get back to our normal training sessions. We can get through this lot in no time."

"I work best with Daniel. If no one objects, how about we do our eight and the other six between the pair of us? That is, if Daniel agrees?"

"Fine by me," he responded amiably. "I was going to suggest the same thing."

"Honestly, you two! Are you sure you aren't secretly married?" Fortan asked, but there was no rancour in his tone.

"We have been, in training, many times," Alex replied with a wink. "Hardly appropriate here, though. Oh, and I'll go for anything that's not aboard a ship. I've had my fill of that."

Daniel concurred.

"Probably best if the Eternals who were there originally didn't deal with those worlds," Almega offered. When the others were confused by his suggestion he elaborated. "If there's one thing I know about all of you, it's that you bore easily. If you're re-running places you've already been, you might rush it or miss something because you're already familiar with it. Fresh eyes have a better chance of spotting problems. We've all shared, which means we know the same information about every world, so none of you will be starting from scratch, but if you move around it will at least be interesting for each of you."

"He has a point," Fortan admitted.

The list of past trips was projected and the Eternals made their choices. Since they could visit any of those worlds once the problems were sorted out, there was no disappointment if one chose a place another had their eye on, and before long all had a list of four trips they were to make, Daniel and Alex, with eight between them, quickly scooping up the remaining six. The others pointed out they were more than happy to do those extras and eight trips for the two of them was more than enough, but Alex and Daniel insisted they needed to play their part here in Anqueria.

"If you're sure," Brega said, "But if you decide you've had enough, just yell out. I certainly don't mind doing another one. In fact, tell you what, identify the ones you really want to do and if I finish before you I'll take on one of the others."

The others all agreed. Each now settled down to examine their targets, using the secondary program to identify the key changes that had to be made.

"OK, Gracti? What in Anqueria possessed you to take the training in the two-dimensional world?" Fortan yelled out.

"I was curious!" she defended.

"Even with the sharing, I'm going to need some help with this one. I had no idea how hard it was going to be. Could you...?"

Gracti nodded and joined him, the two discussing the particular problems when a multi-dimensional being, used to moving without restriction in space and time (and across parallel worlds), was constrained to two dimensions.

"We may have a similar problem with this one," Daniel pointed out, tapping on one of the worlds. "For these beings, time is just another spatial dimension."

"Yeah, let's save that one. Dealing with beings who fancy themselves Eternals just because they've got the hang of self-directed movement in time isn't on my top ten list. Tell you what, though, I wouldn't mind taking a swing at that one."

Daniel examined the world in question.

"Laws of physics are rather different to our recent trips," he pointed out.

"They'd have to be, otherwise those creatures would be impossible. The wingspan to support something that heavy and get it off the ground would have to be far bigger for a start."

"That one interests me," he said, indicating another world.

"A way to stop war marketed as a toy by mistake? Yeah, I can see why that one would appeal!"

"If any have found a way to prevent war, especially one as bloodthirsty as that one seemed to be, I'm definitely interested. Wouldn't you be?"

"Yes, but the point of that one isn't that they found a way, but that the way they found got marketed to children. Whole different ball game."

"I'm sure we can learn how it was supposed to work while we're fixing the error," he returned.

"Too advanced to be used in alternative versions of World War one or two, if that's what you're thinking."

"Oh, I don't know," he mused, leaning back. "Advance computing a bit in an alternative universe so they have the technology..."

"And have self-guided drones available to the Spanish Inquisition? No, ta!"

His eyes widened at the thought.

"Hadn't thought of that."

"How about we investigate what we have to do in a few cases, then come back to look at the rest? No need to do them all at the start. I won't remember the details anyway once we get going."

Using the secondary program, they identified where and when they need to go and the gist of the alterations that would have to be made to get the first four worlds back on track: Alex's dragon world, Daniel's war toys world, a genuinely flat earth in which conspiracy theorists claimed it had to be round (which Alex found highly amusing), and an incident aboard a space station. They decided they'd address the next four when they returned.

"Almega and the others certainly did an excellent job with the secondary program," Daniel said approvingly. "This is going to be a lot easier than our last trips. We'll have time to explore while we're putting things straight."

"A lot more varied," Alex concurred. "It's a good thing we forgot this place while we were in Oestragar. I'd've found the limitations there so restrictive!"

"And we're going to get to see some of those other options first hand. I'm glad Almega suggested we all take on worlds we've not been to. That was a good idea."

Daniel looked up from their viewing hologram and noticed the room was a lot emptier.

"The others seem to have set out already."

Almega strolled over.

"They've been doing this for a while and have become quite efficient at it. I think you're allowed to take a little longer. Personally, I think you should have been allowed to stay out of it and recuperate a bit from your last session."

"We hardly need to recuperate!" Alex pointed out.

"Physically, no, but psychologically?"

"I handle things like that better if I keep busy," Daniel replied.

"This from the Eternal who stayed in his cottage for ages?"

"But I still kept busy," he insisted. "I just didn't do it by going on more training sessions. There's more than one way to occupy a mind."

"Plus in Oestragar it sometimes felt more like a competition," Alex elaborated, "with the winner whoever could do the most trainings. That was encouraged by Fortan and Paxto who were, of course, winning."

"You know it's not like that in Anqueria. The others would have been happy for you to sit this out. After all, your work in Oestragar taught them how to deal with it, and gave them the tools to do it, and now you've cut down their work to a fraction of what it was."

"But it needs to be dealt with before things escalate and start causing trouble at the second levels," Daniel offered reasonably. "If we hang around things could get much more serious."

Almega shook his head.

"You remember Fortan got stuck in the program in Oestragar? That was us. We had to do it so our Fortan could interact with the program separately from that avatar at both levels without causing further programming errors, but since then we've expanded it. Once we identify a world that needs repair, we put it on hold, effectively freezing the first and second levels until we're ready to enter. Nothing will happen in these worlds," and he pointed to the display, "until you step into them. Theoretically, now you've solved the problem of why only specific worlds are affected, we could put them in permanent freezer storage and carry on, provided we didn't visit them again, but I think the others prefer everything to be available to them at any time and they're on a roll. That doesn't mean you have to be."

"Can't be comfortable having your sub-selves frozen," Alex said, wondering how Almega was coping.

"I have an infinite number of sub-selves. Losing access to fourteen or even forty-two of them is hardly a strain. If anything it's almost pleasant. A few less things I have to keep in my mind at the same time."

"Never thought of it like that."

"The advantage of not being me," he grinned.

"Harking back to our previous conversation," Alex said, "If Oestragar or Anqueria is heaven, I guess that makes Almega here god. After all, he knows all about every possible world, exists in all the heavens, keeps everything running smoothly... well, most of the time."

She stopped when Almega's chuckle developed into a full-blown belly laugh. As neither of them had ever seen him laugh quite so hard, they were at a loss how to respond. Eventually he calmed enough to draw a breath.

"Me? Some all-powerful being? For Anqueria's sake, think about what you're saying. If anything, I'm the janitor! I'm... admin! I'm certainly not god! The rest of you fit that description far better than I. Your last sessions must have fried your minds." He walked away, still chuckling. "God! Me!"

Daniel turned to Alex.

"To paraphrase Shakespeare, 'methinks he protesteth too much'!"

"Yes, but let's face it, all of us here are as much god as any, in terms understood by those on the first level."

He drew a breath, rose and held out his hand.

"God or not, we have work to do. Care to join me in another adventure?" He smiled down at her.

"You know I can never resist that smile of yours," Alex grinned, rising to join him. "Quite the journey since this all started. From lowly teachers at Herabridge to Eternals in Anqueria, off to visit parallel universes and alien worlds our colleagues there couldn't even imagine. Whatever happens next, it certainly won't be boring!"

"Hardly, but whatever happens, I'm sure we'll be able to handle it."

"Together? Oh yes!" she agreed.

With that, they vanished from Omskep and began their next trip.

After they'd gone Almega gazed at the space they'd vacated. The laughter that had rendered him speechless had vanished as though it had never been. Instead, a thoughtful and almost sad expression crossed his face.

"Oh, you two," he murmured. "If only you knew."

Shaking his head, he returned to his work station.

The End

Next in the series

The Anquerian Alternative

Book II of Oslac's Odyssey

Alex Oslac and Daniel Lancaster have even bigger problems than they imagined, and the canvas is much larger. In Anqueria, where fictional worlds are made real, anything is possible. Dragons, robots, ghosts… Still, at least they're home now.

Aren't they?

This novel is available as an eBook and paperback.

Thank you...

… for buying and reading *Entrapment In Oestragar*.

If you liked it, please take a minute or two to give it a short review where you bought it.

Reviews really make a difference to a writer like me. They help to promote my books and that helps me put out even more.

If you want to find out more, go to:

https://oslacs-odyssey.co.uk/